Thunder at Sunset

Thunder at Sunset

JOHN MASTERS

LONDON
MICHAEL JOSEPH

First published in Great Britain by Michael Joseph Ltd
52 Bedford Square, London WC1B 3EF
1974

ISBN 0 7181 1191 5

Set and printed in Great Britain by
Tonbridge Printers Ltd, Peach Hall Works, Tonbridge, Kent
in Plantin ten on twelve point on paper supplied by
P. F. Bingham Ltd, and bound by James Burn
at Esher, Surrey

A Julio y Eva, Antonio y Alegría –
españoles, aragoneses, oscenses,
y amigos de corazón.

One

THERE WAS THE big lagoon just up the bay from Trangloek, what was its name? ... Dha-something Sap, ah yes, Dhaphut, named from the village half hidden where the white sand beach gave way to the dark mangroves. Now the curve of Trangloek Bay itself, first sand, then the Gymkhana Club's jetty and boat basin, the concrete-walled Esplanade, the houses growing taller, more massive, made of stone now instead of thatch, the short row of docks – and the city! There was the golden spire of the Old Pagoda, unmistakable on the height of land amid the huddled warren of the houses ... many trees, large and small patches of green – that must be the Residency lawn, or perhaps the palace had a lawn, too. No, that was the palace, farther along.

That was where Kumara lived. Out here she would dress in bright sarongs or something like that, and wear only light sandals on her feet. It would be strange to see her as an eastern princess, with all his memories of her ... as a slight shape huddled against the chill of a bad London summer, caped and booted against the rain as they came out of concerts, always well wrapped against the damp air. Whatever she wore, it would be wonderful to see her again, like being re-offered something that you thought had gone for ever, unrecallable, like one's childhood or first youth. Would he – could he – bear to lose it again?

The note of the Comet's engines dropped to a breathy roar and the plane palpably slowed in air as the deep flaps started to roll out from under the wing. The plane banked and David was looking down on Cape Rataphun, Rataphun Park and, at the limit of the park, the old British infantry barracks. He saw that they had changed – rows of modern three-storey buildings had

9

replaced the ancient thick-walled bungalows and arched verandahs of the old days.

The seat-belt and no-smoking signs lit up. David stubbed out his cigarette and mopped his brow. It was muggy, even in the aircraft, his sunproof suit was crumpled and he felt as though he had been sleeping on a dirty Malayan railway platform in the rainy season. These Comets cut the time down fantastically, but still ... almost twenty hours now since he had left London. A long lazy tepid bath to clean himself, topped with a cold shower, and a couple of ice cold gin and tonics, set the fans going and close the shutters – if the staff had not thought to do those important things long since – then bed for several hours ...

The jet was gliding down, crossing the coast now, over the crawling lines of foam where the South China Sea met the earth of Mingora, over the sand and the palms and the scattered huts of the fishermen who lived along that golden shore, over the railway. To the right here were the other barracks – they hadn't been modernized, of course: they were only for Gurkhas ... that wasn't really fair; they'd been built in 1910 while the British barracks, at Rataphun, were part of an ancient Portuguese fortress, brought 'up to date' about 1820, soon after the original treaty had made the Queendom of Mingora a protectorate of Great Britain.

His eyelids felt heavy as bars of lead. Why could he never sleep on aircraft, like this fat Chinese gentleman next to him, who'd been snoring all the way from Calcutta? He forced himself awake. The Comet was nearly down, there were the white stripes at the end of the runway, there was the jar of touch-down. At once the roar of the reverse thrust pushed him forward against his seat belt. Down. One dirty, tired brigadier in a rumpled, sweatstained civvy suit. Cold water. Cold tonic. Darkness. Sleep ... Tomorrow, he'd telephone Kumara.

As he stepped stiffly out into the embrace of the heat he saw, waiting at the bottom of the ramp, an immensely tall, thin officer in crumpled green slacks and bush jacket, wearing the rank badges of a major and a single long row of medal ribbons, beginning with the purple and white of the MC. His Sam Browne belt was on awry and had never been polished, and a pair of thin steel rimmed glasses hung insecurely on the bridge of his nose. David was not surprised to see that his cap badge was that of the Royal Engineers. Beside this human crane stood a short Mingoran in impeccable white drill uniform, wearing the round black velvet Malay cap called a *songkah*. They were both scanning the faces of the half dozen passengers coming down the ramp. They were probably looking for him, David thought, and were at a loss because he didn't look like a brigadier. That was true even when he was in uniform, his thought continued, a little wearily. His long nose and sad brown eyes and thick, arched brows gave him a resemblance to a certain sort of deadpan comedian ... indeed he had been mistaken for a famous one, two or three times.

At the foot of the ramp he said to the major: 'I'm Brigadier Jones. Are you looking for me?'

The human crane threw him an ungainly salute, and the little Mingoran followed suit. 'I'm Wilfrid Porter, sir. Your brigade major. Do you have any more hand baggage?'

David shook his head. 'Just this briefcase and overnight bag. Everything else is in the hold.'

'May I have the baggage slips, sir? Tuan Yunus here, of the Customs Service, will clear it.'

The Mingoran took the slips and, saluting again, turned away.

'This way, sir,' Major Porter said. He led across the edge of the tarmac, through a gate, past a saluting Mingoran policeman, to a parked Land-Rover, and took the khaki cover off the little flagstaff. A triangular blue pennant with an embroidered red '44' fluttered out in the damp heavy breeze. David felt a small thrill. Childish, he thought, but I can't help it: my first flag. 'May I drive, sir?' the tall officer asked.

'Certainly. I was here for a few months fourteen years ago, right after the war, but I wouldn't know my way around. It'll come back. Just lead me to a cold bath and a cold drink.'

'Yes, sir.' The Land-Rover moved off slowly. 'The Staff Captain has your staff car, and he'll take your baggage to Flagstaff House ...' They were out of the airport now and bowling down a wide road. The major said, 'Sir, there's a mutiny in the British battalion.'

David's heart missed a beat and he felt an emptiness in the pit of his stomach. Not even five minutes of peace and quiet! A crisis before he'd washed his hands. It wasn't fair!

He forced himself to speak steadily – 'That's the Royal Oxford Fusiliers, isn't it?'

'Yes, sir. The CO's John Allen. A VC.'

Why the hell couldn't the sods have mutinied while old Bill Fowler was alive, David thought. Old Bill had been here nearly three years, and must have known everyone and everything intimately. Trouble like this was almost invariably the fault of the battalion's commanding officer ... but with a VC, you'd hardly think ... well, VCs weren't always the best administrators in the world, but usually respect for what they'd done, and awe of the crimson ribbon, would carry them through.

'Tell me what you know,' he said. The Land-Rover buzzed on, not fast, along the paved road, between avenues of palms, towards Trangloek, capital of Mingora.

The major said, 'This morning A Company of the Fusiliers was supposed to go on a route march – twenty-five miles in Field Service Marching Order – because they had ten men fall out on the last jungle exercise they did, a week ago. The company refused to parade.'

'Including the NCOs?' David asked quickly.

'No, sir. All the NCOs except a couple of lance-corporals paraded. When the company commander arrived, the sergeant major told him that the men had refused to leave their barrack rooms. The company commander – Major Spalding – went in and tried to reason with them. He warned them that if they didn't appear on parade within fifteen minutes they would all be guilty of mutiny. They shouted him down and someone even put a shot close by him as he went out ...'

'They're armed?' David cut in.

'Yes, sir. They have all their personal arms ... Spalding went to Colonel Allen, who went to their barracks himself with the RSM. They wouldn't let him in, but he shouted through the door that if they were not on parade by noon they would be attacked. They shouted that they'd shoot back.'

'Who's Colonel Allen proposing to attack them with?' David asked.

'The rest of the battalion,' Porter said. 'He told me that no one else is going to fire at his men. They're going to settle it among themselves ... but I suggested to Colonel Campbell-Wylie that he might keep his battalion standing-to. He's the CO of the 2nd/12th Gurkhas.'

'I know him,' David said, 'I was a 12th Gurkha. Have you told the Resident?'

'There is no Resident,' Porter said. 'One's been appointed but no one thought there was any hurry for him to get here – the Emergency's just about over in Malaya and there's no trouble here ... then Brigadier Fowler died suddenly, and we had no brigadier and no Resident. I told the Residency Counsellor, Charles Nugent.'

'What did he say?' David asked anxiously. Mutiny in a British battalion was a very serious matter. It could have repercussions of the greatest importance throughout South East Asia and beyond. Certainly the civil power, represented here by the Residency, should give their advice.

'Nothing,' Porter said dryly. 'At least, nothing of value. Just – on the one hand this and on the other hand that ... In other words, passing the baby. Well, it's ours anyway.'

'Yes,' David said unhappily. It was true enough. But all the same, advice from an experienced diplomatic type would have been invaluable. He glanced at his watch. Twenty to twelve. 'Drive to the British barracks as fast as you can,' he said. 'Signal Colonel Allen to take no action till I get there.'

There, it was done. It was a bad thing to interfere with a battalion commander when he knew nothing of the situation; but a sort of civil war inside the force which was the backbone of the British Government's support of the Queendom of Mingora could not be allowed to happen without at least some personal observation and deep thought.

The Land-Rover sped through the ragged outskirts of the city, dust flaring out behind its wheels. The Brigade Major, steering with one hand, spoke into the microphone he held with the other. 'Out,' he said finally. 'That's done, sir. Colonel Allen didn't sound very happy.'

David nodded. That's what he had expected. 'Have you informed FARELF?' he asked suddenly. Far East Land Forces had its headquarters in Singapore, and its Commander-in-Chief was General Sir Rougemont Huntingdon, a man who ate major-generals for breakfast, and had been known to reduce a much-decorated brigadier to tears.

'Yes, sir. I sent a Top Secret message, exclusive for COS. I enciphered it myself. Here, sir, I have a copy.' He fished in the pockets of his slacks, pulled out a ball of string, a few pencil stubs, a slide rule and a crumpled message form. David read TO

C IN C FARELF FROM 44 INDEP BDE TOP SECRET EXCLUSIVE
FOR COS FROM BM A COY R OXF FUS REFUSED TO PARADE FOR
ROUTE MARCH 0800 HRS BN CO PROPOSING TAKE STRONG
MEASURES 1200 HRS BRIG JONES DUE ARRIVE 1100 HRS.

What on earth would General Huntingdon expect him to do?
David thought. Lead the charge against the mutineers in person?
See that no blood was spilled? Starve them into submission?

'Have you had any reply?' he asked.

'Just "acknowledged", sir,' the lanky major said, with another
touch of wryness in his voice. 'I believe the C-in-C himself is on
tour somewhere in Sarawak and they won't be able to get hold of
him for a day or so . . . We could wait that long,' he added.

David nodded. Yes, they could wait, indefinitely, if it came to
that; but the question was, *should* they?

They were passing through the centre of the city now, along
the top of the ridge behind the Palace and the Old Pagoda, where
to the east narrow alleys gave vistas down to a distant beach and
a green-white flecked sea.

Major Porter said, 'I thought your piece, *Ultima Ratio Regis,* in
the Army Quarterly was brilliant, sir.'

'Thank you,' David said, gratified. Many officers thought quite
otherwise about that article, written six years ago but still famous
– or infamous.

The major said, 'I expect the Army Council remembered that
when they posted you here.'

David said nothing. General Huntingdon probably had more to
do with the posting than the Army Council but Porter might
well be correct. David's article had been about the necessity of
thinking afresh in the army's relationships with subject peoples,
among which he specifically included the Welsh, Irish, and Scots.
He had recommended much more decentralization, and greater
recognition of cultural heritages: otherwise the British Army's
future would not be on foreign battlefields, but in fighting domestic
divisions, which sooner or later would split the army itself. He
had been DAAG at Huntingdon's divisional headquarters when
he wrote that, and Huntingdon had promptly got him command
of a battalion and sent him off to a remote part of Malaya to
put his theories into practice. They had worked; hence his only
decoration – the OBE. But to many simple-minded soldiers
the last resort of a king was still, as it had always been, the

cannon, and to these David had branded himself a theoretician; more – a weakling who preferred talking to fighting. He thought, unhappily, that Colonel Allen would almost certainly be of that opinion.

After a short downhill stretch a wide gateway appeared, white pillared, with a bronze nameplate on the arch above – SLIM BARRACKS. The multi-storied white concrete buildings he had seen from the air stood in rows behind the barred gate, which was open, but guarded by four British soldiers, two with sub-machine guns and two with rifles with fixed bayonets. A corporal held up his hand and Porter brought the jeep to a halt. 'The Brigade Commander,' he said, indicating David.

The corporal looked doubtfully at the crumpled suit and tie and the battered porkpie hat. A subaltern came out of the guard room, recognized Porter and called, 'It's all right, corporal... The CO's in the orderly room, sir.'

Porter acknowledged with a wave of his hand and drove the Land-Rover into the barracks, across the gravelled drill square, and wheeled to a halt in front of a highly-polished brass plaque reading 'Commanding Officer, Royal Oxford Fusiliers'. David climbed out. He had been feeling exhausted shortly before the plane landed, almost ready to sleep on the tarmac. Thank God that had passed, for the moment at least, though it would come back. He followed his Brigade Major into the building, and through a door being held open for him. The BM announced, 'Brigadier Jones, sir. Colonel Allen, sir.'

David went forward, hand outstretched. The man standing at the salute behind the wide table was big, rawboned, freckled, red-haired. The starched jungle-green bush shirt bulged across his chest and red hairs glistened on his forearms below the immaculately rolled-up and ironed sleeves. His Sam Browne shone a deep, rich ox-blood and the brass rank badges glittered like stars on his shoulders. On his left breast two rows of medal ribbons began with the dull crimson of the Victoria Cross, a tiny miniature of the medal itself dark against the watered silk; then came the Military Cross, followed by a rainbow of colours. David felt glad, now, that he was not in uniform. The single row of ribbons on his thin chest, headed by an unexciting OBE, always embarrassed him. In the presence of this superbly military figure, it would have been worse.

Allen came down from the salute and shook David's offered hand. David noticed that he was wearing a brown leather glove on his left hand: it must be artificial.

'Let's sit down,' David said.

A couple of rifle shots rang loud and clear from outside. Allen said, 'That's the mutineers, probably firing to warn off the men reconnoitring.' He looked at his watch. 'I put H hour back to 1230 after getting your message, sir. We'll be ready to go then.'

The big clock on the wall behind the desk showed a few minutes past noon. David thought, I've got to make up my mind in the next few minutes. Say, ten. Through the window, against the back wall of a tall barrack block across the square, he saw soldiers lining up, dressed for battle in jungle green. They should be carrying gas masks, too, he thought, for CS gas would surely be the best weapon to use. But the mutineers of A Company also had gas masks. It would have to be bullets. Perhaps Allen didn't really believe that the mutineers would resist.

'What's the company commander, Spalding, like?' he asked.

'Not bad. A little idle. Prefers the staff, really, I think. Don't you, Stork?'

'Yes, sir. I've seen quite a bit of him in the last couple of years. He gives me the impression that he's afraid of the men. And rather dislikes them because they're all different, and untidy. He would prefer dealing with paper problems, I think.'

'And the CSM?' David asked.

Allen said, 'Norris. An old sweat, on the wide side. Got into a little trouble with corporals' mess funds about ten years ago.'

David walked to the window and stood there, looking across the square. He didn't see the soldiers lining up there, but the piercing blue eyes and bulging forehead of General Sir Rougemont Huntingdon. The general had torn him off a colossal strip a few years ago in Malaya. Quite rightly, too. He'd made a silly mistake in the siting of an ambush and half a platoon of Communist Terrorists had escaped certain annihilation. A month later he'd made amends, and Huntingdon – then only a major general – had given him a sharp sudden smile and said, 'I see you learn from your mistakes, Jones.' What would the brain behind that domed forehead decide to do here?

He turned round. 'I'd like to see Spalding and the CSM, at once.'

Colonel Allen rang a bell, an orderly stamped in, and Allen snapped, 'Tell Major Spalding and Sergeant Major Norris to come here, at the double .. They're in A Company office.'

A minute later the two hurried in. Major Spalding was tall and studious, and showed signs of strain. Norris was dark and foxy with an imposing moustache.

David said, 'What do you think caused this trouble, Spalding?'

'I don't know, sir,' the major said hesitantly. 'The men seemed perfectly all right yesterday.'

'Do you think there are some troublemakers in there?'

'Definitely, sir,' the CSM cut in, 'Fusilier Lane, Fusilier Packard, Fusilier . . .'

David waved his hand, 'And you haven't been able to get rid of them? Or teach them?'

'Some, sir. But there's rules and regulations nowadays, and National Service men, and we can't do like what we used to before the war.' The CSM had a marked Birmingham accent. He was the real commander of the company, David thought, Spalding putty in his hands.

He went to the window again and stared out. The blue eyes of General Sir Rougemont Huntingdon stared back. Why in God's name was there no Resident here? He turned round.

'I'm going to talk to those men myself.'

Allen stood up. 'Sir, I've given the orders for the attack. I have told the mutineers that there will be no more parleying. Either they come out, without their arms, or we go in.'

David hesitated a moment. Allen was right. It was no good parleying with mutineers. They would mistake compassion for weakness. But the men were . . .

Allen cut into his thoughts. 'There won't be more than two or three casualties,' he said. 'Once we go in, the ringleaders will get it from the others.'

David said, 'I'm going to speak to them.'

Allen's freckled face was deep-flushed and angry – 'Sir, I feel that I am responsible for this battalion . . .'

David wished he could agree. It would be much easier. But, like it or not, he was the brigadier, and he was here. He said, 'Wait here till I come back. Give me an orderly – unarmed – to show me which is A Company barrack block.'

Allen said, 'If anyone is to give them a last chance, I feel it should be me.'

David said, 'I want them to realize that they're not dealing with a closed shop . . . that someone outside the battalion is concerned about them.' He picked up his porkpie hat and put it on his head. Damned silly he'd look, talking to the fusiliers, wearing that.

Allen said, 'If you're going, it's my duty to go with you.'

David said, 'Thank you, but I think it's important that I go alone.' He stopped at the door. 'Porter, who's the senior commanding officer here?'

'Colonel Allen, sir.'

'Then if I don't come back in, say, half an hour – that's one p.m. – you will be in command of the brigade, Allen, and will act as you think best. Personally, I would recommend that you fill the barrack block with CS gas, and keep it filled until they get fed up, and come out. But take no action till one p.m.' He went out into the sun and the hot breeze off the sea.

The orderly marching at his side said, 'Left here, sir. That's A Company's block.' He pointed at a three-storied block, with long verandahs on each floor and a wide double door at each end of the ground floor.

David said, 'Thank you. Go back now.' He walked on alone. As he approached the building he noticed that the barred metal shutters were closed on all floors, and both doors slightly ajar. He headed for one of the doors, and as he got close he saw the dim shape of a person in the half light inside, and the gleam of a weapon. At the door a voice said, ' 'Alt there, pops. What do you want?'

'I'm Brigadier Jones, your new brigade commander,' David said. 'I'm just off the plane from London.'

The voice inside called to someone else, 'Says 'e's the new brigadier, Sandy.' Another shape came to the door, and David said, 'I want to speak to you – all of you.'

There was confused muttering behind the door. Some of the voices appeared to be arguing against letting him in, but a majority were of the other opinion. David distinctly heard a man say, 'We're not against all officers, Sandy, only ours – and that little fucker Norris.'

The door opened. David entered a long room well furnished

with tables and chairs, a ping pong table at the far end. There appeared to be about forty men present, all carrying self-loading rifles or sub machine guns. 'Where's the rest of the company?' he asked.

'Upstairs, sir, on the other floors ...'

'All right. Colonel Allen is not going to take any action while I'm here, of course. Now, can someone tell me, in as few words as possible, what's the matter.'

The voices rose. 'Sir ... it's like this ... we don't want ... Sandy, you tell 'im ...'

A fair-haired fusilier of about twenty-five spoke in an educated voice: 'Sir, this company is being run by CSM Norris. The sergeants can do what they like with us as long as they keep on the right side of Norris. The platoon commanders see a little of what's happening but when they tell Major Spalding he trusts the CSM more than them, and he doesn't see anything for himself.'

'What is there to see?'

'Unfair and illegal punishments. Cheating at weapon classification. Bribes to get your proficiency pay. Or recommended for a stripe ... You know we had ten men fall out on that exercise last week.'

'I have heard about it.'

'Well, the reason was that we'd had no food the day before. The company cookhouse never came up.'

A voice from the back said, 'It's the dirty system. The colonel backs up the officers an' ...'

'It's not Chesty Allen's fault, Packard,' another man protested. 'But 'e can't 'ave eyes in the back of 'is 'ead, now can 'e?'

No, David thought, but to be a good CO he must have, all the same; and he noted that the man called Packard, who had been mentioned by the CSM, was possibly one of the real trouble-makers, and probably a regular; while this man Sandy, whose surname would certainly be Lane, was merely an earnest seeker after justice, probably a National Service man and perhaps university educated.

Lane continued: 'Of the ten men who fell out on that exercise, sir, four were suffering from heatstroke. One nearly died. He's still in hospital.'

David said, 'What do you want?'

The speaker hesitated, then said, 'We want things put right. This was a good company. We're not criminals.'

'Get rid of Norris and Spalding,' the man called Packard shouted. 'Make them apologize to the company. Let the men 'ave the right to go to the CO if they don't get satisfaction in the company. Form a committee inside each company that has the power to get things changed . . .'

Form a soviet and appoint commissars, David thought. Make the high-ups eat dirt, publicly. In some other army, at some other time, perhaps, but now here and now, and the speaker knew it; he didn't want agreement, but war.

He said, 'I don't have to tell you how serious this is, not only for you but for our country. When British troops refuse to obey their officers in a place like Mingora, there's no knowing where the trouble will end. It's your presence which backs the authority of the Mingoran police, of the whole government here. If the foundations totter, the building could fall, burying us all with it.'

'There ought to be different foundations,' a new voice cut in. 'These people ought to be standing on their own feet. Why should we support their queens, princes and sultans?'

David recognized the singsong cadence at once; the speaker was Welsh, like himself, probably from Cardiff. Here was the third element necessary to create trouble in the company – the educated theoretician, the man 'agin' authority, and now the political speechmaker; and all working in soil made fertile for them by the failure of officers and senior NCOs.

He answered the Welshman's question. 'That matter's been decided by Parliament. It isn't for us to discuss or question. We're soldiers . . .'

He stopped. What to do now? What to say? He had used up all the time he had. What was it General Huntingdon had said about him when he was on the general's staff? 'You'll never be a good soldier, David. Because you see everyone's point of view and your head's always in a muddle because of it . . . But you might be a great soldier, also because of it.' He did not add, because he did not have to, '– if you can learn to make up your mind in time.'

David was finding that easier to do as the years went by. All the conflicting interests and emotions still crowded in on him whenever he faced a problem: until the last moment he could never see a good solution. But now, more often, as each occasion came when something at last *had* to be done, he saw clearly what to do, and did it.

So now, without consciously deciding it, he knew what he must and would do. He said, 'Listen all of you. I ask you to return to duty. As soon as you do – and have completed the route march you should be on now – I will set up a Board of Inquiry to look into the causes of this trouble and to make recommendations to me to cure it. All the members of the Board will be from outside this regiment. You can have till noon tomorrow to think it over. I'll be back here at that hour, and I expect to see you all on parade outside there in Field Service Marching Order.'

'And if we aren't?' Packard growled.

'I shall then call this a mutiny. I'm only calling it a misunderstanding, so far.'

A fusilier said, 'Chesty Allen isn't. He called us all fucking disgraces to our mothers and God knows what else, in 'ere a few hours back.'

'What about victimization, reprisals?' the Welsh soldier said.

David said, 'If the officers or NCOs have been at fault, they will be punished. If some of you have been lying or acting so as to *make* trouble, then you're guilty, too. I can't punish them and let you free. The board will get at the truth.'

'But 'ow do we know, sir ... how do we know ... trust?'

David felt the immense weariness of the long flight weighing him down again. He said, half yawning, 'You'll have to trust me. Now, I'm going.'

He headed for the door, the men making way for him. A soldier called, 'Sir, can we 'ave water 'ere. It's been cut off.'

David thought a moment. Allen was trying to starve them into submission, not a bad idea, if carried through – but he was also planning to use force, and the two methods didn't go together. He said, 'I'll see that you get water. What about food?'

'The colonel said we'd bloody well die with empty bellies and bladders,' a man said. David caught the undertone of pride in the voice. These men respected and admired their CO, whatever his faults.

'You'll get food,' he said, 'Till noon tomorrow, at least ... I believe I'm being sensible in treating you the way I am. Now you be sensible.'

He went out. The sun beat down harder and he put his hand over his mouth to cover a yawn. Colonel Allen and the Brigade Major came out of the orderly room as he approached. He said, 'I've given them till noon tomorrow. Until then this is not to be regarded as a mutiny but as a misunderstanding. See that they get water and food.'

'Shall I send in beer?' John Allen said with angry sarcasm.

David thought and said, 'Yes. I want to prove that we're reasonable people. Stand all your fellows down. Let me know at once of any developments.'

He climbed into the Land-Rover. Colonel Allen stood rigidly at the salute, his blue eyes glinting and his face white with suppressed fury. VC, MC, and a row and a half more, and I have to tell him he's wrong about his own battalion, his own men, whom he served with for twenty years, David thought.

As they reached the barrack gate two men came out of the guard room, where another Fitted For Radio Land-Rover was parked. He recognized Alastair Campbell-Wylie and said 'Stop!' The other came forward with a salute and a smile: 'Delighted to see you, sir.'

'You, too,' David said. Alastair was a good soldier. A little smooth, but intelligent and reliable. 'Bad show, this. But perhaps not as bad as it seemed at first.'

'I hope not, sir. My men are standing by, but in barracks. I thought I'd stay here, in case John needed me and I could make some plans while my men were getting here.'

David nodded. 'I think we're OK till tomorrow, and then . . . well, the British soldier is a sensible chap, at base.'

'Yes, sir.'

'I've got to get a bath and some sleep . . . Oh, Alastair, can you provide me with an orderly?'

'Certainly, sir. In this sort of job we like to post some local Lance-naik almost ready for paid. It gives him experience.'

'That'll do me fine . . . What's the matter with Allen's left hand?'

'Blown off at the Rhine crossing in '45 sir. He's got an artificial one, but it hurts him like hell sometimes.'

Porter engaged the Land-Rover's gears, and David said, 'Go by way of the Esplanade, please. I'd like to see how much I remember.'

He settled back. Funny the way he and Alastair still spoke of Lance-naiks – the Indian Army word for 'lance corporal' – though it was eleven years since they'd transferred to the 'British' Gurkhas. Even now, he'd only just got over thinking of permanent rank as *pakka* ... He yawned. Porter would have to carry him upstairs. Should he signal the C-in-C what he had done about the Fusiliers? He'd have to follow up Porter's original signal with something. Talk to him about it later ...

Trangloek was several cities in one. One part of the water front had the solidity of Singapore, the buildings facing the docks ponderously Victorian and unmistakably British. Crowded Oriental lanes curved down to the Esplanade from the human warrens up there on the ridge. The Palace and the Old Pagoda and the Residency stood like islands of space and calm amid the eddy and the bustle. The savoury smells from Chinese peddlers cooking shrimp under the trees mixed with drifting oil smoke and the scents of dried fish and curry and coconut. That tall building, the tallest on the front, was some great commercial house ... oh yes, M & O, Mingora and Oriental, which owned mines and ships and rubber and tin, and bought and sold from Celebes to Yokohama ...

Here was Victoria Square, a big open place beyond the docks. It was full of people, and the cords of innumerable kites ran up glistening into the blue sky, where the bright-painted dragon and snake and eagle forms of huge kites glided and dipped and swirled against the cottonwool clouds high above. A deep throbbing hum from devices fixed to the kites filled the air. He remembered suddenly the favourite sport of the Mingorans and exclaimed, 'Kite fighting!'

Porter said, 'Yes, sir. There's a minor competition today. The Gurkhas have been learning and ... there, that's one of their teams.'

He stopped the Land-Rover and David, smiling, watched the two Gurkhas run to and fro across the square trying to cut the string of a Mingoran kite with their own. A twenty-foot length of each string, about fifty feet up, had been dipped in glue and then coated with finely ground glass to make a cutting edge. The Gurkhas, shouting at each other in Gurung-kura, nearly caught the Mingoran unawares, but the latter was an expert, and when he saw the danger he made a diving manoeuvre that brought his kite swooping across the Gurkhas'. The Gurkhas' string was cut and their kite, after a lurch into the air, sank like a dying bird to earth. The Gurkhas ran off to get it, their faces full of woe.

Porter drove on. There was a wonderful sense of friendship between peoples here, David thought, much better than in Malaya or Singapore or India – better than anywhere he knew. He remembered noticing it fifteen years ago, back in '45 – that you didn't feel a stranger here, still less a guest – though you were – but a Mingoran, as concerned with what was going on, with the present and the past and the future, as all the others, as though you too were short and pale gold-brown, with slanted eyes and lank black hair.

On one side of Victoria Square was the Mingora Club, looking as though it had been shipped here stone by blackened stone from Pall Mall and re-erected facing the dancing green sea, its façade frowning a heavy Victorian disapproval of so much light and air. He recalled that membership was open to all civilians on an entry fee of three hundred pounds sterling and annual dues of three hundred more – but members of HM Forces of the rank of major or above were admitted without entry fee, and paid only half dues.

'Are the dues for the Mingora Club still as high as ever?' he asked.

'Yes, sir. But the membership keeps increasing. They allow Mingorans, you know. And Chinese. Anyone, as long as he's voted in.'

David said, 'They always did. It seemed strange in '45, coming from India. But it's obviously the only sensible – and decent – thing to do. So the Mingora Club is flourishing, while the mighty Bengal Club is dying . . .'

The houses were becoming fewer and smaller on the left now. On the right the sea wall ended and they drove along the top of a wide sand dune, with royal palms and flower beds regularly spaced on the landward side. David saw it all, and remembered it all, through a half numbed haze composed of present weariness and blurred memory, lit by sharper, more recent worry. It was all tidier than it had been in '45, when the Japs had only just gone . . . but had he done right in giving such a polite hearing to Fusilier Sandy Lane, instead of refusing to listen until the original order had been obeyed? . . . That was the Gym ahead, repainted

24

and very comfortable looking, its red roof glowing behind emerald lawns and high hedges.

'The Gymkhana and Yacht Club, sir,' Porter said.

'I remember,' David said . . . but why hadn't he let John Allen make his own decisions and carry them out? Now the responsibility was his own, and whatever the outcome, it would surely be a blot on his copybook.

Porter said, 'There's the golf course, on along the dunes, and beyond that, the Military Beach. Brigadier Fowler wanted every man in the brigade to be a proficient swimmer. We turn up here.'

The Land-Rover turned away from the sea and up a long rise towards the barracks visible on the ridge ahead. A few minutes later Porter stopped in front of Flagstaff House. Mingoran servants came out, saluting with murmurs of 'Tabek Tuan!' A short, slight white-haired man stood in front of them, wearing white tunic and trousers and a songkah. Porter said, 'This is Thomas, your butler, sir.'

'Goanese?' David asked.

'Yes, sah. Fourteen years as steward on the P & O. Your baggage has arrived, sah, and I have unpacked it.'

Porter was standing by the Land-Rover. His work was done and he was waiting for David to dismiss him. But David didn't want to be left alone, or he'd keep on thinking of what he had done, what he ought to have done, and what he should do tomorrow. He would dearly like to ask Porter, who seemed a bright and intelligent young man, whether he thought he had done right, but a brigadier couldn't do that, especially on his first day . . .

The Brigade Major said, 'I'll give you a call if anything develops down there, sir. May I say I think that you did exactly what ought to have been done, sir?'

David said, 'I hope to God you're right.' He felt light-headed with relief that Porter was on his side. He said, 'I gather you're known as Stork.'

'Yes, sir.'

'Well, Stork, send FARELF a top secret message, exclusive for COS, telling him I've given A Company of the Fusiliers till noon tomorrow to end their disobedience, then I propose to take other action . . . Come here after dinner tonight and we'll discuss what that should be.'

He turned up the steps under the high, white-pillared portico. 'Your bath is ready, sah,' the Goanese butler said. He was creaking up the steps at David's side, his back bent by age.

David felt his knees wobble. There was a piano in the big room to the right of the foot of the stairs. Wonderful, even though it would be horribly out of tune. He could play Kumara more Welsh songs. But the piano was levitating, surely? To the butler he murmured 'Bath later, Thomas. Just show me the bed. Wake me at seven.'

Two

THE OPENING SESSION of the Eisteddfod had been held in the open air that year. They'd sat on the grassy hillside looking out over the ruined castle and, beyond, the sea. It had been raining, the grass was wet, and far out on Cardigan Bay a vagrant waterspout linked indigo cloud to steel-sheened water.

Unwaith eto yng Nghymru annwyl
'Rwf am dro ar dir fy ngwlad;
Llawen gwrdd . . .

the liquid voices chorused, greeting the return of the exiles. She sat beside him, knees hunched under her chin, her small face intent, raindrops in her hair, the mountains misty behind.

Rhai ymffrostiant mewn prydferthwch
Gwledydd pell mewn swynol gan . . .

'It sounds beautiful,' she said, 'but it must be difficult to learn. Will you teach me Welsh, if I teach you Mingora-Malay?' And he'd said yes, but soon she had to go back into hospital, for a final operation, and they'd put him on a NATO committee sitting in Oslo and there hadn't been time to learn more than a few words.

. . . those damned shutters on the barrack room windows. They had the same type here in Flagstaff House – steel, to protect the glass against typhoon winds. Not bullet proof, of course, but CS gas grenades or cartridges fired at them would bounce back and explode on the gravel of the square outside. Perhaps they could catch the men unprepared – at night, certainly, they'd want to open the shutters to let the breeze through. But someone in there was cunning and experienced, and had thought the thing out. Someone who wanted an attack and a lot of bloodshed. That's what John Allen really wanted, too – Allen to wipe out the disgrace

27

to his regiment, the other to send a ripple of dismay and distrust through the fabric of the army as a whole.

He peered at the luminous dial on his wrist watch. Just after six. He got up and pushed wide the shutters. Light was spreading, mist tendrils writhing ghostlike across the grass, the sea a palely shining carpet below, the Old Pagoda a silhouetted finger to the sky, the light glinting down one side. He lit a cigarette, went out on to the verandah and walked up and down in his pyjamas. He still felt tired, though not as bad as yesterday. He wasn't as young as he used to be. Porter had come along after dinner, as ordered, and they'd talked till late. Mostly about the Fusiliers, of course. Porter was brainy, like all sappers, but also intelligent and full of common sense. They didn't always go together. He seemed to be the best kind of engineer officer, just the man to be president of the Board of Inquiry, with probably an officer from the 2nd/12th, and the Battery Sergeant Major from the gunners. That is, if he himself was still here to do any appointing when the C-in-C came out of the jungles of Sarawak and heard what was happening.

. . . Gas was surely the answer. But the gas had to be released inside the barrack, on all three floors simultaneously. And there were those bloody steel shutters . . .

He went downstairs. This Flagstaff House was new. The old one used to be near the British barracks on Rataphun Point. This one, two storeys high, red tiled roof, with deep verandahs, and high rooms, was far too big for a bachelor . . . a divorced man, technically. He'd walked through the great rooms and peered up at the silent ceilings last night, lights pouring out over the shaved lawn, the torrent of bougainvillea trailing down the tall front and over the portico, the heavy purple of the jacaranda trees lining the drive. It was lovely, but it needed a woman, children perhaps – not babies, but young people – to dance through the rooms and run, singing, across the parquet floors. It was the sort of place Lucy would have loved, not for its taste but for its grandeur. She was unhappy, poor girl. After the first long rapture the man had turned out to be dull, petty, and – worst from Lucy's point of view – unsuccessful. A semi-detached in Balham had been the final reward of her unfaithfulness; and for his own – what? lack of understanding? inability to reflect the sparks in her shallow nature? – this splendour at the rim of the China Sea; and for

Edward, their only child – London University, a hoped-for career as a journalist. Pavements slimy with damp and dog shit. The growl and stench of traffic . . .

Kumara . . . he sat at the piano in the drawing room and began to play a Prelude, humming to himself. It wasn't that Kumara liked music, as he did . . . and knew the ways of birds, as he did . . . it was some concordance in their natures. They both looked inward rather than outward. They reserved themselves, and their pace was slow. He knew what she would do, and how she would do it, before she acted. He knew what she would say before she said it; and, though he had not dared to speculate, it had seemed that she had the same secret knowledge of him.

He stumbled over a note, and went back and played it three times, until he had got it right. Today, he must go and call. Or tomorrow, once the Fusilier business was settled . . .

'Sah . . . breakfast, sah?'

He turned. 'Oh, hullo, Thomas. Yes, I might as well get up. I only want fruit juice and toast.' The butler bowed and creaked away. David went upstairs to shave and dress.

At half past seven he was a quarter of a mile away, in the office of the Commander, 44th Independent Infantry Brigade. The Artillery Lines and the stuccoed old bungalows of Kandahar Lines, the Gurkhas' barracks, stretched along the gentle slope. The Brigade Major came in, and David pointed to his IN tray, piled a foot high with papers. 'Is there anything there I've got to see to at once?'

'No, sir.'

'We've got higher priorities than bumf for a day or two at least. Anything in from FARELF? Or the Fusiliers?'

'No, sir. I rang Colonel Allen ten minutes ago. Everything quiet there, the mutineers still in the barrack block not letting anyone in except last night some cooks with food . . . Would you like to meet the staff?'

'Just the D/Q and the Brigade IO for now.'

Porter brought them in together; the D/Q was Marriott, Coldstream Guards – small, neat, rosy cheeked, the opposite of Porter in almost every detail. The Intelligence officer was Lieutenant Peter Crawford, medium height, lithe, black thick hair, slanted black eyes. David soon dismissed the D/Q and kept the other two. He said, 'Have you had breakfast, Crawford? Good. I want you to take me round the city, and show me the points and areas which might bring us internal security problems. But I'll visit the 2nd/12th and the gunners first – so warn them, Stork. You hold the fort . . . Can we start out in fifteen minutes? Right.'

They left and he picked up the telephone. He was about to ask for the Residency, when he remembered the time. Diplomats didn't get up at this hour. Whenever possible they preferred to ignore local time and pretend they were still in Whitehall; but here, with some eight hours difference, that was difficult. He must remember to go there before ten, though, to talk about the Fusiliers. But what was he actually going to propose? He sat doodling on his blotting pad until Crawford came in. 'Ready, sir . . . Do you want your orderly to come?'

'Oh yes, I haven't met him.' The Brigade IO brought in a young Gurkha, the single black chevron of a lance-corporal on each sleeve of his faultlessly ironed jungle-green shirt, and the ribbon of the Malayan Emergency on his left breast.

'*Timro nam kya chha?*' David asked.

'*Tulbahadur, sahib. Lance-Corporal, Sikkin Twelf.*'

'*Kya jat ho?*'

'*Gurung, sahib.*'

'*Kya Gurung?*'

'*Charjat.*'

'*Kya Charjat?*'

'*Lama, sahib. Tehsil Char Hazar Parbat.*'

David nodded. Not many Lamas enlisted and it would be interesting to talk to this one. Well, they'd probably have plenty of time together, in the next year or two.

'And one of your drivers, sir. Lance-Corporal Wood, of the Fusiliers.' A British soldier came in, and stood to attention. He was lanky and lantern jawed, with alert eyes.

There was his military family, almost complete. The Standard Vanguard staff car waited outside. He motioned his orderly to sit in front with the driver. The green-painted car moved off, gravel crunching under the tyres.

Within the next hour David had met the five officers of 154 Light Battery, and the CO, second-in-command and all the company commanders of the 2nd/12th Gurkha Rifles. He already knew the gunner major, Paul Stevens, by repute, for he had earned six England caps as a second-row forward, and his appearance was just what one might have expected – a vast solid chunk of man with a cauliflower ear, bruised frontal bones and huge hands – but a gentle voice and innocent blue eyes withal. He also wore a DSO and bar. His battery contained one troop of four twenty-five-pounder gun-hows, and two troops each of six 4.2 inch heavy mortars. Campbell-Wylie of the Gurkhas and his second-in-command George King he already knew, as also three of the six company commanders. Barracks and offices seemed to be spotless in both units, but he'd have to make a proper inspection to find out the inner truth about that. Ceremonial drill parades told a lot about a unit, but it was just as important to inspect the cook-house wastes and under the seats of the latrines.

The staff car turned on to the main road and down towards the city. Lieutenant Crawford seemed shy, huddling as far away from David on the back seat as he could. David said, 'What's the internal security problem here?'

The Brigade IO stammered, 'Sss . . . sir . . . there's really only one, the MPRP – the Mingoran People's Revolutionary Party.'

'Tell me about them.'

The young man gained confidence fast as he spoke – 'It was formed originally by Chinese Communists while the Japanese were still here. After the war they tried to do the same here as they were doing in Malaya – systematic terrorism – but there aren't more than five per cent Chinese in the country, so the CTs – that's Communist Terrorists, sir . . .'

'I know,' David said dryly, 'I was there.'

'Sorry, sir,' the young man said, blushing. 'The CTs were easily wiped out, or driven out of Mingora. Then about three years ago a man called Sujak bin Amin reformed it, in Burma actually, and secretly started recruiting Mingorans, mainly from the western provinces, with promises of a revolution soon. They haven't done much until recently – raided a Post Office and stolen money, killed a couple of constables and a landowner, scattered leaflets promising to redistribute land . . . but now they seem to be on the verge of starting something bigger. The State secret police nearly got Sujak a few days ago. They heard he was going to come to Trangloek, and baited a perfect trap for him . . . but somehow the trap got sprung too soon. The Perdana Menterika, that's the . . .'

'Chief Minister,' David said, smiling.

'Yes sir . . . he's sure there's an MPRP sympathizer somewhere high up in government. Anyway, they never got Sujak. He's a Mingoran, but got a scholarship to the University of California.'

'Why is the MPRP concentrating on the western provinces?'

'The people on this side of the central range are of Khmer and Thai descent, sir. They're Buddhist, with a lot of Brahmin influence. The royal family is Khmer, all the high posts of the government have usually been held by easterners . . . but the people west of the central range are of Malay origin. They're mostly Muslim by religion – Sujak bin Amin was born a Muslim, of course, you can tell by his name. There's always been some discontent in the west, and the MPRP are trying to take advantage of it. But most of the people, even the westerners, are loyal to the Queen and the present set-up.'

The young man spoke with a noticeable Scots accent, quite incongruous with his slant eyes and shiny black hair and the pale gold glow of his skin. Father a Scots planter or engineer, probably, David thought, the mother a Malay girl and the boy raised in the big house with his father . . .

'Do you speak Malay?' he asked.

'Yes, sir, perfectly. My mother was a Malay. The first time I left Malaya was to go to Sandhurst . . . Mingora-Malay is not quite the same, but it's near enough.'

They were bowling along the Esplanade again. The weather was the same as yesterday – warm, humidity very high, a few sunny intervals but mostly overcast, with the brief heavy showers that marked the middle of the north-east monsoon period, which had begun in October and would last till February.

David asked, 'Do we get co-operation from the Mingoran intelligence people?'

'Yes, sir. They're good, too. Brigadier Fowler used to arrange everything through the Chief Minister, and told me to do the same on Intelligence matters. I only have to ask him, and he sees that it's done. He really is a marvellous man, sir.'

'Good. Does he, or the Queen, have a secret police force, too?'

'Not as far as I know, sir. Agents and spies, but not police.'

The staff car turned up into the narrow streets of the city and slowed as the crowd thickened. A riot in these parts would be very difficult to control, David thought. The place was a warren, bolt holes everywhere; the outcome would depend on two things and two things alone – the goodwill and the confidence of the people. If they chose to conceal the troublemakers or were afraid to do otherwise, then the only way to get them out would be the destruction of houses by the score, whole streets. Nearly every building here was made of wood, and fire would be very dangerous, however started. People who might have been friendly to begin with could change their allegiance if they lost their homes and property. On the other hand it was fatally easy for the revolutionary, the troublemaker, to make threats to intimidate, to promise – and carry out – ugly vengeance on any who did not co-operate . . .

'The Old Pagoda, sir.'

David remembered it vaguely. There was no wall. In the centre of the large open space a huge square plinth rose in successive steps to a height of ten feet above the ground. On the centre of the stone plinth the pagoda squatted like an old woman with her skirts spread, a tall tapering golden hat on her head. Gargoyles and eagles and *chinthes* in weathered stone stood in fierce attitudes all round the edges of the plinth and guarding the single entrance into the pagoda. A dozen shaven-headed monks in orange robes strolled or meditated. The sound of tinkling bells and a faint whiff of sandalwood incense wafted out from inside the pagoda, the latter immediately drowned by a pungent drift of cooking oil from a Chinese stall set up beside the steps. Half a dozen peddlers ringed the square, and everywhere women bartered, haggled, and argued.

Nothing had changed.

'Let's look at the Palace, for a minute,' David said. 'Then I've got to go to the Residency.'

The exterior of the palace surprised David by its fortress-like appearance. It was a very large one-storied oblong building, with only a few irregularly spaced and high-set windows facing out over the wide lawns and spaced trees in which it sat. The pitch of the roof was steep, the gable heavily carved, the painted finials in the form of dragons and eagles. The actual roof was of blue and green tiles, everything else of unpainted teak. But why did it seem so stark?

Then David remembered. His mental pictures of enclosed grass plots and bright flowers and long verandahs, the pillars cascading bougainvillea, were all of the interior. 'There are three hollow squares inside, aren't there?' he asked.

'Two, sir. The royal apartments are in the divide between the north and south squares ... That gate we're looking at, the South Gate, is the only way into the palace for vehicles. The North Gate at the far end is very narrow and is only for pedestrians.'

'I don't see any guard at the gate,' David said.

'They have messengers, but no guards. The Prince Chamberlain says it has never been necessary.'

'H'm,' David said, 'I should think the MPRP might take advantage of that some time.'

'Yes, sir – if they ever come into the city, or even over the Central Range ... That building at the far corner of the palace park is Radio Mingora. The steel tower on top is their transmitter.'

'Is the telegraph office there, too?'

'No, sir. That's Imperial Communications, and it's down on the Esplanade, in the M & O Building. The cable goes to sea inside Dhaphut Point, behind the lighthouse. They have radio towers on the hill there, too, just behind Slim Barracks.'

David said, 'All right. Now, the Residency. That's just ahead there, isn't it?'

'Not all that close. About three hundred yards on along the ridge.'

Wood eased the staff car past a pair of cows lying in the street and David sat back. A moment later the car stopped. A policeman in blue cotton trousers, white jacket and blue cap spoke rapidly to Wood who said, 'Sorry, mate, I don't speak the lingo.'

Crawford said, 'He says, will the general please go to the Palace, sir.' After a brief conversation with the policeman he added, 'They telephoned the office, found where we were likely to be, then warned the police in this area.'

'The Palace?' David said, 'Who does that mean?'

'The Chief Minister or the Queen, sir. Anyone else would come to the office or send you a letter explaining their business before-hand.'

'Shouldn't I be in Number Three Dress, or something?' David asked dubiously.

'They always indicate that on the invitation, if it's formal. You're perfectly all right, sir.'

'All right, corporal, back to the South Gate of the Palace.'

A few minutes later, escorted by a royal messenger, David walked down a long wide verandah, many small rooms on his right, on his left a grass lawn seen through the row of wooden pillars and the arches of bougainvillea. In the verandah, on the grass, and in the verandah the other side of the lawn women squatted, sewing and chattering, groups of men talked and gestured, rising to salute him gravely as he passed.

The messenger stopped before a silk curtain and whispered to someone just inside. That someone spoke to someone else farther in. A minute later a man came out. He was in his sixties, dark-skinned, thin, partly bald under the embroidered black cap, with big ears and pince nez. The wrinkled age-flecked hands joined, and he bowed.

'Brigadier Jones? I am Hussein bin Idris, Her Majesty's Chief Minister. She would like to have the privilege of introducing herself informally to our new protector. This way, please.'

David followed him across the room, and through another curtain. He was in a larger room, surprisingly light in spite of the dark wood, the smallish windows, and the further shade cast by the verandah on to which the windows opened. The lightness came from the predominant white and blue of the decor – white silk cushions, ivory tables, pale blue hangings, the gleam of sapphire, points of ruby fire from gold statues and figurines.

Two women faced him at the far end of the room, one seated on a low wide table, the other standing behind. He knew before he focused on them that the standing one was Kumara, but he dared not look at her, though his heart beat faster and he felt his hands tremble. The woman seated cross-legged on piled cushions on the table was wearing a black sarong and a short jacket of light blue. At the bosom, she wore a hooped brooch of diamond and sapphire in the shape of a cobra's head, the hood raised, the mark of Vishnu in sapphire. Like the Minister, she was in her sixties, but where the Minister looked wiry, though thin, the Queen's skin had a clay-like pallor and her body etched a palpable weariness. Her white-streaked hair was drawn back in a bun, the hair shining with oil but of itself listless and dead. The face – heart-shaped, small, wrinkled – was the face of a great beauty, ill and dying.

David walked slowly forward, raising his eyes. Kumara. Kumara of the concerts and the Eisteddfod. Kumara of the London parks and restaurants and walks on the Embankment. But this face was

35

smooth, as though plastered, paler even than he remembered though Kumara was pale-skinned; the eyes were matt black, looking at him without expression, the hands folded hieratically. It was she, though if he had not known it must be, he would not have recognized her . . . He smiled. The composure of the face did not crack, nor the lips move. Only an infinitesimal forward inclination of her head indicated that she had seen the smile.

With a wrench he looked at the Queen, came to a halt in front of her, and saluted. The Minister said, 'Your Majesty, Brigadier David Dylan Jones, the new commander of the British forces in Mingora . . . Brigadier, Her Majesty Queen Valaya VI.'

The Queen looked at him a long time. He did not feel embarrassed, for there was nothing hostile about her scrutiny. She wanted to see him, to know him. At last she said, 'Welcome to Mingora.'

'Thank you, ma'am,' David said.

'You will stay three years with us?'

'That's the length of the tour, ma'am.'

'Poor Brigadier Fowler,' she said. 'He was a kind man. And his poor wife.'

She relapsed into silence. She spoke English well but with an unmistakable singsong accent. David stole a look over her head at Kumara. At the breast, where her mother wore the cobra brooch Kumara wore a huge ruby set in gold. The ruby glowed deep and rich, but her eyes remained still and flat. David felt cold, though the room was warm.

The Queen said, 'This is not the time to talk of our problems, in which we hope you can help us. We will do that when the Prince Chamberlain can be with us. He is my elder brother, you know . . . I would not have asked to see you before our formal meeting, but the Perdana Menterika here told me that there is a rumour in the city that the British soldiers have refused to obey orders.'

David hesitated a moment; but it wouldn't do to start his relationship with these people by trying to sell them palpable lies. He said, 'It is unfortunately true, ma'am. I hope to settle it today without further trouble.'

'We pray for your success,' she said formally. 'If there is any help we can give, we are at your service.'

36

'Thank you, ma'am. I'd like to speak to His Excellency here later, if I may . . .'

'Speak now.'

Again David hesitated, but the Queen said, 'I am a woman, but I have to deal with much that other women know nothing of. As you must know, it is only the daughters of the royal house who can become sovereign in Mingora. Speak.'

David said, 'I think that all Royal Mingoran Constabulary in the city, and throughout the country, should be put on a stand-by basis, in case the situation gets worse.'

The Minister pulled one long ear thoughtfully. 'You mean, in case the rest of the Fusiliers join the mutiny, and you have to use the Gurkhas against them? . . . I will do what you suggest. Is there anything else we can do for you?'

'No, thank you,' David said.

The Queen bowed slightly in sign of dismissal, and David saluted again. The Princess Kumara met his eyes with the same neutrality she had shown throughout: no hostility, no friendliness – recognition, nothing more. He turned and went out, feeling her eyes in the small of his back.

At the staff car he snapped, 'Residency'. Crawford glanced at him and looked away. He tried to wipe his mind of her. She was the heir to the throne, in her own country now. They'd have to meet formally sometimes, but that was going to be all. That must be the message of her expressionless eyes.

It was getting hotter as the sun climbed, and here in the city the wind could not change the air the way it did on the seafront or in the fields. The north-east monsoon was not as bad as the south-west. Though it would never be cool and dry, it was not bad.

The Queen must have been a remarkable woman . . . still was, in many ways; but she was very ill. Kumara would be queen soon. What was that title she had? He'd heard it once or twice in London, but mostly she was called 'princess' there. He asked Crawford.

The Brigade IO said, '*Perdana Binte Mingora*, sir. It means literally "the chief daughter of Mingora", but it's usually translated as the Daughter-in-Line. Was Princess Kumara there?'

'Yes,' David said.

'Her eldest daughter is the *Binte Binte Mingora*, the Grand-

37

daughter-in-Line. She's Princess Salimina, but she likes to be called Sally.'

David grunted. Should he tell Crawford he had known Kumara in a previous incarnation? What business was it of his? Or anyone's?

The car turned in through the open gates of Her Britannic Majesty's Residency. This David remembered much better, for his company had often provided the guard here in '45, immediately after the Japanese surrender. Just as the Palace was unmistakably Mingoran in its material and design and ornamentation, the Residency was unmistakably British. It stood foursquare, a late Georgian country house, wide, deep, two stories high, the windows big and clear, with very large panes. It made no obeisance at all to the climate or the eastern city outside the wall. The lawn in front was English green, water sprinklers playing and three gardeners at work in borders of cannas. The front door was open, and a uniformed Mingoran orderly, wearing on his cap the royal cipher of Great Britain, greeted him with a bow. 'Brigadier Jones to see the Counsellor,' David said.

The orderly disappeared, and he waited. From the high walls Victorian Residents examined him down their high noses – mostly men with the ribbon of St Michael and St George across their breasts, but here and there a scarlet uniform and the crimson of the Bath showed where a soldier had been Resident in earlier days.

A portly man in a light linen suit came out from a door ahead, under the ornate coat of arms. His hair was thin and greying and his double chins shook as he walked, yet David thought they were of about the same age; perhaps this man was even three or four years younger.

'Brigadier . . . so pleased,' the man said, his hand out, his voice weary, bored. 'I'm Nugent, Counsellor . . . Her Majesty's Acting Diplomatic Representative . . . until Mr Wilson arrives.'

'When will that be?' David asked.

'A fortnight. He's still tidying up the Seychelles . . . Shall we go to my little cubby hole? This is Mr Crawford, isn't it?'

'Yes. I brought him along because I only arrived yesterday, and I know nothing, while Crawford . . .'

'Quite, quite . . .' He led back past the coat of arms, down a dark passage, and into a large room with windows opening out on

38

to the same front lawn that they had driven round as they came in. He indicated comfortable leather chairs and himself sank into one by the window.

'I know you're a busy man . . . what about those British soldiers, by the way?'

'That's what I wanted to speak to you about,' David said, 'They're still in their barracks, refusing to come out – as far as I know – I'm going there when I leave here. I've told them that if they continue their disobedience after noon today we shall treat it as mutiny and act accordingly. Of course I want to avoid bloodshed as much as possible, but . . .'

He explained how he proposed to use gas, and ended – 'There may be difficulties, but it's our best chance. I advised the Chief Minister to have all the Constabulary stood-by, just in case we run into real trouble.'

Nugent sat back, twiddling his thumbs and gazing out of the window. At last he said, 'It's entirely a military matter, of course. But HMG will be quite upset if there's anything like a civil war among the soldiery, I fear.'

He sounded bored, but, under the weary manner, wary. A Civilian of the bad type, David thought; one whose motto in life was 'Do not stick your neck out'. He hoped to God the new Resident would be different. He rose, saying, 'Well, I just wanted to let you know what we are going to do. I'll keep you informed.'

'Yes, do . . . Let me see you to the door.'

As the staff car drove away, Peter Crawford said cautiously, 'He wasn't very, er, forthcoming, was he, sir?'

David said shortly, 'No.' The young man seemed to shrink away, and David realized he thought the brusque tone had been addressed to him, because he had spoken out of turn. He said, 'People like that rub me up the wrong way.' He did not add, 'because they throw the responsibility back on me, and I don't like it'. He wished to God they had given him a brigade in a normal division, where the major-general was always at hand to give definite orders – military orders – and accept responsibility. 44th (Independent) Infantry Brigade had sounded splendid at the War office – three years by the sea in the most beautiful spot in South East Asia, friendly inhabitants, peaceful frontiers – and Kumara. It wasn't working out that way.

'Slim Barracks,' he said to the driver.

Now he had come to the next point of decision. A more single-minded man would have ordered the attack for before dawn, for the mutinous soldiers would probably have left the steel shutters open at night. Such a man, say Sir Rougemont Huntingdon, would have leaped out of bed at 4 a.m. and gone straight to battle, with joy, instead of circling round, circuitously approaching the evil hour by way of visits to the City, the old Pagoda, the Palace and the Residency, all way stops, he recognised, designed to put off the moment of truth.

Colonel Allen and his adjutant were waiting outside the orderly room. David climbed out of the staff car, acknowledged the others' salutes, and said, 'Any change?'

Allen said, 'A deputation said they wanted to speak to you as soon as you came . . . I think we should ignore that request, sir.'

'Why?' David said; and he asked, he knew, only to gain time.

'Because you gave them an alternative yesterday – on parade, or else. This is more parleying.'

David closed his eyes. Should he, shouldn't he? Allen was fidgeting impatiently.

He said, 'I'd better hear what they have to say. But I won't alter the deadline . . . Prepare to put tear gas, without warning, into all floors of A Company's block. Firearms will be used only to protect the men putting in the gas, and then only on my order. Make your preparations out of sight.'

He walked off towards A Company barrack block. When he got near he noted that the steel shutters were thrown back. Good, he thought, that'll save some lives and the worst of the aftermath . . . unless they prepare for defence after they've spoken to me.

Fusilier 'Sandy' Lane was waiting inside the door, surrounded by armed soldiers. They all looked tenser than yesterday, David thought, and weary, as though they had been arguing all night. Lane came to the point at once – 'The men,' – he began; he corrected himself – 'some of the men . . . feel they won't obey orders until Major Spalding and Sergeant-Major Norris have been dismissed. And the Colonel promises, in writing, that there'll be no reprisals against anyone . . . no court martials, no punishments, no dismissals or transfers, nothing.'

David thought a moment. The conditions were impossible for any responsible officer to accept; the men who had pressed them – probably Packard and the Welshman, with Lane put forward as

40

figurehead and spokesman – knew that; but they were only some of the men here. Others, perhaps a majority, wanted to go back to their duty, but were being prevented. That majority had to be encouraged and given an incentive to overcome the others.

He said quietly, 'Those conditions are impossible. I might just as well demand that every man here should be given six years in jail . . . I've told you that I will appoint a Board of Inquiry, a tough one, with no officers from this regiment in it, to find out what really happened and why. I have no wish to keep bad officers or NCOs in the regiment . . . or troublemaking fusiliers. One thing I will guarantee – that any man giving evidence before the Board will be absolutely protected, whatever he says . . . When the report of the Board reaches me, I shall take whatever action I think is called for, against people of any rank, and to change the system where a change will help to prevent this sort of thing happening again.' He turned to go. 'That's my last word. Let me remind you – please listen – that you are committing mutiny. The Royal Oxford Fusiliers, after two hundred and twenty years – *mutinying*! We'll have to change the colour of the regimental facings from white to black.' As he reached the barrackroom door he heard the Welsh voice shout 'Close the shutters, quick! They'll try something as soon as he gets out of here!'

And another – ' 'Old 'im! Don't let 'im go.'

A chorus of angry voices cried, 'Don't you touch him, you fucking bastard . . . We promised . . . Let him go . . .'

He went out. Twenty minutes to go. The clamour of voices in the barrack rose higher. He walked slowly back to the orderly room, his palms wet.

Allen said, 'Some of the shutters are being closed . . . I'm going to order the assault now, right away.'

'No,' David said, 'They're fighting among themselves now.'

'Christ Almighty!' Colonel Allen exploded, 'We're wasting every opportunity to get this bloody mutiny crushed, and crushed so that no one will ever try it again . . .'

David, ignoring the insubordinate tone, said wearily, 'I'm sorry you disagree, but I have given you an order. Do not question it again . . . Make preparations to use gas, at twelve noon precisely, as I instructed you.'

For a moment longer the red-haired colonel glared at him, the sun glowing in the crimson silk of the first ribbon on his chest.

41

Then he snapped to his adjutant, 'See that everything's ready,' and strode into his orderly room. David waited, Crawford at his side. On the wall beside him a glittering brass plaque bore the regiment's badge of a flaming grenade, below, the three leopards of England, and a scroll with the single word QUEBEC. David pulled out his old lizardskin cigarette case and offered Crawford a cigarette. They both lit up. Ten minutes to go. Even if all the steel shutters were closed, they were only slatted, and some tear gas would blow through them. Behind a barrack to the right he saw jungle-hatted men in battle order, moving. Where the hill rose at the end of the barracks he saw the coloured dots of women's dresses – the families. Some of those women's men were in A Company. The women had been prominent, probably too prominent, in his mind from the beginning. He'd been trying to save husbands as well as discipline soldiers. And in a few minutes he'd know whether he had in fact done either. Or failed in both by not acting decisively in the beginning . . .

The adjutant of the Fusiliers ran out of the orderly room, saying, 'They seem to be coming out, sir.'

David walked round the end of the block, to a position where he could see A Company barracks. An armed man was coming out of the far door. David saw a score of rifles trained on him, but the man was wearing the jungle hat, slung gas mask, and heavy pack of Field Service Marching Order. Others trickled out, one by one, in threes and fours. The company markers fell in. His heart beat faster and an enormous weight lifted from his shoulders.

John Allen was at his side, silent, staring. David said, 'Get the company NCOs and officers fallen in at once. You'd better command the route march yourself.'

'Yes, sir, 'Allen said.

'As soon as you get back post all sergeants and officers of A to other companies. A Board of Inquiry will convene here at 0900 hours tomorrow. The Brigade Major will be the President.'

'Yes, sir.' Allen appeared to be about to say something, but instead saluted, jumped into his parked Land Rover and raced away.

On the parade ground the sergeants were calling the roll. It was over . . . but David was even now not sure that he had taken the wisest course. The men had mutinied, and they had not been punished; that no one could deny. If anything like this happened again, it would be easy, and perhaps correct, to say that his leniency and caution had caused it. On the other hand, the women up there were gathering in little clusters now, some embracing others, children huddled at their knees, the cordon of regimental police moving away. It was something to put on the other side of the ledger.

'Home, Lakri,' he said to the driver. The driver gave him a dour grin as he drove off. They were all the same, David thought. There wasn't a soldier in the British Army called Wood whose nickname wasn't *Lakri* – the Hindustani word for 'wood' – but they were always astonished that an officer, a senior officer at that – would know such things. Did they think one was born with a red hat, and therefore ignorant of the facts of life?

The Brigade Major was in front of the office when the staff car arrived, a wide smile on his long face. 'Well done, sir,' he said quietly.

'Thank you,' David said gruffly. They went together into the office and he gave detailed orders for the Board of Inquiry. He ended, 'I want to get the whole truth, Stork. There's obviously something wrong within the battalion and it's the sort of thing that has to be ferreted out by outsiders. Be ruthless. Don't spare anyone in asking questions.'

'I won't,' Porter said. 'Colonel Allen will be hard to handle, but when we get down to cases he'll realize that we're trying to help his regiment.'

'I'm going to have lunch and a nap,' David said, 'I didn't sleep well last night. Anything else important?'

'No, sir. Only I've got to issue the orders for the ceremonial parade on the 15th, to receive the new Resident. I've looked up the records and it should be two companies, one British and one other, under a field officer, with a troop of guns to fire the salute. The Resident's entitled to thirteen guns.'

'Where does all this take place?'

'It used to be at the docks on the Esplanade, but last time it was at the airport, so I suppose it will be this time. He'll surely come by air.'

'All right. You fix it.'

'Yes, sir . . . Colonel Campbell-Wylie told me you were a golfer. And there was a set of clubs in your baggage.'

43

'Yes. Not very good, but I try. I had a nine handicap when we were in Singapore.'

'Would you care to play a foursome this afternoon? My wife and I were going to play with the Princess Sally and Freddy Young, the adjutant of the Fusiliers, but he phoned just now to say he was going on the route march, so . . .'

'Delighted,' David said. 'What time?'

'Five o'clock at the Club house, sir.'

They were waiting for him in wicker chairs on the long verandah, where the clubhouse faced the eighteenth hole and, beyond, the curling surf. He didn't know quite what he had expected the Granddaughter-in-Line, Kumara's daughter, to look like, but certainly not this – a curvaceous girl of about twenty-two in white slacks and a Hawaiian shirt. Her skin was brown, but less than Mrs Porter's sunburn, and her hair was short under the peaked white golfing cap. Porter introduced him – 'Princess . . .' he began, but she said, 'Heavens, call me Sally . . . They started it at Stanford where no one could be bothered to pronounce my real name . . . And what do I call you?'

'David,' he said. Kumara, like everyone else, had called him that until she learned that his second name was Dylan; then she refused to call him anything else but Dylan. No one else had ever called him Dylan.

'You met my mother in London, she says,' Sally said.

'Yes,' David said.

The princess said, 'Well, I expect you'll find she's different here. We all are. I wish I were back in Palo Alto . . .'

Then Porter introduced his wife, and the princess said, 'Let's start.'

It was a good course, on the Scottish pattern, a links course laid out along the edge of the sea in the sand dunes, with the sea wind perpetually blowing, except in a few deep hollows where there was an unexpected and almost sinister calm. The caddies were Mingoran boys who trudged along behind chattering to each other and rushing up officiously to offer a club whenever a shot was to be played. David, to his surprise, found himself at the top of his form. He and Sally comfortably defeated the Porters.

At the club house Wilfrid Porter ordered the first round of

stengahs and they settled down in cane chairs, the wind ruffling their hair. 'What was your regiment?' Sally asked David.

'13th Gurkha Rifles, originally. I had family connections with it. But they stayed with India in 1947 and I was transferred to the 12th.'

'The regiment that's here now?' the princess exclaimed.

'Yes, but the other battalion, the 1st.'

'Where were you in the war?'

'North West Frontier of India ... Persia, Italy. Nothing very exciting. I was here for a few months in '45 and '46, after the Japanese surrender, too.'

Now she'd ask about his family, he thought; and he'd have to tell her that his wife ran away from him during the war, taking their only child with her. But the princess started talking about golf. Porter must have warned her, or she was more tactful than she appeared to be.

With the second round of stengahs the princess said, 'Now who knows anything about the new Resident? Sidney Francis Wilson, Esq. CMG, CBE, DSC.'

'DSC?' David said, startled. The Distinguished Service Cross was the naval equivalent of the MC.

'Yes,' the princess said. 'He was in the RNVR, in the war, Mr Nugent told me, and did very well as a pilot in the Fleet Air Arm.'

David thought, even my civilian boss will be more decorated, militarily, than I am, let alone both my subordinate colonels and some of the majors.

Stork Porter said, 'I hear he's a fire eater. He put down that trouble in the Seychelles in double quick time, and only two people killed.'

Sally said, 'Very ambitious, Mr Nugent hinted. *He* wouldn't say a thing like that out loud, would he? ... And brilliant.'

Ambitious, brilliant, and brave, David thought. Well, it would certainly make it easier for him to deal with a man who knew the services, who thought and acted like a sailor.

'But what else is known about him?' Sally cried, 'You don't seem very interested, but to us he's the Big White God for the next three years. What he says, goes. My grandmother can say what she likes but unless the Great Panjandrum approves ... pfft!'

'I believe he's a Roman Catholic,' Margaret Porter said in her pleasant Scots accent. 'His wife's a Lady, the daughter of the Marquess of Romford. They're a very important Catholic family, so I'm sure he must be.'

'Ah, there's the ambition coming out!' Sally cried gaily. 'But I want to know what his weaknesses are … except having children: Mr Nugent said he had five … Does he go for wine, women, little boys, money, ribbons to wear on his chest, what? *That's* what we want to know. It's the duty of my mother … or me … to seduce him for the sake of Mingora, if necessary .. Joke!'

David laughed politely. But was it a joke? He could see how, in this context, it might easily be someone's duty to see that the weaknesses of the British Resident were found and exploited.

'It sounds as though he doesn't have any weaknesses.' Porter said.

'He'll have some,' Sally said. 'Every man does!'

'And every woman, unfortunately,' Margaret Porter added.

Sally said, 'Well, we'll find out … How's your brigade, David?'

Now she's going to sound me out, he thought. He answered, 'One battalion's in Malaya and will remain there, directly under Singapore for another year at least, I've been told. I haven't had time to take more than a brief look at the troops here.'

'You were with the Fusiliers for some time, I hear,' she said.

'I went down there,' he said.

'And what did you find?' It was obvious that she knew about the mutiny; but he would not give her any satisfaction.

He said, 'A lot of British soldiers, going on a route march … I'd better be off, if you'll excuse me. I have piles of paper work to catch up with.'

Sally said, 'If you must … You look as though you'll work even harder than Brigadier Fowler. He was so nice … and such an *awful* bore. Please don't be a bore, David, eh? Then we could have so much fun.'

She was smiling at him over the rim of her glass, her eyes warm. Was it possible that she was flirting with him, in spite of his thinning hair and the grey streaks at his temples? When her mother had apparently dismissed from existence an intimacy between them that had been at the same time something far more and far less than flirting?

The princess said, 'Do you know about the Royal Beach? . . . Well, it's past the Jumbhorn Wat – you know where that is? – on the sea. There's a big changing cabin, and an old couple who live in a palm hut nearby and look after the place and serve fresh fruit and cold coconut juice and Coke. Please use it whenever you want to, you and your . . . well, you. We always invite the brigadier and the Resident.'

'Thank you very much,' he said. 'You'll probably find me there most mornings.'

He liked to swim in the early mornings, whenever he could and this would be a great deal better than sharing the Military Beach with a couple of hundred splashing and yelling Gurkhas. They were wonderful people, but he did not think his body, white and thin and bony, looked very like a commander's, when stripped of its uniform and the crown and three stars on the shoulder epaulettes.

'Thanks,' he said again, and with a wave of his hand headed for his car, leaving them on the verandah. He had a lot to digest, and to worry over, as a dog worries a bone.

At the car he heard running feet, and turned. Stork Porter leaned in through the open window: 'Freddie Young just called, sir – that's the adjutant of the Fusiliers . . . several men in A Company were sporting bunged-up eyes when they got on parade and another a bloody nose. Packard, Hadley and Jones were among them. He asked me to pass the message on to you.'

'Thanks,' David said, nodding. He drove off. Packard he'd seen in the crowded barracks, and heard, too; a troublemaker. Hadley was the bolshie anti-everything fellow. And Jones must be his own compatriot and namesake, the mellifluous Welsh demagogue. The company had indeed found its commonsense, this time. Now it was his job to see that something better, not worse, grew from the trouble.

Three

IT HAD RAINED heavily for two hours after dawn, then, to David's relief, the rain had stopped. Now, at the airport the sun shone, flocks of fluffy white clouds filled the sky, their shadows seeming to graze across the dappled landscape of rice and bamboo, green sugar cane and tall jungle, out towards the sea, invisible behind the slope where barracks and storerooms and the isolated bulk of Flagstaff House lined the ridge two miles to the north.

The northbound BOAC Comet was loading its passengers on one side of the tarmac apron. The other side was occupied with lines of white clad soldiers on parade, standing at ease under the morning sun. Off the apron behind the soldiers a dense mass of Mingorans covered the grass like some muticoloured swarm of bees, brown skins and green and yellow silk, buzzing, crawling, standing, sitting, squatting on the slight rise. Ten thousand of them were gathered to stare at the soldiers, at the row of four guns shining to the right at the edge of the main taxi track, and above all at the silk awning, its edges braided with gold and silver thread, where on ornate Victorian chairs of State sat Queen Valaya VI, her eldest daughter Tuankana Kumara, the Perdana Binte Mingora; and Kumara's only child, Tuankana Salimina, the Binte Binte Mingora. These three sat alone in the front row, their chairs widely spaced. In the second row, where David sat in No. 3 Dress, his sword in its steel scabbard held between his knees, sat the Prince Chamberlain, the Chief Minister, and other dignitaries he had either never seen or met only briefly during his business visits to the Chief Minister. All the Mingorans, men and women, were wearing full Mingoran costume, the men ornate short jackets, headdresses and sashes, with silk trousers, and the women embroidered bodices over long skirts. A jewelled tiara crowned Kumara's small head over her severely drawn-back black hair, her slender neck rising from bare honey-coloured shoulders. Her skirt was of blue and white, silver-threaded. She was wearing the same ruby brooch and the Queen the same diamond cobra head that they had been wearing in the palace.

She was sitting a few feet to his right and in front of him. She was keeping her reserved distance from him. He had seen Sally several times at the Royal Beach and the Gym, and once she'd invited him to a small dinner at her quarters in the Palace; with Kumara there had only been two meetings, the first that one with the Queen, the second a chance brush on a verandah of the Palace. Then, she asked him if he were comfortable in Flagstaff House: and he replied, 'Quite, *tuankana*,' and she said, 'If there's anything we can do for you...' and he said, 'Nothing, thank you, *tuankana*'...He must forget that their past had ever happened, which was hard when a tune from the Eisteddfod ran in his head, a tune they had sung together, softly, in the car on the way back to London.

The Queen was old as well as ill. Everyone in the government was old. The Prince Chamberlain had a wise mind and a gentle hand, but he was old and tired. The Chief Minister allied integrity with shrewdness, both qualities much admired by Mingorans – but he was not young. The ruling class, and the people as a whole, were bathed in a general good will, a gentle tolerance, which rendered their mild wish for improvement lethargic. Younger people might provide the energy to make necessary changes, but unless something was done, the younger people would gravitate into opposition.

The Comet pilot started up his engines and the crowd oohed and ahhed. Pretty girls at the edge of the crowd put their hands over their ears and made delighted grimaces. Jet aircraft were not old hat here, and as a people Mingorans liked noise, a lot of noise. It was really remarkable that ten thousand of them should have come out, on foot, four miles, to see the arrival of the British Resident. The Queen had made it known that she wished as many people as could to come to the airport, and declared the day a holiday...but still, it was an impressive indication of the Queen's position, and the general popularity of the regime.

The Comet taxied slowly out and turned up wind. David had another look at the guard of honour, a company of the Fusiliers on the right and a company of Gurkhas on the left, the whole under Major Powell of the Gurkhas. The Gurkha Pipes and Drums and the Fusiliers' band, fifes and drums, were fallen in to one flank. Some of the soldiers were looking towards the north, where perhaps they could hear something he could not. The Resident was due, and apparently he was the sort of man who could impose punctuality even on aircraft.

The BOAC plane opened up for take-off and then David saw something glinting in the sunlight to the north, moving in a rightwards sweep that would bring it to land. The Comet passed, the air shuddering to the thunder from its four tail pipes, the nose tilted. For two seconds the slender craft rode with nose high, tail dragging, then it arrowed into the sky. The commander of the guard of honour turned round to face his men. The sound of the departing plane's engines grew less, superseded by the screaming whine of the other coming in from the east.

The new plane, another Comet, landed and, as it slowed, clearly showed the Royal Air Force roundel on its wing. A minute later it was taxiing slowly towards the airport building, the lines of soldiers, and the ceremonial awning. The pilot swung the craft sideways and cut his engines. The whining scream died, and airport staff pushed out the ramp. Queen Valaya rose and walked slowly forward, leaning on the arm of the Chamberlain, her brother. Her daughter and grand-daughter followed three paces behind, and David took his place with the Chief Minister and the Residency Counsellor three paces behind again.

The door of the aircraft opened and after a brief pause a tall figure in white, the collar of an order glittering at the high gold-embroidered throat of his tunic, strode out two steps and stopped on the top of the ramp, the breeze fluttering the plumes on his cocked hat. David jumped to the boom of a gun and the Resident's hand rose to the point of his hat. *Boom! If I wasn't a gunner I wouldn't be here, Fire TWO,* David muttered under his breath, repeating the age-old phrase that artillerymen firing a salute use to make the proper interval between guns. *Boom. Boom* ... The Queen's head was up in the hot sun, Kumara's ruby brooch glowing like a redhot coal against her breast. *Boom* ... *Boom* ... *Boom* ...

As the echoes of the thirteenth gun died the Resident brought his right hand slowly down from the salute, put his left hand to the hilt of his diplomatic sword, and paced down the steps. As he reached the foot of the ramp the Fusilier band struck up 'God Save the Queen'. The Resident again came to the salute, turning to face the band, as Queen Valaya already was. The guard of honour stood rigid at the present.

The music ended. The Queen went forward two steps, the Resident came two steps to meet her. The Queen bowed her head and murmured something which David could not hear; then the Resident bowed in turn, and taking both her hands in his, bowed low over them. They turned and came on side by side, now, the Queen resting her arm in that of the Resident, her brother walking a pace behind. Shouted orders, and the guard of honour came to attention, ready for inspection. Side by side the Resident and the Queen moved slowly along the front rank, Major Powell at their side with sword drawn, while the Gurkha pipes wailed a slow march. Meantime, at the aircraft, a large woman wearing a blue silk dress and a wide-brimmed garden party hat came slowly down the ramp, followed by four children, the last a toddler, and a nanny with a fifth child, a baby, in her arms. Mr Nugent introduced David and the princesses to the Resident's wife, Lady Anne Wilson. Then the whole group waited while the Resident and the Queen turned at the end of the front rank and came back along the rear rank.

The Queen was very tired, David saw, really leaning on the Resident now, not just the touch that protocol demanded. She ought to have cut out this part of the ceremony, but she had courage . . . inviolate courage, that everyone agreed on. The Chief Minister had warned him that nothing would persuade her to give up any part of this ceremony, for it underlined in terms of pageantry, the truth of Mingora's existence – an independent queendom protected from foreign aggression by the arm of Britain, under a perpetual treaty that had already been honoured for one hundred and forty-nine years.

The Queen and the Resident returned slowly to the aircraft. The Queen said, 'Your Excellency, I have the honour to introduce my daughter, the Perdana Binte Mingora, Her Royal Highness the Kumara.'

Kumara sank slowly in a formal curtsey, her palms joined in front of her breast, her head bowed. Slowly she rose again, with serpentine slowness and perfect balance, then raised her head.

David saw the Resident's eyes stare, and for a long moment he stood as though frozen; then slowly, almost as slowly as she, he bowed. There was suddenly a peculiar tension in the group, and for that moment it was centred in the two figures, the man and the woman, linked to each other in formal contrast. As the Resident straightened, his eyes were still on Kumara's. Then... 'My grand-daughter, the Binte Binte Mingora, Her Royal Highness...' the Queen's tired voice unstrung the bow. The Resident moved sharply a pace to his right, and everyone seemed to sigh.

As the introductions ended a Daimler landau, its back down, and three large Austin saloons, swept round in front of the awning. The Resident helped the Queen into the landau, and the two sat side by side in the open back. David stepped into one of the Austins with Kumara, the Chamberlain, and the Resident's wife; Sally entered the third car, with Mr Nugent, the Chief Minister and another Mingoran whom David did not know. The nanny and the five children piled into the last, with another Mingoran official. At once the procession moved off. The crowd on the grassy slopes, all standing now, cheered and shouted and little boys and girls ran alongside the slow-moving limousines.

'It's really wonderful,' Lady Anne said. 'I mean, how popular your family must be. So much enthusiasm!'

Kumara said, 'My mother is very popular. The people remember what she did and suffered for them under the Japanese ... She never pretended to give up the special relationship we have had for so long with Great Britain. The Japanese did everything to try to make her – starvation, humiliation, threats of death ... she suffered it all.'

'How wonderful,' Lady Anne murmured.

David thought, how similar were the two women's tones and accent, both English-County, though Kumara's was a bit more marked, and Kumara also had the faintest trace of the Mingoran lift at the end of phrases. It was funny to hear the same accents coming from two such dissimilar bodies – Kumara's small, slim, fine-boned and high-breasted, Lady Anne's large and strong and heavy in the bust.

Lady Anne turned to David: 'Your wife must take me shopping here, brigadier.'

'I'm afraid I'm a bachelor,' he said.

'Oh, what a pity! Then we must find a wife for him, eh,

princess?' She was nice, probably very nice, David thought, a girl brought up on a big country estate, her humour simple and a little elephantine.

Kumara did not look at him as she said, 'Brigadier Jones would not be an easy man to marry.'

'Oh dear,' Lady Anne said, 'Why not?'

'There is more to him than meets the eye, and we women too often look only with the eye . . . Don't you agree, uncle?'

The old Chamberlain gave them a wizened smile and said nothing, as though he had not understood, though David knew by now that this posed ignorance of English was merely one of his little pleasures; in reality he understood it very well, though he spoke little. But David, stealing a look at Kumara, wondered why she had said what she had. It was a personal reference – the first; she was not looking at him. If he had not been able to understand someone as simple-minded as Lucy, how could he expect to fathom this experienced, intelligent – and foreign – woman at his side?

The cars were rolling into the outskirts of Trangloek now, the crowds thick along the verges of the road and among the shops and stalls and booths. As they crossed the railway just outside the station three steam engines, lined up as though for inspection, let loose with their whistles and railwaymen standing on the buffer beams, yelled and waved their hands. In the landau David could see the Queen and the Resident acknowledging the crowd, the Queen's thin brown hand turning slowly in air, the Resident's white glove touching the peak of his hat, the cocks' feathers ruffling in the breeze. The crowds grew denser yet, the cars' speed slowed, and the noise increased, with bells and horns and trumpets and human voices all at full volume.

'Goodness,' Lady Anne said, 'I never expected anything like this! A British Resident or ambassador is just as likely to be met by people shouting "English, go home!" these days, isn't he?'

'Not here,' Kumara said. 'We are linked for ever, and the people like it so.'

Then they could not speak, unless they leaned forward and bellowed in each others' ears, for firecrackers were exploding all round, and a band jammed in among the people was playing a tune which David, after some thought, recognized as 'God Save the Queen', followed by 'Mingora Ala-kir'.

The cars crawled past the Old Pagoda, the steps of the great plinth lined with monks and, inside, horns blowing eerily muted hollow blasts . . . past the Palace, scores of liveried men and bright women bowing on the grass outside the long wall, . . . through the Residency gates. The landau stopped in front of the main door, where the Residency staff, thirty in number were lined up. The Chamberlain scrambled out of David's car and hurried forward to help the Queen down. She in turn handed the Resident down. David, by now saluting beside them, distinctly heard her say, 'Welcome to your home in Mingora. The earth is yours, the air is ours. One cannot live without the other.' The Resident bowed deeply over her hands and stood saluting while she climbed slowly and painfully back into the landau. All the other British were out of the cars now and standing behind the Resident.

The cars swept slowly out, the Queen alone in the landau in front. As they passed the Residency gates and re-entered the streets of Trangloek the roar of the people rose to a new height. 'She goes back alone to the palace,' David heard Nugent tell the Resident, 'to prove that although we protect them, she is her own mistress inside the country.'

The Resident said, 'How ill is she?' The voice was sharp, the tone incisive but not rude. He was a little over six feet, well built, with brown hair, a square jaw, and an incongruously wide and sensual mouth. His skin was pallid and his eyebrows thin-arched over the pale blue eyes. He looked about forty, David thought, the same age as Kumara; five years younger than himself.

'Very ill, I believe,' the Counsellor murmured, 'though there has been no official announcement, and no private notification to us.'

'We'd better find out.' He turned on David: 'The guard of honour was very well turned out, brigadier. Congratulate the COs, please. Come and have dinner on the eighteenth. Friday. Eight thirty . . . No one seemed to know much about you at the War Office, but someone did say that golf and squash are your games. You don't by chance play chess, too, do you?'

'No, sir.'

'Nugent, do you?'

'Good heavens, no. Far too cerebral for me.'

'Well, I expect I'll find someone.'

David said, 'Kumara plays . . . the Perdana Binte Mingora.'

'I know,' the Resident said, 'Near international level. Come, Anne. Introduce us to the staff, Nugent.'

David backed off. His staff car should arrive any minute now, once the streets had cleared a bit, then he could change, get to the office and do some work. Her Britannic Majesty's Resident at the Royal Court of Mingora had been duly installed.

He pulled the next document out of his IN tray and looked at it with distaste. It was the report of the Board of Inquiry into the Fusiliers' mutiny, and David had already read it, carefully, twice. Porter had done an outstanding job: he was coming to realize that his Brigade Major was an outstanding officer, although in some respects he lived up to the old saw that all sappers were mad, married or Methodist. And the battery sergeant-major had obviously been invaluable on the board, getting worried young fusiliers to speak where they would have frozen in front of an officer.

The report left no doubt that Major Spalding was not suited for regimental duty; he would probably make a good staff officer in a big headquarters, or the War Office, but he should not be allowed to serve with troops. The first step there was to have him severely reprimanded and transferred out of the Fusiliers. A 194 E would see that he was kept away from troops. Next, CSM Norris was a crook and should be courtmartialled for accepting bribes. Two of the platoon sergeants were weak and should probably be reduced to the ranks. He'd have to tear a strip off John Allen, who must bear a large part of the blame. The CO should have seen what was happening. He would have to make that quite clear, and John Allen wouldn't like it at all. He wouldn't like it himself, for it was not pleasant to berate a war hero. He ought, really, to initiate a 194 E on him, too, but he'd be a coward and let the C-in-C decide that, when he read the Inquiry report and knew what he himself had done about it.

He scribbled a note on his memo pad and picked up the next paper. After reading a couple of pages he touched the bell on his desk and said to the orderly, 'Brigade IO, please'.

Crawford came in. He was more at ease now and his face, instead of being closed and cautious when speaking to David, was open and alert. 'What's going on in Kusalung and Moirang,

Peter?' David said, tapping the papers now before him.

'I don't know how serious it might become, sir,' the lieutenant said. 'So far, the Constabulary can handle it easily. But the Chief Minister apparently thinks it might be the beginning of a programme by the MPRP to organize their platoons in the western provinces and start the sort of campaign that caused the emergency in Malaysia.'

'You say a prominent landowner of Kusalung was killed, but . . .'

'He was . . .' Crawford cut in; then, realizing what he was doing, he flushed and said, 'I'm sorry, sir.'

'No, go on.'

'He was a strong supporter of the royal family, sir, and a Muslim of almost pure Malay descent. His loyalty to the royal house meant a great deal in the western provinces.'

'But there's no proof that he was murdered by the MPRP is there? Don't these political terrorists always make it very clear that a killing is their work, when it is?'

'Sometimes, but the Chief Minister thinks they don't want to tip their hand yet – they want people down there to doubt and worry . . . The murdered landowner was a great womanizer, sir, and it is also possible that he was murdered by a jealous husband. In fact the governor of Kusalung reports that the Constabulary arrested just such a man . . . though he swears he didn't do it. He wanted to, he says, but he didn't.'

'Well, the Constabulary can surely handle it.'

'Oh yes, sir. '

'Good . . . Where did Sally go to school? She has a slight American accent, sometimes.'

'She went to Cheltenham Ladies' College, sir, like her mother the Princess Kumara, but afterwards the Queen decided she should be sent to an American university as she thought America was going to play a big role in South East Asia. She went to Stanford. It's in California, near San Francisco.'

'Didn't I read in that summary that Sujak bin Amin, the head of the MPRP went to Stanford, too?'

The lieutenant's eyes gleamed. 'No, sir. He got a scholarship to the University of California at Berkeley, which is close. He was there from 1949 to 1953, and Sally didn't go to Stanford till 1956. Sujak was hired by the royal family to cram Sally for Stanford – Sally's not very good at books – and to tell how she should eat, dress, and live. It didn't help much. At the end of her second year Stanford said she'd have to leave. She came home in early '58.'

'What was Sujak then?'

'When they hired him to help Sally he was an assistant professor of philosophy at Mingora University here. He disappeared soon afterwards and founded, or re-founded, the MPRP in Burma. I hear – this is only rumour, sir – that Sally was attracted to him. She talks like a socialist, sometimes.'

'H'm. Socialist monarchy? . . . Well, we've got one in England, haven't we, so there's nothing impossible about that.'

He nodded in dismissal. Nothing else important in all that bumf, except the DO from the Chief of Staff hoping that the report of the Fusiliers' Board of Inquiry would soon be on its way with his recommendations. That would be answered to-morrow, with the report. It was clear, reading between the lines, that the C-in-C was still unhappy about the way the mutiny had been handled. When he emerged from the Sarawak jungles and heard what was happening in Mingora, he'd spoken direct to David by radio, and expressed some concern about the ultimate effects of such apparent clemency on the mutineers. But by then the thing was over, for better and for worse. As for the long term effects . . . they'd all have to wait and see.

Lunch, a nap, an hour with Marriott on the drainage problem in Kandahar Lines, then golf with Sally. She was really very flirtatious. Well, it didn't do an old man of forty-six's ego any harm. Dinner with the Resident at eight-thirty. He smoothed down the hair over his bald spot and went out.

The Resident pushed back his chair and said, 'We won't be rejoining you, Anne. I'm going to take Brigadier Jones along to the study.'

Lady Anne stood up. 'Oh dear, are you going to play chess all night?' She smiled uncertainly. There were only the three of them at the table, two servants waiting in the shadows.

'The brigadier doesn't play. Just business.' The Resident picked up his brandy and motioned David to follow suit. David thought he ought to bid some more formal goodbye and thanks to his hostess if he wasn't going to see her again, but Wilson had vanished through the tall doorway and he didn't know what to say, so he threw Lady Anne a hurried smile and followed her husband. From upstairs he heard children shouting, and the wail of a baby.

The Resident's study was large and airy, with three sets of french windows opening out on to the secluded lawn at the back of the Residency. His desk was set near the centre of the room, but he was standing now by the empty fireplace under the lifesize oil painting of Queen Elizabeth. The fireplace would always be empty, for fires were never needed in Trangloek, but an English room had to have a fireplace, and this was very English.

The Resident said, 'Nugent swears that there are no eaves-dropping devices, but I've had this room re-checked. We can talk freely. You've only been here two weeks, so I suppose you don't know the country yet.'

'I was here briefly in '45 – '46,' David said. 'I went on some flag marches with my company in the eastern provinces.'

'Simdega, Machin, Lepet, and of course the capital district, Trangloek,' Wilson said. He sipped his brandy. He was wearing the proper local evening dress, David noted – white dinner jacket and black trousers; in some parts of the east one wore black tops and white trousers, but Wilson had taken the trouble to find out the correct wear. Bareheaded, he seemed as tall as he had with the cocked hat and ruffling plumes. He was a burly man and his hands were big; probably a rugger player in his days at the university.

Wilson said, 'The total population of Mingora is 3,065,000, of which 1,685,000 are easterners, mainly Buddhist-Thais, and 1,380,000 are westerners, mainly Muslim-Malays.'

'Yes, sir,' David said. The Resident's homework had included more than finding out about his brigadier's sporting inclinations and the local dress. The pallid blue eyes were fixed intently on him but that was a habit of Wilson's. He stared at anyone he was talking to, including his wife or a servant.

'Our connection with Mingora dates back to 1810,' the Resident continued, 'when the then Queen begged the British government to protect her queendom from Burma and Thailand. At that time Mingora became a Protectorate of the British crown, its independence, the integrity of its borders, and the continuity of its form of government guaranteed by HMG. It could have no policy dealings with foreign countries except through the British representative, that is, the Resident. It could have no army, only a constabulary, not to exceed one thousand men and armed only with small arms ... Your troops are here to fulfil the terms of the Treaty of Trangloek, and because there is at present no other suitable place in the Far East from where they can carry out their second role as a small strategic reserve in the area.'

'Mingora will be very important when the Singapore base is phased out and Malaya takes over its own defence,' David said, 'I wouldn't be surprised if we put more troops in here.'

The Resident ignored his observation and continued: 'So there has been no change in our military commitment in Mingora, although there have been immense political changes all over South East Asia – over nearly one hundred and fifty years.'

David drank some brandy, wondering where this was leading. The Resident said, 'The royal family of Mingora, and its advisers have not changed their ways of thought in all that time – because they have not had to. They have rested secure under British protection, both external and internal. The threat from outside is now nil, but the threat from inside – revolution, insurrection – is great and growing greater every moment ... and we would be dragged in to save the regime by force.'

David opened his mouth and said, 'But——'

The Resident raised his hand. 'You are going to say that the Royal Mingoran Constabulary could do it.'

David said, 'They have a hundred men in each province and ...'

'... a central reserve of two hundred and fifty here in Trangloek,' the Resident interrupted. 'I know. But they would be useless in a real revolution. After any initial rebel success many of them would turn their coats. In any case we would be called in, as we were in 1837 and 1890.'

'Probably,' David agreed. 'The MPRP must have learned a lot from the CTs in Malaya. They'd be a tough nut if they were to get any local support.'

'That's just what they are getting,' the Resident said decisively, 'because the ruling clique here think there is no need to change, to progress. The governors of every province are easterners. There are no elections for any office, whether at the village, city, provincial, or national level. Change is supposed to come through the traditional channels here – and they aren't wide enough or deep enough. If something isn't done, the dykes will break ... and drown *us*.'

The Resident's voice had an astringent quality, a harshness that tingled like a rebuke, though he was not rebuking. It was stimulating to listen to him. The pale eyes were fixed on him. 'What I am about to tell you is known only to the Cabinet, the Permanent Under Secretary, the Commissioner General of British Dependencies in South East Asia, the Commander in Chief FARELF, and now you ... Her Majesty's Government have decided to reduce British military commitments east of Suez as rapidly as possible, with the aim of ending them altogether. As a first step in this East of Suez policy, as it has been called, they have decided to terminate the Treaty of Trangloek as from 1 June, 1960, which will be the one hundred and fiftieth anniversary of its signing. All British forces are to be out of the country by that date, except a token force to take part in the ceremony, on 1 June, at which I will declare Mingora fully independent, and will step down as Resident and become ambassador. Today is 18 December, 1959. Your task in the next five and a half months is to prepare the Mingorans to stand on their own feet in all matters of defence, external and internal. Think about it.'

The words were spoken in a tone of finality. David put down his empty brandy glass and said, 'I will, sir ... Has Queen Valaya been told?'

'I just told you – no. I will tell her in two or three weeks, when I judge the moment ripe, and when I have had time to study this country more thoroughly. At that time I will be able to tell Her Majesty what she must do, in such a way and with so much supporting data that she cannot argue ... That's a military maxim, isn't it? Never send a boy to do a man's job? Because there cannot be any argument. None. The Cabinet has made up its mind ... Let me show you out. Your car is waiting, I think ... See you at the squash courts.'

David sat back in the staff car, rubbing his chin. The seduction of Mr Sidney Francis Wilson, which Sally had jokingly declared to be necessary for the salvation of Mingora, was not going to be easy. Unless perhaps 'they' had decided that Kumara was the one to do it. He shook his head violently, trying to shake out the thought ... An intense, ambitious man. Brilliant, as they had all said. High strung. His master. And what a bloody mission the Government had given him. He himself had never studied the actual text of the Treaty of Trangloek but he was sure it said something about 'for ever'. Now it seemed that 'for ever' meant 'a hundred and fifty years'; or, actually, from the point of view of today's Mingorans, five and a half months. It wasn't going to be easy to create an adequate defence set-up here in the time available. In fact it was going to be impossible. He'd have to decide first what *was* possible, and then try to get it done. And it would siphon out of the economy a great deal of money that could be used for other things like education, better sewage for the capital, modernizing agricultural methods in the provinces, better medical services everywhere. Still, the defence money was now being provided by England, which was no longer rich . . . but some of those old riches had come from this very treaty, by which England had gained immense mercantile and strategic advantages. Now, England was going to try to keep the trade advantages but give up her side of the bargain – the defence and security of the country.

On an impulse he spoke at the back of his driver's head – 'How long have you been in Mingora, corporal?'

'Two years, sir,' Wood said over his shoulder.

'How do you like it?'

'I'd rather 'ave the Holloway Road on a Saturday night, but you can't complain. There's much worse.'

'What about the people? How do you get on with them? I don't mean just you, the fellows in general.'

'They're good blokes, sir. They really seem to like us, none of this smile to your face and stick a knife in your back sort of thing. A lot of fellows want to marry the girls and some do, but they don't take 'em 'ome. Because they don't want to go. I mean, the fellows don't, nor the girls. That's been going on for a hundred years. You look round when we 'ave a ceremonial parade. Look at the crowd, sir. There's 'alf a 'undred girls, kids, old fellows in the front of the crowd, that's 'alf castes . . . children of blokes from regiments that was 'ere donkey's years ago, and stayed. And of course, when we 'ave Christmas next week, there'll be thirty, forty old sweats eating in the company messes with us, from the Rifle Brigade we took over from, from the Welch before them, and the Devons, and there's one that was 'ere with the 2nd DCLI in 1894! . . . It's more like 'ome than it 'as a right to be,

61

this place, in spite of the palm trees and the 'ot wind off the land and the cool wind off the sea and the fruit and the smells in the bazaar.'

David wondered. All good things must come to an end, but this seemed a pity. A shame, almost. Indeed, shameful.

Four

AT THE MILITARY BEACH David got out of the Land-Rover, which he was driving himself, and told his orderly to join the others in the sea, and go back to the Lines with them. Tulbahadur saluted, tore off his uniform, revealing swimming trunks beneath, and ran down into the sea. David saw approvingly that life guards were perched on high chairs at either end of the Military Beach, with lifebelts and cord ready, and also rifles. He beckoned to a Gurkha officer standing nearby and said, '*Sab thik chha, Captain Sahib?*'

'*Thik chha, huzoor!*'

'Did you have the shark net inspected?'

'Yes, sahib. It is in good order.'

'Why do the lifeguards have rifles?'

'They fire them in the air, as well as blowing a whistle, if they see sharks' fins inside the net, or close outside. Those *shaitans* patrol the net, sahib, waiting for a man to put an arm or a hand through by mistake ... And the guards also fire the rifles at the sharks.'

'I don't suppose that would do much good.'

'No, sahib, but it makes the men in the water feel better.'

David smiled and moved on along the beach. The 2nd/12th seemed to be keen on swimming. Their training programme showed that each company spent one hour here twice a week. Nearby, a score of learners wallowed waist deep in the light surf. The noise was tremendous, close to, but as he moved away from the capering brown bodies the soughing of the trade wind, the hiss of the sand and the whisper of the bent grass on the dunes gently smothered it, reducing it to no more than the murmur of sleepy birds in distant trees.

He got back into his Land-Rover and drove on northward. The road turned away from the beach and ran parallel with the metre gauge railway that linked Mingora with Thailand to the north and Malaysia to the south. After a couple of miles an iron signpost pointing to the right announced *Jumbhorn Wat*, and he turned down the dusty road. The great temple was a national monument, but long since abandoned, and now not guarded, nor used in any way as a place of worship. It bore a resemblance to its famous, and larger, relative Angkor Wat far to the north; but, in the long terraces and the sheer bulk of some of the buildings, it also resembled Borobudur in Java far to the south. The jungle had not seriously encroached on it, for the local farmers grazed their cattle freely between and inside the massive blocks of the buildings, but there was no sign of human habitation and, this early morning of mid December, there were no cows and no cowherds. The flat eastern light shone low and full on the luscious apsaras, the rows of pillars, demons and gods in a gigantic tug of war. David had never looked at it properly. In 1945 he was young, and not very interested. Now, he must make time. There would surely be time . . . three years in this gentle paradise by the sea.

He drove on, passed through a gate heavily posted with the legend, PRIVATE–ROYAL PROPERTY–NO ADMITTANCE, and more, presumably with the same portent, in Mingora-Malay script. A few minutes later he drew up in front of the wide-verandahed hut which was the royal beach house. He looked out at the royal beach. A car was here already, an open MG. That was Sally's, and that must be her head in the water now. The old caretaker came out of his hut at the edge of tall trees behind the beach house and, recognizing David, asked whether the presence wished anything. David shook his head, went into the beach house and changed into his trunks. Near the edge of the sea he broke into a run, and plunged through the first small breaker as it rose up, green and soft in front of him. He came up, blowing and wiping his eyes, in front of the Princess Sally. Her voluptuous body was barely contained by a yellow bikini.

'Ah, the serious brigadier,' she cried, 'You're not wet yet.' She started splashing water into his face, laughing happily.

She's still partly a child, David thought, in spite of that body or perhaps because of it. He threw water back at her and she dived under the surface, grabbed his ankles and after a struggle, pulled him over. When he surfaced she said, 'Race you to level with the big palm.'

'Wait a minute,' he said, 'Have you checked the net?'

'Oh, no,' she said. 'It's all right.'

'I don't want to end up as breakfast for one of those beasts,' he said and swam off to the net. She followed close, swimming with lazy ease. 'I suppose you're right,' she said. 'How did your dinner with the Great Panjandrum go last night? What do you think of him?'

'A very high-powered man,' David said, cruising along the net and peering down into the translucent water for signs of holes in the wide steel mesh, and looking for glass balls missing out of the line that stretched the net taut, upwards, from the lengths of steel rail on the sand to which it was tied at short intervals.

'Those eyes!' Sally exclaimed, 'What on earth made him marry *her*? Well, we know that's because she's a marquess's daughter. She's like a great big worried cow. She was here yesterday with the nanny and all the children. Like something out of a Victorian novel. He didn't come, though . . . He's discovered my mother is a good chess player.'

'He knew that before he arrived,' David said.

'A friend of ours had some business with him and do you know what? He spoke several words of Mingora-Malay. When on earth has he had time to learn it?'

'He has a very quick mind,' David said. 'And far seeing. Or he wouldn't be good at chess.'

'He's invited my mother to play tonight. He'd better know what he's doing. If he thinks my mother's just a simple straight-forward product of Cheltenham Ladies' College, he'll wind up losing his shirt . . . or his trousers.' She shrieked with laughter and dived under water. She came up again, 'The net's OK. Now will you race me?'

Afterwards, still in their swimming clothes, they sat in cane chairs on the verandah of the beach house, drinking coconut juice and eating persimmons which the old man brought to them from his hut, and the princess said, 'Will you play golf with me this afternoon again, David? I want you to show me what I'm doing wrong with my chip shots.'

'I can't, I'm afraid. The Resident has booked me for squash.'

She moued in discontent, 'Beastly man,' she said. 'Tomorrow then?'

'That'll be fun,' he said. She leaned over, pressed her damp, cool breasts against his shoulder, and kissed him on the ear. 'I like you,' she whispered.

'Thank you,' he said, holding her gingerly round the waist. 'I'm a little old for you, I'm afraid.'

'Not for me,' she said. 'The subalterns are . . . so callow, aren't they? And everyone else is married.'

'What about the young Mingoran men?'

'The old-fashioned ones daren't – can't – act naturally with me, because I'm the Binte Binte Mingora. The younger ones are – unsophisticated, I suppose. Their interests and experience have been so different from mine that we have nothing to talk about. Our points of view are different. Except for one or two . . .'

He stood up. 'I have to go now. Work,' he said.

'Kiss me,' she said, holding up her face. When he hesitated she said, 'Please!'

David stooped, wondering what General Sir Rougemont Huntingdon would have to say if he happened to be watching from the bushes, and kissed her gently on the lips. She was a sexy young woman and he was not so damned old. Sexual urges stirred in him and he kissed her harder as she clasped her hands round the back of his neck. The face he saw behind his closed lids was not Sally's, but Kumara's.

'Presence, does the presence want . . .' the old caretaker's voice spoke behind him.

He broke away, and went into the men's changing room to dress.

As he followed the Chief Minister's round black hat down a narrow alley he wondered whether the minister had already heard that he had been kissing Princess Salimana two hours ago. He'd certainly hear sooner or later . . . but then perhaps Sally kissed a lot of men and no real notice was taken of it.

'This part of the bazaar is full of Moirangis and Powlangis – westerners,' the minister threw over his shoulder. 'Look here' – he stopped in front of a narrow stall displaying rolls of cane mats. 'This weave of the matting is only used in the west . . . over there's

66

an eastern one, probably from Lepet. Do you see the difference?' He spoke rapidly to the first storekeeper in a dialect David did not understand. The minister said, 'I am a Moirangi myself. This man knows my wife's family. He was from the same village . . .'

He moved on. The alley ended in a wider street. At the end of that, an empty space of beaten earth suddenly opened up. Beyond the dusty emptiness stood a group of whitewashed stone buildings with green tiled roofs. 'Trangloek University,' the Minister said, 'And that red building you can see through the gap there is the railway station. This area is our biggest danger in Trangloek – many westerners who, as you know, are not altogether content – and the university, with many young men – and women – who want to change things but don't know why, or how.'

'I took a cursory look at it with my Brigade IO,' David said.

'Lieutenant Crawford? A capable young man.'

'Yes . . . Now you've shown me where the police posts are, and I've met the inspectors, I think we can make a sound plan for emergencies.'

'These are the city police, you understand,' the Minister said, 'They are armed only with long staves and truncheons. We have two hundred and fifty Constabulary – stationed here, but they are not supposed to be used in the capital, though they could be. They are the central reserve to be sent out to support the Constabulary in any threatened province . . . Now, I will show you the university more closely.'

He walked slowly across the open land, where one or two men were practising flying their war kites. Outside the university buildings a number of young people were lounging under a shaded patio. As the Minister began to tell David that this was the Humanities Building, a motorcycle orderly buzzed up on a Vespa, stopped his machine, and spoke briefly in Mingora-Malay. The Minister nodded and the motor cyclist wheeled his machine round and buzzed away. The Minister said, 'I have to go back to the palace. There is a report of more trouble in Kusalung. I will telephone you if it is anything serious.'

'I can look round here by myself,' David said. If there's anything I want to know I'll ask the Constabulary Commissioner, or the Chief of the city police.'

'No, no, come to me, brigadier.' He walked away, his old legs moving a little faster than usual, his back a little bent.

David began a leisurely inspection of the university and concluded that the buildings offered no great internal security problem in themselves. The whole group of them was easy to contain or cordon off, and the individual buildings could also be isolated, though storming one might be a messy business if it became necessary. The big problem would be the students, if they were to support anti-government riots or violence, and spread out through the city. But why should they do such a thing? Barely 10 per cent of them were paying any tuition, or even board, the minister had told him – all the rest paid for by the state. They were from all over the country, selected as those whose graduation would most benefit the nation. The Queen had been talking about forming an elective council, even a parliament, and these young people could reasonably expect to be the future leaders of Mingora . . . but all were young, most were impatient, and some were foolish. He would speak to the minister and make it clear that he did not want to use his troops in the city of Trangloek if it could be avoided; he'd rather take over the rural areas, so that they could concentrate more RMC here.

His car came for him at the agreed rendezvous and he returned to his headquarters. Half an hour later, as he was discussing the new sewer plans with his D/Q, the telephone rang. It was the Chief Minister who began without preamble, 'There have been three more murders in Kusalung, brigadier. Not in Kusalung city, but in and near a village about twenty miles to the east, called Ban Dhrai. One of the murdered men was headman of the village, one was the local agent of a landowner, and the third was a peasant. The murderers carved the letter R on the peasant's forehead with a knife blade.'

'R?' David asked.

'For *rangfun* – it means tattle tale.'

'Oh. The man had told the RMC something?'

'They've heard nothing, and don't know the man. He may have spoken to one of the other two victims.'

'This is the work of the MPRP?' David asked.

'They have not claimed it yet, but yes, we are sure . . . I am going down there tomorrow, but there is no need, that I can see now, for any military action. There is no threat of force that the Constabulary cannot deal with. I will keep you informed.'

'Thank you.'

David hung up thoughtfully, sent for his Intelligence Officer and Brigade Major, and told them the news. Porter said, 'It looks as though the MPRP are concentrating on Kusalung.'

'That's strange, sir,' Crawford said, 'because it is the furthest from Burma where the MPRP have re-formed. And the Kusalungis are less fanatically Muslim, less "Western", than the Powlangis or the Moirangis.'

'I suppose they think Kusalung is ripe and the others aren't, for some reason . . . or they have some particular places they can hide in. Is the country different there?'

'No, sir. All the provinces are very similar – the same amounts of jungle, paddy, crops, hills, coast – only the hills are along the eastern border of the western provinces and along the western border of the eastern provinces . . .'

Stork Porter said, 'They may be trying to get us to concentrate on Kusalung at the expense of the others. I don't mean only militarily – I mean, put more money into it, better administrators, introduce reforms, take more notice altogether . . . while they're working just as hard, but underground, in Moirang . . . and here in Trangloek.'

'Possible,' David said. 'That's a matter for intelligence. How good is the Chief Minister's intelligence network, Peter?'

'Very good in the east, sir, not too good in the west. It's partly lack of money, particularly recently. The Queen has been putting a lot of money into the university, roads, rural credit. The intelligence budget is secret, but I know it was heavily cut last year.'

David shuffled the papers and pursed his lips and stared at the inkwell. The telephone on his desk rang. He picked it up – 'Allen here, sir . . . There are rumours going round that there's been some sort of trouble in Kusalung.'

'It's true. Not very big. Three men murdered. The RMC aren't worried.'

'I wanted to be sure, because we're on stand-by and we're having our pre-Christmas children's party tomorrow, which will involve the whole battalion. We've started preparations already but we can stop now without any real loss. But in another couple of hours we'll have committed a lot of our regimental funds.'

David said slowly, 'I don't see how we can be pulled in . . . unless of course something drastically worse happens in the next forty-eight hours. The Chief Minister told me himself, half an hour ago, that the RMC could deal with whatever's happening down there. No, you go ahead.'

'Thank you, sir.'

David returned to his files. After an hour he found himself wishing that the troubles in Kusalung *were* bad enough to call in the brigade – all of it; anything was better than spending your days wallowing in the swamps of paperwork that the modern army seemed to think necessary. Proposal to set up regimental boards to study the methods of teaching theoretical subjects to recruits . . . return wanted of all men with experience in repair of outboard motors, in sextuplicate . . . revised safety regulations for field firing exercises . . . rights of men being held for court martial in stations where no member of the Army Legal Service available . . . alteration in pay scales for nursing orderlies at military hospitals outside the UK . . . He gritted his teeth and read carefully every paper. Those who had been set in authority over him, both civil and military, had got there by superior merit and longer experience. What made him think he could do any better if he were to be put in their shoes? Grumbling was useless and also bad for everyone's morale, to none more than to the grumbler. He read on.

At half past four, as he was getting into the abbreviated shorts he wore for squash rackets, the telephone rang in his bedroom at Flagstaff House. It was the Resident.

'Brigadier? You've been informed of the situation in Kusalung?'

'Yes, sir.'

'I consider it is important to take strong action now – before this spreads, as it did in Malaysia. I have told the Chief Minister that we will send troops as soon as possible. How many do you consider we will need?'

David said, 'The Minister told me he was sure the RMC could handle it.'

'I know' – the Resident's tone was brisk – 'but when I made it clear that we wanted to be involved, he said he would welcome us taking over.'

David thought of all the Fusiliers getting their children's party ready. The troops loved such parties so much. He said, 'I can't see how we could use more than a company, at the most.'

The Resident said, 'That's not enough, brigadier. This is not a military matter. It is political. I want to show our immediate and overwhelming support for the Queen's government. And I want to convince the MPRP that we will act firmly – very firmly – against them once we do decide to act.'

It was on the tip of David's tongue to add, 'While we are here'; but he remembered that the planned abrogation of the treaty was still top secret. He said, 'Very well, sir, I'll send the stand-by battalion – that's the Fusiliers. They can move in an hour, less detachments left to look after the barracks.'

'Good. Do you propose to go yourself?'

'I wouldn't go with the battalion. Colonel Allen's capable of handling it . . . but I would normally go down in a day or two to see for myself what's happening.'

'Do that.'

'Is our squash game still on?'

'Of course. It won't take you long to issue the necessary orders, will it?'

'No, sir.'

The Resident hung up. David stared unhappily at the phone and then, girding himself, picked it off the hook and asked the operator for the Fusiliers. When he got through to John Allen he said, 'I'm sorry, but I'm sending your battalion to Kusalung. RASC transport is available.'

There was a long silence; then, in a taut voice, 'The whole battalion?'

'Yes. Move as soon as possible. On arrival at Kusalung contact the governor. If he declares martial law, act as you see fit to restore confidence in the province, particularly in and around the village of Ban Dhrai. If he does not declare martial law you have to act with his advice and consent. We do *not* want martial law declared unless the situation changes radically for the worse.'

'I understand,' the voice said. 'Could this move not have been foreseen? My regiment has been sweating all day preparing for the children's party, and I've been authorizing expenses for perishable items which . . .'

David cut in: 'No, it could not. I'm sorry. That's all. I will be with you in a day or two. Sitreps every four hours by radio.' He hung up.

Why couldn't he have told Allen that the move was a direct

71

order from the Resident? Then they could have commiserated with each other as simple soldiers being buggered about by civilians who couldn't make up their bureaucratic little minds... But it was always wrong to put the blame for unpopular acts on 'orders from above'. You had to take it yourself, just as you expected your colonels and corporals not to pass on orders like automata, but to *give* them, with their own force and personal backing. And this time it wasn't a case of the civilian dithering or trying to pass the baby: Wilson knew exactly what he wanted, and was willing to take the responsibility of ordering it to be done. Also, he was probably right. Never send a boy to do a man's job... Unfortunately, the MPRP terrorists in the Kusalung area would certainly go into hiding when they saw a whole battalion arrive. They wouldn't come out in the open, where the army could get at them, unless they thought they had some hope of victory.

Cursing, he picked up his racquet and gym shoes and hurried downstairs. He found the staff car waiting under the porch, Tulbahadur at the wheel. 'Where's Corporal Wood?' he growled.

'Had his inoculation this morning, sahib,' Tulbahadur said stolidly.

'What's that got to do with it?'

'Twenty-four hours off duty.'

David got into the back, grumbling under his breath, damned scrimshankers, going to bed for an inoculation. What would they do if it were their turn for sentry... or if there was a big attack due for dusk? Well, they'd do the job that had to be done.

He said. 'While I'm playing squash, *keta*, you can take the car to the civilian beach and have a swim, as long as there's a guard.'

The Gurkha said, 'I have to take it back to the MT lines sahib. It's due for grease and an oil change.'

He took the sharp corner leading back along the Esplanade a little tightly. At the same moment a big black Austin took it even more tightly going in the opposite direction. Brakes squealed and the two cars scraped sides with an ugly scream of metal and tinkle of broken glass. David found himself on the floor, his head ringing from a bump against the side pillar. He picked himself up, opened the door and jumped out. A large redfaced Englishman in his sixties climbed heavily out of the driving seat of the Austin, and fanned his face with a white panama hat. His hair was white and thick, his tropical suit was white, he was a vision in white except for the mottled dark red face.

David said, 'You were coming round the corner on our side of the road.'

At the cars, Tulbahadur took out the driver's notebook and began to record the damage.

The fat man said, 'I could say the same of your Gurkha.'

David snapped, 'Look at the tyre marks. We were on our side of the road.'

'Sometimes,' the other said. 'Well, it's no matter. I expect your little man's had a tot or two for lunch, eh?'

David's suppressed frustration burst out into cold rage. He said venomously, 'Tulbahadur has had nothing to drink since last night, if then – which is more than I can say of you, judging by your breath.'

The other raised his head and reared back and said, 'Coom lad! Aren't tha' being a bit insulting, like?' As he had spoken fairly standard English before, this heavy Yorkshire accent was obviously put on.

David said, 'Yes.'

The other said, 'Well, Ah could be insulting too, lad, if Ah wanted to be. It's easy enough, tha' knows . . . But tha' doesn't like tha' little man being insulted, eh? . . . Aye, I've had a good lunch. Lasted till just now, as a matter of fact. But however much he's taken, Harry Johnstone can drive well enough, as plenty here in Mingora will be willing to tell you . . . The truth is I let my chauffeur go to a wedding . . . We were both wrong, eh, me and your little fellow. And I shouldn't have said he'd had a tot too many, eh? How's that?'

David's anger evaporated. He said, 'I'm sorry. I lost my temper.' This man, whom he had been on the verge of punching in the nose, was the most powerful British commercial figure in the east – Sir Harry Johnstone, creator and owner of Mingora & Oriental. Like everyone else, he knew the name, but he had never met the man before. He said, 'I'm Brigadier Jones.' He put out his hand.

Sir Harry took it in a large damp paw and shook it energetically, and said, 'I know. I've seen you. I've been meaning to introduce myself . . . not like this, eh! . . . so we could have a chat . . . You look as if you're going to the Gym, will you drive me there, lad,

73

so that I can telephone someone to look at this car? And we can fix a date for a meal. Lunch at the Place some day – that's what we call the Mingora Club, don't ask me why – I have a private dining room permanently reserved there . . .'

'3–5' the Resident said. He threw up the ball and served, smashing the racquet down with a fierce grunt. With the follow through he leaped into centre court. The service whistled so hard into the back corner that David could take it easily off the wall. He laid a low drive that ran down the left wall. It was a good shot and would have died in the front left corner if the Resident had not reached it with a tremendous bound and grunt, scraped it off the floor with a loud hammer and clatter of his racquet, and got it back on to the wall. It came back easily and David laid it in the opposite corner. The Resident dived over and scooped it out, again just in time. He tore across court, expecting David to put it again down the opposite side, but David laid it dead, back where it had come from, easily passing his opponent.

'5–3,' the Resident said shortly. He waited, crouched, teeth clenched, racquet held across his body. Sweat dripped steadily from his face and forehead on to the red composition floor. His shirt was dark and wet. He lashed out at David's service with all his might. The ball ran round the court, David helping it on its way with an unplayable kill.

'6–3.' the Resident said. The muscles stood out on his jaw as he waited. David served an ace.

'7–3.'

David served again. Wilson was, or could be, a good player – but he hit everything much too hard, and ran about too much. He seemed to be using the racquet and the game itself not to play, but to work out physically tensions that were mental or moral. David was an above average player, but by no means top-class; and he was nearly forty-six years of age. Sidney Wilson was forty, strong, fit, with an excellent eye, but this need to employ maniacal violence overcame both his games sense and his eye.

'Game,' David said two points later.

'Another,' Wilson said.

'Don't you want a breather?'

'No. Serve. Go on.'

David served.

This game lasted longer, for Wilson was wearing him down. When it ended, thirty minutes later, David had won 9–6, but he thought that Wilson was going to demand another game ... and another ... until he had won one. He was clearly not a man who liked losing. But Wilson said, 'That's enough. I have some work to do before dinner. Thanks for the games.'

They went into the changing room and changed back into their street shoes. The Resident said, 'Have you heard any more about the Queen? How ill she is? Sally's a close friend of yours.'

David tried to hide a flush. He said, 'No one's said anything.'

'I give her five months,' Wilson said, 'It's cancer. No, no one's told me. But I've seen quite a bit. My mother ... That means the Princess Kumara will be queen in mid May.'

Just before we are due to leave, David thought.

'Which makes her more important than she would be otherwise. Much more important,' Wilson said.

'Yes.'

'It's fortunate that she is a chess player. Very fortunate.'

'Yes,' David said. Wilson was telling him that he was going to use long evenings of chess with Kumara to pump information out of her, to lead her thoughts the way he wanted them to go, to put the right ideas, his ideas, into her head. He was a very clever man, Sidney Wilson, Esquire.

Wilson stood up, 'Confidentially, I've been told I can expect to stay on here for a year after the change, as ambassador. Then somewhere rather more grand.' He laughed slightly.

'Congratulations,' David said, and meant it. But he felt unhappy, for a picture of Kumara, listening with anxiety and fear to what Wilson was telling her, came into his mind and would not go away.

'See you this evening,' the Resident said, and they parted.

David raised his hand as the servant began to refill his wine glass. He had never been a great wine drinker, and the climate of South East Asia made even the best wines seem livery and heavy. He wished he could ask for a cold beer, but that would be unthinkable amid this imperial splendour. The great dining-room

75

of the Residency was loud with the chatter of talk, and the clatter of knives and forks on plates. Portraits of eight British sovereigns gazed down on coruscating rows of men and women in green and black, white and red, blue, violet, primrose. David in white mess kit with miniatures, sat between Lady Anne Wilson and the Princess Sally. Opposite, he faced the host, the Resident, who had the Queen on his right and the Princess Kumara on his left. The ribbon and cross of Saints Michael and George hung round the Resident's neck. On his left breast the miniatures stretched out near to the shoulder, headed by the blue-white-blue of the DSC. He was the picture of dominant certainty, of health and vigour, the big head raised, one big hand resting lightly on the mahogany. The old queen had obviously been made up with touches of rouge to hide the pallor of her cheeks. On his other side Kumara talked with each, not moving much – as her daughter Sally did, always wriggling – her gestures small and economical. She was wearing a bare-shouldered golden dress, the ruby brooch at the breast.

Sally muttered, 'Can't you take your eyes off my mother?'

He turned, caught off balance: 'I was thinking . . . I was looking at the ruby.'

'That's the Jumbhorn Ruby. It's supposed to have been found at Jumbhorn Wat when Vishnu gave a miraculous sign. It's worn only by the Perdana Binte Mingora. I shall wear it when . . . You're not the only one who thinks she's still beautiful.' She lowered her voice still more. 'Watch the Great Panjandrum.'

'The . . . ?' David began.

'Yes. Shhh! Yes. You know what funny pale eyes he has? Well, when he turns to speak to her, they light up, and the muscles on the back of his hand tighten. You watch.'

David began to watch uneasily, but Lady Anne engaged his attention, and it was not until near the end of the dinner that he had a chance to observe the Resident closely. Then, though he could not detect the glowing of the eyes that Sally had seen, he did see the tightening of the tendons in the back of the hand. But there could be a hundred explanations for that.

They rose, glasses in hand, as the old Queen proposed the toast of Her Majesty Queen Elizabeth II. Immediately afterwards, the Resident proposed the toast of Queen Valaya VI of Mingora. The old Queen sat, head bowed, while they looked towards her, glasses

76

raised. When they had sat down she again rose slowly and stood, her thin right hand resting on the table. She spoke in a small thin voice: 'I say only, thank you. Now I ask that you all drink with me to the future of the friendship and love between Britain and Mingora, that it may continute for ever, as it has lasted so many years.'

Again all drank. Now what would Wilson say, David wondered. Knowing what he knew, perhaps he had better just sit down, saying nothing. But the Queen, again seated, was looking at him, and so was Kumara. It was with no noticeable hesitation that Sidney Wilson rose and said, 'Your Majesty, on behalf of Her Britannic Majesty's Government, I second your toast. To the friendship and love between our two countries. May it continue for ever, as it has lasted so many years!' He raised his glass towards the Queen, then drained it. All down the table the guests clapped and banged their hands on the mahogany. David thought, how can he do it? How can he keep his face serious when he knows he's come to break the treaty that all this is based on? Well, it wasn't any of his business, thank God. Who was it who once described an ambassador as a man sent to lie abroad for the good of his country? Anyway, perhaps one could talk of perpetual friendship and love without meaning that you were actually going to be tied by treaty, or firm commitments of military support. That *could* be read into the words.

The Resident was rising again and the murmur of talk died away. When all were silent Wilson said, 'It is unfortunately customary for the Resident to say a few words on these occasions. I don't want to keep you from the garden for long – we have a cool breeze now, an excellent group of Lepeti dancers and a *gamelan* band . . . This is the year 1959. The world is changing fast. The problems we will have to face in the 1960s are not the same as those we faced in the 1950s. Some will be easier, as the world finally recovers from the effects of the last war. Some will be harder, as that very removal of the most urgent physical needs, like food and shelter, allows more emotional matters to surface. We have faced many difficult times together in the past hundred and fifty years, and together we will face those of the future. And together we will overcome them. Thank you.'

He sat down to prolonged applause. David watched him with something like awe. There was nothing in his face or demeanour to show his real thoughts. He did not hum and haw but grasped the nettle firmly. He obviously had to lie or tell the truth and he'd chosen, perhaps unavoidably, to lie. And he'd done it as well as it could be done.

Thoughts of Kusalung returned to his mind. What was John Allen going to be able to do if the CTs had vanished into the jungles? And what...? Sally was pulling at his elbow and he caught a glimpse of the old Prince Chamberlain, down the table, eyeing him with a faintly paternal expression. 'Swim tomorrow morning?' she said.

'Well...'; he ought to be going to Kusalung. But it was only a hundred miles, and he didn't want to arrive so hot on Allen's heels that Allen would think he was peering over his shoulder. Nor would Allen really have had time to find out what was going on, and make a plan. If he went swimming with Sally he had an uneasy certainty that he would kiss her again. Nothing more, though; that would cause God knows what complications. He wished he knew whether she was flirting with him because she liked him; because she liked all men; or because she wanted something out of him... or all three. He caught Kumara's level eyes on him. He flushed, and turned to Sally.

'All right,' he said.

She said, 'Half past seven.'

Five

THE LITTLE CONVOY of scout cars and Land-Rovers came out of the jungle as the Central Range flattened into the western plain, and at once turned south on to a narrow cart track, deep in yellow-red dust. The dust formed a long sausage-like cloud in the still air, so that David, glancing back from his Land-Rover, saw the one behind, Lieutenant Crawford's, only as a murky moving shape in the gloom. The village of Ban Dhrai ahead began to stand separate from the clumps of palms and small patches of cane scrub that dotted the plain.

Tulbahadur, perched in the back with his sub-machine gun across his knees, said sharply, 'Shooting, sahib!'

David had heard it too, and from the scout car ahead the corporal shouted back, 'Shooting, in the village!'

They were almost on Ban Dhrai then. A pair of fusiliers were crouched at the sides of the track, one holding up his hand, the other glancing back over his shoulder. David's driver, Wood, said, 'Brigadier here, mate.'

The fusilier said, 'There's some CTs in the village . . . they were firing just now. Better not go in any farther.'

David jumped down, Tulbahadur following without orders, and walked into the village. Fifty yards past the point where the convoy had been stopped, he came to the village square, an open place on the banks of the Kusalung River, here a clear stream only just out of the hills. The space was ringed by houses made of palm thatch, all standing on tall wooden legs. On the ground under the houses pigs rooted for food, chickens pecked and darted, and dogs scratched themselves.

The body of a man, a Mingoran in peasant's clothing lay face down in the mud at the edge of the river. A large hole had been

79

blown out of the back of his head. A dog sniffed at his hand until a fusilier swung his foot at it and it ran away howling, though it had not been touched. Half a dozen other fusiliers stood round, leaning on their weapons. To one side a British captain talked with a uniformed constable and two old peasant men. David walked over to them.

'What's happened?' he asked.

The captain glanced round and stiffened to a salute. 'We've just killed this man, sir. A few minutes ago.'

'Is he a CT?'

'Apparently not, sir ... 2 Platoon was carrying out a sweep of that patch of jungle there across the river. Part of 1 Platoon was guarding the river. They saw a man run out of the jungle ahead of 2 Platoon, and cross the river ... it's shallow ... They thought he was armed. One of our men fired and killed him with his first shot.'

The constable said, 'Tuan, the elders here say he is a good man, who was returning from visiting his daughter in the next village. He was not armed. Only, he had a stick that looked like a rifle.'

'What do you think?' David asked.

The constable hesitated, then said, 'I think it was a mistake, tuan.'

The Fusilier captain said, 'I gave my men orders not to hesitate. If there's anyone to blame, it's me.'

His voice was taut and ready to be belligerent. He was a man of about thirty, of medium height, wiry, dark, and intense, faintly resembling the Resident in manner rather than appearance. He wore a parachutist's badge on his right upper sleeve.

David said, 'What's your name?'

'Whitmore, sir.'

'Ah, this is A Company and you've just been brought back from the Special Air Service to take it over ... I thought I recognized some faces.'

'Yes, sir.'

'It's a pity about this but I don't want the men blamed. When you're operating against CTs you have to learn to shoot quickly, at fleeting targets ... Constable, tell the headman they can take the body away now. What can be done about compensation?'

The constable said, 'The headman will go to the Governor in Kusalung, with the widow. I will explain to them.'

David said, 'And tell them how much we regret what happened.'
The constable said, 'I will, tuan.'

David turned back to the captain, walking slowly across the square with him, away from the river and the motionless body. 'How do you find the company?'

'They'll be all right, sir,' the captain said briefly, with a snap of his jaw. He looked like a man who would lead as well as drive, David thought. A Company were in for a hard time. 'I'd like to meet the new CSM, too,' he said.

'Sar'n't major!' the captain called. From across the square a voice bellowed, 'Sah?'

'Come here a minute, please.'

A burly figure in jungle green came across the square at the double, stopped in front of the captain and banged his hand against his rifle with a fierce crash. The captain said, 'Sar'n't Major Berg, sir.'

The CSM turned and saluted David, his back arching more stiffly yet. He was just under medium height, with a long oft-broken nose, cauliflower ears and slightly bowed legs. David said, 'Are you any relation of Kid Berg?'

The mouth broke into a wide grin, showing missing teeth and two prominent gold caps, 'Yes, sir! Me uncle. That's what they call me, too – Kid.'

David chatted briefly with the captain and the CSM. The latter was a typical Whitechapel Jew, as cockney as they came – and a perfect balance for Whitmore's rather humourless intensity.

Half past ten. He'd be in good time for the conference, but he'd have to go now. The convoy formed, and fifteen minutes later, its trail of dust lying dense over the track and the now distant village, turned on to the tarmac and headed for the capital of the province, Kusalung.

It was a pity about the wretched villager, David thought. He had ordered John Allen to act aggressively – aggressive patrolling, sweeps of the jungle areas, anything that would show the Mingorans the army was present, and able and willing to defend them against terrorism – all this as he understood the Resident wished it. But all the same, one innocent man was dead, and the beginnings of fear of the soldiers implanted. The enemy, if they were anything like as clever as the CTs in Malaya, would not fail to nourish and increase that fear, that doubt . . .

They were waiting for him in the big audience room of the provincial governor's house – the governor himself, the Chief Minister, the provincial superintendent of RMC, and John Allen. As soon as the introductions were over, 'I'm sorry about that man A Company shot,' John Allen began aggressively, 'but Whitmore told me on the radio that he didn't stop when challenged, and . . .'

'It can't be helped,' David said. 'No one's fault. It isn't serious, yet. The people here aren't on edge, as they were in Malaya – yet.' He looked round the table and realized that the three Mingorans were waiting for him to say something; even the Chief Minister, normally a decisive man, was waiting. The message came through – the military had taken over. Strong action, David repeated to himself. But what?

'Where is the rest of your battalion?' he asked Allen.

'Bivouacked in the park at the edge of the city here.'

'Is there any area where we could usefully employ the troops, Governor?'

'There are two big jungles beyond Ban Dhrai,' the governor said haltingly. 'The gang who did murders might be there.'

'And, superintendent, can you send more constables with the battalion, to interrogate? They don't have to speak English. All the soldiers need to know is whether the men they pick up should be arrested or let go.'

'Yes, sir. We can send constables. How many wanting?'

The Chief Minister said, 'Not too many, I think. If the army will sweep the jungles, there will need to be blocks on nearby roads, police posts to catch anyone who moves out of the jungles . . .'

David nodded. The governor said, 'This is terrible thing. All people here love our Queen. This is not work of true Mingorans, but traitors . . . mad men . . .'

'Anything else we could do?' David asked.

Allen said, 'I think they should offer rewards for information.'

The Chief Minister said, 'It is not a good idea usually, I think, colonel. Wrong information can be given, for private purposes. Also, it is the duty of every subject to help, without reward. Now, that is how our people . . . most of them . . . are still thinking. But I will reconsider, if there is more of this murdering.'

'When can you start?' David asked.

'Tomorrow,' Allen said. 'We'll have to do a recce this afternoon and get the troops into position . . .'

'Can you do that at night?'

'Yes. Ready to start the sweeps at first light. The governor was showing me these areas on the map before you came. The sweep will take three days – half the battalion in each jungle area, doing the two areas simultaneously. That'll take us to the 23rd, late.'

Two days before Christmas. Allen was hinting: the Gurkhas might be brought out on the 24th so that the Fusiliers could go back, and celebrate Christmas with their families in their own comfortable quarters in Trangloek; but that was a waste of government petrol, and unsound tactically. Either nothing would happen, in which case they could go back; or they'd uncover a nest of MPRP and have to stay. It would be a bad idea to replace them with troops who did not know the ground.

He did not comment on Allen's remark, but said, 'All right, then.'

When the others had gone the Chief Minister said, 'I don't think the soldiers will find anything, brigadier . . . but it is good practice for them, eh? . . . I have to return to Trangloek. Will you stay to supervise the operations?'

David shook his head. 'Colonel Allen can handle them without me . . . but I want to have a look at the country round here – the back country, the jungle patches. I want to look at some of the villages right off any road. But there are a lot of irrigation ditches with no bridges, or just log bridges that are the wrong distance apart for the Land-Rovers.'

'I'll tell the governor to lend you a horse,' the minister said, rubbing his hands with pleasure.

'Better have one for Crawford here, too, then,' David said.

'And your orderly?'

David glanced through the open door at Tulbahadur sitting on the verandah steps outside, and smiled. 'Yes,' he said.

'They won't be thoroughbreds,' the minister said, 'just our local Mingoran ponies . . .'

An hour later, after eating some rice and fish that the governor pressed on him, David was riding along a dusty track between rice paddy, Lieutenant Crawford on his right and Lance Corporal Tulbahadur Lama on his left. The sun was high and the day hot and damp. The Central Range shimmered in a dull blue haze to the east.

They rode into a village, and two or three men and women came out, smiling, hands touching their foreheads. Crawford said, 'This one's the headman, sir.'

'Let's dismount. We don't want to talk down to them from horseback.'

He swung down, followed easily by Crawford. Tulbahadur swung his leg over the pony's crupper so energetically that the momentum carried him clear off the horse. He fell to the ground with a clatter of equipment. The pony turned and looked at him in amazement. Tulbahadur muttered a Gurkhali expletive, took the bridles and led the three horses into the shade of a tree.

The headman brought coconut milk and fruit. David spoke in his slow Malay: 'Is all well here?'

'It is well, tuan.'

'Do you fear trouble here, such as there was in Ban Dhrai?'

The headman said, 'I pray not, tuan. We are loyal subjects of the Queen. We are not rich, but no one starves. We are happy.'

Other villagers were gathering as they spoke, a silent, squatting audience in front of them. The headman acknowledged their presence, and spread his hands towards them: 'Is it not true, what I say?'

'It is true,' they murmured.

'But that's what the headman of Ban Dhrai felt,' Crawford cut in.

The headman nodded, his mobile face looking unhappy. 'It is true, tuan. These devils come from outside, kill, and go away. What can we do?'

'Could you not go after them?' David said, 'They are not many, are they?'

'I do not know how many went to Ban Dhrai. Are not these things done at night, tuan?'

'Sometimes, but the devils are nearly always seen by some-one . . . to know how many there are at least.'

'We have no weapons, tuan. We are tillers of the soil, husband-men. We are helpless in the face of these leopards . . .'

They ought to form village protection groups, a sort of Home Guard, David thought, as Crawford began to talk about the crops.

The RMC could not be everywhere . . . yet the CTs could be, or so it seemed.

Fifteen minutes later they rode on towards the next village, two miles away, its roofs nestling in a dense growth of palm. 'They seem very friendly,' David said, 'but nervous.'

'They don't know what's going to happen next, sir,' Crawford said, 'They don't have many radios, but news gets about very fast and sometimes it's accurate, sometimes it's not.'

David relapsed into silence, thinking. If the villagers could be given arms . . . would it merely provide more arms for the MPRP to steal? Or have given to them by disaffected elements? Or would it enable each village to turn itself into a little bastion?

'Someone else is riding into the village,' Crawford said. 'I think it's a woman.'

David stared over at the road coming in at an angle A horseman was trotting down it, the hoofs kicking up a trail of dust that hung behind the horse in the hot air. It was a woman wearing a bright pale blue blouse, and black trousers, like a coolie woman's, and a big conical straw hat. The sun caught a gleam of red at her throat and David muttered, 'Kumara! The Perdana Binte Mingora.'

The two tracks converged. Kumara nodded slightly, as David saluted. 'So,' she said, 'you are seeing for yourself.'

'Yes,' David said.

'Do you speak Mingora-Malay?'

'Ordinary Malay,' he said. 'People seem to understand. My Intelligence Officer, Mr Crawford here, speaks Malay perfectly.'

The conversation sounded stilted and false to him. She knew perfectly well he spoke Malay, but knew little of the Mingoran variations. She had taught him some while he was teaching her Welsh, after the Eisteddfod. Now the four horses were walking side by side into the village. Again they dismounted, again men and women came running, but this time David kept back, as the women touched Kumara's feet, and the men made low obeisance.

'How do they know who she is?' he muttered to Crawford. 'Did she send word ahead?'

'I don't think so, sir. They might recognize the Jumbhorn Ruby, and I suppose they've seen pictures of her.'

And, David thought, she must have a name for travelling about by herself, seeing for herself . . . She asked much the same questions as David had at the previous village, and after fifteen minutes, refusing all the offers of refreshment, made ready to remount. She looked at David, who had not spoken during the visit, and said, 'I'm going on to other villages, that way.' She pointed east. 'Are you going the same way, or not?'

What did that mean, he thought? Was she inviting them to go with her, or hinting that she'd prefer to continue alone? Well, he'd ignore her hints. He'd learn more with her than he would without. He said, 'We'll come with you.'

She nodded, swung up easily into the saddle, waved her hand at the people and put the pony into a walk. David fell in beside her, Crawford and Tulbahadur behind. She said, 'What would you say if we proposed arming some of the men in each village?'

'It would depend on what likelihood there was of the arms getting into the wrong hands,' he replied.

'If we don't trust our own people, when they are loyal, we will play into the enemy's hands . . .'

'It would take time.'

'We need time for everything we're trying to do,' she said. 'My mother has started redistribution of some of the very large estates . . . there aren't many, and we're paying compensation, but it takes time. *We* want to have the headman elected in every village . . . but most of the villagers don't seem to. They're more interested in electing members to rural councils, which don't exist at present. What else have you seen, that you think we ought to do?'

He said, 'I don't really know. I've only been here three weeks.' Why was she asking him these questions? What right did she have to involve him? He said, 'I'm not a politician. All of us have to work out our own problems.'

It seemed that he had given her an opening for which she had been waiting. She said, 'Yes, but what if we are attacked by men organized, armed, and supplied from outside the queendom . . . men determined to see that our plans for progress fail, determined to cause chaos and confusion . . . so that they can step in?'

David said, 'Everyone has to protect themselves.'

'We can't,' she said. 'We agreed to let Britain protect us, in return for strategic and commercial advantages. In time, we could, but are we going to be given time?'

Her eyes were on him, sparkling with concentration. The sweatband of his wide-brimmed Gurkha hat, with the red cloth folds round it to show his rank, was soggy on his forehead and sweat ran down the side of his head and inside his shirt. She looked cool and comfortable, though determined. Are we going to be given time, she had asked. Did she mean, by the MPRP, or by Britain? She must have heard somehow about the impending abrogation of the Treaty. Or feminine intuition had worked it out for her during a chess session with Wilson.

He said, 'I hope so. The MPRP . . .'

'We must have time,' she said firmly. 'Given that, we can look after ourselves.'

'How much time?' he asked.

'To make an army, from nothing? About ten years, I suppose, but most of the British troops could leave much earlier than that. Our new soldiers would learn more quickly if they could work alongside yours for a time. And I suppose we'd need senior British officers for some years after that . . . It's a pity about that man who was killed in Ban Dhrai.'

'Yes,' he said, 'I wish there was some public occasion, or place, where we could say we're sorry, because . . .'

'It doesn't matter,' she said. 'The villagers know it was a mistake. And they're beginning to realize that more mistakes of that kind will happen if terrorism increases. I have been told that your soldiers are going to sweep the jungles beyond Ban Dhrai.'

'You heard that?' he said, dismayed. 'It was supposed to be a secret.'

'Don't worry,' she said, smiling a little grimly, 'We have people watching to see if anyone tries to pass that news into the jungles. Do you think the sweeps will produce results?'

David shook his head. 'Frankly, not much. Personally' – her huge, wide-set black eyes were looking through him, the heart-shaped face below was full of intelligence. He blurted out, 'It's the Resident's idea. He's very keen to show the people that the army's ready and willing to help them.'

She said, 'It's unusual for politicians to urge soldiers to do more than they want, isn't it? I thought it was always the other way round.'

'It usually is,' David said.

Kumara said, 'I think the jungle sweeps may perhaps be useful . . . . but it is very important now, before the Communist campaign gets worse, to keep the villagers on our side. It might be better to let some terrorists get away than have the peasants think the army doesn't care whether it shoots innocent people or not.'

David said unhappily, 'It's easy to say that, but one terrorist who does get away may then kill a dozen more equally innocent people ... and these things happen in dense jungle, or at night, to men overwrought and tense and tired, men who've seen their comrades shot in the back by murderers disguised as peasant women.'

'Poor Dylan...' She laid her hand on his arm. 'It's such a shame the terrorists don't wear a proper uniform and come out and fight like men, isn't it?'

'Yes,' he said with heartfelt energy. Then he saw that she was laughing at him; and she had called him by the name she had always used in England. He turned to her, ready to smile at her as he used to, confident of her warmth and companionship, and surely something more – affection at least.

She withdrew her hand and her face settled back into its neutral determination. She said, 'Do not worry, brigadier. Between us, we will beat them.'

His heart, which had begun to rise like a singing lark, fluttered back to earth.

'Yes,' he said.

They rode on in silence. A village was taking form ahead. Crawford and Tulbahadur were talking behind. Crawford was getting Tulbahadur to teach him some Gurkhali words and phrases.

Kumara said, 'Do you see that long ridge on the skyline there, with a rounded end on the right?' Her hand was outstretched, pointing. 'It's very faint.'

'Yes,' he said.

'That's the Maliwun Forest Game Preserve. It's on the headwaters of the Kusalung River, fifteen miles above Ban Dhrai. There's a small village there and a big rest house for the use of people who are allowed to shoot in the Reserve.'

'What game is there?' he asked, not caring what the answer might be.

'Tiger,' she said, 'Leopard, several kinds of deer ... and seladang.'

'Selandang!' he exclaimed, startled out of his unhappiness. The seladang was the giant wild bison of south-east Asia. Standing six feet at the shoulder, nine feet from nose to tail, almost black in colour, and enormously horned, it was one of the rarest and most dangerous of game trophies.

She said, 'When you get back to Trangloek you will find a letter from me inviting you to a seladang shoot there. One bull seladang per gun, limit. We'll be well looked after.'

'I'm sure,' he said. 'I'd love to, but . . . there may be something important in Trangloek . . . and, of course, if an emergency . . .'

'Of course,' she interrupted, 'but otherwise, please come. We'll go out on 17 January, for three days. The Resident is coming. And Sally.'

They rode into the edge of the village. Out came the people, running, smiling. Rain began to fall.

Three villages later, at four in the afternoon, David decided he must start back. It would take him an hour to reach Kusalung, then something under three hours on the tarmac road to Trangloek, depending on the number of carts and stray bullocks to be met. He parted from Kumara with a salute, which she acknowledged with another of her small smiles, and turned his horse's head. She was two people, he decided, the woman and the princess, and here in her own country the woman was not permitted to make more than fleeting and unimportant appearances. The princess had given him much to think about. In her talk early on she had been hinting to him that she knew that Britain was preparing to abrogate the ancient treaty. Then, as they spent more hours together, and visited more villages, she seemed to speak more directly at him. At first, he felt that she was using him as a relay station, to pass on her opinions and advice to others – to the Resident, obviously; perhaps to the C-in-C. But if she were going to play chess regularly with Wilson, why couldn't she tell him directly, in her own words, what was in her mind?

He shrugged his shoulders involuntarily. It was all too bloody devious for him. But he'd have to think very hard about three proposals which would affect the military situation here. Two were immediate – the forming and arming of village Home Guards, and the provision of helicopters to give the Constabulary mobility. The third was long range – the raising and training of a Mingoran

Army. For that he'd need good training, sound administration . . . and time. But time, Wilson said, they were not going to be given.

It was wrong for a rich and powerful country to break its ties with another, without mutual agreement. After taking money for a century and a half, it was wrong, when times became a little hard, to say, OK, finished, we're off, sink or swim. It was dishonourable!

'I'm looking forward to a cold beer, sir,' Crawford broke into his thoughts.

'Me, too. Just a quick one, if we can find one, then we must get back to Trangloek . . . When we get to Kusalung, go to Colonel Allen, ask him if there's anything he wants and tell him we're leaving. Usual sitreps. Then come back to the governor's – I'll have beer for you.'

They reached the gardens of the governor's house in dusty evening light, and David swung down stiffly. Kumara, for all her delicate, thin-boned appearance, must be made of whipcord. She never showed any sign of weariness, never looked untidy. Well, he'd learned that in London. He climbed the steps up on to the wide verandah. The governor's servants were bringing him cold beer in a tall glass. He waved them on to Tulbahadur and sank into a cane chair. A minute later he had a beer in his own hand, and fifteen minutes later again, Crawford was drinking beside him.

'Colonel Allen said he didn't need anything, sir,' Crawford reported. 'The battalion's marching at six. They're ferrying in one company to a point north of the north jungle area, and then going in across country. The southern area is fifteen miles from here, by village tracks, and the company allotted there is marching all the way. A Company will march from Ban Dhrai to join them.'

David nodded, stood up, and finished his beer. He'd have to thank the governor for the loan of the ponies, and say goodbye, then they could start. The Land-Rovers were waiting in the dusk, the drivers standing beside them, and signallers seated in the third one.

Twenty minutes later the convoy was bowling through the night towards Trangloek, the headlights boring into the warm night air, myriad insects fluttering and whirling by in their bright light, or dying against the windshield. David, in the passenger seat beside Wood, sat with his head dropped into his shoulders, thinking. Barracks for the Mingoran recruits. Rifle ranges. Training areas. Medical facilities. Instructors . . . what language would they instruct in? Selection of officers. What . . . ?

The Land-Rover slowed violently with a scream of brakes. Wood muttered, 'Bloody bastard! Tired of life, eh?'

David said, 'For God's sake don't let's kill another innocent man.'

'He stepped right out in front of me, sir,' Wood said, aggrieved.

A Mingoran was standing in the middle of the road, shading his eyes. trying to peer into the glare of the headlights. He shuffled round to the driver's side of the Land-Rover and David saw in the bright light of the following vehicles that he was a youngish peasant of medium height, with a square fat-cheeked thick-lipped face, dressed in a tattered shirt and trousers. The peasant saw the red band round David's hat, waved his hand in a sort of salute, and backed away, muttering, as Crawford came up from behind.

'What's he saying?' David asked.

'He says he's sorry, he didn't know it was the military.'

'What's he want?'

Crawford spoke rapidly; the man replied. 'He's trying to get to a village up the road. He's heard his mother is dying.'

Let's take him, David thought. The man smelled slightly of garlic and his lips were red-stained with betel, but he was dusty and tired, and needed help. The main business of the army now was to make friends with the Mingorans, to convince them that it cared: it was only this morning that he'd said that.

'Tell him to squeeze in the back here with Tulbahadur,' he said.

The man clambered in, Crawford ran back to his own Land-Rover, the convoy moved on. David returned to his thoughts.

Sally: a nice girl . . . wished he were fifteen years younger, but even having her flirt with him was flattering. Big round breasts, bursting out of the bikini top. Kumara's were small and firm and high . . . Would he be able to get the Fusiliers back for Christmas? Depended on what happened in these next three days. John Allen despised him. A pity. Campbell-Wylie knew him better but probably thought that if their seniorities were reversed he would be the better brigadier. Probably right. The beer was making him sleepy. He dozed. Soon the Land-Rover stopped and the

Mingoran climbed out with profuse bowings and obeisances. The Land-Rovers purred on between dusty verges. The road began to climb . . . This was the Central Range . . . the jungle . . . the Maliwun Forest Game Preserve was somewhere in there to the south . . . What did Kumara mean by inviting him to the seladang shoot, after pretending for three weeks that she had never set eyes on him before? And, worse, making it clear that he was to be there to amuse Sally while she, the great Perdana Binte Mingora, settled matters of state, at least, with the Resident. He'd make some excuse . . . regret it was impossible . . . pressure of work . . . sudden emergency in the drainage system of Kandahar Lines . . . He dozed off again.

Six

DAVID TOOK A last look up and down the track, and to right and left. Stevens had no objection; he'd said he could get his guns up on to flat beds or dropsided ordinary wagons, if a loading ramp was built. O'Grady had said he could build a ramp in a couple of days. The Mingoran man from the railway civil engineer's office had no objection. This site was as good as any they had selected on this two-day railway reconnaissance. And it was one of the best in being very well concealed from random observation. They had looked to find sites in or near a cutting, or where the line ran through dense jungle, though there always had to be a car road coming close. O'Grady's sappers would make spurs from the roads to the actual loading ramps in the process of building the ramps.

'All right, gentlemen,' he said. 'Record it as Number One North... And now I think we might head for Trangloek...'

'And cold drinks I have waiting for us in my refrigerator,' the railway engineer said.

They all climbed up on to the flat car coupled to the front of the old steam locomotive hissing on the line, and sat down on the cane chairs parked all over it. It was not a comfortable way to travel, and it restricted the speed to 20 mph, but it was the only way to carry out this sort of reconnaissance, where one needed to see in all directions at once. The engine chuffed pompously into motion and the flat car ground down the track towards Trangloek station four miles away.

Ten emergency loading platforms chosen; also twenty-five important rail protection points agreed on between himself, the Commissioner of Constabulary, and the railwayman. Now there'd be discussion as to who was to do the protecting – the Constabulary, or the army. He would fight strongly against tying down any of his men in such a role; it was perhaps too static even for the RMC. Excluding a few of the most important points – two big river bridges in Lepet and one near the Malaysian border, and perhaps two others, all of which could be allotted to the RMC, why shouldn't responsibility for guarding all the minor danger points be given to the Home Guard of the nearest village? It would all have to be settled, and soon. Here it was 15 January, 1960, and the MPRP campaign of terror had not been stopped. It had not increased much in scale either, a murder here, arson or robbery somewhere else, all in the name of revolution, . . . but he felt that the communists were rehearsing their men, carrying out training cadres, as his own battalions trained their NCOs. He could imagine MPRP junior leadership course No. 4 – how to break a working relationship between landowner and peasant: No. 5 – how to make villagers keep their mouths shut . . .

The engine whistled shrilly behind him and he looked up. They were clattering over the level crossing. There was Trangloek station, the university buildings green and white beyond. Hundreds of would-be passengers crowded the low platform, and they rode slowly through a babble of chattering, calling, shouting, cries of fruit and food vendors, whine of beggars. 'The northbound express is due in five minutes, brigadier,' the railwayman murmured in his ear.

Behind them there was a hiss of escaping steam from the locomotive, and the flat car's brakes ground and squealed. They stopped at the far end of the platform, outside the railway's administrative offices. David climbed down the steel steps at the end of the flat and jumped to the platform, landing in front of half a dozen Mingorans of both sexes. The man closest to him turned round as he landed and David knew he had seen him before. 'You're . . .' he paused. Then he remembered, and said in Malay, 'I hope your mother is better.'

He turned to the Constabulary Commissioner and said, 'We gave this man a ride outside Kusalung last month.'

The Commissioner, a portly gold-skinned man of fifty, who had just landed with a heavy thud on the platform, looked at the Mingoran peasant, then he stared, a choked sound escaped his throat and he fumbled for the revolver at his uniform belt. 'You . . .' he gasped; but the man had turned and dived into the

94

dense crowd. 'That's Sujak!' the Commissioner gasped, breaking into a run, 'Police, where are the railway police?' Behind them the engine whistled and clanked into motion, pushing the flat car farther up the line. From the south another whistle answered loud and imperious. The already great animation on the station redoubled as everyone seized their boxes and bundles and fought for places at the edge of the platform. The express appeared, still whistling. David and Stevens and O'Grady drew their pistols and forced into the crowd, shouting 'Way...make way!' The head of the man was difficult to see. He was off the end of the platform now, dodging among groups of people coming out of the city and the university buildings, and others flying kites or selling their wares in the dusty open space. O'Grady was gaining on him fast when David, pounding along twenty yards behind, saw a foot come out of the crowd and the captain went sprawling. He ought to catch the man to whom the foot belonged, now sprawled on top of O'Grady and his gun, as though he too had tripped... but one thing at a time. He ran on.

They had left the railwayman and the Commissioner far back. As the quarry reached a corner in the University Stevens stopped, aimed, and fired two shots. The bullets knocked chips out of the stone, and the running man disappeared round the corner. They ran on, turned the corner...the man was vanishing round the next corner. O'Grady, who had caught them up, made ready to fire, but now five girl students swept into sight, laughing and joking; the man plunged between them, knocking one to the ground. David ran on...but at the next corner there was no sign. For five minutes they searched the area, but did not find the man they were looking for.

They turned back towards the station. 'That was good clean fun,' the burly gunner major said, 'What was it all about, sir?'

'Apparently that man is Sujak bin Amin, the head of the MPRP, and wanted for murder. We gave him a lift out of Kusalung last month...Worse than that. I've just realized that the village where he said his mother was ill is opposite Ban Dhrai, the other side of the road. We took him as close to the jungle areas that the Fusiliers were going to sweep the next day as he could get on a main road. Bloody idiot I was.'

Stevens said, 'He doesn't look like the pictures of Sujak I've seen.'

'I didn't make any connection when we gave him the lift,' David said, 'Nor when I first saw him just now. But as soon as the Commissioner said he was Sujak, I realized . . . He's been stuffing his cheeks with cotton wool, and putting blotting paper or something between his lips and gums. Far more effective than a false moustache.'

True, but no excuse. This explained why the Fusiliers had had no luck with their sweeps, although they had found recently abandoned camp fires and sleeping sites in the south area. Sujak had got to them in time. Also, there had not been enough security of planned moves and intentions. There'd have to be a tightening up all round. The MPRP might not be popular but they had supporters. One or two were enough . . . like that man who'd tripped O'Grady. Without him, Sujak would be dead now.

Inside the railway administration buildings they found the Commissioner, a city policeman, and a handcuffed Mingoran. The commissioner said, 'This is the man who tripped Captain O'Grady. I was close behind you then, and got him.'

The man whined and held his hands up, and David made out that he was saying he had done nothing, he was a poor man, he had not seen the tuan coming, he had just been turning, nothing more . . .

'Silence!' the commissioner rapped. 'We'll have his fingerprints in soon, and find out whether he's known. Then we'll start questioning him. The city police have a hundred men on their way to the university to look for Sujak.'

The railwayman said, 'Now what about those cold drinks . . . ?'

An hour later, changed into civilian clothes, David passed through the heavy double doors of the Mingora Club into the cool of revolving ceiling fans, and the purr of their motors and the rustle of the white starched uniforms of the club servants and the soft pad of their bare feet on the stone floors. It seemed dark in there after the brightness outside, where the sunlight danced off the sea, and he stood a few moments while his eyes became accustomed to it. The great visitors' book of the Club lay open on a mahogany table under a lifesize portrait of Queen Victoria and the Prince Consort, the queen carrying the future Edward VII as a babe in her arms. Through the heavy glass doors to the right, in the main reading room, a few gentlemen were reading old copies of *The Times* and a thin Chinese in western clothes was reading yesterday's *Mingora Times*, Mingora's own daily. Faint in the hall there, below the smells of furniture polish and old wood and cigar smoke, was the smell of cooking, the food of many races, good and solid smells.

The place was incredible, like a perfectly preserved dinosaur, the outside a spiritual replica of the Bank of England transmigrated from Threadneedle Street to Victoria Square; the inside materialized as directly from the mercantile splendour of Calcutta ... but it was no dinosaur, for it was alive, as those smells testified.

A stately old servant said politely, 'Does the tuan want anything?'

'No, thank you. I'm having lunch with Sir Harry Johnstone, but I'm early.'

'Sir Harry has not come in yet. I am sure he would wish you to have a drink at the bar, tuan.'

'I will.'

He went down a passage, turned into the cool gloom of the Long Bar, and sat down with relief in an overstuffed chair. Two days on the chairs on that flat car had given him a square backside, and sore eyes from staring down the endlessly glittering rails.

A servant appeared beside him, 'Stengah, please,' he said, 'Long, weak.'

The drink in his hand, he sat back and took a long pull. The beer at the station had assuaged his thirst, and the dryness in his throat from the excitement of the chase; this was pure pleasure ... not needed, just wonderful.

'Brigadier ... just back from your tour?'

He looked up and saw Sidney Wilson, the Resident, looming over him.

'Yes, Resident,' he said, 'An hour ago.'

'Mind if I join you? ... I have a three o'clock audience with Her Majesty. At my request.' He threw David a meaning glance. So this was the day, David thought; today he's going to tell them they're to be cast adrift.

The Resident swirled his drink round in his hand. 'One of these, then a game of squash ... then I'll go.'

'No lunch?'

'Not today. Food dulls the mind ... You've seen a lot more of this country than I've been able to. How do you like it?'

'Very much.'

'So do I. I was able to visit Moirang and Lepet, between Christmas and the New Year. Wonderful people, so easy with each other.' He spoke almost dreamily. 'They disagree about politics, obviously, but they have a peace at the core ... deeper than politics, something in here.' He touched his chest. 'There's no pressure from inside. Some from outside ... they can deal with that. Anyone can. It's easy. It's pressure from inside that can lead to ... anything ... can destroy ...'

David had not seen the Resident very often, and except for the squash games their meetings had been business sessions to discuss the MPRP, and the military consequences of the forthcoming British withdrawal. On those occasions Wilson had been severe, brilliant, incisive. David had never met this other man, who talked almost elegiacally in the cool gloom. He said, 'I agree, sir. I felt something of that even in 1945. That was why I was glad to be posted here ... for three years.'

The Resident ignored the reference and said, 'One thinks of staying for ever. Surrendering to the peace. Joining them. Going to a village and saying, Let me in ... give me some of whatever it is you have ... Why not? We're giving them whatever it is that we have ... techniques, disciplines, scientific methods. No one starves, as they used to.'

'They can't give us what they have,' David said thoughtfully. 'We have to find it ourselves. We can give them our things because ours are concrete ... theirs isn't.'

'What would happen to a man's character if he did surrender?' the Resident said. 'An Englishman's ... or a Welshman's? Struggle is in our bone. Advance. Move forward ... These people are moving forward, too, but not on the same plane.'

David thought he understood, but had no comment to make, so kept quiet. The Resident seemed to awaken from a reverie. 'There's no time,' he said, his voice again sharp edged. 'I've just been talking metaphysically. In practice, there can be no surrender, no passing on of this supposed peace ... because it's another name for lethargy, or acceptance. If we surrender to that, we're finished.' He drained his glass and stood up.

David stood up with him for it was nearly time for his

appointment with Sir Harry. He said, 'Will Princess Kumara be there . . . at the Palace this afternoon?'

The Resident said, 'I'm sure she will. Why?'

David said, 'I wondered how much the Queen lets her share in decisions.'

'Enough,' the Resident said. 'Sometimes, too much. The Princess is very intelligent.' David thought he detected a gleam in his eye, the sheen in the pale blue that Sally had pointed out to him at the state dinner.

The Resident said, 'See you the day after tomorrow at Maliwun, then?'

David said halfheartedly, 'Unless something crops up . . .'

The Resident said, 'Don't let it! You don't want to miss the chance of a seladang.'

He went out with a final brisk nod. David sat down. He had sworn a dozen times that he'd find an excuse to say he couldn't make it to Maliwun; now it was getting too late. He'd be there with Sally, and Wilson with Kumara, and poor nice Lady Anne floundering out of her depth on the outskirts.

Sir Harry Johnstone strode ponderously into the Long Bar. He was wearing the same white tropical suit he had been wearing at the time of their first meeting. The hand engulfing David's was as large and strong and damp as before.

' 'Ave a drink, lad.'

'Thanks, Sir Harry, I've had one.'

' 'Ave anuther. It woan't kill tha'.' The Yorkshire accent was being laid on thick and strong as Sir Harry lowered his bulk into a chair opposite. 'Ah will . . . that's why tha' can smell the booze on my breath, didn't tha' say?'

His eyes were twinkling and David, smiling, said, 'We'd better both forget that little accident.'

'Reet! . . . Good 'ealth, lad. That's t' onny thing that matters in t'East . . . How are you settling in?'

'Pretty well, I think. I've visited all the provincial capitals, at least, and have toured a few village areas.'

'Like round Ban Dhrai, eh? The governor down there's not a bad chap, for an Easterner.' He was speaking almost standard English now, his Yorkshire antecedents no more than a slight broadening of some of the vowel sounds. His voice boomed through the gloom, which David was by now so accustomed to that

99

it seemed a pleasant pale light. A Mingoran at the bar caught Sir Harry's eye and raised his hand in greeting; two middle-aged Englishmen passing by said, 'Morning, Harry.'

Sir Harry continued: 'The Westerners are more energetic, more efficient all round – look at the Chief Minister, started out as a Moirangi with no education, no money, no family . . . but he's the only Westerner the palace people trust. Here, drink up and we'll go upstairs. I think I told you I have a private dining room there.'

Five minutes later, in an airy room on the second floor, tall french windows open on to a wide verandah overlooking the Esplanade and the sea, Sir Harry said, 'How long are you going to be here?'

David started, recovered himself, and said, 'The tour is officially three years.'

'I don't mean that, I mean what are those boobies back in Westminster up to?'

David tried to look puzzled, without much success. Sir Harry boomed, 'Ay, you can't talk. But listen to me . . . if this fellow Wilson has come to tell the government that we're going to break the treaty, he ought to shoot himself before he agrees to do it. It'll be a damned disgrace. No Englishman will be able to hold up his head in the east again . . . Hey, Chengku, *dua stengah.*'

He settled back with the new drink when it came and spoke in a lower voice. 'I've met him twice – once at some damned official lunch, and once when I went to find out what British trade policy was going to be out here for the next few years. It affects business, you know. He talked a lot, said nothing . . . Do you like him?'

David glanced at the Mingoran waiters standing immobile at the end of the room, their hands behind their backs. Sir Harry caught the look and said, 'Chengku has been here twenty-five years, Noor twelve. They hear everything, say nothing. Chengku worked for me for twelve years before he came here . . . How's that eldest daughter of yours doing, Chengku?'

'Not well, tuan. Her husband likes lying in bed better than working.'

'She should get rid of him. She's a good looking woman.'

'I have told her the same thing.'

Sir Harry turned back to David. 'Wilson's not my boss and he's not yours. Come on, what do you think?'

'I think he's very capable ... brilliant,' David said cautiously, 'I've never seen anyone who can learn so much in so short a time – history, geography, languages, names, everything ... And he must have guts.'

'His medals? Perhaps.'

'I don't think, myself, that ... I may be wrong – I've only known him a month ... but I don't feel he's very warm.'

'A cold fish, eh? All ambition and no heart? You may be right. Appearances are that way, but I have the idea he's not so cold as he looks ... or as he would like to be, perhaps. He's cooking inside.'

David knew exactly what Sir Harry meant, for he had felt the same thing; Wilson's introspective mood of their meeting in the bar an hour ago could have been the expression of a yearning to escape from inner pressures.

Sir Harry said, 'I was sitting near him at that state lunch, for the business community here ... never seen such mountains of food as the Palace served, incidentally. Men only, except the two princesses, Sally and Kumara, as hosts. He had something on his mind then.'

David said, 'What do you think is the matter ... what is it he's cooking about?'

Sir Harry slurped energetically at the peppery shrimp soup. 'Built in, perhaps. I mean, born that way. Roman Catholic, so half the time feels that he's full of sin. Confession helps some people like that, others not. How do you confess rage at yourself? ... It might be that he feels disgrace at what he's been told to do ... Might be something personal. A woman ... Lady Anne looks lost. Something's going wrong there.'

For a time they ate in silence, except for the sound of Sir Harry's mastication. David marvelled at the amount of food and drink the man put away. It was astonishing enough to watch the piled plates empty, the heavy glasses set down light, but to realize that this had been going on for forty years ...

The younger servant brought coffee in small cups and Sir Harry motioned David to a comfortable chair by the french windows. The sea air blew gently on his face. Sir Harry said, 'I have a feeling that we – England – are going to disgrace ourselves. I suppose you know as a fact, but I'm sure. There are clues. Reading between the lines of the government statements. The cackle-cackle of the boobies at Westminster. The strong action you were ordered to take at Ban Dhrai. Of course I know about that, man! Do you know what that really was? A warning to the MPRP to wait till the British have gone, then they'll be free to do what they like. I want to tell you that I'm not going to take it lying down. I'm a rich man – very rich – I have a lot of power in the east now, and I can exert plenty in England, if I pull all the strings I have in my hand, or can get hold of. I suppose you'll do just what you're told . . . have to, don't you, in the army? but I don't, and I won't. So I'm telling you that you may find me or my newspaper saying a lot of rude things about you and the army. It's not personal. It's because I think what we're going to do is a damn disgrace. If the boobies fight dirty – and you can't get dirtier than break a treaty the other side's kept like a gold watch for a hundred and fifty years, can you? – I'll fight dirty. Have a brandy.'

'Thanks very much, but I really can't. I'll have to play an extra set of squash to burn off what I've had already.'

'Play squash, eh? Played with Wilson?'

'Yes. Why?'

'Nothing. One of my assistants has played him a couple of times . . . But I'm told that chess is really his game. Chess, with the Daughter-in-Line. Two or three times a week, in the evening. He thinks he's getting something out of Kumara, I suppose, but I'll bet you a Chinese dollar to all the sterling in the Bank of England that Kumara will get more out of him.'

'She's very keen on chess,' David said.

Sir Harry's suffused face looked up: 'Know her personally, eh? It might be that's the only reason. I doubt it. You should get more of an idea at Maliwun. They'll feel freer than they do here. Not so many eyes on them.'

'Lady Anne will be there,' David said stiffly.

'No, she won't, lad. She'll develop a touch of dysentery to-morrow. You'll see . . . I hear you nearly got Sujak bin Amin this morning.'

David thought, this self-made old Yorkshireman keeps his ears closer to the ground he treads on than does Mr Sidney Francis Wilson, CMG, etc. The Resident had not heard of the incident at the station, or he would have asked about it in the bar . . . but then, why hadn't he himself mentioned it? He could imagine the Resident's look when he told him that he'd given Sujak a lift near Ban Dhrai. Perhaps that was the reason he had kept quiet. He was afraid of the Resident.

Sir Harry said, 'The MPRP isn't strong. It's weak in fact, but it does exist and the few members are dedicated . . . mostly recruited here and trained in Red China over the past three, four years. But they'll get more members if we break the treaty. Because if we go all of a sudden like, we leave a vacuum, and people won't want to be left out in the cold. There'll be plenty of jobs going . . . from cabinet ministers to hamlet commissars. The university students and graduates are the natural people to fill those jobs, if you throw out or kill the sort of people who are filling them now . . .' He pulled a gold watch from the fob pocket of his ample trousers, displaying the end of a pair of black silk braces, and said, 'Back to t'roody office. Anything I can do for you – as long as it's not helping us disgrace ourselves I will. Otherwise, look out!' He held out his big hand and waddled out, the servant Chengku holding the door open for him.

In his office, David glanced at the clock on the wall. The Resident would have been nearly twenty minutes at the Palace by now. The truth would be out, at least as far as the Queen and Kumara and probably the Chief Minister and the Prince Chamberlain, the inner circle. What was the phrase? 'Perfidious Albion'. He had felt much the same when pulling out of India in 1947, breaking some five hundred 'perpetual' treaties with the Indian princes in the process; or rather, instead of facing the opprobrium of publicly abrogating the treaties, pretending they didn't exist, and sneaking off by sea, scattering the worthless pieces of parchment to sink slowly in the wake of the departing ships. Now he was being ordered to do it again, and told it was all perfectly legal: the Cabinet had decided.

He picked up the note from Crawford that he had seen when he first came in after his lunch: *Bde Comd: The man who tripped Capt. O'Grady at the station has been identified as Shukor bin Yunus, ex-lawyer's clerk, a member of the MPRP and wanted for inciting to commit a breach of the peace here a year ago. The police are 'questioning' him about Sujak's movements and other details. PC Bde IO. Jan 15/60.*

David put the paper down. Questioning, in inverted commas, was right. He wondered what he would do if he captured such a man, and it was vital to get information out of him. Send him off into the jungle with a pair of RMC probably, thus shuffling off the responsibility for what would be done. CTs didn't play by the rules of law. They despised the law, calling it a bourgeois trick to keep the masses subjected. They bullied, murdered, tortured, punished without trial ... but if we did the same, what was the difference between them and us? The end, our purpose, the thing we wanted to achieve was different. So, am I saying, that the end justifies the means?

He slammed down the courtmartial review proceedings that lay open on his desk and called, 'Anything more, Stork?'

'No, sir.'

'Gilbert?'

'No, sir.'

'I'm off. I'm playing squash in case you need me. With Paul Stevens.'

After a hard game which Stevens won, David felt the need of fresh air. He drove slowly out of the Gymkhana Club gate and on to the coast road. The quickest way home was to turn right here, and at once up the gentle hill towards Kandahar Lines and Flagstaff House; but the evening was balmy, with a breeze off the sea and a cooler breath in the air that had made him put on his blazer. He was washed and showered and the game had sweated out the drinks Sir Harry had pressed on him. He drove appreciatively along the Esplanade towards the docks and the centre of the city. The low sun turned the water of Trangloek Bay pink, and the white lighthouse on Cape Rataphun into a pillar of reddish gold. In the streets and on the beach children ran about. Young men strolled along the Esplanade, fingers intertwined. A dozen girls were playing a game of tag on the sand, their lithe bodies twisting and turning, their high birdlike cries cutting across the murmur of the traffic and the calls of the street vendors. Farther along, the buildings grew taller, the traffic heavier, but still the cheerful calm and noisy order of the place prevailed. Here a Chinese couple strolled on the front, there three Gurkha soldiers haggled over the price of a huge fish they were buying from an old Mingoran woman with a wheelbarrow. The spire of the Old Pagoda rose out of the houses on the ridge to the right. The sun sank into the sea behind Cape Rataphun.

The Resident would be back in the Residency long since, his message delivered. The air become cooler, as though blown from a dank cellar. David headed for home, possessed by doubt and unhappiness.

Seven

THE DISTRICT GAME WARDEN stopped the Land-Rover and said, 'Now, if you will please get out, gentlemen . . . Oh, Your Royal Highness need not move. You have seen this many times.'

Sally said, 'I want to stretch my legs anyway,' and scrambled down with David and the Resident. The Land Rover was parked on the side of a hill, where a break in the trees gave a long view to the east. The immediate foreground, of brown grass savannah country thinly scattered with tall trees, slopeed gently to the valley floor three miles away. Along the river and on the farther slope the jungle was much thicker – a dense, dark green nubbled carpet, here and there reflecting the afternoon sun. In the hazy blue distance an indistinct horizon marked the watershed and the top of the descent to the next stream.

'The seladang are now resting in that thick jungle,' the Warden said, pointing across the valley. 'When it is getting dark some come out on to this slope – others on to the slopes beyond, fifteen miles away – and graze all night on the *lalang*, unless they are disturbed. At dawn they start moving back into the thick jungle. We will be in blinds down the slope there before dawn, and should get good heads . . .'

'Their sense of smell is excellent, I understand,' the Resident said. 'What if the wind is blowing in the wrong direction?'

'We have another set of blinds at the other end of this open country, sir,' the Warden said. 'And another road we can reach them by . . . I'm afraid we must walk the last two miles in any case. The noise of car engines disturbs the seladang.'

They stood a few moments longer, surveying the scene before them. Kumara was coming out tomorrow, to share a blind with

Wilson; but this afternoon, after their lunchtime arrival from Trangloek, she had retired to a desk with a box full of official papers, saying she had seen the area many times, and deputing Sally to accompany the British guests. Now Sally said, 'Seen enough, Mr Wilson?'

'Yes,' the Resident said, while David wondered again why he vaguely resented Sally's deference to the man: if she called him 'David', which she had done from the beginning, why didn't she call Wilson 'Sidney'?

They drove back to the base at Maliwun. Here five modern chalets, each with two bedrooms and a bathroom, were grouped round the large Rest House, one-storied, with the usual wide verandah and containing the dining room, kitchen, billiard room, and a comfortably furnished reading and smoking room, with card tables. A little beyond, the few houses which composed the hamlet of Maliwun lined the stream on stilt-legs, their palm thatch roofs matching the roof of the Rest House. As David stepped down from the Land-Rover, he saw Kumara's head silhouetted in one of the front windows of the reading room. Her Land-Rover, painted the distinctive blue of Mingoran royalty, still stood at the foot of the steps. She'd been working all the time, and still was. Wilson ran up the steps, throwing his safari hat at a peg as he went. David turned and headed for the chalet that had been allotted to him.

Sally called, 'Hey, David! Aren't you coming in for a cup of tea?'

'I don't think so, Sally. I have to check my guns. I didn't have time in Trangloek.'

The girl glanced briefly at the silhouette of her mother's bent head in the window; and the back of Sidney Wilson disappearing through the open outer door; and said, 'See you for drinks before dinner then. We eat early when we're going out for seladang the next day. Six for six-thirty.'

'Right,' David said, and walked off. Tulbahadur, putting new laces into his canvas jungle boots, rose smiling as he approached. It was all very well for Tule to grin: he was twenty-two, unmarried, and a lance corporal. 'Get me the Winchester and the shot gun,' he snapped, 'I'm going to clean them.'

The Gurkha said peaceably, 'But, sahib, I already have, just now, while you were out.'

David said, 'I'll clean them again.' Damn it, he had to have something to do, to occupy his mind.

At the end of dinner they wandered back into the reading room where the servants brought them coffee. The young Game Warden, obviously ill at ease in the exalted company, excused himself on a plea of work to do, and bowed out of the room and away to his chalet.

'Excellent dinner, princess,' the Resident said, sipping his coffee. 'Rather elaborate for the jungle, perhaps . . . but excellent.'

'The elaboration is just for you,' Kumara said. 'We can't serve anything but the best to Her Britannic Majesty's Representative, can we?'

'Mr Henderson would have complained, in writing, if he'd been served on anything but the best plate, anywhere, any time,' Sally said.

'Come, Sally,' Wilson said, smiling, 'You're exaggerating. Personally, I prefer the simple life, in its place.'

'I don't see you as the simple outdoorsman, somehow,' Kumara said, looking at Wilson over the rim of her coffee cup. She picked a small thin cigar out of the box the servant was holding for her. Wilson made a motion of feeling in his pocket, but Kumara said, 'You still don't smoke, so you still don't have matches or a lighter.' By then David found his own lighter aflame in his hand. He looked at it in surprise as he held it to the end of Kumara's cigar. That had been a reflex action, left over from their time in London. She had been in a good deal of pain in those days from her operations, and had smoked a lot.

Kumara said, 'Thank you,' and at once looked again at Wilson. She made a small gesture towards the servant with the cigar box, and said, 'Won't you change your rule, and try one? They're very good.'

Wilson said, 'I never smoke – anything. Never have.'

'Because,' Kumara said, 'if you did you would become a victim of the drug . . . a weakness. That's why you don't change any of your rules, isn't it? You don't trust yourself.'

'Oh yes I do,' Wilson said, sitting back, the coffee cup in his hand. His face was smiling, but the smile was only on the surface, David thought; below, whatever he was really feeling, it was not the mild amusement the smile tried to indicate. And Kumara was openly flirting with him. Her words, written down, would give no idea of the way she was drawing him into intimacy with her eyes and her tone and the small movements of her hands and head.

He felt excluded, as though shut outside, looking in – alone with Sally, who was watching her mother with a strange expression. He glanced surreptitiously at his watch. Barely eight . . . he could hardly leave yet, and if he did would certainly not get to sleep.

Kumara said, 'I brought our last game, where we adjourned. Shall we finish it now?'

'It'll take some time,' Wilson said. 'You think you have me where you want me . . . but you don't.'

'We shall see.'

She rose, drawing deeply on the cigar. Those thin cheroots of hers had caused a sensation in England. The looks of amazement on people's faces as they saw this slender, very feminine woman drawing on a cigar had never ceased to amuse him; but he had quickly got used to the fact of her smoking. He saw in Wilson's face that the Resident had not. His expression was part vexation that she should be breaking the rules of conduct for ladies, and part awe at the personality that made the act seem both ladylike and provocative.

Kumara walked to a card table and opened up the chests board set on it. Glancing at David she said, 'We meet here at half past three. There'll be a light breakfast ready. We must be on the move at four.' She picked up a piece of paper and began to set out the chessmen, looking at the paper from time to time.

Sally said, 'When my mother gets an idea into her head she never lets go.' She looked moodily across the room. The Resident was standing beside Kumara now, their heads close, both bent over the board, their hands picking up pieces, putting them down. Sally said, 'Oh hell! . . . I've got an idea. Come with me!'

'But . . .' David began.

She took his hand and tugged him out of the room into the lamplit passage and out on to the verandah. 'Moonlight,' she said, 'Balmy tropical night. We can't go to bed at eight o'clock. We'll go for a moonlight joy ride.' She ran down the steps, still pulling him after her.

David thought, why not? Neither of the others inside had a thought for him; nor for Sally, come to that. They didn't even want to see them until half past three in the morning. So be it.

Sally said, 'There's my mother's Land-Rover . . . but she always leaves it locked, and keeps the key . . . careful, my mother is.' She ran past the first chalet to the second. 'We'll use this. It's the Warden's. Besides, it's an open one.' She banged on the door. The Warden came out, a notebook in his hand and Sally said, 'We're going to take a moonlight ride.'

'Certainly, princess,' the young Mingoran said, trying to bow in the Mingoran fashion and stand to attention in the British manner simultaneously.

Sally jumped into the driver's seat and David climbed up beside her. She drove off, heading past Maliwun village on a dusty road to the west.

For a little while David's unfocused anger stayed with him; but it was an enchanted night, and gradually, under the caress of the invisible breeze, his frustration died, and became instead an appreciative, observant calm. The moon, a few days short of full, hung near the zenith, now shining on his cheek, now on Sally's, as the narrow forest trails swung through every direction of the compass. At first she drove fast, then more slowly as though some resolution of mood had come to her too. The dust which had been racing behind, now and then sucking forward to envelop them, sank low, and they smelled the heavy night scents of the jungle. The headlights flooded long green avenues ahead, the tree trunks so many pillars supporting the arched canopy above. Orchids flashed white and purple in the deep folds of lower boughs. Twice a pair of jade jewels glowed in the middle of the trail, and Sally whispered 'Leopard!' before the jewels vanished and a barely discernible yellowish blur bounded into the jungle. Huge fruit-eating bats fled down the forest aisles, just in the light, low over their heads. They crossed clearings and open places, but there was no distant view, for the lower air was of a dense pearly opaqueness, moon-suffused. They forded three streams, the water gurgling against the hubcaps; and never stopped until, after almost two hours, the headlights showed two figures ahead on the trail, going the same way. They were a man and a woman, in the simplest of peasant clothes, both old, both bent under heavy loads of sacks and jars.

When the lights played on them they stepped quickly into the edge of the jungle and waited. Sally stopped the Land-Rover and asked them: 'Are you going to Maliwun?'

The man answered, 'Yes, your honour.'

Sally said, 'Get in the back.'

'But, your honour, it is only a mile now. We are dirty, our clothes are dirty, we will spoil . . .'

'It is nothing. Get in!'

The old couple heaved their loads over the side of the vehicle, and gingerly climbed in. Sally started the Land-Rover forward again, throwing over her shoulder 'Where have you been?'

'Ban Nau, your honour. We went with my nephew in his cart, but he decided to stay another day. We could not, so it was necessary to walk.'

'Sixteen miles,' Sally said in English to David. Then, to the old couple, 'How is it in Maliwun?'

'Not bad, your honour. Like every year. The rains were not good . . . but not bad. We are not hungry . . . often. Our eldest grandson has become a monk. Our granddaughter will have a baby next week. We are old, but not sick . . . yet. We are happy.'

The houses of Maliwun loomed in the headlights, and Sally said, 'There. Get down now.' David glanced at her in surprise, for her tone was quite curt.

When the old couple were on the ground with their belongings the woman peered closely at Sally, and exclaimed, 'Idiots that we are! It is the Binte Binte Mingora! How did we dare to . . .'

'Quiet!' Sally snapped, jerked the car into gear and drove across the open grass to the Forest House. 'Idiots, is right,' she muttered. 'They're the sort who are holding us back. What's ever going to improve if people are satisfied with what they've got?'

'Yes,' David said, 'but . . . there has to be a limit, surely, otherwise everyone would always be unhappy. There are a lot of things I'd rather put up with than try to change.'

'Oh, but you're so . . . careful! If you don't sometimes take risks you just pass your life in a rut.'

'An old stick-in-the-mud,' David said, smiling. 'You're right. That's what I am.'

She turned and put her arms round his neck. The Land-Rover was parked outside her chalet. The moon bathed the houses and the grass and their faces in silver. 'Let's go to bed,' she whispered.

An immense physical desire flooded David's mind and body.

Her large soft breasts were pressed against him, her thighs spread, her head thrown back, the full young lips apart, moist, waiting.

He leaned forward to kiss her. At that instant she opened her eyes and half turned her head. She was looking at her mother's chalet, and beyond, at the Rest House. The latter was dark, all lights out: a light glowed in the window of Kumara's chalet; Sidney Wilson's was dark.

Sally sighed and closed her eyes again, but all the lust which had just now run like a hot flash through David's being, had vanished. Sally didn't really want him. He had been an idiot to think that she did. She only wanted to get even with her mother who, she obviously thought – or perhaps knew – was now in bed with Wilson. It was that last thought which had turned David's desire to bitter ashes.

He slipped free from her arms, and said, 'I'm sorry, Sally. I can't.'

He thought she would be angry, but she opened her eyes wide, looked at him, and said, 'Perhaps you're right.'

They got out of the Land-Rovers at twenty past four, and began walking east down a well-defined gravelled road. The moon had sunk and it was almost totally dark, for high drifting clouds hid most of the stars. The Game Warden led the party, followed by Kumara with the Resident, Sally with David, and two grizzled forest rangers. All but the rangers carried heavy rifles. After walking for twenty minutes the Warden stopped, and said in a low voice – 'We leave the road here and go on a game path. Keep close, please. I will walk more slowly. We should reach the first blind in ten minutes.'

'Where are the seladang?' Wilson whispered.

'That way, sir,' the Warden said, his dimly seen arm pointing. 'On that savannah we saw yesterday afternoon ... but they'll be moving slowly towards the jungle quite soon now.'

He led on. The jungle began to thin, and a faint breeze arose from the south – their right – the same direction as the seladang. The Warden stopped again and David could just make out the irregular shape of a leaf-covered blind, a short, semi-circular wall about four and a half feet high. The Warden whispered, 'Princess Salimina, will you and Brigadier Jones please take this blind?

Ranger Abdul will be with you.' He and the others disappeared into the darkness.

Sally muttered to David, 'You take the first shot ... if we see anything. Abdul here will point out the best target, and won't let you fire at a bad head, or in the direction of the other butt ... unfortunately.' She laughed quietly. They subsided into silence.

David waited with the loaded rifle rested on top of the wall, looking south into the strengthening breeze. The sky began to pale. Slowly the skeletal fingers reaching across the dawn became the branches of tall scattered trees, clouds appeared, then faint colour came, the ground emerged from the universal slough of the lower darkness and took shape as tall waving spears of grass, and it too took colour and was browny yellow, green underneath where the young shoots were rising.

Abdul peered across the savannah, a worried expression now discernible on his face. After a time he whispered something to Sally. She said, 'He says we ought to have seen at least one group by now ... Still, they do sometimes come down in full daylight.'

They waited. Three minutes later a single rifle shot boomed out from farther down the slope. Abdul lifted his head sharply. Sally said, 'You can't see the other blind from here. I suppose ...'

Another shot interrupted her and she said, 'Well, *they* seem to have seen something.'

They waited another half hour. The sun rose and the whole great slope of grass and trees, anthills and bushes, became golden in the bars of light streaming flat under the clouds. Abdul spoke again to Sally. 'That's it,' she said. 'I am sorry you didn't even see one.'

She unloaded her rifle, propped it against the wall of the blind and lit a Lucky Strike. David followed suit. Abdul listened with head cocked to a distant shouting from down the slope. 'That's the other ranger,' Sally said, 'He says they got a bull ... good horns ... old ...' She snorted and threw one hand in the air – 'Mother got it! She must have shot it out of Mr Wilson's eyebrows. He was supposed to have first shot.'

Abdul ran off up the hill with a muttered word, and she said, 'He's gone to get the Warden's Land-Rover.' She relapsed into silence, puffing hard at her cigarette.

Kumara appeared, with the Resident, walking steadily up the gentle slope through the grass. They stopped at the blind and

Kumara said, 'We saw nothing, until just now. An old bull, dying of old age. He had no cows any more.'

'I missed it,' Wilson said, 'A clean miss at a hundred yards.'

Those hands of his often trembled when he was with Kumara, David thought; served him right.

Kumara said, 'I killed it, to end its life quickly and without suffering . . . Why did you not want Mr Wilson or Brigadier Jones to get a seladang, Sally?'

'I don't know what you mean,' the girl said sullenly. She threw down her cigarette and stubbed it out with her foot, head down.

'Look at me, Sally! You know well what I mean. The Warden told me you had borrowed his Land-Rover – when I asked him. The tyre tracks are on the road down there . . . and I am sure they will be on the trail across the savannah.'

David felt a flush of embarrassed shame mantling his neck. In that long drive last night he had had no idea where they were going; but Sally knew. They had started out in the opposite direction from the seladangs' haunts; and had returned from that direction, too; but in between Sally had deliberately driven through and across the seladangs' feeding areas in order to disturb them . . . but surely not to spite himself or Wilson.

He said, 'I'm terribly sorry, Kumara. It was my fault. I didn't realize . . .'

She looked at him the same way she had been looking at Sally: tranquil, impersonal, unangered. She did not answer David's stammered excuses.

Sally burst out, 'The seladang ought not to be preserved for us. They belong to everyone. The people should be allowed to kill them for food.'

'How long do you think, then, that any seladang would survive?' Kumara said.

'The people matter more than the seladang,' Sally cried.

'They both matter,' her mother said, 'But there is a difference . . . The people do not need to be protected against the seladang . . . The villages round the Preserve get the meat of the animals we shoot, as they always have. But by restricting the kill of seladang to ten a year we ensure that the villagers' meat supply – and the seladang – will last for ever.'

Forever's supposed to be a long time, David thought: but it

sometimes turned out to be only a few months. It would for the seladang, if Sally had her way.

Kumara said, 'Now let us hear no more about this. We will try again tomorrow.'

She moved on up the hill, Wilson following and, after a moment, David with Sally. Sally was weeping.

David sat at the battered upright piano in a far corner of the reading room and started his third piece, Polonaise No. 3 in A Major. The piano was out of tune, three of the keys were stuck and one was missing altogether, but that was not what was making him play badly. He was out of practice, his finger joints stiff and his fingers feeling like sausages. He'd never be very good, but he could be a great deal better than this. Damn it, he'd have to practise. No time. He'd bloody well find time. He banged his hands flat on the keys in a jarring discord, slammed the lid shut, and swung round on the piano stool.

'Very good,' the Resident said, clapping. David stared at him in amazement. To say that, even out of politeness, the man must be tone deaf.

Wilson was sitting on a wicker chair behind the piano stool. It was half past five, raining, the sun obscured, the fans whirring softly in the ceiling. Wilson said, 'I hope we see something tomorrow. I for one can't stay here another day.'

'I don't think any of us can,' David said.

Wilson said, 'You were with Sally last night, but the joy ride was her idea, wasn't it?'

'Yes. I didn't know where we were. And of course I never dreamed that she would go through the seladang area, after the Warden specifically mentioned that car engines disturbed them and made them break their routine.'

'Of course not. She seems to be in a bit of a muddle over the beasts, anyway. She tried to prevent us killing them, but wants the peasants to do so.'

'That's because she's against the idea of preserving,' David said.

The Resident said, 'As a general principle, so am I. If the seladang can't survive, let better-equipped species replace them. She's a strange young woman, though. Not quite stable, I think.'

David said, 'She's young. And she's the heir. Princes always fight with their fathers ... and, I suppose, princesses with their mothers. Her heart's in the right place, though she seems to have a lot of the usual half-baked political ideas, even though she is going to be queen one day.'

'What do you mean?' the Resident said.

David said, 'Well ... she wants things changed, because she sees the bad in what they have now, but not the good. She doesn't give weight to things like peace of mind, tranquillity, decorum, beauty ... the only things that matter are material – better wages, electric light, hospitals, drains, votes ...'

'Votes aren't material.'

'If they are given to the politician who promises them the most money, or jobs, then they are.'

'I disagree with you about her. I think her head's all right, but not her heart. You see a lot of her. I advise you to be careful.'

David said, 'What do you mean?'

'Be sure that she cannot compromise you, or even appear to. Or, of course, get any information out of you that she should not have.'

'That will not happen, Resident,' David said stiffly; then: 'When is the official announcement of the abrogation of the treaty being made?'

'The day after tomorrow. It will be announced then that Mingora will achieve *Merdeka*, independence, on 1 June this year ... Did you by chance mention anything to Sir Harry Johnstone about this when you had lunch with him the other day at The Place?'

David said, 'No.'

'He had the insolence to call me the next morning, and say he was damned sure we were going to rat on the Treaty – his words – and if I had any sense of honour I'd refuse to carry out the policy.'

Good for him, David thought: and only just suppressed his impulse to say it aloud.

'I told him that I was carrying out, and would continue to carry out, the policy of Her Majesty's Government, of which I was a servant and he a subject. I did not say, what is true, that his concern is purely commercial.'

'You think so?' David ejaculated, surprised.

'Of course! He and people like him have been battening for centuries on these undeveloped countries. We've gone to war more than once for the sake of their profits. That's coming to an end, and he doesn't like it. Don't get the idea that he's concerned with anything but money.'

He rose, the pale blue eyes looking straight into David's. David wondered, first, whether Wilson could have got a report on his talk with Sir Harry at lunch; and second, whether what he said could be true. Could it be that the bluff Yorkshireman was not really an honest English merchant offended by the politicians' evasions and lies, but a man simply out for his own selfish interests, the embodiment of a cartoon capitalist in a top hat grinding the faces of the poor?

'Have a drink,' Wilson said.

'Thanks,' David said: and after that there'd be dinner, and he'd watch Sally pretending not to be aware of Kumara; and then he'd watch Kumara and Wilson playing chess; and worry . . . and wonder . . .

Eight

IT WAS THE first day of February – two weeks since the near capture of Sujak bin Amin at the station ... 120 days to the desertion of Mingora by Britain ... four hours to the arrival of General Sir Rougemont H ntingdon on a brief visit of inspection ... four minutes to another meeting with Sally at the Royal Beach, his first since the incidents at Maliwun. He had been afraid of what might happen; but then he found himself missing her youth, her offhand voluptuousness. Or was it that he needed a boost for his masculinity?

Perhaps she won't be here, he thought ... but she was, sitting on the verandah of the beach house in her bikini, smoking, staring at the sea. She greeted him with a wave: 'Long time no see. Are you afraid I'll blame you for the Great Betrayal? That's what my grandmother calls it.'

'She's right,' David muttered.

'I don't know,' Sally said, getting up as he went in to the men's changing room. She spoke through the swing half doors as he took off his uniform slacks and shirt. 'I think it's about time we stood on our own feet.'

She ran down the sand, David after her. For a time neither spoke but swam round the shark net, then splashed and played together in the steady rollers. The waves were bigger today than he'd seen them before, so that the big glass balls holding up the shark net rhythmically rose and fell and the waves passed under them and rode on towards the beach, towering up, breaking in white foam.

Sally said, 'Has Shukor bin Yunus talked yet? The man who tripped up your officer near the station?'

'I don't know,' David said. 'I don't think so, or I'd have been told.'

'Not necessarily,' she said. She looked at him keenly for a moment. 'You do know something, don't you?'

David said, 'No, Sally,' but she insisted: and she was right, because in fact Shukor had talked, after long careful persuasion. He had given useful details of the organization of the MPRP in the city, and rumours of help from Thailand; but he knew nothing of the present whereabouts of Sujak bin Amin, or of the detailed plans of the Party in the provinces.

'You don't have a dishonest face,' Sally said, 'I suppose that's why I like you. If you do ever lie convincingly you'll catch everyone out ... Of course the man has said something – after two weeks of starvation and torture and psychological bullying.'

She swam slowly towards the beach on her back, her arms falling rhythmically behind her head, her breasts thrusting like rounded hills out of the sea, the water flowing past their bases. 'I'm glad my mother prefers the Resident,' she said.

'He's a chess player, too,' David said defensively.

'And she's helping him with his Mingora-Malay' ... She laughed. 'I wouldn't stand a chance if she decided to get you, would I?'

David duck-dived and swam under water for a few strokes. Of course, if Kumara lifted a finger he'd crawl to her on his belly, like an ecstatic puppy. It hurt to think of it.

They walked up out of the water and she felt for his hand. 'Don't let them make you feel you're doing something dishonourable in leaving Mingora,' she said. 'It ought to happen.'

They went inside the beach house and separated to the changing rooms. David had just stepped out of his trunks when the swing doors opened with a creak. He looked up. Sally was standing there, naked, the water glistening on her golden skin and drops pearling the small dark triangle of her loins. She put her arms round his neck. Her breasts were cool against him. She said, 'I suppose I would have loved my father, if I'd known him.' She pulled his head down and kissed him on the lips. Her tongue moved into his mouth. As at Maliwun David's sexuality stirred and he felt an artery pounding in his forehead. But it was only an animal response to her femaleness, and her offering of it to him. It was Kumara who filled his thoughts. Kumara, whom he – Christ, there was no denying – loved.

He pushed her away, harder than he had intended. She almost fell. 'I'm sorry,' he said, holding her hand. 'You're sweet, Sally . . . and kind.'

'But I'm not my mother,' she said. 'I'll get dressed.'

'I'm sorry,' he said, 'I really am.'

She threw him a half smile before disappearing. He went slowly into the shower and turned it on. He felt depressed and frustrated.

Ten minutes later, as they were getting into their cars, the Residency Rolls came down the dusty road through the palms. The chauffeur brought it to a stop, and Wilson handed Kumara out. Kumara looked closely at her daughter and momentarily, just visibly, her lips tightened. She had noticed something, David saw – and it hurt her. His feeling of frustration vanished.

He reached his office, after breakfast, by nine o'clock, wondering whether it was written on his face that he had almost made love to a woman young enough to be his daughter. And Kumara thought that he had actually done so.

'Anything urgent?' he asked his Brigade Major.

'Here's a copy of the C-in-C's programme, sir.'

David looked at it to check that he'd got it right: arrival at 1100, reach Fusiliers in jungle demonstration area at 1200, ambush demonstration to begin at once, lunch in Fusiliers' camp mess at 1400, with Campbell-Wylie, Stevens, and O'Grady invited, plane departs 1600.

Porter said, 'The Chief Minister asked that you call as soon as you come in.' David picked up the phone.

The Minister came on at once. 'Brigadier Jones? Can you come to the palace, at once? There are some matters we ought to discuss.'

David said, 'I have the Commander-in-Chief arriving from Singapore at eleven.'

'We will be finished before then,' the Minister said. 'Only you need come, brigadier. There will be no need of staff.'

David hung up. 'They want me at the palace. No staff.'

'That's unlike the Minister,' the Brigade Major said thoughtfully, 'There'll be more in this than meets the eye, sir.'

'There always is,' David said, 'Call Wood with the staff car.'

When the servant squatting outside the hanging curtains went in to announce David, the Minister himself came out to greet him. Inside the curtains David took a couple of steps and paused. At the far end of the room Queen Valaya VI was seated behind the Chief Minister's desk. The Prince Chamberlain, her brother, stood at one side, and Kumara, the Daughter-in-Line, at the other.

David turned to the Minister and said coldly, 'I was told *you* wanted to speak to me.' Really, it was impossible the way these people sprung things on you.

The Minister said apologetically, 'Please excuse me, dear Brigadier – Her Majesty needed to speak to you, not as a soldier, but as an English gentleman.'

'Welsh,' David said.

The Queen said, 'Brigadier, Mr Wilson told me two weeks ago that the British government intends to break the Treaty of Trangloek. He called it "the grant of independence to Mingora". We did not ask for this sudden total independence, and in the days that have passed since Mr Wilson's visit we have been studying what it will mean. It will bring disaster to our people. I ask you . . . I beg of you . . . to prevent this shameful thing from coming to pass.'

'Ma'am, I'm a soldier,' David said. 'I have to obey orders.'

'Why?' the Queen said sharply, 'Did you not try some German generals for obeying orders? Minister, you speak English more freely than I, and I am tired. Explain to the brigadier how we feel.'

The Chief Minister, standing now halfway between David and Kumara, almost like a go-between or interpreter, said, 'The Prince Regent personally signed the Treaty of Trangloek for England, and the Queen's ancestor, Queen Valaya II personally signed for Mingora. The treaty was to be good for ever. England protected us, and in return received cheap raw materials, employment for many of her educated people in our service, paid for out of our revenues, even to their pensions. England still buys our raw materials cheap, makes them up in her factories, and sells them to the world, at a profit. We still employ British men and women in our police, customs, judicial system, railways, public works, hospitals, universities. We still stay in the sterling area, placing our reserves of wealth in the hands of Britain, to back her currency. What has changed?'

David said, 'I suppose our government thinks it's time Mingora stood on its own feet.'

'Inside four months?' the Minister said politely, 'In the end we shall aim at a regional defence group here in South-East Asia, but the immediate fact is that to find more money for defence, we will have to cut back on the essential services which we have been building up. Nor, of course, do we have the trained officers or technical people in any field ... I believe the Perdana Binte Mingora spoke to you of these things, and others, near Ban Dhrai, before Christmas last year.'

David said, 'I suppose Parliament feels that we can't afford it any more.'

'But, brigadier,' the Queen broke in, 'it is a small part of the profit England has made out of the association.'

'What can I do?' David burst out. Kumara's big eyes were veiled, half closed, the thin-skinned face impassive.

'Understand what we feel, brigadier ... that this action is unworthy of Her Majesty Queen Elizabeth, and of England's past reputation. You will shortly be seeing your Commander-in-Chief, I believe. You may tell him of our thoughts.'

The Queen rose, starting up with an easy motion out of the big chair, then beginning to fall back, a spasm of pain on the painted face, to be caught by the arm of her brother. She went through the curtain at the back, leaning on his arm, followed by Kumara. David remained, head bowed.

The Chief Minister's hand fell on his shoulder, the voice was gentle. 'Do not think this is personal. It is just that we are so ... shocked. Britain and Mingora were showing to the world something different – a continued loyalty and co-operation, through thick and thin. We were demonstrating to South-East Asia another way for developing countries ... not dictatorships or military juntas, not communist massacres and thefts. Why can we not continue on the same path?'

David could not answer. After a moment the Chief Minister took pity on him and changed the subject. They discussed briefly the provision of helicopters for the RMC; then the formation of a committee to work out the size, organization, and equipment of the Mingoran Army.

'We'll need a financial adviser,' David said.

'Someone who knows the world markets and currencies,' the

Minister said, 'Could we ask for Mr Nugent? He is a financial expert.'

David said, 'You could. But I think it would be better to start breaking away from British governmental advice.' The Minister gave him a keen look as he continued. 'I would ask Sir Harry Johnstone.'

'An excellent idea! My last point is – I would like you to accompany me on my forthcoming tour of the provinces. I want to see what progress is being made with our reforms, and how the village Home Guards are working. We should also see for ourselves what is the situation in Moirang. The governor there is nervous.'

'He has the whole of the Burma and some of the Thai border, doesn't he?'

'Yes.' The Minister led towards the swinging shimmering curtain of the passage to the verandah. 'Once more, brigadier, please be assured that we do not hold you responsible for the terrible predicament in which we find ourselves.'

'Thanks, but I do,' David said, as he went out.

He reached the airport fifteen minutes before the Chief's aircraft was due, to find the Resident already there. Wilson greeted his salute with a nod – 'The plane's been delayed ten minutes,' he said. 'They should have told me. I have better things to do than wait around on hot tarmac.'

Rain was threatening, the sky full of heavy clouds, and a damp breeze blowing up the slope from the sea and the city.

David made to go inside the airport building, but the Resident said, 'Let's walk outside for a bit ... Have you had any reaction from the Mingoran government people to our new policy?'

David said, 'Yes. I've just come from the Palace. The Chief Minister said he wanted to see me, but when I arrived the Queen was there, too, with the Perdana Binte Mingora. They are very upset.'

'What did you say?'

'What could I? Nothing.'

'Good. The truth is that Britain can't afford to support the commitment here.'

David said, 'Well ... they say that we're making a lot of

money out of the raw materials we buy here, manufacture and resell.'

'We can always buy the raw materials somewhere else. We don't have to saddle ourselves with a military commitment in order to get raw materials.'

'But the commitment was supposed to be for ever. It seems wrong that we can just break it. If it were the other way around, and they said, get out, we wouldn't go, just like that.'

'Not in the past. Nowadays, we probably would. In any case, HMG can no longer afford to be in a position whereby this military commitment to Mingora can put them into a confrontation with Burma, Thailand, or even China.'

'But I don't think this country can stand without our support. Malaya certainly couldn't have survived the Communist Terrorist movement without us. They had a population of millions, a majority of them Malay by race, and only a very small minority were communist. All in all only 12,000 men and women, practically all Chinese, passed through the movement, yet they nearly made the whole of Malaya Red. It took *us* twelve years and 60,000 trained soldiers to beat them. Mingora hasn't got a hope in hell of surviving anything like that, alone ... And the people don't want us to leave.'

'How do we know? The Queen and her ministers tell us, but how do we *know*? The MPRP would tell us differently.'

The mutter of a jet engine intruded quietly on their talk and the Resident slightly raised his voice: 'My dear fellow, the truth is that the British people are tired of so-called greatness, and responsibility. That is why no argument will make the Cabinet change their decision ... And you, as my military adviser here, must be very careful what you say, even what you allow people to say to you. Loyalty is the first requisite for all of us.'

'I am well aware of that, sir,' David said, but the Resident turned his back and walked purposefully towards the place where the aircraft ramp was being wheeled out.

Sir Rougemont Huntingdon held more firmly to the windshield bar as the Land-Rover bounced along the rutty road towards the distant jungle. His red-banded cap did not conceal the bulge of his forehead, nor could the dark glasses fully hide the glitter of his blue eyes. His left leg was stuck woodenly forward, jammed in under the dashboard. The yellow dust was settling more thickly every minute on his olive green uniform and the four bright rows of ribbons above his left breast pocket. A large American automatic pistol hung in its holster from the left side of his belt and he held a short thick leather-padded swagger stick in his free hand.

He spoke over his shoulder to David jammed in the back seat with Tulbahadur: 'I'll think over the helicopter plan, and talk to the Air Marshal about it. It seems sound, but I would say it was nothing to do with us – purely a civil responsibility.'

'They can't raise and train an army in four months, sir,' David said vehemently. 'We owe them at least this, to get the Constabulary more mobile so that it can, a bit, replace us when we go.'

'The Queen and ministers been getting at you? I've heard they can charm a wounded tiger into licking their backsides, if they want to.'

'It's a matter of justice, sir. We *are* breaking the treaty, whatever the Resident tries to call it.'

'Wilson's a very capable fellow, Jones, and very powerful too. Don't forget it. We're soldiers . . . we've got to keep out of politics. We have a civil government, and half of them are pompous nincompoops, and some are plain crooks, but they're our bosses, and we obey them.'

'What about Nuremberg, sir?' David said. 'Suppose we were ordered to do something, well, criminal?'

The Commander-in-Chief twisted his head to look at him. 'You are hot about this, aren't you? Perhaps I'd better pull you out and put someone else in.'

'I wish you would, sir,' David said desperately.

The general bent his wooden leg with an audible creak but did not speak for a long while. Then he said, 'No. You've got to learn to bite the bullet. As you wrote in that excellent article of yours, the *ultima ratio regis* in dealing with his own people is not force, because if he has not been able to make them understand and agree with him, killing them won't help. . . . I could put some insensitive blockhead here, but you have a feel for the place, and you'll do a good job. It's not my responsibility to see that my brigadiers sleep well at night . . . Anything else you want

125

to say about what the Resident was discussing with us there at the airport?'

David thought, and said, 'He seemed to play down the urgency of getting their army raised and trained. He thought we could do it all with my brigade, but we can't. The Chief Minister's forming a committee, but I'm already sure we're going to have to have crash courses run in Singapore for the more technical subjects. We're going to have to give immediate commissions to Mingorans who have no military background at all, and it may need a special school to familiarize them with the military system in general, before they even look at a weapon. These helicopter pilots . . . where do we find them? From constables whose highest contact with machinery is to ride a bicycle? Or from university graduates who have no desire to become constables? And . . .'

The general said, 'You needn't elaborate. I get the idea . . . I'd better have something from your committee by 1 March, even if it's not the final report. One more thing. Our secret intelligence tells me that you go swimming alone with the young princess – Sally, they call her, don't they? – nearly every day.'

David said, 'I do, sir. Not as much as that.' He waited, wondering what would come next.

The general said, 'Just be careful, Jones. You're a conscientious chap, like the Reverend Mr Davidson. Don't come to the same end.'

'No, sir,' David said. If the Chief's Intelligence people were reporting that to him, they were also probably telling him about Wilson's private hours with Kumara; but if the Chief knew, the Commissioner General knew, and Wilson was the latter's responsibility.

'We're nearly there now, sir,' David said.

'Oh. Slow down a minute, driver. I want a special report on John Allen, by 15 May. Not on his work as CO of the battalion, but on his fitness for promotion. I'll tell him about it, and you get him to initial your report before you send it to me.'

'Yes, sir . . . This is the place.'

The Land-Rover slowed and stopped. The following vehicles loomed out of the dust cloud. John Allen and a group of officers and senior NCOs of the Fusiliers stood beside the road where it entered the trees, all in jungle dress.

Sir Rougemont hopped out stiffly and strode forward, his leg

126

creaking at every step – 'Morning, John. Everything ready?'

'Yes, sir. This way, sir.'

'Right. Before I leave I want to meet the new company commander and CSM of A – Whitmore and Berg, I think. Spalding's doing well in my AAG's office. He rides a good desk.' They passed into the jungle down a narrow path, David following with the Fusiliers' adjutant. He could hear Allen explaining the live-ammunition exercise that the C-in-C was about to see: 'Half a platoon of CTs somewhere within this square mile, represented by hidden dummies. One company searching . . .'

'Exits blocked?'

'Yes, sir . . . company and a half . . . mobile patrols on roads to three miles out . . . radio touch . . .'

'Interpreters with forward troops?'

'Two RMC per platoon . . . advanced RAP moving down centre axis . . . It will last an hour and a quarter, then we have half an hour's post mortem, and then lunch, in the jungle.'

'Good. I have to be back at the airport at four.'

'I know, sir. May we begin the exercise?'

'Go ahead.'

A few minutes later irregular lines of green-clad men began to move, wide spread, through the jungle, others following the paths. In a clearing nearby the battalion signallers muttered into the microphones of their radios. Soon the sound of bursting grenades echoed dull and heavy among the trees, with the sharp stutter of sub-machine guns. The sounds of battle increased, and by the strange acoustics of the jungle, seemed to be coming from all directions at once.

Nine

AS DAVID TURNED the Land-Rover off the main road and drove past the silent dark mass of Jumbhorn Wat he reflected that he had not been to the royal beach since the day of the C-in-C's visit. The Chief's warning with its mysterious reference to some person called Davidson, had made him nervous, that was the truth. But now he wanted to see her. There was no law forbidding him to swim in the sea with an attractive young woman, as long as it did not interfere with his work, and personally he thought that it helped. Sally was the only person he knew who was in a position of power in Mingora, but who thought differently from the Establishment. She'd change her views as she grew older, of course – everyone did – but meantime she was an engaging mixture of Mingoran traditional and American liberal: earnest, well meaning, concerned more with theory than practice; but a nice girl . . . and he'd keep away from sex.

He drove past the sign marking the limit of the royal domain and in a few minutes reached the beach house. Sally's MG was parked there and he ran up the steps calling 'Sally?'

As he pushed open the slatted half doors and entered the central lounge part of the beach house he found himself looking down the muzzle of a small automatic pistol. After a fraction of a second he recognized the square cut face of the man holding the automatic. Those level brows, that crewcut hair, those blazing brown eyes had haunted many of his nights. He had taken out the cotton wool that had thickened his lips and cheeks, but there was no doubt who it was – Sujak bin Amin. In the far corner two other men, Mingorans in peasant clothes of faded coloured shirts and black trousers, conical straw hats on their heads, were standing by the Princess Sally.

'Raise your hands,' Sujak said sharply.

David did so. His revolver was in its holster, but one of the two men in the background was coming forward to take it out. They had been holding Sally ... no, one was holding her now, but he had not been before, just standing near her.

Sally said, 'When they got me, I was praying that if anyone else came here this morning, it would be mother and the Resident ... You haven't come for over a week.'

Sujak bin Amin spoke to the other Mingorans, without taking his eyes off David. Then he said, 'They think we should kill you.'

'No!' Sally said sharply.

Sujak continued as though she had not spoken. 'But I think not. Nothing personal, you understand – the killing – but it would bring your army in. It might even persuade your government to continue their imperialist intervention here beyond the date you have now set for your departure. Then they suggested we tie you up with the old couple in the hut ... but I've decided to take you with us.'

David said nothing. Sally said, 'They're kidnapping me as a hostage until the police release Shukor bin Yunus, the man who tripped up Captain O'Grady at the station.'

Sujak said, 'Also as a hostage against any use of torture or force against our people. If the police or army kill any of our people, she will die.'

David looked at her; she did not look very alarmed, rather more attractive than usual as excitement had put more colour into her cheeks and set her full breasts to heaving under the coloured American blouse.

'Turn round,' Sujak ordered. David felt his wrists being securely tied behind his back. Sujak said, 'Later, we'll gag you, but don't make a sound anyway, or you'll both suffer for it. This way.'

David said, 'I'm going on tour with the Chief Minister to-morrow.'

The MPRP leader stared at him for a long moment, then said, 'And you think that makes it improper for us to kidnap you?'

David said nothing. That was just what he'd been thinking; but it was foolish to have let the words come out.

Sujak said, 'The Minister will just have to go without you... This way, Sally.'

David started involuntarily to hear him call the princess by her English nickname; but, of course, this was the man who had helped prepare her for Stanford University a few years ago. They had known each other well then.

Sally followed Sujak on to the beach, along to the north, away from the old couple's hut, and then into the palms. David followed, the two men behind him, the nearest one with David's revolver in his hand. A narrow path wound through the palms for a couple of hundred yards, then water appeared shining between the tree trunks. They stood on the edge of Dhaphut Sap, the shallow water calm and green. Two large boats, like huge elaborately decorated canoes, were moored at a small jetty, and near them, a simpler boat of the sort peasants used to transport rice and other crops along the canals of the flatlands. Sujak motioned the prisoners to get into the small boat. A moment later the boat glided out under the urge of the two men's paddles. They moved north along the western rim of the great lake, mostly passing under the shade of the trees lining the bank, now gliding through reed beds and past occasional tiny coves. Across the lake to the east a line of palms marked the sand dunes which separated the Sap from the sea. In the middle of the lake, three miles off, an island sat dark and green on the water.

After nearly an hour, without seeing a village or a human being, the boat entered a thick growth of mangroves. It was almost dark in there, the water seeming black and the myriad roots of the mangroves an impenetrable forest all round; the boat glided on, sliding between the reaching arms under the closed canopy of leaves.

At last the paddles turned the boat's bow to the left. They entered a narrow creek with steep mud banks. The mangroves ended, replaced by big trees lining the creek. The creek narrowed, and the boat ran aground in soft mud.

Sujak said, 'We cross the road and railway here. Open your mouth.' David did so and a big cotton cloth was tied round his head, passing inside his open mouth. The same was done to Sally. They got out of the boat and worked through bushes for ten minutes. Twice David heard the grind of a truck engine, the first one faint, the second loud and close. Through the bushes he saw the tarmac'd ribbon of the main road ahead, dark red, for it was made of crushed red laterite bound with tar.

Sujak crouched at the side of the road behind a tree. From where he stood ten yards farther back David thought that the road had a curve in it to the north, quite close, and a long straight stretch to the south. The CTs had chosen a good place, for the pursuit would come from the south, the direction of Trangloek; and in that direction they could see an approaching vehicle from much farther than anyone in the vehicle could see them. Sujak rapped an order; one of the men took Sally's arm, stepped out on to the road, crossed it quickly, and vanished into the jungle the other side. Sujak cocked his head, listening. David thought he heard the distant sound of an engine but Sujak said 'Now!' and it wasn't until they were well into the far jungle that a filthy old diesel truck loaded with bulging sacks, passed with a blatting roar and a cloud of black smoke.

They moved on again, to come almost at once upon the railway. Nothing was in sight in either direction, and they crossed as before, in two parties. A few minutes later they picked up a cart track and Sujak muttered, 'This is it.' He turned left on to the track and they walked for half an hour; then, tucked into a patch of thicker jungle, they found a cart, the two wheels solid blocks of wood, the body of the cart half loaded with cut sugar cane. Two tethered buffaloes lay at ease in a circle of green fodder, and more cane was stacked beside the cart.

'Good,' Sujak said. 'Get in. We have a long way to go.'

He reached up to pick a few objects out of the fork of a branch and David saw, inside his left upper arm, the long scar which was the only real distinguishing mark in his police description. Then the two men made him and Sally lie down on the sugar cane in the cart, covered them with a tarpaulin, and loaded more cane on top of the tarpaulin. It was a heavy weight on them finally, and Sally made a muffled sound of protest. They heard Sujak, close on the outside of the cart, say, 'Too heavy? Sorry, you'll have to put up with it.'

They heard the buffaloes being yoked in and soon the cart moved off, the solid axles making piercing squeaks and long drawn almost human groans.

He wanted to say something to Sally, but could not speak for the gag. He would have liked to touch her, tell her not to worry, but both their hands were tied behind their backs. Dust was filtering under the tarpaulin and he wanted to sneeze. It was hot, and getting hotter. The sweat trickled down his neck and round his ribs.

What time was it? About half past nine, perhaps ten. When would someone at his headquarters start a hue and cry? Perhaps they already had ... He'd have to institute the same rules about escorts and movement generally as had been in force during the Emergency in Malaya. But was it as bad as that? He seemed to have stumbled by accident on an action the MPRP was taking against the royal house. Would it really affect the rest of the country? Would it not be worse for their cause, overall, to show that the CTs were having so much effect, so early?

He lay silent, his eyes closed. He thought he dozed. He awoke suddenly hearing the sound of an aircraft engine. Sounded like a Auster, an artillery spotter, not very close. But that meant that the alarm had been raised. The aircraft noise faded. The cart ground on, moaning and groaning. Sujak and the two men were talking close beside his ear, but he could not make out what they were saying.

What was needed for a search operation like this was helicopters, but there weren't any in Mingora. By now some had probably been asked for from Malaysia ... ought to get here in say two hours ... but these country roads were full of carts. He had heard two passing already ...

He heard Sujak say clearly, 'Bicycles!' The word was the same in both languages. Then, in Mingora-Malay, 'Are they police?'

'Yes,' one of the men answered.

David waited. The RMC used bicycles for their patrols. The cart was coming out of the area where the kidnapping had taken place, so the constables would surely search it.

Five minutes later Sujak said, 'They can't have heard. They have probably been on patrol all morning and haven't contacted their headquarters.'

David's heart sank. The constables had ridden by, silent in the dust. He thought, later, that the cart was turning. Later still, it stopped. Some of the sugar cane was removed, and the tarpaulin lifted. They staggered and slipped to the ground, and Sujak untied their gags. 'We're deep in the jungle,' he said, 'And no one will hear you if you do shout.'

David thought from the sun that it was past noon. Sujak and his two followers moved a little away and huddled under a tree, their heads close, but one of the men kept his eyes on David and Sally where they sat on the ground, their backs against a wheel of the cart.

'Can you hear what they're talking about?' David asked in a low voice.

'No, but I think they're planning what to do next. They didn't expect to be followed so soon.'

'How do you know?'

She seemed nonplussed as she answered, 'Oh . . . well, they didn't expect to catch you, too . . . and perhaps they knew that I was going on to spend the day with a friend in Machin.' She fell silent as Sujak rose from his squatting position and came over towards them. 'A couple of constables saved their lives back there,' he said. 'We had our guns on them, but they rode past.' The distinctive beat of a helicopter's rotor thrashed the heavy air from somewhere to the east. Sujak said, 'Helicopters up from Alor Star. I wonder if you'd have sent them if we'd only got Sally here.'

David said shortly, 'Yes.'

'Oh, you are sure! But of course you would have been the one with the authority to ask for them, and you are fond of Sally, I hear.' David said nothing. The sound of the chopper died, to be replaced by the steady light throb of the Auster's engine. It got closer and as David looked up through a gap in the interlaced foliage above, the little plane passed overhead at about a thousand feet. Sally said, 'There'll be more soon, and soldiers on the ground. The Central Range is a long way off, Sujak.'

Sujak said, 'Quiet!' He turned to David: 'I told you that the only reason I'm not killing you is that we are not ready to do so yet. When we are, we will. And I give you now official warning that the Mingoran People's Revolutionary Party is a national movement, military and political. Our members are soldiers, and must be treated as such. If any of our people are treated as criminals, or outlaws by the military, we will hold *you* responsible. It will be to no avail to say that you are only obeying orders. We do not recognize the validity of those orders.'

David said, 'Nevertheless, I shall obey orders given to me.'

'To the letter?'

'Yes.'

'Whatever the effect – good or bad – from your own personal point of view?'

'Of course. A soldier has no choice, constitutionally.'

'You can't imagine a case where . . . ?'

David cut in, 'A soldier has no imagination.'

Sujak stared at him, slowly nodding his head. Then he said two words to Sally, in Mingora-Malay. David thought, I must have sounded a pompous ass in that exchange just now. Things could be much more complicated, inside a soldier's mind, than he had given Sujak to understand. It was no use going back now and trying to explain. Sujak was still staring at him, the lips just parted in an ironical smile. Nettled, David snapped, 'No imagination is needed to see that you're doing your best to destroy a system that only needs some improvements, which are being made, to be as good as any in the world, and just what the great majority of the people want. And no amount of imagination will produce a sensible, or decent reason for it.'

'The people don't know what they want,' Sujak said, suddenly irritable, the level brows down-bent. 'You can make buffaloes pull any cart contentedly, yours or mine.'

'Why don't you try to persuade them that your system's better, instead of murdering innocent people?'

'The people we punish are not innocent. They are supporting capitalist imperialist aggression and royalist oppression. The farmer who employs labour is as guilty as Sir Harry Johnstone. Votes don't put that situation right, only power. As Chairman Mao said, "All political power grows out of the muzzle of a gun." '

David said, 'So we'll just see, in the end, who has the most guns. That's a barbarous way to run a country.'

Sujak said curtly, 'I don't intend to discuss it any further. Stay there, and be quiet.'

He crossed the little clearing. Sally muttered, 'It's no use arguing with him. He's a fanatic . . . but he's not all wrong, you know. There do have to be changes here.'

David said shortly, 'He's doing his best to see that there are none, only destruction.'

'So that they can start again,' she said defensively, 'building on cleared ground.'

David grunted and said, 'What did he say about me?'

Sally hesitated, then: 'He said, "A perfect specimen".'

David grunted again.

One of the men went out by the way they had come into the clearing, presumably to act as sentry on the track outside; after a time Sujak dozed, the third man watched the prisoners. David closed his eyes and went to sleep.

The afternoon drifted slowly by. The light under the heavy trees took on a pinkish tinge, then went faint. The sentry came in and spoke urgently to Sujak. Sally whispered, 'He says a villager told him there were soldiers in the village three miles west of here.'

Vital information, David thought. The villager may have been a member of the MPRP; but probably not – the people of Mingora had no idea yet of how to cope with revolutionary violence. They were innocent and honest, and innocently and honestly answered any question put to them. Of course, the villager would later say, if asked, that he had met a man at such and such a place, who had asked such and such questions . . . but *only* if he were asked. Would he be? Probably. So someone might arrive to search this area of jungle, which did not seem very large, within a couple of hours. By then it would be dark.

Sujak seemed to reach the same conclusion at the same time. He came over, followed by the two men, and with more rope tied the prisoners' feet securely together. After making sure the gags were firmly in place, and their hands tied behind their backs, Sujak stood up. 'We're leaving you here. You'll be found sooner or later. Your revolver's by that tree. We use different ammunition. Remember my warning.' To the princess he said, 'I'm sorry it's ending like this. It was him, coming to the beach. Otherwise we would have got you clean away and forced some changes without out bloodshed. Now, the blood will flow.'

As you want it to, David thought, staring at the revolutionary leader in the fading light. He wanted to remember that face even to the set of the shoulders, as long as he lived, in case they met again. Sujak raised his hand towards Sally, then walked fast into the jungle, and disappeared. The two men vanished with him. Night fell. David lay still for half an hour gathering his strength. The local commander of troops would probably post his force to block all roads and tracks as soon as he had any information of the area where they might be; but he would not

135

begin a search until daylight, for it would be too easy to pass by the captives, and perhaps the kidnappers, without seeing them – which would be disastrous, for then the searchers could never be sure whether they had forced the party on westward, or whether they had doubled back through the cordon towards the east or south.

He began to work steadily at the knots of the ropes that tied him. They were well tied, but the rope itself was old and frayed and he thought that in time he would be able to free himself. Hours passed. His wrists and shoulders and arm muscles throbbed with the pain of the continuous effort. In the end Sally's youthful suppleness beat him. Out of the darkness she said, 'I'm free. Wait.' She came to him, and in a minute he too stood up, his legs and arms free, the gag out of his mouth. He found his revolver, looked into the chamber and saw that it was empty, and carefully reloaded from the ammunition pouch on the other side of his belt.

Sally touched his arm: 'I am sorry . . .'

'It's not your fault. Come on.'

He peered at the luminous dial of his watch. Midnight. The moon setting. After a last look round the clearing at the silent trees and the silent cart, and the cud-chewing buffaloes, he headed back the way they had come. They came out of the trees after half an hour's steady careful plodding; the moon had gone, and in starlight David turned right. Twenty minutes later again a voice from the blackness at the side of the road rapped, 'Halt!' and the same message in Mingora-Malay. It sounded like a Gurkha and David stopped, saying, '*Gurkhali-haru ho? Ma Brigadier sahib ho.*'

A light flashed in his face and then a Gurkha corporal ran out, '*Brigadier sahib! Sab thik chha?*'

'*Thik chha, corporal. Timro commander lai bula.*'

Three hours later he was in his headquarters, speaking on the radio telephone with General Sir Rougemont Huntingdon in Singapore. 'So you're back?' the C-in-C said, 'Have you caught the kidnappers?'

'No, sir. I doubt if we will. They had nearly six hours to get away. They abandoned us at dusk and as they know the country they'd have been able to slip through any cordon in the dark. The troops weren't particularly thick on the ground there because

Alastair – Colonel Campbell-Wylie – had no idea which way we'd been taken. He was holding most of the battalion in reserve until he got some definite information from the RMC.'

'H'm! Cheeky devils . . . You'll have to tighten up security. Get back to Emergency rules.'

'I'd like to wait a bit, sir. There's no emergency yet and I'm afraid it will only cause anxiety if we go around with armed escorts for every round of golf. As far as the army is concerned, this was pure chance. They were after the Princess.'

'Whom you were with again.'

'Yes, sir. Not by arrangement.'

'It looked like it.'

'It wasn't, sir,' David said, reflecting that it was four o'clock in the morning. The Chief had a right to sound peevish.

The general said, 'I'll believe you, but for God's sake, be careful.'

'Yes, sir.'

'Is she all right?'

'Quite, sir.'

'She's a lot younger.' There was an extra bite in the C-in-C's tone. 'Well, get to bed, and think about security.'

'Good night, sir.'

David hung up and looked at his Brigade Major, sitting across the desk. 'Do you have any whisky here, Stork?'

'Yes, sir.'

'Pour me a double . . . make that a triple.'

Porter brought the whisky, a glass, and a jug of water, and poured two drinks. David took a large gulp, breathed deeply, and said, 'There were some unpleasant bits in there. Sujak bin Amin has got to be put out of business.'

'Yes, sir.'

'And there were some odd bits, too. Things which didn't quite ring true . . . Have you ever heard of a person called Davidson?'

'Davidson, sir?'

'Yes. I gather he came to a sticky end.'

The Brigade Major laughed and said, 'You must mean the Reverend Davidson, in *Rain* by Somerset Maugham.' He seemed surprised at the question, and David said, 'I read a lot, but only non-fiction. That's what makes me so dull, I suppose . . . What happened to him?'

'He committed suicide, over a woman.'

'H'm . . . I'm off. Tomorrow morning I want to have another look at the notes we made on desiderata for a recruit training centre. In my opinion that'll be my No. 1 priority on this tour that I'm making with the Chief Minister. Oh God, it's not tomorrow, it's today!'

As he rose the telephone rang. Stork Porter picked it up. David waited, as Porter said, 'Yes' and 'I see', and finally, 'All right.' He held the phone away from his mouth. 'It's a superintendent of the city police, sir. They've got Captain Whitmore of the Fusiliers in jail there and want to know what to do with him.'

'What's he in for?'

'Beating up a Mingoran civilian.'

'Is the superintendent still on the line?'

'Yes, sir.'

'Ask to speak to Whitmore.'

He sat down again, waiting wearily. He was very sleepy now, but this sort of thing had to be dealt with at once.

'He's on,' Porter said.

David said, 'Brigade Commander here, Whitmore. What happened?'

'We . . . my wife and I . . . went out to dinner and a night club, sir. There was a youngish Mingoran in there who I thought was making remarks about Nancy, but I didn't say anything. When we left he and two or three of his friends followed us out, and stamped in a big puddle, splashing mud all over both of us. Then he called my wife a British whore, so I hit him.'

'Any witnesses?'

'Just the other Mingorans – his friends. And Nancy, of course. The man I hit has filed assault and battery charges against me.'

David thought, this'll have to be sorted out by the D/Q in the morning. For the moment, the thing was to get Whitmore out of jail. He said, 'Let me speak to the superintendent, please . . . Tuan, Brigadier Jones here. I'd be grateful if you'd release Captain Whitmore now. I guarantee that he'll appear for trial when you want him . . . Thank you. Yes.'

He hung up. 'Tell Gil to deal with it in the morning . . . Goodnight.'

The little convoy reached Simdega at 7 p.m. the next day, 10 February, having started at five and made a leisurely trip down the main road. David and the Chief Minister rode in David's Land-Rover in front, with Wood and Tulbahadur, followed by a scout car. The Minister's large Austin followed, carrying Crawford, the Minister's secretary, and two armed constables of the RMC: last came a Land-Rover with four Gurkhas, and another scout car. This much protection David had decided was necessary, for the Minister's tour had been well publicized for several weeks, and if the CTs were going in for kidnapping, he would be a prime target.

Simdega, close up against the Malayan frontier, offered little of interest; the population were loyal, of Khmer race, the province was fairly rich, and Malaya posed no threat. Next day on to Kusalung. Here David spent an hour in Ban Dhrai, to find that the Home Guard system was working well, there, at least; but the governor was the same man as before, an amiable fellow, but indecisive, and, of course, an Easterner.

When he was alone with the Minister later that evening, in the Rest House, he said, 'I thought you were going to replace the governor here with a Kusalungi.'

The Minister said, 'I want to. But we have no one trained.'

'Who trains the present people?'

'They all come from families that have been in government for generations . . . centuries, some of them. Most are from Trangloek, where they learn in and around the central government before they are appointed to a province.'

David shook his head. 'You'll have to do something about that.'

'I know,' the Minister said, 'I know. There is so much to do, all at once now. We should be training administrators, not soldiers.'

David did not answer; for he thought the minister was right.

On 12 February to Powlang, another Eastern governor in a Western province, though this man was a much stronger character than the one in Kusalung. They had not been in the town fifteen minutes before he was leading them in his little Morris to a disused factory site which he believed could be converted for use as the Mingoran recruit training centre. David inspected it with a sinking heart. There was the shell of a huge building, roofless, which could have served as the mess hall for a thousand men, but for nothing else. There had been workers' houses, accommodation for about two hundred men, built originally of concrete, now in a bad state. But the worst point about it was the absence of any place to parade for exercise.

'I'm afraid this won't do,' he said to the Minister afterwards.

'We'll keep looking,' the latter said, 'But we don't have much . . .'

'Time,' David finished for him. 'I know, Excellency.'

The next day to Moirang: as the convoy headed into the gravelled drive of the State Rest House, the Chief Minister muttered, 'The Perdana Binte Mingora!' He pointed at the blue Land-Rover drawn up outside the sprawling house – 'No one knows where she will appear next.'

'Will there be room for us?' David said, 'I can sleep in the town somewhere.' He had no wish to be forced to socialize with Kumara.

'Oh, there's room. Rest Houses are all the same pattern – six bedrooms.'

Wood stopped the staff car behind the Land-Rover and David climbed down stiffly. It was near noon and he felt hungry and thirsty. The road from Powlang had been dusty, with a furnace wind from the south following the cars.

Kumara came out on the verandah. The Minister bowed deeply, and David saluted. She said, 'Have you come with all those soldiers to protect *me* from kidnapping?' She laughed silently.

David flushed; the Minister said, 'Do you have anyone with you, tuankana?'

'An escort? Of course not!'

'I think you should, tuankana,' the Minister said, 'After what happened to the Tuankana Salimina . . .'

'I cannot have soldiers or constables round me,' the princess said firmly. 'They would frighten the people I must talk to . . . I have left the rooms on that side for you.'

This was Moirang, the province closest to Burma, the most Muslim and Western in its ways, the one where any real dissatisfaction with the Queen's régime could be expected to break out. Like Wellington, Kumara always knew where the decisive point was, and made it her business to be there. And, also like Wellington, she didn't trust her subordinates to do their job without her presence.

She seemed to read his thoughts, for she said to the minister – 'I got word early this morning – just after Sally came home – that a man-eating tiger had killed a woman of Ban Khao. I started out at once, and got here just before you.'

'Ban Khao?' the Minister said in a shocked voice, 'Your Highness is not going there?'

'Certainly I am,' Kumara said. 'I'm going there now to see the situation for myself, and hope to sit up for the tiger tonight.'

'But, tuankana, Ban Khao is a criminal village. Even the RMC never enter it. And people from Ban Khao are arrested on sight anywhere in the queendom. Their only contact with the outside world is with Burma, where they have promised not to rob in return for safe passage.'

'I know,' Kumara said. 'But now there's a chance to change that. They're frightened and they sent word they would receive me.'

She turned back into the building without another word or gesture.

After lunch, David and the Minister set about their business: talk with the governor, arrange for the selection of a recruiting officer and staff, visit a village or two to inspect the Home Guard, talk with the provincial superintendent of RMC, and continue the search for a site for the recruit training centre of the Mingoran Army-to-be.

The governor showed them two places, one an old rubber plantation, and one a large private estate, but David did not like either – the one was too remote, and the other would have cost too much, for a great deal of extra accommodation would have to be built. Then, as they were nearing the town on their way back, David saw a group of wooden buildings with thatched roofs, on the west of the road.

'Stop ... what's that?' he asked.

'The prison, tuan,' the governor said. 'The Japanese built it originally as a concentration camp. It will hold six hundred men, but we usually have less than one hundred prisoners in there, and thirty guards. The other buildings are in ruins.'

'I'd like to look at it,' David said.

The Chief Minister turned round from the front seat of the car where he was riding, and said, 'One moment, Brigadier ... Even if we can find another place to put the prisoners ... and I don't know that we can ... this is Moirang, the province most in danger of attack, the one most likely to be disaffected. Do we want recruits from other parts of the country to be tainted by possible treason here?'

'Also,' the governor said, 'If the army comes here, it will spend a lot of money. Most of the recruits will be Easterners and their money ought to be spent in the east.'

'If that's what you think,' David said angrily, 'why have you been wasting my time looking for sites in the western provinces? Besides, you are wrong! If you don't trust the Westerners of course they will think they're not welcome, and they'll regard the army as another tool of the East to keep them down. I think it's the best thing that could happen to put the recruit base here. The Moirangis will get richer, the more money they make the less likely they are to be disaffected. More Westerners will join the army, and you will get the proportion you must have – half and half, instead of perhaps five to one if you put the recruit base in Trangloek. Now, let's have a look.'

An hour later he came out, satisfied that with some work from O'Grady's sappers, plus local labour, the prison could be made suitable as a recruit base. As to the prisoners . . . let the real bad hats be transferred to other prisons, and let the rest be pardoned – another gesture towards Moirang and the Westerners.

It was dusk when he reached the Rest House, dark by the time he had bathed and changed. The Princess Kumara was studying a file in the common room, and in the corner Tulbahadur was pouring a drink. He felt much better with the problem of the recruit base settled, and, almost for the first time since coming to Mingora, could regard Kumara without thought of their previous association. As she was working here at this hour, she could not be going to sit up for the man-eater tonight. 'A drink, princess?' he asked her; and when Tulbahadur had brought the whiskies and soda: 'What's happening about the tiger?'

She said, 'He had carried the woman's body into a dry stream bed before starting to eat her. He ate most of one leg, then left her. He'll come back.'

'Tonight?'

She shook her head. 'He's eaten too much for that. Tomorrow. But the body is in a place where we can't set up a hide or get a shot from the ground. The villagers are building a hide in a tree about a hundred yards away. Then they'll take the woman's body there, tomorrow early.'

'And you think the tiger will come back?'

'They usually do. This is a young male, quite big. Lame in the left fore – the usual reason, probably.' Seeing David's interrogative look she said, 'Porcupine quill. He tried to kill a porcupine and got some quills in his paw. He can bite off the ends, but the rest stay inside and fester.' She picked up her glass, drank, and shuddered. 'Oh! Some more water, please! Do Gurkhas always take their drinks as strong as that?'

'Usually yes,' David said, 'but I keep trying to teach Tulbahadur to make them of a reasonable strength. He's not the quickest man to learn something, but . . .'

'. . . when he does, it stays learned?'

'Yes. *Tule, aru pani le!*'

The princess sipped the watered drink. The wide almond eyes were fixed on David over the rim of the glass. She said, 'How did Sally behave during the kidnapping?'

'Well,' he said. 'She didn't panic or lose her head or anything. You should be proud of her.'

'Thank you. And Sujak?'

'Tough, but not brutal. He didn't molest Sally or threaten her. He seems to lack a sense of humour.'

'How so?'

'Well, you know I actually gave him a ride near Ban Dhrai before Christmas, without recognizing him. And then I was staring him in the face on Trangloek Station a little later. He never mentioned either incident, though I think most people would have made a joke about it.'

She said, 'I think you are right. He is not very sensitive, which might be his downfall . . . Would you like to sit up for the tiger with me tomorrow?'

David felt as though he had walked into a wall without seeing it. He sat, stunned, contemplating the invitation. Why should she suddenly ask him? What did she want out of him now?

He'd refuse. He was supposed to be going to Lepet tomorrow with the Chief Minister, and returning to Trangloek the same night. That would make a good excuse.

'Please, Dylan,' she said.

'I have my Winchester with me,' he said weakly,' but I don't know much about this sort of thing. I'll be in the way . . . or do something to scare the tiger off.'

'You will be all right,' she said.

Then the Chief Minister came in, bowing, and soon they were seated round the dining-room table, talking with animation about the kidnapping and Kumara's reception in the criminal village of Ban Khao, as the Rest House staff served food and Tulbahadur poured water and later whisky, and all the time the measured tramp of boots outside told where a guard of the Royal Mingoran Constabulary, ordered by the Chief Minister, was pacing the verandah.

Ten

SHE BREATHED EVENLY, quietly, so evenly and so quietly that he could not have heard if his ear had not been so close to her. They sat side by side on the hide, eight feet above the ground, the flat bamboo platform barely concealed among the thin branches and scanty leaves of a small peepul tree. She was wearing forest green slacks and bush shirt, her head bare, the Jumbhorn Ruby this time left in the bungalow so that it would not catch the light. It was near one o'clock in the the morning, the low moon bathing with dull gold light the farther bank of the dry stream fifty feet away, painting the shadows of the jungle patch beyond a luminous impenetrable purple, and creating grotesque demons by its interplay with the scattered bushes and trees around their hiding place.

Twenty feet from the base of the tree the woman lay, naked from the waist down, the tattered black blouse hiding only her breasts and dragged up to cover her neck and part of her face. The left leg was a red mush, white bone sharp in the moonlight, beginning and ending at her loin. The right was twisted round under her at an angle that showed the knee joint was broken. An unseen chain round her waist was fastened to a wooden spike driven far into the ground underneath her. The tiger could not come, seize her in his jaws, and bound away with her to some more secluded spot. He would settle down and eat the meal where it lay.

The woman was young – the slim and graceful body showed that – but David had never seen her face clearly for she had been arranged like this before he and Kumara arrived. Men from Ban Khao had lifted the body out of the dry stream bed where the tiger had first taken it, and dragged it along the ground – so that the tiger should not fail to find and follow the scent – to this place.

The drive out to Ban Khao in Kumara's Land-Rover had been like a triumphal procession. Every person in every village seemed to know that the Daughter-in-Line was coming through, and all were out of their houses, the women bowing, boys and girls running beside the car, and the men waving with cries of 'May God put the tiger in your way, *tuankana*!' Half a dozen villagers of Ban Khao had been waiting by the nearly completed hide when they'd arrived at two in the afternoon. The oldest made a perfunctory obeisance and said, 'This is the woman's husband, *tuankana*.' He was a young man, as slim as his wife, dry-eyed. Kumara spoke a long time to him, her hand on his shoulder, he nodding occasionally, his face expressionless. Then she climbed up into the hide, and David handed up her rifle. It was a double-barrelled Purdy .510 magnum. It would stop a charging elephant in its tracks, even if the bullet didn't hit a fatal spot . . . but he couldn't imagine how she would be able to lift it to her shoulder; and surely, when she fired it, the recoil would kick her flying backwards off the hide. He handed her his own Winchester, and scrambled up.

The villagers went away. It was half past two in a burning, still afternoon. 'We have a long wait,' Kumara said, 'But it is necessary. People who get up into a hide at dusk will never get a tiger, or a leopard. He will have been watching, and listening, for two hours before that . . . Now, we must not speak, and move as little as possible.'

That was over ten hours ago. He stared at the woman's body: motionless, pink tinged, white edged, gold dyed with the last of the moon. Was it moving, the shadow moving, creeping towards the foot of their tree across the short grass? He gripped the butt of the Winchester and tried to hold his breath steady. He had been staring at it since two in the afternoon. In the harsh daylight the agony of the broken joints was evident, piercing his own comfort. Just visible under the drawn-up blouse, her lips were folded back in a snarl. Her hands, so tightly clenched, were full of yellow fur. Her head was twisted round back to front where the tiger had killed her with a blow of his paw. The flies crawled over her all afternoon, laying their eggs. Thousands of ants came. He had watched lines of ants forming up, marching towards her across the grass, disappearing under her body. By dusk the heat of the sun was beginning to make her swell, her second dusk in death. At that time, two vultures had circled a long time overhead, then one planed down to land fifty feet away, and stand on the stream bank, its naked head cocked. After five minutes it had flown heavily away. So, in the dusk the vulture had seen them in the hide . . . perhaps now, in the moonlight, the tiger would; and they were both facing the same way, barely eight feet up a small tree. Tigers can jump eighteen feet. His back felt cold and twitchy. The moon sank. The sky blazed with stars.

The shadows were moving, creeping, now he could swear it. He closed his eyes twenty long seconds, and opened them again; a shadow, purple black, alone, separated from the stream bank, that had not been there before. Another . . . he nudged Kumara and pointed wordlessly with his chin. She put her mouth to his ear and whispered, 'Half wild dogs.'

How many dogs would there be, he wondered. If a score came, they could eat most of the woman before the tiger arrived; and then he might not even come. He counted four, five . . . five dogs, creeping, now trotting in short diagonals towards the pinioned body. The chain would prevent them moving it, which they could otherwise do if they seized her arms and dragged. She had weighed less than seven stone, less than six now with the leg gone. The dogs reached the body and at once began to attack it. Now they tugged and ripped at the flesh, the growls deep in their throats – a sound of worrying, deep rumblings, snarlings, teeth buried in the woman's loins. David's hair curled and crept . . . vile, ungodly, his hands burned on the butt and forestock. He could not allow this desecration to go on.

Kumara's mouth was at his ear again, louder this time – 'Don't move! Please, Dylan . . . It won't be long.'

He felt like a horse before a race, trembling, sweating, but her mouth and voice soothed him. The dogs were all over the woman now, at her face, her breasts, tugging at an arm, ripping at the soft brown belly, that was new with child, the husband had said.

A coughing roar shook the leaves in their tree. David started, and a twig snapped, fell on his lap, thence to the ground. The dogs' heads rose, all together. A long dark shape came out of the dry stream bed, appearing on the bank at the end of an upward bound, steadying, coming on at an easy trot. The dogs snarled, backed off, ran away in a pack to the north, howling now all together, the eerie cackling like madwomen laughing in concert, dying away in scrub towards Ban Khao half a mile away.

The starlight showed the tiger's barred body now. Kumara did not move. David turned his head and stared at her, in case she had not seen. She nodded: she had seen. She sat immobile, the heavy rifle where it had been motionless for nearly eleven hours, the butt resting on the bamboo floor of the platform, her right hand below the trigger guard, her left holding the barrel tilted slightly back against her shoulder. The tiger paused in dense shadow twenty feet beyond the woman, and roared again. Another warning, David thought: let there be nothing, no one, no animal, near my prey. He appeared again, closer, walking now. When he reached the woman, he sank slowly to his haunches, and sniffed the lower part of the body. Then he rested one huge paw on her belly and buried his jaws in her side, where the dogs had torn open the flesh. As David heard the first crunch of the tiger's teeth Kumara began to raise the butt of the Purdy. The barrel tilted down, the butt slid up her body and settled into her shoulder. The tiger was crunching on the bottom of the woman's ribcage, the ribs cracking like thick wet twigs. The Purdy was in Kumara's shoulder, the barrel aimed at the long shape, crunching and snarling deep in its throat in the starglow.

The tiger sharply raised its body, and at precisely that instant a tremendous explosion blasted David's ear, and Kumara's body slammed back against the tree trunk. The tiger bounded straight up ten feet into the air, and even as it landed was racing in heavy lurching bounds for the lip of the dry ravine. Kumara fired again, but the tiger vanished.

She brought the rifle down and began to reload. 'I'm sorry,' she said in a normal conversational tone.

'What happened?'

'He heard something . . . some more dogs coming, a leopard moving close, I don't know . . . but it was just at the moment that I fired. I hit him, but lower down than I meant to. The second barrel missed altogether.'

'What do we do now?'

'Wait till dawn, then I'll track him down. Meanwhile . . .' she reached across the hide, opened a flask, and handed it to David. 'Tea. And sandwiches.'

David drank and ate. He thought it would be safe to get down at least to the foot of the tree, but Kumara made no move, and he said nothing: this was her show. Either she had been much more comfortable than he had, motionless and barely breathing for a dozen hours on this hard and rickety platform, or she had an amazing capacity for endurance.

She put away the half empty flask and the uneaten sandwiches and settled back against the tree trunk in the same position as before. She said, 'If you don't mind my saying so, I think that's a very good idea, to have the recruit base for our army in Moirang.'

'Thank you.'

'It will do a lot of good where it's most needed ... if it's allowed to come to fruition.'

'What do you mean?'

'You know what I mean, Dylan. We will not be given the time we need – not unless Sujak bin Amin has lost his mind, and I don't think he has.'

'Nor do I. He seemed very sane to me. But fanatical.'

'They're all that. I wish *we* could be ... but it's hard to get fanatical about ordinary decency, ordinary progress.'

David said, 'I wish we could go faster with raising the army – but we can't.'

'How long will it take, in all?' Her voice was gentle, but he thought it edged. He stared at the corpse below, now pulled into an S shape, the tattered blouse back over her breasts, the head still back to front on the torn shoulders, the thighs spread, the only leg twisted underneath ...

'Two, three years,' he said. 'We've got to put the Recruit Centre buildings in order, find the men, train them, train NCOs and officers, set up the administration ... at the same time, choose and buy equipment, and arms, build and stock arsenals, devise military law and pay codes, and ...'

She said, 'So if the MPRP attack soon after you've gone, what are our untrained recruits supposed to do?'

His inner tensions snapped – 'I'm not responsible for this state of affairs,' he cried, his voice quivering. 'I strongly disapprove of it, if you must know, but I am a soldier.'

'And you will obey your orders,' she said, 'But you wouldn't kill innocent people, on order, would you?'

'I hope not.'

'Then why are you ready to leave defenceless innocent people to be killed by others?'

'It's not the same,' he muttered, but his own conscience told him that it was; and that was the only conscience he could deal with.

She didn't speak for a long time, so long that David was almost dozing where he leaned back against the tree. Then she said, quietly, and this time without that edge of steel behind her voice, 'I don't think it will be a matter of staying on for months. The south-west monsoon usually comes about 1 June – that day we become independent. Movement except on good roads is impossible for five months, sometimes longer, depending on how bad the north-east monsoon, which follows, is. By then we will have a sort of an army. I think the MPRP will try to make their move immediately before the British leave.'

'Then we will be able to deal with it,' David said.

'Not if their timing's right. They will aim to be in possession of some provincial capitals before and during the big monsoon. Then they'll have a territory which they can announce as the People's Republic of Mingora or some such title, get recognition from Communist nations abroad, and have a firm base from which to attack the rest of the country after the rains are over ... I think the vital period will be just before you go – only two, three days at the most ... What's the time?'

'Three.'

'It'll be light in another two hours. Then I'll start tracking that poor beast. He's probably in great pain.'

'I'm coming,' David said.

'You haven't stalked wounded dangerous game before, have you?'

'Yes,' he said grimly, 'CTs.'

'What? Oh! You're right. It's not so different, except for the sense of smell.'

'But tigers don't have sten guns or grenades,' David said.

'Let's try to sleep a bit. We'll need to be very much awake soon.'

She closed her eyes and in an instant, so it seemed to David, was asleep; but how could he know? Asleep or awake her breathing was quiet and regular, she never twitched or moved suddenly or made any unpatterned sounds. He tried to make his own mind blank but the jungle was full of sounds, the moon gone, the stars obscured. The tree creaked without cause, the leaves stirred, brushing his sleeve like supplicants who dared not speak. Beyond the ravine an owl called suddenly, a long-drawn screeching moan that made him stiffen, then relax in shame, for Kumara had not stirred a muscle. Later he heard the pad of feet, soft feet swishing through the grass, and thought it might be dogs returning, but the soft rhythmic *pad pad* went on its way, past the woman, without stopping. Perhaps the animal – dog or leopard – had smelled the tiger's wounded blood, smelled its shock in the moment of being struck, and known that this was no place to stay and wonder. That made him think of the tiger itself ... 'poor beast', she had called it. Not an adjective he would have used, after seeing the woman's body; but she was right. Why should the tiger be branded as a criminal for doing what it must? It had been wounded and could not hunt its normal prey. The deer never thought of it as criminal; why should man, when it turned its claws and teeth on him?

The breeze came as a forerunner of the dawn, not a strong wind, but a stirring of the dark, an unseen black slow river of air that moved through the grass and made it hiss and rustle, that stirred first the boughs of the tree they were in, then all the mass of the jungle across the dry ravine, a low long sigh as of a deep breath; then the cautious greening in the east.

Kumara said, 'Dawn ... Let's get down and stretch.'

David said quickly, 'I'll go first.' He had a cold feeling that the tiger was waiting in the pool of darkness at the foot of the tree; but he could not let her go down first into that danger.

She said at once, 'All right.' He handed her the Winchester and slid down the twisted trunk. He almost laughed as his boots touched the ground: if that tiger, or any other, had wanted to get at them, it could have walked up the trunk with the greatest of ease. Kumara passed down the rifles and then he held up his hands and helped her down. They stood together under the hide. The corpse was taking shape twenty feet away.

She said, 'The light's not good enough yet. I'm going to have a smoke.' She pulled out a case of glistening silver, and lit a match. The flame showed a thin cigar between her pale lips. David lit a cigarette, and inhaled deeply.

They walked up and down, flexing and unflexing stiffened muscles. The greenish tinge in the sky turned more and more rapidly to yellow, then orange, then began to pale. David, measuring the distance to bushes and trees nearby, found he could see clearly for a hundred yards, though there were as yet no shadows. The red of the woman's blood and part of her entrails, the white spears of her thigh bone, formed a macabre still life composition at his feet.

Kumara threw down her cigar, carefully stubbed it out with the heel of her boot and said, 'Ready?' She checked that both barrels of the heavy Purdy were loaded and cocked, pushed off the safety catch, and lifted the gun into a ready position across her body, her left hand supporting the stock, her right forefinger outside the trigger guard. David made sure that he had a full magazine and a round in the chamber, the weapon cocked and the safety catch off.

She said, 'I'll lead . . . just at first . . . we'll take turns if it goes on for a long time. You follow a few paces behind, but looking more to my right and left, and behind you.' She licked her finger and held it up: 'The wind's very slight, but there is some . . . from the east, that way. Unless he's so crippled that he has no choice the tiger won't stalk us downwind, because he thinks we have a sense of scent like his, and can smell him. He'll come upwind . . . if he can stalk at all. Of course if he just has to charge, it could come from anywhere. But I'm not sure he'll be able to. The wound should have stiffened by now.'

They moved off. The first blood splash was at the spot where Kumara's bullet had hit him, a long spurt, with a white bone splinter in it. The next was ten feet away, and after that an almost continuous trail led to the bank of the ravine. David came up to the edge, they both looked right and left, then the princess slid down, crossed the sandy bed, peering at the blood trail, and with some difficulty climbed up the farther side. Then she waited, rifle ready, and David crossed. The blood trail led into dense trees, and progress slowed. The small dawn breeze continued to blow from directly in front and David searched back over each shoulder every ten seconds.

Glancing at his watch he saw that they had been gone fifteen minutes. His hands were damp on the rifle grip, sweat beading his bare forehead. But if he were already feeling the strain, she must be in worse case, going in front. He went up close and whispered, 'Change places.'

She stepped aside without a word and David took the lead. The blood trail was still easy to follow but becoming less so. The flow seemed to have been slowing about here. Now the danger was presumably in front of him, and yet he had to keep his eyes down to make sure that he did not lose the trail. The pace slowed still more. They were moving through fairly open jungle, big trees every ten yards or so, their lower trunks clear, above, the heavy creepers twined among the branches. Above the treetops there was full daylight, though the sun had not yet risen, but under their canopy it was almost exactly as at the moment they had started out from beside the woman's body.

At the base of a tree ahead he saw a large patch of dull red. The pool of blood had been over a foot square. Most had drained into the earth, but some had clotted, and the fallen leaves were dark red with it. The grass around was flattened, and four long fresh raw scores marked the tree trunk. Kumara whispered – 'He clawed the tree here . . . then lay down . . . quite a long time. He may not have moved on till he heard us . . . or saw us . . . I'll lead again.'

David stared slowly round the circle of the trees and down the shadowed aisles between them. Was the great beast watching him now? He could see nothing. His nerves taut, he followed Kumara. The wind was coming from the left now, not from behind. But it was not the wind that had changed direction, surely, it was the tiger wheeling slowly as he moved away from his resting place. Downwind was now to their right, so the tiger would come from there. Or perhaps it had doubled back. Hadn't he read somewhere that they circled round and lay up beside their own track, farther back, so that anyone behind, head down to follow the track, would be an easy prey for a sudden upwind pounce? He must look right . . . right . . . he was looking at an orange and white head, flaring yellow eyes.

'Right!' he yelled, throwing up his rifle.

Kumara swung with him, her foot slipped on damp leaves and she staggered to her right, across David's line of fire at the charging tiger. The tiger's roar hurt his head. He stepped one pace left and fired at the tiger in the air, a snap shot at the centre of its chest as it took off, jaws wide and claws extended. Kumara dived forward, throwing herself flat. The long striped body arched gracefully through the air and landed with a heavy crunch almost at David's feet, the hind legs across Kumara. David aimed at the head below him, and fired one more shot into the skull at three feet range.

He ran round and tried to heave the tiger's hindquarters off Kumara, gasping, 'Are you all right?'

She stood up, her face smeared with dirt, and carefully unloaded the Purdy. Then she said, 'Yes. Thank you . . . I slipped turning.'

'I think he was doubling back on us, but wasn't quite in time.'

'I should have guessed he might do that,' she said, 'But my mind was elsewhere – which was very stupid. Fire three shots into the air, please, Dylan, at five seconds interval. That's the signal for the people to come out from Ban Khao. They'll go to the hide so we must get back there.'

They walked back through the jungle, and recrossed the dry ravine. As they climbed out David saw men and women coming down from the direction of Ban Khao. Kumara turned to him: 'Thank you again, Dylan. And please forget what I was talking about, in the hide. It's not your business.'

She put out her hand, the huge eyes steady on his. Then she turned to the oncoming villagers, now running.

Lance Corporal Wood took the staff car carefully along the winding road between Moirang and Lepet. It was well surfaced, but here where it traversed the central range there were many curves and inclines and bridges across small streams, now mostly dry.

David said, 'It was good of you to wait that extra day for me in Moirang.'

The Minister said, 'It was nothing, brigadier. Besides, we are in your hands. It would not be much use my going to Lepet on a military reconnaissance without you. Furthermore, the details of turning the Moirang jail into a recruit base occupied the day most usefully for me. I didn't get back to the Rest House till eight o'clock.'

David said, 'You know, thinking about that affair of the tiger, what strikes me most is the quality of the intelligence. The fact that the woman had been killed was learned very soon, the body located, the facts about the tiger passed first to Moirang and thence to the princess in Trangloek very expeditiously. Then when she got here, she was told of the tiger's background, where he had probably gone to sleep, what he'd do next . . .'

'And so . . . ?'

'We must have an intelligence system as good as that, against the CTs. A web like a spider's, where if any part is touched, accurate news of what's happening goes at once to the centre, and of course to other parts of the net at the same time.'

The Minister pulled his prominent ears. 'H'm . . . The intellegence system here is motivated by the people's sense of self-preservation. They know that if they don't have accurate information about the tiger, he will kill them. But with the CTs, the people feel that if they *do* get accurate information, they will be killed.'

David said, 'We must overcome that. We can use loyalty. The sense of self-preservation, even, once we have made them understand what would happen to them under the MPRP . . . We can use money, but carefully. There's always a danger that if money is being offered for information, the information will be created, somehow. But safeguards can be worked out.'

'Yes, with money,' the Minister said, 'And with . . .'

'Time,' David said testily. 'If we don't stop talking about the shortage of time, we'll lose what time we do have. I think that the improvement of the local intelligence network, all over the country, is vital, and urgent . . . but it should not be under the military. It should be a provincial civil responsibility, with a strong central organization to coordinate.'

'I'll look into it,' the Minister said, suppressing a sigh – 'We do have financial reserves. Of course we have plans for that money, but this emergency of self-protection will have to come first. The Resident is very positive that the date for our, er, independence, cannot be set back.'

'He is,' David said.

'He repeats to Her Majesty and to me – in official meetings, so I presume that is what he reports back to London – that the programme will go through as planned.'

155

'I suppose so.'

'But . . .' The Minister's eyes wandered to the backs of the two heads in the front seat. David said, 'They are trustworthy completely.'

The Minister said, 'It is possible that another Resident might see the matter in a different light . . . might agree with our point of view, that full independence for us this moment means collapse. We need another year at the least, and preferably three. Such a man might be able to persuade London to change its mind.'

'I suppose it's possible,' David said, 'But Mr Wilson's only just been sent here.'

'Quite,' the Minister said, and was silent for several minutes. Then he said, 'The Resident is meeting some person, or persons, secretly.'

'Secretly from whom?' David said.

'From everybody,' the Minister said, 'He goes out into the country in the Rolls Royce with two or three Residency servants, whom he drops off to stop anyone following. We know, because we've tried. Then he drives on to the meeting place, wherever it is, spends about half an hour there, and comes back.'

'You don't really know what he does, at all,' David said, 'if the Residency servants stop your people getting close.'

'In theory, no, brigadier.'

'But . . . ?'

'To speak practically, the Resident would have cause to engage in secret negotiations with only one group or party.'

'The MPRP.'

'Precisely.'

David was silent. Was it any business of his if Wilson was making secret contacts with the MPRP – or any other political group?

The Minister said, 'We may never learn any more . . . until or unless we find out from someone on the other side. But I thought you should know.'

'Thank you.'

'There is more I would like to talk with you about, brigadier . . . but not now.'

It was not till later that evening that David heard the rest. The Minister knocked on his door as he was dressing for dinner after his bath, alone in the bedroom allotted to him. The Minister said, 'I could not finish what we were discussing in the car, not even before those two excellent soldiers ... The Resident visits the Princess Kumara nearly every other evening.'

'To play chess,' David said.

'And learn the finer points of our language,' the Minister added smoothly. 'The princess is sure he is infatuated with her. He has so far controlled himself, and made no advance or proposal to her ... but she is sure.'

'Yes,' David said.

'The princess has pointed out to me that if she were to encourage Mr Wilson, and the resulting connection were to be uncovered ... with suitable publicity ... our Queen would be fully justified in asking for the removal of Mr Wilson ... if indeed the British Government did not remove him first.'

David whistled softly through his teeth. A most capable woman, the Minister had often said. He'd seen that, this morning, and earlier, a score of times. Unscrupulous, too, apparently. Ready to pull a really dirty trick that would ruin a man's career. For her country, she felt. And if Wilson was ass enough to have an affair with the crown princess of the country where he was Resident, he deserved whatever he might get. But was he? Surely ambition would keep him on the tracks if nothing else did ... Yet, the man was not so solidly controlled: the involuntary muscle movements, the way he played squash; and there were other indications that his nature might sometimes be too violent for his brain to guide.

Kumara, willing to whore herself. Perhaps she already had. Breaking all the strictest rules of her upbringing – of her inmost beliefs. For her country.

'Why did you tell me this?' he asked coldly.

'The princess asked me to. I advised against that. What can *you* do, one way or the other? It is best that you should not know. But the princess insisted. This morning, after breakfast, before we left Moirang. I have done my duty.'

'What was her husband like?' David asked.

'A remote relation. An amiable man. Quite fat even when young. The Princess Salimina resembles him ... The Japanese killed him, for no reason that we could learn, except as policy, to terrorize the people. They were on the point of shooting the Princess Kumara with him, when the Kempei Tai chief was able to persuade the general here that they'd have the whole of Mingora in active rebellion if they did . . . It's time for a drink.'

'I'll be with you in a minute, Excellency,' David said.

When he was alone he shrugged into his clean bush shirt and began to brush his hair. Getting a little thin on top, he noted . . . If Kumara were willing to be caught *flagrante delicto* with the Resident, for the sake of the country, Sally certainly would do as much for her principles, which were . . . what? These royal women were trying to get something out of him. Because political power grows out of the muzzle of a gun. And he had the guns. Under the Resident. Well, his military boss was Sir Rougemont Huntingdon, a different kettle of fish. Not easier, just different. And farther away.

It struck him, as he was going out of the door, that if these people were trying to use him, it might be possible, and certainly permissible, for him to use them.

Eleven

DAVID DROVE THE Land-Rover along the familiar sandy road towards the royal beach, but this time with Tulbahadur, armed, sitting up in the back and another Land Rover full of armed Gurkhas following at a hundred yards. Normally he hated having to be escorted but the presence of all these men would surely put a damper on Sally's continued determination to seduce him, if she were here at the beach. He didn't want to hurt her feelings but she no longer excited him – at least, not beyond a point where he could easily control himself. When Kumara had finally looked into his eyes outside Ban Khao he had realized that there was no other woman for him.

He had held off ordering these extra security measures for a couple of weeks after his own abduction a month ago, but the increase in terrorist activity had finally forced him to it. The attempted murder of a signals officer on shooting leave with his wife in the jungles of Simdega had been the turning point: after that David issued the order – all military personnel and their families will go escorted outside the city limits of Trangloek.

One encouraging fact about the signals officer incident was that he and his wife had escaped with their lives, after he had been wounded, because the nearest village Home Guard turned up, having learned what the CTs planned to do. They drove the CTs away, killing one. Another fact, not encouraging but strange, about the new wave of violent communist activity was that it was taking place in Kusalung and Simdega, the two southernmost provinces of the country. So the MPRP was launching an offensive in the south. But why? Perhaps he'd better get Crawford to make a reverse appreciation, as from the CT point of view, arguing back from the known results to deduce what policy would have led to them.

There was the royal beach house, the old man popping his head out of his door to see who was coming; a salute, and the head disappeared again. But there was a car parked at the beach house . . . not Sally's or Kumara's; a grey Austin saloon. As he stopped the jeep he tried to remember where he had seen it before. Of course it was Lady Anne Wilson's; he had seen it parked in front of the Residency, and several times at the Gymkhana and Boat Club. She must have brought some of her children here for a swim. He glanced down the beach and stopped dead. A head showed clearly in the green translucent water – outside the shark net. Three fins cut the water in lazy circles a hundred yards beyond the head.

'Quick! Who can swim strongly?' he called to the escort in Gurkhali, 'Clothes off, follow me!' He tore off his shoes and outer clothes and wearing only his underpants ran down the beach and into the sea. A moment later he heard splashes as a couple of Gurkhas followed him. The sand sloped evenly and after a few heavy ploughing strides he was swimming hard, and out of his depth.

'Come towards the net!' he yelled as he swam, but the person was swimming away, out to sea, not fast, but definitely, and could hear nothing. The dorsal fins seemed to have vanished – no, he saw one about fifty yards beyond the swimming person . . . the hair was long and blondish: it must be Lady Anne herself.

He reached the shark net, threw himself over the supporting cable between two glass balls, and continued swimming. She would have heard if he called now, but he had to save his breath. One of the Gurkhas was a very strong swimmer and was coming up on his right; they would reach the woman together. The other Gurkha was splashing mightily some way behind. Lady Anne turned. They were barely twenty feet from her, where she had been swimming straight towards one of the cruising fins. Her mouth was open, her face contorted with misery, her eyes red, streaming, her heavy hair wet across her neck and shoulders. Seeing them she cried out and turned again towards the shark, but she was almost exhausted now, and David and the Gurkha reached her simultaneously. David grabbed her upper arm and shouted 'Turn back!' She struggled feebly, still trying to get out towards the sharks. David gritted his teeth, and smashed his closed fist against her jaw. She gasped and sank for a moment below the surface; but the Gurkha had her from behind, his arms under her armpits and was swimming strongly on his back towards the shark net and the beach, dragging her with him. David and the second Gurkha followed, zigzagging from side to side, kicking their heels and splashing as much as they could. David had heard that such splashing scared away sharks; and also that it attracted them . . . but there was no question of attracting these three – they were already here. The only hope was to persuade them that the humans could defend themselves. One of the fins was cruising along effortlessly twenty feet to the left; he could see the long grey body shimmering just below the surface. The other two were somewhere behind – he had neither time nor energy to look for them or wonder what they were doing. In any case he could not defend himself against them.

The Gurkha who was supporting Lady Anne reached the shark net and David swam to him; together they forced her body over the net, the other Gurkha following; then David and the life-saver went over. The sharks cruised by in line ahead just outside the net and now David could clearly see, as he hung exhausted on the cable, the glinting little eyes and the huge down-gashed mouths.

Five minutes later he said gently, 'Ready to swim ashore now?'

Without a word she began to swim in. She was a good old-fashioned swimmer, using the trudgeon, but there was no strength in her strokes and David and the two Gurkhas easily kept up with her. She reached the sand and stumbled wearily up out of the water. She was wearing an ill-cut one-piece suit, that accentu-ated her clumsy build and movements. He turned to the Gurkhas: 'Well done, *keta haru*, well done indeed! Your commanding-sahib shall hear of what you did today. Give me your names.' The Gurkhas stood to attention, knee deep in the sea, beaming. He patted them on the shoulders and said, 'Go now, dress, and wait in the shade by the little hut there.'

'*Hunchha, hazur!*'

The two brown men ran up the beach, their huge hillmen's calf muscles glistening wet. David said, 'Are your clothes inside the changing room, Lady Anne?'

She nodded and he said, 'You'd better get dressed.'

She went up the steps on to the verandah and into the women's changing room without a word. David sat down in one of the wicker chairs – last time he was here Sally was stroking his hair and telling him he wasn't really going bald. He wondered if he should keep an eye on Lady Anne, but he could hardly insist on watching her dress herself. How odd it was to put on a bathing suit to commit suicide. Good God, now he'd said it, that's what it was ... must have been! Either by drowning, or by shark. What a death, in either case!

Perhaps she'd just been careless, didn't believe there were really any sharks here, didn't believe all this nonsense about staying inside the shark net. She could say it, and anyone who hadn't seen her might believe her; but he couldn't and wouldn't – not after seeing her face, and feeling her struggle out towards the sharks.

She came out, her long hair hanging dank down the sides of her long face. 'Thank you,' she said, her head down. 'I'll go home now.'

David stood aside to let her pass; then remembered the utter misery in her face, when he first saw it out there beyond the net. He put out his hand, caught her arm, and said, 'Stop. What's the matter?'

She tugged momentarily to free herself, but he held fast, saying again, 'What's the matter? Please tell me.'

Then she turned and almost fell into his arms. 'Oh my God, I must! I haven't been able ... not being able to talk to anyone because ... we are what we are, here ... it was ...'

'Sit down,' he said. He picked a towel off a hook on the wall and said, 'Dry your hair. It doesn't look too nice like that.'

'Thank you,' she said automatically. She took the towel and began to rub her back hair in it. As she did not speak for several minutes, looking at him but through him, David said, 'Well?'

'Sidney's going to leave me. Oh God, he'd kill me if he knew I was talking to you.'

'That would be better than you killing yourself,' David said. 'And anyway ... of course I don't know him very well, but surely he wouldn't do anything violent, would he?'

'He would!' she cried vehemently. 'He controls himself so carefully most of the time that people don't realize what there is underneath ... You should read how he got his DSC. It wasn't an action done calmly but in a frenzy, when he'd dropped his torpedo and missed, ramming the German submarine with his aeroplane. He hit the conning tower with his undercarriage and it couldn't dive. God knows how he survived . . . No, he'd kill me.'

'Well,' David said, 'I'm sure he wouldn't dream of leaving you.'

She said, 'It's Princess Kumara. They play chess . . . I've sneaked in to see and they really do play chess. That's when they're at the Residency. But the expression on his face when he looks at her. When he thinks about her. I know when he's thinking about her, and it's all the time. She's never out of his mind, even when he's in his office. She has obsessed him. Yet I don't think she's a bad woman. She hasn't done it on purpose. Or has she? What happened on that trip to the Maliwun Forest Game Preserve, when he told me to make an excuse not to come? He said he had important policy matters to discuss with her, but . . . And then again, another time, to Powlang, three days together, only two weeks ago . . . It must be on purpose . . .'

She was speaking fast now, almost gabbling, the towel rubbing vigorously, colour coming into the pale cheeks.

'She's done it because they, the royal family, don't like the policy Sidney's come to put into effect. She's going to hypnotize him so that he'll tell the government it's all wrong . . . that we must stay . . . then he can stay here longer, with her.'

David said carefully, 'I can't say whether your husband is infatuated with the Princess Kumara or not . . . but as to her, I doubt whether she returns the feeling. I don't believe that she wants to marry him.'

'Why not?' she said with head raised, almost belligerently – 'I wish I could believe you. But you don't know him. Once he wants something, he gets it. Always. Sooner or later. By any means. Like the German submarine. And . . . she's been in the Residency late at night.'

'After the chess?'

'After she's supposed to have gone home,' she said with bitter triumph. 'I've woken up and found Sidney not there. That's not unusual – he's always getting up in the middle of the night to work . . . I'm not supposed to go and find out what he's doing. I learned that right after we were married. He hates it. But after this had happened a couple of times this month, I crept down to his study – not the big one he receives visitors in, a small one he does private work, mainly financial, in . . . I heard her talking inside. I listened . . . I couldn't hear exactly what she was saying – it was in Mingora-Malay, but it was her voice and it was soft, tender . . . so was his . . .'

She continued drying her hair, looking now through the open door towards the calm sea, where a solitary shark still patrolled beyond the net. David thought, what do I do now? This bears out what the Chief Minister told me last month on the way to Lepet. Had Kumara decided to carry out her plan and ruin Wilson? Should he hint as much to Lady Anne? But she firmly believed it anyway. Should he warn Wilson? . . . Perhaps. But Wilson was always reminding him to keep his nose out of politics. So he would. The worst of this was the sorrow here before his eyes, this large kindly miserable English countrywoman, fundamentally as simple as a plough girl, though a marquess's daughter . . . enmeshed in passions and intrigues conceived under the Asian sun, born beside the Chinese sea, nurtured by ancient Khmer goddesses.

'Have you talked to the priest?' he said.

She laughed shortly. 'Father Crouch? He worships the ground Sidney treads on. He wouldn't believe me, or if he did, would be sure Sidney had good reasons . . . But I suppose I'll have to confess that I tried to kill myself. When I think of that, I feel worse than ever. I was ready to abandon the children, even Sidney . . . I wish I could believe that Kumara really doesn't care. Then my mind would be at rest. But the tone of her voice . . . in the Residency at two in the morning . . .' She got up abruptly. 'May I come to you again, brigadier . . . if I get desperate? I have nowhere else, no one else. I'm alone with what I see, with what I think . . .'

'Of course,' he said, 'We'll escort you as far as the city limit . . . You won't come out here again without asking for a RMC escort, will you?'

She said, 'Not unless I have the same intention, when an escort wouldn't be what I wanted, would it?' David followed her out and down the steps. As she started up, David walked over to the Gurkhas in the escort jeep and said, 'Make no mention of what happened here to anyone, not even to your *sathis*. It is important. Is it understood?'

'*Hunchha, hazur!*'

He motioned Tulbahadur to drive the Land Rover and settled back beside him, his knees up, staring moodily at the dust cloud raised by Lady Anne Wilson's car ahead.

David closed the heavy file and put it down. It was labelled SECRET – US ARMY INTELLIGENCE REPORTS, THAILAND, Vol. 5. No. 9, February 1960. He picked up the next volume, labelled MALAYAN EMERGENCY INTELLIGENCE REPORT, March 1960, TOP SECRET. He began to read. The clock struck ten thirty. He yawned. He'd been here nearly two hours, since the incident at the royal beach and a light breakfast in Flagstaff House.

The northern frontier worried him. The Chief Minister had assured him that the short border with Burma was absolutely secure. The Thai border, stretching the whole northern length of Lepet, and half of Moirang, was a different matter. The local Thai authorities were more interested in nightclubs they owned in Bangkok than in their responsibilities. And the central stretch of the border was dense hilly jungle. It was doubtful whether the Thais would know what was going on there, or be able to do anything about it even if they wanted to.

He made a note on a pad: call Crawford and get the latest on his private intelligence net.

He opened another intelligence file: CIA reports on Communist personalities of South East Asia – early lives, where they had been trained, what schools of Communist doctrine they subscribed to; battle and administrative experience ... He looked up Sujak bin Amin. H'm ... Showed tactical and organizational skill at Berkeley in setting up communist cadres designed to destroy the functioning of the university; failed because the cadres were infiltrated, but Sujak's involvement was not known until two years after he had graduated. So, good at covering his tracks ... More pragmatic than doctrinaire, but at base dedicated to Marxist theory. Considerable charm of manner when he wants to exert it ... as when cadging a lift from an army vehicle; one might say, great nerve, too. Ruthless ... like all of them; nothing unusual there ... he himself was alive not because Sujak had scruples about killing him, but because he wasn't ready to have the British really turn on the heat; and the corollary to that, surely, was that he soon would be ready . . .

The phone rang and the clerk said, 'The Brigade IO would like to see you, sir.'

Crawford came in with a slim folder. David motioned to him to put it down, and said, 'I was going to send for you. How's our private intelligence net coming along?'

'It's all set up, sir,' the young man replied, 'but we've run out of available funds. We'll have to make an urgent application to FARELF for more.'

'How much?'

'Ten thousand pounds for the rest of this year . . . that is, until we leave.'

David drummed his fingers on the table. The day he'd got back from his tour of the provinces, he'd sent Crawford up north, with an official of the Chief Ministry, to set up an intelligence organization that would report not so much what was happening inside Mingora – that was the responsibility of the Ministry's own intelligence people – but over the border in Burma and Thailand. This was tricky work politically and the sources of the money had to be concealed, the agents had to have no connection with the British Army. So far he had been able to find the money needed from training funds, contingency allowances, and regular intelligence allotments. Now he would have to ask FARELF for money – a lot of it – and he'd have to explain just what it was for.

Suppose FARELF said No? Suppose they told him to shut down the whole operation – which they probably would? Then Mingora would be at the mercy of Sujak and the MPRP, because no one can win a fight blindfolded. He began to feel uneasy, for he could sense that his thoughts were leading him towards dangerous territory, a future filled with morasses and swamps, wherein reputation, career, life itself could be lost.

'All right,' he said, 'I'll see what I can do about it.'

'We need some of the money within a week, sir.'

'I know,' David said testily. 'I've got to think what's our best way to tackle this.'

'Yes, sir . . . Sir, have you seen one of these?' Crawford opened his folder and handed David a postcard-sized glossy print. It showed Nugent, the Residency counsellor and Sir Harry

Johnstone, a small Mingoran official between them, seated at a table groaning under elaborately composed mountains of rice, chicken, pork, fish, vegetables, fruits, wine, liqueurs. The photographer had caught the two Englishmen, both portly, in the act of stuffing more food into their mouths. The effect was of luxury amounting to gross greed.

Crawford said, 'The legend says "Your taxes pay for this".'

'Where was it taken?'

'At a state banquet.'

'By a servant? Through the window from outside?'

'No one knows, sir. But this is being distributed secretly in Trangloek and the two northern provinces – Lepet and Moirang. The Minister's people think distribution only started yesterday.'

Effective, David thought. More effective still if there was a bad crop. Crawford went out. David sat staring out of the window. The staff car was waiting in the shade, Wood and Tulbahadur playing cards on the grass. His red-banded SD cap hung on the peg behind the door. Outside, the board read *Brigadier D. D. Jones, OBE*. By the time his tour was up, Wilson had hinted, those last three letters might be *CBE*. If he kept his copybook clean there was no reason he shouldn't be a major general soon after that. If . . .

He grabbed the telephone and snapped: 'Get me Sir Harry Johnstone at Mingora & Oriental, please.' He fumbled for a cigarette. 'Sir Harry? Brigadier Jones here. It's rather short notice I know, but could you join me for lunch at Flagstaff House today? Just the two of us . . . Oh . . . It is, rather . . . I see . . . That's very kind of you . . . Twelve-thirty on the *SS Tunku Kala*, in Dock Three, then.' He hung up. He found his hands were damp, and dried them on his handkerchief.

The D/Q came in with a file. 'Sir, Colonel Allen's been calling about Captain Whitmore.'

'Yes,' David said wearily, 'What's he want?'

'He wants you to deal summarily with him, sir. Or send him to Singapore for the C-in-C, if necessary.'

David said, 'Is Colonel Allen in his office?'

'Yes, sir.'

David picked up the phone: 'Get me Colonel Allen . . . John, Brigadier here. What's your point about Whitmore?'

The colonel's normally powerful voice sounded tinny at the far end of the line. 'It was a put-up job. Those people attacked first by deliberately kicking mud and water over the Whitmores.'

'Then that will come out in the trial,' David said.

The thin voice at the far end showed the exasperation that David was finding familiar in his dealings with Allen and the Fusiliers: 'It should, sir, but it won't. The man was an *agent provocateur*, and he'll have his witnesses to prove Whitmore attacked him without reason, when he was drunk. Paul's got a hell of a temper, and he'd had a drink or two, but he was wasn't drunk.'

David said, 'I think we must let this thing go to a civilian trial, John.'

'We don't have to. We have the right to reserve military personnel for military trial for any crime in Mingora.'

'I know,' David said, 'but I don't think we should use it in this case. The MPRP are increasing their propaganda against us, and if we spirit men away from their courts, for a crime against a Mingoran, although comparatively trivial . . .'

'They can give Whitmore six months,' Allen said.

'. . . we are giving them a handle,' David continued. 'I spoke to the Chief Minister about this a couple of days ago, and said that we would allow Whitmore to go to civil trial.'

'Very well, sir,' the exasperated voice grated. The phone was hung up with a bang. David lit another cigarette and said to Marriott, 'Captain Whitmore will go for civil trial. Tell the Fusiliers that he's not to leave Mingora without brigade permission. And call the Chief Minister's assistant and say we'd like the trial put on as soon as possible. See Whitmore and arrange to get a good lawyer to defend him.'

'Who'll pay the lawyer, sir?'

'Whitmore will have to. The judge may award him damages or costs, but my whole point here is to make clear that this case is the Queen of Mingora *versus* Captain Whitmore, not *versus* the British Army . . . If you want me, I'll be inspecting the Military Ward at the hospital for the next hour. I'll look into those complaints about the food that you reported.'

He picked up his cap and went out. In the staff car he thought about A Company of the Royal Oxford Fusiliers . . . Whitmore was a fire eater, given to bashing Mingoran civilians in street fights. That certainly wouldn't turn his men against him . . . unless he was inclined to do the same to them. He'd have to take a look at the company again, soon, and have a talk with CSM 'Kid' Berg. And he'd have to think very hard about John Allen. The special report on him was due in a couple of months. He'd stage an exercise or two with complicated staff-type problems, and put Allen in as brigade commander. He was not staff-trained, and that might be a weakness, unless he had the sense to recognize it and rely on Stork and Gil Marriott . . . Well, none of it would affect him, soon enough, the way he had now set his course.

The derricks clacked and hammered on the foredeck, bowing and sweeping in crane-like ritual, as David watched through the heavy glass of the cabin portholes. The little ship shook and heaved and settled as the bulky cases were lifted out of the holds fore and aft. Every blow of steel on steel anywhere echoed through the ship and turned the officers' dining saloon into a metallic drum, gently beaten by a distant giant. The rubber-bladed fans set in the ceiling and on the edges of the forward sideboard whirred busily.

Sir Harry motioned to the Chinese steward to fill his brandy glass. The captain of the ship and the third mate, the only others present, rose and left, the Third bowing uncertainly. Sir Harry said, 'New skipper. Was First with McLean McNaughten, but they're going out of the shipping business.'

The brandy came, with a splash of soda. David sipped his iced water. Sir Harry had apparently come down to see how the new skipper organized his command, a Mingora & Oriental coastal steamer, for unloading. When David arrived he'd been up on the bridge, staring down into the forward hold; then he'd taken David down into the hold itself, which was like a boiler factory. Now they'd had lunch, and were alone.

Sir Harry said in his broadest Yorkshire, 'What's t'problem, lad?'

David glanced meaningly at the open door to the stewards' pantry, and Sir Harry picked up his glass and said, 'Let's take these to the stern. There's a good breeze there.'

And plenty of extraneous noise, David thought, when they reached the curved stern platform, under the filthy Red Ensign fluttering feebly over the murky water below. The vessel was moored head in to the dock, the rust-stained bows reaching out almost over the Esplanade. A spur from the railway ran along the seaward side of the Esplanade here, sending off stubs down each side of each of the four basins. Travelling cranes stood like giant storks along the edge of Docks 1 and 2 to the east. Beyond the fussy superstructure of the little tramp, with its derricks and cabins and lifeboats and funnel and funnel stays, the city of Trangloek rose like a backdrop from the Esplanade – below, the heavy grey of the Victorian and Edwardian commercial buildings, above, brightening in smaller blocks of colour to the twisted golden spire of the Old Pagoda on the crest of the ridge.

David raised his voice against the clangour: 'We need money Sir Harry. It's for Intelligence.' He explained his plan for getting military intelligence along and over the northern border during the vital period now beginning. Sir Harry sipped his brandy and soda, a thin perspiration spotting his red face under the wide-brimmed panama. 'And you don't want to go to General Huntingdon for it?'

David said, 'I'm afraid he'd say No. He might approve of the idea, militarily, but he'd have to ask the Commissioner General, who'd refer it to London . . . and the answer would be, No.'

The old merchant said slowly, 'I don't know that I ought to get involved in this undercover stuff. I'm putting money behind a group who are organizing people against the British policy – but openly – and . . .'

'You are involved,' David said. He pulled the photograph out of his pocket and gave it to Sir Harry. Sir Harry's congested face turned purple and he gasped. 'T'roody bastards! They should show a photograph of me eating only twice a week so I could pay my men, when I was starting! How much do you want?'

'Ten thousand pounds will last until 1 June. After that, it'll be Mingora's responsibility.'

Sir Harry snapped, 'You can 'ave it. Send that young man of yours – Crawford – round to me and I'll have my accountant work out the best way of getting the stuff to you, under the table. Send him this afternoon.' He nodded towards the solid bulk of the M & O Building a little farther along the Esplanade. He studied the photograph more closely, and said, 'That was the commercial dinner. There was a servant standing about where that was taken from, all evening. Right behind Sally . . . Hear anything about the Wilsons' private life?'

'No,' David said, trying to keep his face immobile.

'My information is that Lady Anne is going off her rocker. Acting very strange.'

'Oh?' David said.

Sir Harry shot him a glance. 'Coom off it, lad! . . . You know Wilson's gaga over Kumara. He hasn't done anything foolish yet, but he might. Then we can get him.'

David said, 'But, Sir Harry, even assuming that Wilson could be replaced as Resident, what guarantee would anyone have that the new man would not be even more determined to carry out what the cabinet say is their policy?'

'None,' Sir Harry said, 'but desperate people might think it's better at least to jump out of the frying pan, where you *know* you're being cooked. The fire might go out, or be put out, before you land in it . . . That Kumara's a lady to be careful of, lad. She's got more brains than's safe for a woman with her looks. And all she cares about is Mingora, and don't get any other idea into your head, the way Wilson seems to have . . . Why do you think Sujak kidnapped Sally?'

'Blackmail, of a sort, I suppose,' David said slowly, 'She would have been a hostage in case we got rough with them. Or captured someone important.'

Sir Harry's fat belly wobbled as he started to walk forward. 'I don't believe it, he said. 'I'm leaving for the Satul mine at four, so send that young fellow along right away.' They passed along the clamorous deck and eventually down on to the dock side, and parted.

The Resident swung his racquet fiercely and the rubber ball whizzed down the court. David watched it with a feeling of intense rage, and swung as hard, smashing it back – an easy return; but Wilson did not attempt to kill it or lay it dead in the front corner. In his turn he smashed it straight against the centre of the front wall, six inches above the tin. David smashed again. There went his commission . . . *smash* . . . taking money from a civilian . . . *smash* . . . for an illegal, unsanctioned intelligence operation . . . *smash* . . . in a friendly foreign . . . *smash* . . . country!

The Resident's shot angled down into the corner and David was left with racquet poised, but no ball to play. He felt aggrieved that the rally had come to an end. It was the Resident's fault. Glancing at Wilson he thought he felt the same way; for there was a sort of momentary apology in his face, but all he said was '6–5', and served again, right above the service line, in the centre of the wall. *Smash . . . smash . . . thwack . . .* Sir Harry might give him a job . . . Sir Harry might find himself squeezed out of Mingora by a programme of Mingora for the Mingorans.

The rubber ball hit him on the right cheek, a glancing blow that stung viciously. It showed what happened when you had other things on your mind. He concentrated on the game, finally winning it 9–7 after he had calmed down, taken some strength out of his shots and used his head instead of the muscles of his forearm and wrist.

The Resident said, 'Another set.'

David mopped his forehead with the terry towel hung outside the court. 'Sorry. I have an early dinner date with the princess.'

Wilson's pale eyes stared, his lips tightened. Sweat ran off the end of his nose. He said, in a harsh flat voice, 'You're seeing too much of the princess.'

They were face to face in the little changing room behind the squash court, towels in one hand, racquets in the other. David's hand had tightened on the grip of the racquet; and so, he saw, had Wilson's. They were staring at each other – no, glaring was the word; men in their forties, responsible men, the civil and military heads of the British community here.

David said, 'I think I am the one to decide that.'

The Resident controlled himself with an enormous and visible effort of will, and said, the voice grating, but the tone meant to be pleasant, 'Well, you saved her life, she says, so I suppose no one will see anything amiss in it if she invites you to dinner from time to time.'

David thought back to the kidnapping, and their hours as Sujak's prisoner, and said seriously, 'I don't think we were ever in danger.'

'Not when the tiger charged? Don't be modest,' the Resident snapped, 'Though personally I suspect she would have killed it with her first shot if you hadn't been there in the hide . . . You must have moved, breathed, done something to make it raise its head just as she fired. She doesn't shoot animals for pleasure, but when she does shoot, she never misses.'

By then David had understood. He said, 'It is Sally who has invited me to dinner, and an exhibition by a troupe of Thai dancers.'

For a moment Wilson looked as though someone had hit him with a sandbag. Then he recovered himself and said with sudden cheerfulness, 'And I'm sure Sally will flirt with you and try to get information from you about our plans for handing over our military responsibilities to the Mingorans.'

'I expect so,' David said in a neutral voice.

The Resident said, 'And you will be as silent as only a good Welshman can be. Kumara tries to pump me over our chess. Is Sally just backing her up, in another area? Or is she working for herself? For some third party? Whom?'

'I don't know,' David said, struggling into his cardigan, 'unless she's working for her mother and the Queen, the Chief Minister's intelligence people will be on to it. They watch everyone, you know, including the Queen . . . in case her illness deranges her . . . and including Kumara, twenty-four hours a day.'

Twelve

A S HE TURNED in past the black bulk of Jumbhorn Wat, the low sun in his face, he was thinking that it was Tulbahadur's turn to swim today. The escort of four Gurkhas in the following Land-Rover knew by now to work out among themselves as to who should swim and who should stand guard. He had wondered, since ordering the extra security measures, whether he should stop going to the royal beach; for the Queen had invited only himself, the Resident and their immediate families to use it, not squards of soldiers and armed police . . . but a few days ago Kumara had sent him a note asking him to continue using the beach, with whatever escorts were necessary; for one thing, the occasional and unpredictable presence of soldiers would help to protect the beach at all times.

He had not seen Sally here since the kidnapping, but a week ago, in the evening, he had found Kumara. He had thought, when he first saw her, that she had just arrived, but it turned out that she was just leaving. Now, as the road wound out of the palms he saw that he was going to have company again. A blue Daimler saloon was parked outside the beach house and as the Land-Rover stopped David recognized the Daimler as Kumara's state car; he had only seen it two or three times because she usually used her blue Land-Rover.

She came out of the beach house and stood on the verandah at the top of the steps up from the sand. She was wearing formal Mingoran daytime costume. He saluted her, hoping she would smile. Her face remained without expression as she said, 'My mother is inside, waiting for you, brigadier.'

'The Queen?' he said in astonishment. 'She is going swimming?'

Kumara said, 'No. She wishes to speak to you. We are going to Pulo Pattan – the island in the middle of the lake.'

'I saw it when we were kidnapped,' David said. 'And from the air.'

'We have a small palace on it – a sort of pleasure dome. There are guards there now, so your soldiers can wait here.'

David saluted again as the Queen came out, slowly, leaning on the arm of the Chamberlain, and followed by the Chief Minister. She threw him a weary smile and said in her precise lilting un-English English, 'Good morning, brigadier . . . We will all be back here in two or three hours.' She hobbled down the verandah steps and past the guardians' hut where the old couple stood in the doorway, bowing deeply. At the end of the path through the palm grove one of the big canoe-like boats was ready at the dock, six men at the sweeps and the skipper in gold and blue sarong holding the steering oar. They got in, sat on the thrown cushions, and at once the steersman cast off. The rowers began a smooth strong stroke and the boat surged out on to the clear shallow waters of Dhaphut Sap.

The Queen said, 'We have some important decisions to make, brigadier. We need your advice.' She looked at the Chief Minister, then closed her eyes.

The Minister said, 'The day before yesterday our security police captured Masam bin Mohammed. They were acting on information received – for money.'

David nodded. Masam bin Mohammed was the No. 3 man in the MPRP. The water gurgled and chattered along the side of the boat, and the rowers grunted quietly in unison as their oars struck the water.

The Minister said, 'We know that Masam is jealous of Sujak, and were able to persuade him to tell us much of great value.'

I bet, David thought.

The Minister said, 'They – the MPRP under Sujak – are planning a rising, to take place a few days before the south-west monsoon sets in, which is usually about 1 June. You and your soldiers will have gone, or be packed ready to go. If you went out after them they'd either hide in the jungles until you had to turn back – or they might start a battle from which you'd have to disengage, which would look like a British defeat.'

David thought, they're right; the Resident would never permit him to take troops out so late, because they might get committed to a battle from which they could not disengage for a long time.

The Minister continued, 'Masam says that a rising will take place in all six provinces and the capital, but that is to tie down troops and constabulary. In fact, they plan to capture only the three western provinces – Kusalung, Powlang, and Moirang. There the rising will be supported by a force of so-called Mingoran Freedom Fighters, who are now being raised and trained somewhere in south Thailand. Masam doesn't know exactly where. These Freedom Fighters are mostly Mingorans from the western provinces – also some Chinese CTs who fled there from Malaya – and a few Vietnamese.'

'How many in all?' David asked.

'They're planning on five hundred, Masam said, but he believes they only have three hundred now and won't reach more than three hundred and fifty by the time they have to act.'

David said, 'That's a lot of men. Does he know what sort of arms they have?'

'Sub-machine guns, grenades, a few anti-tank rockets – what are they called?'

'PIATs, bazookas,' David said.

'Yes. And a few light mortars like the Japanese used.'

The Jap knee mortar, David thought; a useful little weapon.

'And rifles and automatic pistols, of course.'

Ahead the island was close now. Through towering royal palms David saw the verandah of a wooden house, its ridge pole curved up to end in carved heads of the mythical lion-like *chinthe*. Bougainvillea smothered one wall and trailed along the top of the wide verandah, and scores of poinsettia bushes bordered the path leading up to the house from the landing stage. Men in the royal uniform of blue sarong and embroidered coat and round blue hat came running down. The boat slowed, turned and swung silently alongside.

'Welcome to our island retreat,' the old Queen said.

A few minutes later they were sitting round a polished mahogany table, bowls of iced durian before them. The Queen was looking very frail, David thought – more make-up on her face even than usual.

Kumara said, 'The question is, what are we going to do? Sujak intends to overrun our three western provinces while we are busy putting down the risings in the east. Then the rains set in, and you go. In a week or two he can announce that he has liberated half of Mingora. Russia or Red China will send him a big radio transmitter – he has one or two small ones already, which he's using to send out propaganda and coded orders from this base inside Thailand – but then he'll be able to reach listeners almost anywhere in the world. And we will have no army ready . . . I'm sorry I have to bring this up, Dylan, after I swore at Ban Khao that it wasn't your fault, but we're . . . *I'm* desperate. Our forces will consist of a hundred Constables in each province plus what we can spare from Trangloek . . . less deserters. It's not enough.'

David did not attempt to argue. The figures from the Malayan Emergency proved she was right.

The Chief Minister said, 'I have advised Her Majesty that we should strike about two weeks from now – that is, the middle of May. We should arrest every known member of the MPRP. We have a long list by now, and Masam is giving us more names.'

'But the invaders, when they come, will still be able to over-run the provincial capitals, at least,' David said, 'and then take on the village Home Guards – those that stay loyal – a few at a time, all through the monsoon.'

'We have brought you here to beg you to attack and destroy the invading force at the same time – in mid May,' the Minister said.

David gasped. 'You mean, attack them inside Thailand?'

The Minister said vehemently, 'There they are – somewhere, close over the border, preparing to invade our country! Doubtless they are wearing black trousers and jackets, and claiming to be peaceful civilians. When they cross our border they will put a red star on their coats and claim that they are uniformed soldiers, entitled to treatment as such. Why should we not dress your Gurkhas in grey trousers and shirts, and send them over as civilians? Once they find the invaders, there would be a disagreement. Thailand has no troops near enough to interfere before the Gurkhas could have done their work, come back to Mingora, and put on their uniforms again.'

David said slowly, 'It's the right answer, from a military point of view. But we'd never be allowed to do it.'

'Could a patrol wander over the border by mistake?' Kumara

asked, 'They would be fired on, and would have to defend themselves.'

'A patrol, yes,' David said, 'A battalion, or two battalions, with artillery support, no.'

'We must do something,' the Queen said, her voice quivering, 'We cannot merely wait, like rabbits, for the snake to come and kill us.'

The Chief Minister said, 'Leaving that proposal aside, what do you say to the rest of our plan – to arrest all the known revolutionaries in the middle of May?'

David thought carefully. A servant removed his empty plate and put down another, with fresh cut pineapple. The long boat rocked gently by the stage at the end of the avenue of poinsettias. The clouds overhead were heavy white, tinged with slate and possessing a great sense of mass.

He said, 'It might be better not to act until the last minute. Then, the important point will be to concentrate the Constabulary. If you left, say, twenty constables in each province, and a hundred in Trangloek you'd have over six hundred at Moirang. That's a big enough force to meet the invaders, break them up – with luck, destroy them.'

The Chief Minister said gently, 'That would be very good, brigadier, if it were possible . . . but twenty men is not enough to guard a province, or a hundred the capital, against determined and ruthless revolutionaries who are at least as well armed as the Constabulary.'

David said, 'Well, it's certain defeat to remain scattered in penny packets.'

Kumara said, 'I think we should set up check points on all main roads, and have village Home Guards do the same on small roads and paths. The MPRP will have to move about a lot from now until they act – passing on orders, grouping ready for action on their D-Day. We should put sentries on all main bridges and Radio Mingora. They will see that we are on our guard, which is perhaps a pity, but I think we will gain more than we lose.'

'Princess,' the Minister said, 'I fear we don't have enough Constabulary to do these things, and at the same time maintain the necessary strength in Trangloek.'

David said, 'Suppose I made two companies, that's two hundred men, available as a central reserve, until we leave. Then you wouldn't have to keep all those RMC in Trangloek, would you?'

Kumara threw him a small smile: 'No. I've suggested to my mother that she should pardon all prisoners not guilty of major crimes. It will be a popular gesture . . . and it will make room in the provincial jails for the MPRP we'll be rounding up.'

The Queen said, 'I will do it on 11 May.'

They all looked at David as though expecting him to say something. Puzzled, he finally asked, 'Why that date, ma'am?'

The Queen said, 'On 12 May I am holding a plebiscite, as to whether my people wish our connection with Britain to end, or wish it to continue.'

David had a feeling this must have been Kumara's idea.

No one could have thought of a better way to embarrass the Resident and the British government. He said, 'Has the Resident been told of this?'

The Queen was leaning back against an ornately carved rosewood pillar behind her, her brother whispering solicitously in her ear. It was Kumara who answered, 'No. He is being received in audience at noon today . . . Mother is feeling tired, and we should get back in time for her to have a rest before Mr Wilson comes. If you have had enough to eat . . .'

Everyone rose. Down the long aisle of flowering bushes the boatmen appeared and took their places.

As soon as he reached his office David sent for Lieutenant Crawford, and told him all he had learned on Pulo Pattan. Then he said, 'Go up to Moirang at once, and pass this on to our new agents there. I want to know exactly where these Freedom Fighters' camp in Thailand is, how many of them are in it, and what they're doing and planning to do – all about them. See if we can infiltrate them. Possibly fit one of our men with a radio transmitter.'

'It'll be hard to get a man in whom they'll accept,' Crawford said, 'A woman might be easier.'

David said, 'All right. Get cracking.' He turned to the files piled in his IN tray.

At a quarter to one, as he was tidying his desk, the telephone

179

rang. He knew whom the call would be from, and it was: the Resident.

'Brigadier Jones? Come to the Residency at once, please.'

'Should I bring any staff?'

'No.' The line went dead.

David put on his hat and went out. The Gurkha escort was ready, for he had been expecting the call, and in a few moments they were heading through Kandahar Lines towards the city spread out below.

The doorman at the Residency greeted him with a salute, and he passed through the open doors into the central hall. He turned to go along the passage towards the Resident's office, and Lady Anne came out of the door to the right. With a gesture she invited him into the room. She left the door half open as he followed her to the window. She spoke in a low voice: 'I overheard Sidney call you ... I've spoken to the Princess.'

'What did she say?'

'She said that her intentions were quite innocent. She wasn't very forthcoming ... I feel miserable.' She looked haggard, the big face mournful in the strong light at the window, the red hands clasping and unclasping. She said, 'I wish ... I wish she'd fall in love with someone else ... get married ... You'd better go. He seems in a bad temper.'

David went out, without speaking; he could think of nothing to say to assuage Lady Anne's unhappiness.

The Resident stood up as he came in, saluting, and said abruptly, 'I've just come back from an audience with the Queen. She is proposing to hold a national plebiscite on 12 May to ask the people whether they want the British connection to continue or to end.'

'It seems a reasonable thing to do,' David said.

The Resident snapped, 'It is not, because the people of Mingora have no say in the matter. It's the people of Great Britain who have decided, through their elected representatives, that the connection shall end. This plebiscite, if it goes against us, will merely cause bad publicity in the world press, questions in parliament and so on.'

'Against us?' David said.

'Against our declared policy,' the Resident said impatiently. 'I did all I could to make the Queen change her mind, but she was determined. After a few minutes she left, saying she was feeling very tired. I had to talk, after that, to the Daughter-in-Line, the Chief Minister, and the Prince Chamberlain ... couldn't persuade them, either.'

'Can you not forbid them to hold the plebiscite?' David asked.

The Resident said, 'No. I can indicate the great displeasure of HMG. In the past I could have made threats of economic or diplomatic reprisals, but as we're going, what threats mean anything? Did you know about this?' he suddenly shot at David with a cold glare.

David hesitated only a moment. Lying was a sign of fear and though he had to admit that he still stood in a soldier's awe of his civilian master, he must not allow that awe to affect his judgment or his probity. He said, 'Yes. This morning.'

The Resident said, 'Why didn't you tell me?'

'I hardly had time. The Princess said you were going to be received in audience immediately afterwards.'

'The Princess Kumara?'

'Yes, sir.'

Wilson strode round his desk and sat down in the high-backed chair. He said, 'I am Her Majesty's representative here. I am to know everything, at once ... The Chief Minister told me that you had agreed to place two companies of your troops in reserve to release Constabulary for action against the MPRP.'

'That's right.'

'Why wasn't I told?'

'I haven't had time.'

'Why didn't you ask my permission first?'

'I considered it within my competence as military commander here.'

'It is not. There is no such thing as a purely military decision here any more ... Sit down.'

David lowered himself into the plain chair opposite the Resident. Wilson's lips were tight, but he was making an obvious attempt to control his anger. When he spoke there was still a bite in his voice, but his words were gentler. 'They told me about the capture of Masam bin Mohammed, and the information he has been giving. They presumably told you, too.'

'Yes, sir.'

'I think the report of the force gathering in the jungles north of the border is exaggerated – if there is any truth in it at all.'

David thought, our new intelligence force, the one Sir Harry was paying for, would find out soon now; but he could not mention that to Wilson.

Wilson said, 'The Minister asked me whether I would authorize you to move against these Freedom Fighters. I said it was out of the question. Did they ask you?'

'Yes, sir.'

'What did you say?'

'The same.'

The Resident said, 'Good! As we are responsible for Mingora's foreign policy until 1 June, I was able to tell the Minister that no force of any kind was to cross the northern border. And that that applied to intelligence agents, too. If you have any military intelligence operating in the north, see that it keeps inside Mingora . . . The Minister told me that the Queen would make a formal request that the Freedom Fighters should be attacked. They want it on record that they asked for this action while our forces were still available . . . This promise of yours to allot two companies to aid the civil power in Trangloek releases Constabulary for other action . . . political action . . . which the government could not have taken without your help. That's why I say that there is no such thing as a purely military decision any more. What is your reason for doing this?'

David said, 'Our treaty is with the royal government, and I think it's our duty to help them, as long as we're here.'

'That's precisely why we're leaving,' the Resident said; 'One reason, at least.' He was silent a minute, looking down at a paper on his desk. He looked up: 'All right. The secret of this next month is to act very firmly wherever we can, on the principle that if you are planning a retreat, you attack just before, so the enemy won't follow you up too closely. We have an opportunity to do just that, now, in Lepet. Communal trouble is brewing there . . . riots and damage last night and this morning. The report reached the Chief Minister actually while I was in audience, so I know you haven't heard about it. I want you to go up there and take strong action, in a way that the constabulary may not want to. They live here, we're going. Visit the Chief Minister when you leave here – he's expecting you – decide what force to send up, and go as soon as possible. When you get there, force a decisive action. Don't patrol the streets with armed men so that no one comes out, but keep your troops out of sight, so that the trouble-makers are tempted to do something that they have been forbidden to – hold a procession, or a meeting, or whatever ... then open fire.'

'I understand,' David said.

The Resident said, 'It sounds brutal, but it will save lives in the long run. Go yourself.'

David said, 'Either of my battalion commanders could handle it.'

'This is a political matter,' Wilson said, 'Politico-military decisions will have to be taken. I want you to be there in person, handling it.'

'Very well, sir. Is that all?'

The Resident nodded. 'Give me a call before you leave.'

The scout cars of the Royal Oxford Fusiliers rolled ahead, due north up the main road. David followed with his escort and the Land-Rover with the command radio set. Behind again came John Allen and B Company of the Fusiliers, in RASC three tonners. C Company was at this moment entraining at Trangloek and would reach Lepet an hour and a half after the road column. It was five o'clock in the afternoon of 30 April, 1960. The heat was becoming more oppressive every day now, though the thermometer showed only a small rise in the actual temperatures.

David sat with his knees hunched up, as he often did. The wind of their passage was preventing the sweat forming on his face, but he felt damp under the arms and round his waist, under his belt. Get tough in Lepet, the Resident had ordered. In order to frighten the MPRP. But the MPRP agents would take care not to be in the firing line. They'd only point out afterwards what atrocities the army had committed. The object was surely not to kill Lepetis, but to make sure they stayed loyal, and actively on the right side.

How could he get at those bloody Freedom Fighters? A sudden swoop across the border, once he had learned exactly where they were? Landing from the sea ... no, they weren't near the coast, and he didn't have any landing craft. Air? Parachute drop? Air strike, with small bombs, machine guns and napalm?

183

He had a flat order not to cross the border, even with Intelligence agents. And he had a feeling that Wilson knew something – not much, but something – about his private Intelligence organization. So why had he not brought it up? Why was he insisting that he, David, should go north himself, instead of leaving the job to one of the colonels?

David saw the Resident's face in close detail, as though he were sitting on the front of the Land Rover, staring at him through the raised windshield. It wasn't an official stare, but a personal one. Wilson was duelling with him – and Wilson didn't want to wound, but to kill. He was being given latitude, so that the thrust, when it came, would not be the reprimanding of a man who was *planning* to do wrong, but the execution of a man who had *done* wrong.

Thirteen

THE OPPRESSIVE HEAT faded as the sun set, and a small breeze began to blow in from the east. It carried a breath of the sea, though here on the southern outskirts of Lepet it had already crossed thirty miles of paddy and cane. The heavy cloud masses that towered up the evening sky were limned by gold along the upper edges, the lower parts indigo, between a dazzling white that was being washed over by successively duller tints of slate as the minutes passed. A monsoon shower, pressed out of the high clouds a month before its time, had dampened the earth and left puddles on the verges under the double avenue of trees that ran towards Lepet's tall pagoda.

David twisted and stretched for the hundredth time. The tyres hissed on the red road; ahead the Fusiliers' scout cars were pulling off the road. Here were three constables, headed by the superintendent for the province. David signalled for Wood to stop the Land-Rover. The superintendent saluted. David remembered him from his reconnaissance here six weeks ago with the Chief Minister – a thin man of about forty, tall for a Mingoran. John Allen drove up and the superintendent said, 'Brigadier, these houses here have been cleared for the soldiers' – he indicated a row of bamboo huts on stilts to the east of the road, set along the bank of the stream ahead.

'Whose are they?' David asked.

'Peasants who work in the fields here to the south,' the superintendent said; then, seeing the look on David's face, hastily added, 'They have only moved to relatives there across the road. It will not be for long, will it?'

'I hope not,' David said, 'Did you hear that, John?'

'Yes, sir.'

'Move your chaps in.'

The superintendent said, 'And, brigadier, the governor is awaiting you at his house.'

Fires began to show their presence in points of red light along the river. David turned to Allen. 'Hand over and come with me.'

They drove off, the superintendent on his motor cycle leading the Land-Rovers, across the concrete bridge, left into the warren of the city, past the pagoda, and to a long low house, made of bamboo and palm like all the others, but much bigger and with a wider verandah, and lit by electric light inside and flaming torches on stands along the road.

As they went up the steps the governor came out. After the formal greetings, David said, 'We had better start at once, Excellency, as we have another company arriving by rail in an hour and a half, and I must decide what to do with them ... Is anything likely to happen tonight?'

The Governor, like almost all men in his position in the government of Mingora, spoke English accurately but with a stilted accent, and when speaking to other Mingorans, as to the superintendent sitting on his left, often broke into Mingora-Malay. Now he said, 'I do not think so, though we cannot be certain. Three men and a woman were going about urging an attack on the Moirangis tonight, but we arrested them.'

'The Moirangis?' David said, 'Moirang's sixty miles away.'

'There is a small Moirangi community here,' the governor said. 'They work hard and are mostly well to do, and live together in the western part of the town. It is there that the trouble originated. This morning early a Lepeti youth, that is a Khmer, an Easterner, was found dead in the canal that runs through the Moirangis' quarter. The Moirangis say he was drunk and fell in and drowned, but the Lepetis say he was pushed in. The death was due to drowning – the provincial chief of health services ascertained that at once – but there was high feeling – more among the Moirangis than among the Lepetis, which I do not understand.'

David said, 'They did not like being accused of murder without proof. It shows mistrust – which is what the government has been showing to Moirangis, and all Westerners, for centuries.'

The governor said, 'I agree that we have been foolish in that respect, tuan ... The Moirangis' anger became greater when a leader of their community was found stabbed to death this afternoon – in the main part of the city, the Lepeti part. Now the Moirangis have established road blocks all round their quarter, and allow no one not a Moirangi to enter. When this became known the hotheads among our own people determined to break in and exact punishment . . .'

'For what?' David asked.

The governor shrugged: 'You know crowds, tuan. They were going to do it tonight, which would have led to great slaughter, but we imprisoned the ringleaders, or some of them.'

'Do you know them?' John Allen cut in.

'One of them, colonel – he is a known MPRP member who has been in hiding for the last two months. The others we assume are also members, although they were not previously known to be.'

'So now everything is calm,' Allen said.

'Far from it . . . the people are preparing to march into the Moirangi quarter at eleven a.m. tomorrow. We expect the crowd to number eight to nine thousand, with five hundred Moirangis inside their quarter.'

'Arms?' David asked.

'Knives, daggers, scythes, bayonets left behind by the Japanese, a few guns in the hands of the ringleaders . . .'

'What are they going to do?'

'It is hard to find out, as there is no acknowledged leader, but most people think they are going to proceed peacefully through the Moirangi quarter with the body of the drowned youth, on their way to the burial ground, which is beyond . . . but they expect they will have to force the barricades, and when that starts, with concealed revolutionaries to cause trouble, no one can say where it will end.'

'I can make a damned good guess,' John Allen said.

'We are in your hands, brigadier,' the governor said with a slightly unctuous tone.

David looked at him with distaste – this was the sort of man who should never have been put in this sensitive and responsible post. He said, 'You're still the governor.'

The governor said, 'I declared martial law an hour ago, tuan. You are the dictator in the province now, and I your willing servant.'

David said, 'I'll give my orders when I have more information. What do you think ought to be done, Excellency?'

The governor spread his hands and said, 'I agree with the advice the superintendent here gave me this afternoon.'

The superintendent, seeing that everyone was looking at him, said, 'We must confront them, tuan. The streets are narrow – the river is on one side of the road they will be using – my constables can box them in on two sides, and when they have gone far enough in, if you will block the road in front with soldiers, they will have to turn back . . .'

'Or, if their blood's up, they will charge,' John Allen said, 'Then we can really show them what's what. They won't be able to get away.'

Like the Jalianawala Bagh in 1919, David reflected: a crowd, told to disperse, and unable to do so, being mown down; whether a mistake or done on purpose as an example, the turning point in relations between England and India, a point after which there was little trust and less affection.

'You agree with that?' he said to the governor.

'Whatever you military gentlemen think best.'

David said, 'Thank you, superintendent . . . I'm going reconnoitring, and will issue orders on my return. Superintendent, please come with me. You too, John . . . signal that your rail company is to bivouac at the station.'

The governor said, 'The Rest House is ready for you, brigadier. The cook there is very good.'

'Thanks,' David said, 'I'll eat later.'

He went out. Standing by one of the tall flares, he said to the superintendent, 'Show us along the road the procession will take tomorrow, from where they will gather, to the Moirangi barricades – on foot.'

'Very well, sir. '

As David started walking he realized that they were being followed by the three Gurkhas of his escort, and the three Fusiliers of John Allen's, self-loading rifles and sub-machine guns crooked in their arms. He said, 'Escorts stay here. I want only the three of us.'

'Pretty risky, sir,' John Allen said.

'I doubt it. We have to show the Lepetis we have nothing to fear from them, and, I hope, vice versa.'

They turned out of the gates between the flaring torches, the black smoke briefly visible in the lurid short-lived glare. John

Allen rather ostentatiously unslung his carbine and carried it ready in his right hand. The flare of the governor's lights dropped back. It was still early evening, and as soon as they had passed the end of the governor's grounds, lights of shops blinked and glittered down the street, to the right a row of close packed stores and shops, to the left vendors' stalls set up on barren ground at the top of the slope down to the river. On the opposite bank a few scattered houses showed a dim light, but mostly over there was nothing but the shape of palms, and a few darkened houses on stilts rising out of the unknown of the water below.

The crowds were dense but a little quieter than David would have expected at this hour. There was nothing sullen about them but an excitement, partly hidden, that made them gather in small groups, huddled by the corners of the shops or beyond the barrows along the river, talking earnestly but quietly. The street opened up into a large square. 'This is where they propose to gather,' the superintendent said.

David stopped and examined it. Four roads led into it ... no, five; all wide and unobstructed ... those roads could easily be blocked and then the procession would never have a chance to form. Then there'd be no confrontation. John Allen would think, once again, that he'd backed off from facing the vital issue; the civil authorities would not get the chance they wanted to show the people the strength of their military backing; the Resident would not have his strong action.

The superintendent led on again, still west along the road by the river; but now the shops were becoming few, and to the right private houses were jammed together, without pattern, only haphazardly divided into blocks or groups. Here there were one or two houses on the river side, but in general that side was unoccupied. He said to the superintendent, 'This might be a good place to stop the procession, but it looks as though they could easily escape among the houses there –' he pointed north, where a rare street lamp, or the light from an open verandah, served to accentuate the labyrinthine quality of the quarter.

The superintendent said, 'Come with me, sir.' He led north. Less than a hundred yards in from the river, invisible from the main road, a canal ran among the houses parallel to it. It was twenty feet wide, and steep sided. A light reflected from gleaming black water. 'It is nearly six feet deep,' the superintendent said. 'There are very few bridges . . .'

'Perfect,' Allen muttered. 'We'd have 'em cold.'

'It looks like it,' David said. 'Lead on, please.'

There was no change in the character of the area, or of the road along the river, or of the parallel canal set back a hundred yards to the right, for another quarter of a mile. By now the people met in the road were very few, and they moving fast, none westward, until under a street lamp David stopped, looked carefully all round and saw that the three of them were alone, the river silent at their left hands, houses silent at their right. The superintendent said, 'The Moirangi barricade is between this light and the next, sir. You can hardly see it, for it is in deep shadow.'

David said, 'They can see us here, I suppose?'

'Certainly, sir.'

He took the revolver from his holster and gave it to the superintendent. 'Wait here with that, please. John, give him your carbine.'

'Sir, we don't know . . .'

'Come on.'

Unarmed, the two officers walked into the darkness. After thirty paces David heard a voice say, in Mingora-Malay – 'Wait, tuan'; then the patter of running feet and a low call. His eyes became accustomed to the gloom and he saw that they had erected the barricade under two heavy branched trees. Faces shone palely behind the boughs and carts that had been dragged across the road, weapons glinted. Beyond the barricade, two men approached. They reached the barricade and one of them said, 'Who is it, please?', in English.

'Brigadier Jones, commanding the British troops in Mingora.'

'Ah, I saw you here six weeks ago with the Chief Minister. I heard it was you who ordered that the recruit base for the army should be set up in Moirang.'

'It was,' David said, 'And I've come to protect you now.'

'They are many,' the man said. 'Wait, come inside.' He gave orders and some boughs were moved. David and Allen passed through. The man led them into a lamp-lit house and turned to David: 'Tuan, that boy was not killed, he drowned.'

'I'm sure.'

'Why do they mistrust us? Why are they ready to believe the worst of us? Have we not always been loyal subjects of Her Majesty?'

'There are men about, in these times, who wish to set brother against brother, father against son,' David said.

'It is true,' the other said, 'but their task is made more easy by the foolishness of many in authority.' David saw by the light of the oil lamp set on the floor between them that he was an oldish man, perhaps about sixty, small and grizzled. David said,' The Queen is making changes. The Perdana Binte Mingora will make more, when she becomes queen. Meantime, we are here to protect you.'

The old man said again, 'They are many, tuan.'

John Allen cut in, 'The more the merrier. We can give them such a bloody nose that they'll remember it for a generation.'

David said, 'The Westerners are important, but it wouldn't help to gain their support at the expense of turning the loyalty of the Easterners into hatred.'

John Allen said, 'We won't, sir. That's why they want *us* to do the job, not the Constabulary. They can say afterwards that it was all our idea. I don't mind. It won't be any skin off our noses. We won't be here by then. And it certainly ought to be done by someone.'

David said to the old man, 'You have lost a Moirangi, too?'

The other said, 'My elder brother, tuan. The most loyal to the Royal House of any of us. A leader – *the* leader – of our community. The balance wheel against all evil or ill-considered counsel.'

David thought at once of the Indian Mutiny – another, earlier turning point in the relations between Britain and India. The refrain of the leaders of the mutineers in those far off days had been, *kill the best officers first* – not necessarily the best soldiers, but those best loved by the sepoys.

It was the same here. This murder was the work of the MPRP, the victim carefully chosen to deprive the community of its leaders at the critical moment. Perhaps the drowning of the youth had also been deliberate, though on balance that was probably an ill chance, quickly and efficiently taken advantage of. If there were heavy bloodshed tomorrow – if either the Moirangis felt they had been left without protection, or the Lepetis felt they had been massacred – the winner would not be the army but Sujak and the MPRP. Yet, the governor wanted strong action to frighten his people into passivity, the superintendent wanted strong action, John Allen was thirsting for it, the ground was perfectly suited for it. And his civilian overlord, the Resident, had ordered him to make an opportunity to use it.

He said, 'Wait here a minute, please.' He went out, crossed the road, and stood by the river. He heard bare feet close and knew that the old man had sent someone to watch over him, in case an over-zealous guard pounced on him. He wiped that distraction from his mind. The river made tiny lapping sounds at the foot of the bank below him; behind he heard the muted sounds of the Moirangi quarter. A light shone yellow across the water, and below it an unseen person was filling a bucket from the river. Gradually he cleared all these messages from his senses out of his mind.

The facts of geography and politics he understood. The threat from the MPRP he understood. But the fact of emotion here, the emotion of the people, was something different: they were nervous and unsure, needing leadership. The arrested MPRP members had been trying to provide that leadership – march, fight, destroy – with the aim of causing a massacre in the Moirangi community here. Such a massacre would have tremendous repercussions in all the western provinces, where in less than a month, Sujak would arrive at the head of several hundred armed men, relying on local support. The Lepetis had not followed the agitators' original goadings – attack at night, when massacre would have been certain; but they were going to come by day, when, at best, the outcome would be a matter of chance, and the smallest incident could create tragedy. And there were certainly men and women here ready, trained, and eager to cause such an incident, as the murder of the old man's brother showed. What should he do?

'Leadership,' he said aloud; then, to himself, 'don't say, don't do it – they won't obey; say, do this instead: *follow me*. Follow me . . . yes, but where to, what for?'

An idea came to him. He stayed a few moments longer and then walked back across the road. To the old man he said, 'To-morrow there will be a funeral procession for the Lepeti youth and for your brother. They will be buried side by side in the cemetery, which is to the west of here, I know. At ten o'clock tomorrow morning remove this barricade, and the one leading out towards the cemetery. Soon after that, British soldiers will arrive to line the road, to do honour to the dead. There will be a procession. When the Lepeti people have passed with the body of the youth, let all your people follow on with the body of your brother.'

After a time the old man said slowly, 'It might work . . .'

'If it doesn't, we can say we have tried,' David said.

John Allen said, 'My men are going to be in the worst possible situation if anything happens, spread along the road, too close to the crowd to use their weapons effectively before they can be rushed.'

David said, 'I don't think anything is going to happen.' Again, to himself, he added, 'except to me, when the Resident hears about this.'

The superintendent said dubiously, 'My constables would be able to help somewhat there . . . though they are not armed or trained for this sort of work.'

David said, 'Your men – all of them – will be providing a guard of honour for the bodies.'

'But, tuan . . .'

David said, 'What has been lacking here is trust. Tomorrow we're going to show the people we trust them.'

'There'll be MPRP agitators there,' John Allen said, 'They're not going to respond to trust.'

David said, 'What we want to achieve is that the agitators are jumped on not by us, but by the people themselves. I'm going to have something to eat now. I'll give out orders at the Rest House at . . .' he peered at the luminous dial of his watch '. . . eleven p.m.'

David waited impatiently. It was nine o'clock and he had had his breakfast, but the staff car had not yet arrived. The Fusiliers' vehicles, Allen had told him, had arrived at five a.m., and the men were getting dressed now. But here he was, still in jungle dress, and . . .

He heard a car engine and went out on the verandah, then frowned, for it was not his staff car but a Land-Rover. Lieutenant

Crawford jumped down and ran up the steps. 'I only heard at midnight that you'd arrived, sir,' he said. 'I thought I'd better come over in case you wanted me.'

David grunted. Where the hell was that staff car? Crawford was looking hurt. He pulled himself together: 'How are you getting on?'

Crawford looked around, then spoke with lowered voice: 'The general intelligence set-up is good, sir, and the local head has got men who are operating inside Burma and Thailand. But he can't get anyone to actually go and find the camp of the Freedom Fighters. It would be suicide, the agents say, and he agrees.'

David was about to speak, when he heard another car. But this was a blue Land-Rover. Kumara stepped out and came up the steps. She said, 'Good morning, brigadier. You're looking anxious.'

'I'm waiting for something.'

'I've come from Moirang,' she said. She looked him seriously in the eye. 'They are very perturbed there, as to what will happen here.'

'Have you seen the governor?' he asked.

She shook her head. 'I thought I'd speak to you first. I know he has declared martial law in the province, so you're now the responsible authority.'

'I am,' he said, 'and no one can relieve me of that responsibility, unless they have power to remove me from my command.'

'You are thinking of Mr Wilson,' she said, 'who does not have such power.'

He did not answer. She was looking at him in a way he had not seen since London – a look direct but open, no longer reserved.

She said, 'Can you tell me what you propose to do? I passed many groups gathering as though for a procession.'

He said, 'Well . . .' The staff car turned into the drive. David said, 'Look, when I'm dressed, will you come with me?'

'Yes,' she said.

'Do you have formal clothes here suitable for a funeral?'

'Yes.'

'Get into them at once, please.'

A soldier ran up the steps with a suitcase and a long bundle wrapped in cloth and David said, 'At last! What happened?'

'Had to replace the fan belt, sir, and mend a leak in the radiator,' the young Gurkha said.

David nodded, took the bundle and hurried into his room.

Half an hour later he stepped out in No. 3 Dress, white, with scarlet waist sash, the sword in its dress scabbard hanging in the black leather slings of a Rifles officer, his five medals clanking on his left breast. Kumara was eating a mango in the dining-room. She stood up. She was wearing a white dress trimmed with the royal Mingoran blue, her shoulders bare, her feet in high-heeled silver sandals, her hair piled up, oil sheened, and afire with scattered diamonds. The Jumbhorn Ruby glowed at the cleavage of her breasts. David's heart jumped. She still had the direct, open look, her armour set aside. Finally she bowed her head and held out her hand. He led her to the staff car, and helped her in. At the river bridge the adjutant of the Fusiliers was waiting. 'Everything ready, sir. They'll be here in . . . four minutes.' He saluted, and hurried away.

A band struck up from the scattered huts where the Fusiliers had been bivouacked the evening before. Kumara looked inquiringly at David, who said, 'I sent for the Fusiliers' band, and No. 3 Dress for the two companies up here. We're not going to fight a battle but take part in a ceremony . . . and the Fusiliers are damned good at that.'

The music of 'The British Grenadiers' rolled across the paddy. The drum major swung into sight down the road to the south, his ornate staff rising and falling across his chest. Ranks of white-clad bandsmen followed in the measured swing of heavy infantry, the big drum thudding, the side drums rattling.

David said, 'One company's following the band. They'll lead the procession, and the Constabulary will bring up the rear. The other Fusilier company is marching by back ways to line the streets near and through the Moirangi quarter.'

'Are they all in white, too?'

'Yes. The governor's had men out since dawn announcing that there will be a funeral procession starting from the square down there at ten.'

She looked at him a long time. Finally she said softly 'Dylan, there was something I wanted to tell you in London, but didn't, because it was going to be so short a time, and we'd never meet again. Then you came here, and I couldn't tell you, because you were going to be the instrument to destroy us. Now I must say it. I love you.'

David said, 'I know. I've tried a hundred ways to tell myself it can't be true . . . but I've always known.'

'And you love me.'

'Yes.'

'What are we going to do, Dylan? Oh God, what *can* we do?'

'Get through today,' he said. He wanted to touch her, but if he did, he'd kiss her, hug her, make love, even. He dared not start, yet, what could not be controlled.

They got back into the staff car and headed down the crowded road towards the pagoda and the centre of the city. People were listening to the approaching thud of the drums and the swinging rhythm of the music, beginning to swirl along westward, like leaves in the eddies at the sides of a river. At the square two or three thousand people were already gathered, and in the background, in three ranks, a hundred men of the Royal Mingoran Constabulary, also in their full dress, which meant simply that they wore blue trousers instead of khaki, and their caps were blue instead of black.

The band approached. The governor was there, surrounded by his staff, sweating visibly with anxiety. To one side, by the river, the corpse of the drowned youth lay on a light bier, eight men stripped to the waist ready to carry it on their shoulders. The body was wrapped in a blue winding sheet, firmly tied down by thin white cords to the bier.

The band appeared, the crowd slowly making way for it. The drum major twirled his staff and the band halted. The big drummer was six feet five inches tall and his leopard skin towered above the heads of the small side drummers on either side of him. John Allen halted with the company behind.

Kumara went slowly forward. The governor prostrated himself on the ground, put his hands to her feet, then rose and followed her. She gestured slightly to the men at the bier, and they lifted it up. Behind it stood a man and a woman in middle age, dressed in the white of ceremonial mourning. The princess took her place between them.

This was the moment, David thought, waiting tensely. If an MPRP agent in this crowd did the right thing now . . . when all was taut, everyone was ready, but the actual final movement had not yet begun, the crowd not yet hypnotized by the music into a sort of processional discipline, sandwiched between the soldiers in front and the Constables behind . . .

A shot exploded close to his left. At Kumara's side the dead youth's mother spun round, crying out, her hand clasped to her side. Kumara was unhurt, her arm round the woman's waist, helping her. To the left, where the shot had been fired, there was commotion, a rising and falling of arms. David waved his hand energetically at the drum major. With a barked command the big drum began the heavy thud of a slow march. A few beats later the trumpets wailed into the 'Dead March'. David began to run to Kumara's side, but at once broke into a walk: no one should run now, least of all himself. When he reached the bier he saw that the woman was bleeding from the side. Kumara was holding her upright, and whispering fiercely in her ear in Mingora-Malay, 'Just a few paces more . . . a few steps!'

'I can go on, *tuankana*,' the other muttered.

David could not see whether the woman had suffered a flesh wound or something more serious. Blood stained her side and Kumara's dress. The governor, immediately behind, shouted to him above the sound of the band, 'The crowd held the man who fired. A constable's guarding him.'

David nodded. Good. More information . . .

Minutes passed. Looking over his shoulder he saw that behind the company of Fusiliers thronged an immense silent crowd, swaying onwards almost in step with the slow pace of the infantry. The white bier rose and fell ahead of him, behind the band. The dead youth's mother, wounded by a shot obviously meant for Kumara, was grey under the coffee-coloured pigmentation of her skin, but walked on. Kumara's face was stern but even more lovely in its severity of line.

They came to the place where the Moirangi barricade had blocked the road. There were the ruins of it, pulled to the sides, and the thin lines of white-clad Fusiliers, arms at the present, red and white full dress hackles in place above the cap badges.

Kumara said, 'The danger's over now. We must get this woman to hospital.'

But the woman, as though she had understood, said, 'I am all right. I will stay with you, *tuankana*, and my husband and son.'

The old Moirangi was waiting at the side of the road, and David muttered, 'The brother of the man who was murdered.'

Kumara said, 'I know him. He's a widower . . . Join us, friend.'
She held out her free hand.

The old man stepped forward. A second bier was carried out
of a side street and took its place beside the other. The band,
which had been marking time, moved forward again. Moirangis
began to emerge from the side streets like people groping to
light from imprisonment. David heaved a long slow sigh, took
off one black glove, found his handkerchief in his sleeve and
mopped his brow and face with it.

Kumara glanced across at him and said in her own language,
'My lord!'

The old Moirangi and the middle aged couple looked up in
astonishment, stared a moment at their princess's radiant, exposed
love, then looked down, foot following foot through the red dust.

All about the square in the centre of Lepet cooking fires burned
under great black pots. The smells of coconut oil and baking
fish and roasting meat drifted among the aimlessly moving throng,
mingled with the sharp tang of fresh cut fruit. The band of the
Royal Oxford Fusiliers was seated on rows of benches against
the shops on one side, playing a medley from *The Merry Widow*.
Other British soldiers, by now in jungle green uniforms, wandered
among the crowd, buying from stalls, and exclaiming over the
strange food they had bought – octopus, snails, queer-looking fish.
The noise – of the band, of three thousand people talking, of
singing and the beat of Mingoran drums from the city all around
– was thick enough to cut with a parang. David sat on Kumara's
right hand, the governor on her left. An endless stream of men
and women came before them where they sat behind a long low
table, to bow, smile, touch hands, and drift back into the crowd.
One group of five men came together, and Kumara said – 'These
are the principal men of Ban Khao, where we shot the man-
eater.'

The governor exclaimed, 'The criminal village in Moirang!'

Kumara said coldly, 'The village is no longer outlawed. These
people are our subjects, and friends.' To David she said, 'They
came over by bus after they heard what happened this morning.'

She spoke quickly to the five men, gesturing towards David
as she did.

'I have told them that you saved many Moirangi lives today. They ask what they can do for you.'

'Nothing, thank them,' David said automatically, smiling at the men: then an idea flashed into his mind and he said, 'Wait!' Ban Khao was full of men and women who had lived for generations by robbery, murder, smuggling, banditry. They had been able to travel anywhere, at will, through their adeptness at concealment and disguise.

He said, 'I'd like to speak to them, alone, please.'

'They don't speak English,' Kumara began, but David interrupted – 'I think they'll understand me, though I might not get everything they say – but Crawford's here, and he can interpret for me.'

Five minutes later, in a room at the back of a store, the five men from Ban Khao were squatting in a half circle on the earth floor, their lined brown faces impassive. David and Peter Crawford sat with crossed legs facing them.

David said to his Intelligence Officer, 'Tell them, under oath of secrecy, that we have a military Intelligence organization in the northern part of Moirang.'

A few moments later the young subaltern said, grinning – 'They say they know that, sir. They say they know who our agents are, and do we want any of them killed.'

David said, 'Explain to them about the Freedom Fighters in Thailand, and tell them I want to know everything about those people.'

Later, Crawford said, 'They say it will be dangerous, but for your sake and the Perdana Binte Mingora's, they will arrange it.'

David said, 'I must have full and accurate information by the fifteenth of this month.'

'They ask, what of the families of any who are killed in this task.'

David considered a moment, and said, 'They will become wards of the royal family.'

'They are content.'

'Good. Make sure they have contacts in Moirang City, so that urgent information can be phoned or telegraphed to us at any hour of the day or night.'

After more rapid talk between Crawford and the Moirangis, they all returned to the open air. The Moirangis bowed low before

Kumara, and disappeared into the crowd. She said to David, 'I don't know what you want of them – but they will not fail. Come, I'm hungry. They have Siamese delicacies here in Lepet you won't see anywhere else in the country . . . Where's Colonel Allen? Wasn't he supposed to be here with us?'

'I expect he's busy seeing his men are being properly looked after,' David said. 'He's a very conscientious officer.' But, privately, he thought John Allen is avoiding me; he thinks I took the easy way out this morning, merely laying up trouble later for all of them; that I have no moral courage.

Girls brought plates of spiced rice and shrimp soup with a tang of chili and garlic, and heady wines in halved coconuts. The Fusilier band marched out and away to the thumping rhythm of 'Men of Harlech'. Gamelan bands appeared from the side streets, and the crowd coagulated round a group of dancers, faces and bare arms painted dead white, who began to sway and twist directly in front of their table. Kumara leaned towards him, a tidbit in her fingers and held it up to put into his mouth. She said, 'It's a piece of lobster, cooked in wine and spices . . .' She looked into his eyes, putting the piece of lobster between his lips . . . 'and this is how a Mingoran woman feeds the lord of her soul.' David took the lobster on to his tongue and began to eat it. The gamelan dancers seemed to be bent over them, frozen in hieratic poses, like priests blessing a wedding.

The moon, two days old, was a thin orange crescent above the palms. The lights began to go out in the houses, and the un-countable comings and goings of the earlier part of the evening gradually concentrated into the slim bodies and gesturing legs and arms of the dancers. They danced for half an hour, and after a pause, for another half hour. Then Kumara said, 'I'm tired . . . They'll be going on all night.'

'I'll take you back,' he said.

As they crossed the square towards David's car, parked on the river bank, the people bowed, smiling. John Allen, accompanied by his adjutant, appeared from the direction of the main road bridge. He saluted and said perfunctorily, 'Sorry I couldn't make the feast, sir . . . and *tuankana*. There was a lot to do. You still think it's necessary to send a company over to Moirang for a week, sir?'

'Yes. I want the recruits to see some real soldiers.'

'Very well, sir. The rest of us will move off at 0600, by rail.'

'Good.'

'One thing, sir. Has a date been fixed yet for the trial of Captain Whitmore?'

'No,' David said shortly. 'I've spoken about it twice to the Chief Minister and he says two judges are sick and the courts are overloaded.'

'It's hard on Whitmore, sir.'

'I know. Good night.'

He helped Kumara into the staff car and climbed into the driver's seat. Wood and Tulbahadur had been dismissed long since. His escort Land-Rover started up its engine. David drove carefully through the deserted streets. To run over a careless or drunken pedestrian now would undo much of the good that had been accomplished.

At the top of the steps leading up to the Rest House verandah, after the escort had dismissed, Kumara put out both hands to him. He took them, realizing that she was signalling with her hands: stay at that distance, come no closer. She said, 'Not here, Dylan. We've waited so long, we can wait for perfection . . . Will you stay here a few days, with me? I want to show you Mingora – *our* Mingora.'

David said, 'I can stay two . . . three days. I must be back in Trangloek on the sixth.'

She bent slowly, and kissed his hands, first one, then the other. She whispered, 'This has been the happiest day of my life.' She turned and ran into the black silence of the building.

David stood, staring into the darkness that had swallowed her, then at his hands. The slow beating of his heart became heavier, not faster, but a steady heavy pounding, till his temples throbbed in rhythm to it.

Tulbahadur awakened him with a knock on the door. David looked at his watch and called, 'It's only seven o'clock. I wanted to be called at eight.'

'*Resident sahib ayako chha*,' the voice answered, '*Salaam bhanccha.*'

David sat up and ran a hand through his thin hair. A moment ago he had been dreaming of Kumara, her large dark eyes looking seriously into his, the imprint of her lips warm on his hand. He shook his head, shaking the vision away; the image of Sidney Wilson replaced Kumara's. He called, '*Das minute ma aunla*.'

'*Hunchha, hazur.*'

He washed perfunctorily, shaved, dressed and went out. The Resident was pacing up and down the verandah. David saluted carefully as he wheeled round and snapped, 'What happened yesterday?'

David said, 'We were able to convert the procession into a ceremonial funeral. Both Lepetis and Moirangis took part.'

'There was no bloodshed?'

'One man who tried to assassinate the Daughter-in-Line was badly beaten up, but they think he'll survive. He wounded the dead youth's mother, but not seriously.'

The Resident said, 'I explained to you, before you left Trangloek, why it was essential to take strong action here. I ordered you to take such action.'

David said, 'The governor had declared martial law by the time we got here. I was responsible. I took the action that seemed best to me.'

'In the interest of whom?' the Resident said coldly.

'Everyone.'

'Everyone except Her Majesty's Government – of which you are a servant. I told you that the malcontents here must be given memories, examples, which will make them hesitate a long time before taking any hostile action again.'

Perhaps, David thought; it was also possible that the Resident wanted the people of Lepet and Moirang to have a recent example of British military brutality before them when they went to the polls in two weeks' time, to give their opinion of the British connection.

The Resident said, 'I also think your action – or lack of it – has been harmful to the government of Mingora. I am dissatisfied with the weakness you have shown here.'

'I'm sorry,' David said.

'I shall report the facts, and my opinion, to the Commissioner General.'

David said nothing. The morning sun shone on dewy grass. Clouds were already building in the high blue, and there was a damp heat in the air that made his shirt sticky against his back.

Kumara came out on the verandah with a cheerful, 'Good morning, Sidney.'

'Good morning, Kumara. I've come to take you back to Trangloek. I heard you were . . .'

'That's very kind of you, but I'm staying here for another day or two.'

Wilson turned to David. 'You're returning to Trangloek, aren't you?'

David said, 'Not just yet. I want to inspect the recruit base at Moirang, and check some bridge guards and have a general look round these two northern provinces.'

Kumara said, 'I'm going to have breakfast. It's ready.' She turned into the building.

The Resident said, 'Let's take a bit of fresh air.' He walked down the steps and on to the gravelled drive, David following. The Resident seemed to be searching for words. After a while he said, 'Sally didn't come up?'

'Not that I know of,' David said.

'So you'll be alone here with Kumara. I'm not sure that's a good idea . . . nothing personal . . . people might talk . . .'

David realized that Wilson was nearly bursting with an emotion held back by a will that was itself on the point of breaking. The muscles at the side of his jaw were like knots, and his knuckles white. There was only one explanation. Insane jealousy, and that based on infatuation.

He said formally, 'I'm afraid I can't help that, sir. I have a job to do. And there's nothing for people to talk about.'

Wilson swung round and headed back for the bungalow. 'I'll speak to the princess . . . privately. She doesn't realize how much harm this sort of thing can do.'

'Very well, sir,' David said. At the top of the steps he turned along the verandah and went to his room. The sound of a man's voice, urgent, but too low to make out the words, trembled in the wooden walls and susurrated in the curtains. Ten minutes later the Resident's car shot furiously out of the drive, the wheels grating on the gravel, the tyres screeching at the curve where the drive entered the road.

David went to the dining room. Kumara looked up: 'Eggs and bacon?'

Fourteen

D YLAN? ARE YOU ready?'
'Coming,' he answered, watching Tulbahadur fasten the last strap on his valise. He went out on to the verandah. She looked cool in pale green, though it was eleven o'clock on a hot morning, the sun behind cloud but a universal heat oppressing the low-roofed bungalow and the dense green lawn.

'Time to go,' she said.

'I suppose so . . . I wish we could stay here for another week.'

'Is that all?' she said, smiling.

Her Land-Rover was waiting beside his at the bottom of the steps, Tulbahadur stowing his valise. The Gurkhas of the escort waited beside the other Land-Rover five yards behind. David had sent the Command Set Radio car to Moirang with C Company of the Fusiliers.

David said, 'Didn't I hear a motor cycle come in just now?'

Kumara said, 'It was from the Resident, with a message for me . . . Would you like to drive?'

He nodded and climbed into the driver's seat of the Land-Rover. This car had been their daylight home for the past two days, always alone, except for the following escort, which he had insisted on. She had shown him the byways of her country, the inner life of the people, as no amount of personal observation could have revealed. They had talked little of politics or the forthcoming problems of Mingora's independence, much of flowers and fish, of animals and crops and burials. They had attended a wedding in a village of the border hills, and for an hour watched the work of a check post at a big road bridge close to the Thai line. In the evenings she had played the gamelan and sung Mingoran songs, the two of them on the verandah, the young moon hung like a decoration over the city below. And at night she had held his hands, bowed to kiss them, and said, 'Not yet, Dylan.'

The little convoy rolled off. David suppressed a sigh. The laterite road stretched southward under the high sun to Trangloek, Flagstaff House, and routine.

Near three o'clock, having stopped for a light lunch with the governor of Machin, they were within five miles of Trangloek.

'Turn in here,' Kumara said.

David said, 'The road to the Royal Beach?'

'Yes.'

'Do you want to have a swim?'

'Yes . . . but later. Stop here, Dylan.'

He braked to a stop and followed her to the ground. She said, 'I want to show you Jumbhorn Wat. Let the escort wait here.'

Once, returning to Malaya from a leave taken in Japan, David had stopped off in Cambodia, and visited Angkor Wat. The memory of the great temple surrounded by its wide moat, and the ruins of the city, struggling like an animal in the coils of a python to escape the stranglehold of the jungle, was still vivid in his mind.

Angkor was always full of life and the movement of monks and visitors. Here only the creepers slithered along the ground and clambered up through broken windows, and only the thick green of the jungle relieved the black of the walls.

Kumara led down a long cloister, the regularly spaced pillars on the outside casting shadows like marching automata against the wall on the inside. The wall was carved with ethereally beautiful figures of girls, bare-breasted, winging like birds up and across the expanse of stone. Here and there grass and small red flowers grew in the cracks of the masonry.

'This is what our Khmer ancestors made when they came here from the north,' Kumara said.

What would England leave, after a hundred and fifty years, David thought? The Mingora Club and the M & O Building, shrines to their goals, Commerce and Trade? The appallingly ugly church, a neo-Gothic horror translated by Victorian muscular Christianity from Clapham to the gate of the old Portuguese Fort?

'The Khmers left us two other things,' Kumara said. 'Their name. And their vision of beauty. Everything else they did or made is forgotten here . . . but we see with their eyes, still.'

On the wall, in low relief, a dozen mighty demons pulled at a huge pole, a dozen angel-like figures pulled in the opposite direction. David at once recognized the theme of the Churning of the Milky Ocean from Angkor Wat, also built by the Khmers. Like everything else here, this version was smaller and more weathered, but still powerful – the unresolved conflict between Good and Evil; unresolved because the Khmer universe was not under the sway of an all-powerful all-good God, but at the mercy of the forces of Good and Evil, which struggled perpetually for the mastery . . . and the outcome depended not on the whim of a Being above, but on the decision of each man, as to which side he joined, or whether he sat like the spectators and waited for others to write his fate.

Kumara stopped and he stopped beside her. She leaned her head on his shoulder without a word. They stood beside a square pool at the farther end of the Wat. The stonework of the rim had broken down but the pool retained its form, and it was full of water to within six inches of the rim. The water was clear, lotus flowers floated pink and white on it, and in it were reflected to one side the tower that finished the long line of a wall, ahead, the massed ranks of the trees that had advanced to the lip of the pool, and, over all, the cloud masses drifting across the blue sky.

She turned her face up to him and they kissed, long and gently. Then, her hand in his, they went slowly back, through the deserted squares, along the empty cloisters, past the silently warring bas-reliefs, to the cars.

'Now to the beach,' she said.

David did not argue, but did as he was bidden. At the beach house the old couple seemed to be waiting, but Kumara only nodded to them and walked past into the grove of giant palms on the path that led to the landing stage on Dhaphut Sap. At the lake shore David blinked in astonishment – the big canoe-like barge was waiting, the crew in their places, the steersman in the stern, the sun gleaming on their oiled torsos.

'Get in,' she said, 'The escort too.'

He paused: 'They can wait here till we . . .'

'We aren't coming back . . . not tonight,' she said.

'But, Kumara ...'

'They are not expecting you in Trangloek. Your Brigade Major knows where you are – but there will be no emergency.'

He got into the boat. Kumara followed and then the four Gurkhas, impassive as though embarking on ornate royal barges was part of their daily routine. The steersman called a long, singing order and the boat moved out on to the lake.

She said, lying back on the cushions beside him – 'Look at the sky, Dylan ... the colours ... they are angry seeming, but it is not real anger, it is the promise of the monsoon ... It is always like this, in the middle of May.' She trailed her hand over the low side, the ripple fading in the bubbled wake. David thought he ought to say something, ask something – but why, what? He had done his job and now he was in her hands. Until some dim time in the future, that was hidden from him by the night to come, he held no responsibility for anything. All had been sloughed off him as though by a ceremonial exorcism – he was not a brigadier, not a Welshman, nor young nor old, just a being floating without effort across the sunlit water, green and silky.

At the royal island, Pulo Pattan, as she started up the aisle of poinsettias he said, 'Where are the Gurkhas sleeping?'

'The boatmen are taking care of them,' she said, 'There are large quarters for servants and guards behind the house, you know.'

She opened a door, and said, 'This is yours.' The room was airy, the walls of finely split cane, the floor of the same, covered with brightly coloured mats, a lamp set on a low table, the bed low and furnished with only one sheet and a pillow, and a mosquito net hung from the palm beams above. A Mingoran royal servant stood, arms folded, bowing, at one side of the room. Kumara said, 'I'm going to have a shower and then ... will you join me on the front verandah in – three-quarters of an hour?'

Again, as she had at the Lepet Rest House, she seemed to vanish into the shadows, but he heard her light footsteps and the creaking of the cane floor as she went on down the passage. He dropped the screen over the door – like the walls, it was a thing of fine-cut cane – and stretched luxuriously. The servant was at his feet, beginning to unfasten his shoes. He wondered where Tulbahadur was and what he was doing, out there in the village of palm roofs he could see through the hibiscus. It was like Kew

Gardens out there – beds of dark red cannas, pink oleander bushes, allamanders, the hibiscus white and pink and red, frangipani trees, purple morning glory, and, thick outside the window, deep violet bougainvillea.

The servant was murmuring, 'How hot does the tuan want the water?' He began to undress.

Later, as he walked towards the front verandah, he heard music. For a moment he didn't recognize it, and then it came to him – it was *Y Bwthyn Yn y Cwm*, 'The cottage in the valley', an original composition that had won a prize at the Eisteddfod. It was a lovely tune, being played now on a piano. He quickened his pace as a tenor began to sing over the piano.

She was alone on the verandah, standing over a wind-up gramophone on a table.

She turned, and smiled: 'Did you think I'd invited another man here? You looked jealous.'

'I would have been,' David said. She sank into a chair beside the table. David sat on the edge of the table, listening till the end of the tune. Then he found a record of the Preludes, wound up the machine, and put it on.

'You taught me to like Chopin,' Kumara said. 'And some Welsh. And other things.'

David looked at her, half listening to the trills of the piano, half to the wind in the palms. 'Such as what?' he said.

'What honesty means ... absolute honesty ... Despair.'

'Despair?'

'I told you. At Lepet. There seemed to be no hope.'

David said, 'Is it any different now?'

She said, 'This time, when it came back stronger than ever, I knew that nothing else mattered ... I want a child of yours, Dylan.'

He said, 'I thought you couldn't have one any more.'

'Oh, those operations I had in London. They thought I had cancer of the stomach, but I didn't. It was peritonitis – nothing to do with my womb.'

The sun was low behind the big house, the light dull reddish-yellow on the lake and the distant palms of the sea beach. The pianist began another Prelude. Kumara seemed to think all would be plain sailing, now they knew what they wanted. But what of her position, obviously soon to be queen? What of his career? It was all too difficult to be faced just now, in this wonderful peace and beauty.

He said, 'All these people don't live here all the time, do they?'

'There is a telephone from Lepet to Trangloek,' she said with a faint smile.

She must have made these plans yesterday or the day before. What would she have done if urgent military business had come up? Or heard that the C-in-C was coming on a flying visit? Her stars must have told her that nothing would happen; or if it did, that she would find a way to deal with it.

She said, 'There was a message from the Resident.'

He started, for she might have been reading his thoughts: 'For me?'

She nodded: 'That dispatch rider who arrived at Lepet just before we left... There was a message for me, as I told you, but there was also one for you. Mr Wilson said he wanted you in Lepet at four p.m. for an important conference. He said a representative of the Commissioner General was coming to Trangloek. I tore it up.'

'Good God!' David exclaimed, 'they'll court martial me.'

'I don't think so. Mr Wilson gave the impression that the Commissioner General's representative was coming for this conference ...but I know he's not coming till next week. Mr Wilson wanted you back.'

'And you too.'

She said, 'No. He apologized for what he had said before, and hoped I would continue the work I was doing in Lepet and Moirang. Are you sorry I tore up the message for you?'

David said, 'No. There'll be some unpleasantness, but I think that's going to come anyway. The only thing I shall be sorry for is if he gets angry enough to have me replaced. But he doesn't seem to want to do that.' He added suddenly, 'Did you bring *him* here, too?'

The music stopped, the needle grated on the record. She looked at him sadly as he turned over the record, wound up the machine, and lowered the tone arm. He felt cold, not angry, but determined.

She said, 'Here – no. Everything with him was ... dynastic, political ... for the good of my country and family, not for me. Thousands of women have done as much ... more ... No, no, don't ask me whether I was his lover. When he arrived I already

209

knew I was more in love with you than ever. And saw even less hope. I went out for Sidney, partly because he is what he is, partly to get you out of my mind. I never dreamed what would happen . . . that Sidney would become infatuated with me.'

'He certainly is infatuated,' David said. 'I can't blame him.'

She said, 'It's worse than you – than anyone else – imagines. He asked me to record Mingoran poetry – so that he could appreciate the beauty of the language, and perfect his accent, he said. It was all love poetry that he chose. He tells me that he plays the tapes over and over to himself, late at night.'

'So that's what Lady Anne hears!' David exclaimed, 'She thinks it's you in there. And after all this, have you done any good for Mingora?'

'I don't know. We have spent hours talking together, in the Residency late at night, in the Palace, in Forest Rest Houses, on drives through the provinces. I know him now, I think. I have convinced him that the British government's policy is wrong, but he will not – cannot – press his views on Whitehall, because it would count against him. He'd never become Permanent Under Secretary. He's been sent out to do an unpleasant job and they're not going to like it if he backs away from it.'

'The poor bugger must be ready to explode,' David said.

'He is,' Kumara said quickly. 'I dare not think what it's doing to him, inside . . . And now, I have shown him that it's you I love.'

He walked the length of the verandah and came back. 'Did you tell Sally that I was her responsibility while you took on the Resident?'

She said, 'Sally did that on her own. No one told her to. I thought she was being foolish, and . . .'

'But me, much more foolish. A half-bald old fool being twisted round the finger of a girl. A figure out of the cartoons. You must all have had a good laugh.'

Kumara said patiently, 'You are trying to make yourself angry, because you are jealous of Sidney. Dylan, dearest, I have been ravingly jealous of my own daughter for the past five months. Have you been her lover? I could scratch her eyes out!'

The record ended and she jumped up, took off the tone arm and said, 'Come!' He walked at her side down the avenue of poinsettias to the water's edge and turned right. The sun was a red ball sinking into the lake shore to the west, its lower edge serrated by the outline of mangroves and taller trees. From the east he detected a heavy grumbling beat and under it the long hiss of dragged sand on miles of the outer beach. 'The sea's rising,' Kumara said.

They were in a small cove, the sand glowing through the translucent water, cloud shadow upon them and the tall trees curved round them like an arm.

She said, 'Let's swim.'

Her hands reached round behind her neck, she moved her body and the dress fell off her. She was wearing no brassiere and only the skimpiest of bikini underpants. She stepped out of her sandals and the underpants, and stood, waiting. David felt as clumsy as a bull buffalo as he struggled out of shoes and socks, shirt and slacks. Her body was straight like a boy's except for the small firm breasts and their big dark areolas, and the neat black triangle between her thighs. He had waited a long time – years, he now acknowledged – for this moment, and expected a sexual arousing in him, that he would present himself at last naked to her, and priapic; but there was nothing – yet. He felt that she had not willed him to sexuality – yet. She walked into the water, holding her hand out to him. 'It's brackish ... but there are no sharks.'

They swam silently side by side for a while, then she turned on her back and said, 'Hold me ... as though you were rescuing me ... There.'

They swam together, coupled now by his hands under her armpits, their bodies touching from chest to groin, legs kicking lazily. Again, he waited for the arousal of his physical desire, but nothing happened. She whispered over her shoulder, 'Hold my breasts.'

He did as she asked, saying nothing. She said, a little later, 'You are a good life saver. I was nearly ready to kill myself, like poor Lady Anne.'

'You know?' he said in surprise.

'She told me. And that you rescued her. Since you came to Mingora I have often dreamed of you rescuing me. I need it.'

She released herself and swam towards the little cove. In the shallows she began walking. She said, 'I have had no man for eighteen years. It is not sex that I miss, though I do ... but love.

I admired my husband, who was chosen for me – but did not love him. I have loved no one . . . till now.'

'What can we be to each other?' he said harshly, 'You will be the queen. I am a foreign soldier. I love you, but all we can be is playmates, for a few days, a few hours.'

'My God, Dylan,' she whispered, 'You don't know what you're saying, whom you're talking to. I've suffered tortures for six months and now I know the truth. You are everything to me. I don't care what happens to Mingora. Just look at me like a husband and lover. Love me. Take me.'

David bent slowly, kissed her, and carried her up the beach.

Fifteen

DAVID WATCHED THE play of expressions crossing John Allen's face as he read the report – a frown, a tightening of the lips, a flush, a whiteness at the jaw. He put the paper down and looked up.

'Initial it, please,' David said.

'I don't think that's a fair report,' Allen began.

David said, 'You're not initialling it as agreeing with it, but as having seen it.'

Allen looked for a pen and David handed him a ballpoint. It had been the devil of a report to word so that it accurately reflected his opinion of John Allen's fitness for promotion. If the question had been 'Fit to command an infantry brigade in war?', he would unhesitatingly have written 'Yes'. But above his present rank Allen would have to spend more than half his time in rear headquarters staff appointments, and he was not staff college trained. Even that would not have mattered if he had the temperament to realize his shortcomings, and use the technicians, instead of despising them, and showing it. Above all, it seemed to David that his inability to grasp the large picture and understand how his own command fitted into it was not merely the fierce regimental pride that a battalion commander needed, but a failing of character which he would carry with him to higher places – if he were allowed to reach them.

'I want to appeal against this report, sir,' Allen said.

David nodded. 'Right. I'll forward that request with the report to the C-in-C. He may ask for your appeal in writing, but he'll probably call you for an interview.'

Allen stood up, his freckled face still pale beneath the reddish tinge. 'Anything new on Whitmore's trial, sir?'

213

'No,' David said. 'Please, John, realize that the very reason we are allowing Whitmore to go to civil trial prevents us putting too much pressure on the Mingorans.'

Allen saluted without a word, swung round and strode out.

Stork Porter came in: 'That's all for the day, sir.'

David glanced at the clock. Half past five. He said, 'You got anything to do for the next hour? Let's go and see how the people are taking the result of the plebiscite. The last I heard the Queen was getting a ninety per cent majority.'

They drove down in the staff car, followed by the inevitable escort. They parked the vehicles near the docks, leaving Tulbahadur and the escort with them, and walked up into the old city. They were both in plain clothes, light-weight grey trousers and white shirts. From time to time rockets rose into the velvet sky, bursting in puffs of grey smoke. Huge bangs from deep in the alleys shook the houses and sent half-naked small boys running in search of the sound. In the more open places men and women were dragging out old boxes, cardboard cartons, all the debris of the streets, and lighting bonfires.

Porter said, 'They seem very happy.'

'I don't know quite why. We're still leaving on the 31st.'

'Most of us, sir. Some before that. A warning movement order came in just before we left the office.'

'What's it say?'

'The families start down to Taiping on 15 May, in RASC transport, as we already know. They've only got one company of three-tonners available, so we have to move one battalion at a time. The first one goes on the 24th . . .'

'Make that the Fusiliers,' David said.

'Right, sir. The three-tonners come back here and the next lot move on the 31st – that's all the rest less you yourself, the guard of honour for the independence ceremony and one twenty-five-pounder troop to fire the salutes.'

David nodded. If he ordered the Fusiliers to carry out training exercises en route they might not be too far away when he needed them. Even if they were, he would still have an adequate force in his hand. The problem would be to hold them here until the MPRP made their move.

The crowds grew thicker. They were gathered twenty deep, dense as flies outside the palace, where a large poster displayed the latest returns in English and Mingora-Malay.

'There's Sally,' Porter exclaimed, 'In that window ... taking pictures of the crowd.'

'I'm surprised there's enough light,' David said.

'She must be using a pretty fast film.'

The princess disappeared from the window as they went forward to look at the notice board. The voting booths had opened all over the country at five in the morning, and closed at noon. The votes had been counted on the spot in each hamlet and village, the results put on paper and sent by runner or bicyclist to the nearest market centre and thence by telegraph to provincial capitals. The figures had started to reach Trangloek soon after one in the afternoon.

Porter said, 'It's still about nine to one in favour of the British connection.'

'Who do you think the ten per cent anti are – Westerners?'

'I don't think so, sir. Not after what you did for the Moirangis in Lepet. I imagine it's the people who would benefit most immediately by our going – graduates from the university without jobs, some revolutionary sympathizers, socialists or communists who are hoping to run the government if they can overthrow the queendom and set up their own sort of bureaucracy.'

'So, very few, but some of the best educated people in the country. I suppose that's inevitable.'

'They didn't hear about what the Sultan of Johore said a few years ago when the Malayan politicians were pressing for immediate total independence. He said, 'What are we going to do for aircraft, pilots, ships, tanks? If the British leave tomorrow, someone else will come in the day after." '

'I remember ... the politicians were so cross they refused to attend the banquet he gave for them. Politicians don't like to deal in truth, but in what they can persuade the people is truth.'

'Yes, sir ... The Resident's not going to be pleased with the plebiscite result.'

'No, but he's been expecting it. There was no chance that a majority would vote against the Queen. Anything close to fifty-fifty would have counted as a defeat for her.'

They moved on, past the long façade of the palace, back towards the Old Pagoda. The crowds were as dense there, but quieter. Inside the temple the monks were blowing on their long

horns, endless notes that echoed and re-echoed and carried in their
deep tones a sort of mournful triumph. The light was fading fast
and the rockets now burst in explosions of sparks which drifted
slowly to earth as golden rain. Half an hour later they were
driving back along the windblown Esplanade towards their houses.

Thomas the butler bent over him where he was eating his
curried lamb and murmured, 'Telephone for you, sah.'

'Who is it?' David put another spoonful in his mouth. He
hated food that was supposed to be hot, to be cold.

'Tuankana Salimina, sah.'

David wiped his mouth with his napkin and got up. At the
telephone he said, 'Sally?'

'Oh, David, there's the most marvellous celebration going on
here. Food and champagne galore. Come along!'

David said, 'I'm sorry, Sally. I don't feel like anything more
exciting than going to bed. I'm not as young as I used to be,' he
added, hoping to remind her not only of the difference in their
ages, but of the fact that his years had perhaps taught him some
wisdom – at last.

'You'd come if my mother asked you, wouldn't you?' she said.
She sounded cross.

'No, I wouldn't,' he said, knowing that he was lying.

'We don't have to stay all night,' she said. 'We can slip away
. . . to the beach. A midnight swim.'

'I'm sorry, Sally. I really can't . . . Was that colour film you
were using?'

There was a silence, then in a strained voice, 'What do you
mean?'

'You were taking photos from the palace this evening, early.'

'And you saw me? Yes, that was colour. Anscochrome 200
and you can push it to 400 ASA as long as you tell them when
you send it in for processing. I do want to see you soon, David.'

'Come and watch the soccer match with me tomorrow afternoon. The Fusiliers' A Company against the University.'

'You don't feel safe with me except in a crowd now? Oh, all
right.'

'Four o'clock on the University *padang*.'

David returned slowly to the dining-room. A midnight swim

... he imagined Kumara's slender body, her hardened nipples catching the starlight ... not tonight, though: there would be a big sea running, for the winds had been blowing all day. When driving along the Esplanade this evening the waves were breaking high against the wall, and spray blowing across the roadway.

He ate another two mouthfuls of the lamb and rice, and added more mango chutney. Thomas bent at his ear: 'Lieutenant Crawford giving salaams, sah.'

'Send him in,' David said.

The IO came in and glanced significantly at the butler. David said, 'Wait outside till I call you, Thomas.'

When they were alone Crawford said in a low tone, that could not hide his excitement. 'I've got the first report in from Ban Khao, sir. They sent two men up into Thailand to find out about the Freedom Fighters. They located them easily. It seems that they're getting desperate for more men in their invasion force. The Ban Khao men were able to enlist with them. Yesterday they sent a message out, by another man who'd gone up with them but stayed hidden in the jungles ...'

The Resident's lips were tight drawn, the corners of his mouth turned down. He said, 'Before we discuss this intelligence, can you assure me that you were not responsible for sending these men into Thailand?'

'I was responsible,' David said. 'I arranged it while I was in Lepet for the riots.'

'Ah, Lepet,' the Resident said, 'When you were martial law administrator, and your own master.'

David thought, now Wilson's finding excuses for me. Why didn't he ask the C-in-C to relieve him and get it over with? But, as before, he had a sense that Wilson didn't want to get rid of him, but to destroy him, which he could only do if he remained.

The Resident said, 'You still had no right to send agents into a foreign country. What reason do you have to think that this information is accurate?'

The rockets were still exploding close all round the island of British territory which was the Residency. David said, 'It makes sense. The only thing not certain is the number of Freedom Fighters, and how they're armed. The Ban Khao men said there were four hundred there now, with over three hundred firearms, some bazookas, and a dozen knee mortars. They said that the flow of recruits was getting less, in spite of the inducements that were being offered. My guess is that four hundred and fifty men will enter Mingora on the date the Ban Khao men gave – 28 May.'

He wondered whether it was any good asking once more for permission to make a raid across the frontier and destroy or disrupt the invasion force before it got started. But he could tell by Wilson's face that the answer would be a curt No.

Wilson said, 'I've thought of making an official protest to Thailand but nothing would be done. The Thais don't want to antagonize the MPRP which, they probably believe, will soon be governing this country.'

David said, 'And they'll be right, unless we find a way to stop them.'

The Resident said, 'As I have told you many times already, brigadier, Mingora's future constitution is not a responsibility of Her Majesty's Government – in spite of Queen Valaya's plebiscite. It is a matter for the Mingorans to decide for themselves – *by* themselves.'

'Can we put in an urgent request, on the basis of this hard intelligence, to postpone our departure until the middle of the monsoon, say three months? We would have advanced a great deal in training the Mingoran Army by then. There might be . . .'

'No,' the Resident said. 'You're wasting your time and mine. You should do what you failed to do a fortnight ago – take a strong force up north, and root out the MPRP sympathizers in Moirang, making a stern example of anyone caught with concealed arms or the like. The Governor will certainly declare martial law if you ask him to.'

David said, 'I think I've already said that that would antagonize the loyal, and fail to catch the disloyal.'

The Resident said, 'I am not giving you an order. I am only trying to indicate a course of action which would lead towards the result you wish to attain. That's all.' He nodded in dismissal.

David drove back to Flagstaff House, through a city still celebrating, but slowly preparing for sleep, the lights fewer in the long narrow streets, the bonfires only glowing embers in the squares and along the Esplanade, where still the wind roared and the spray burst up out of the dark below the sea wall and laid wet streaks across the road.

At Flagstaff House the lights of the staff car showed a blue Land-Rover parked under the high portico. David's heart gave a great leap. He forced himself to speak normally, 'Thanks, Wood. That's all for tonight ... Escort, dismiss.'

He ran up the steps. Thomas in the doorway, bowed expressionlessly. 'Her Royal Highness the Perdana Binte Mingora waiting for you in the drawing room, sah. I have given her whisky soda.'

'Thanks, Thomas. That'll be all.'

'Good night, sah.'

He closed the drawing room door carefully behind him as she ran across the tiles into his arms.

The combers rolled in towards the beach in long grey-green lines, spray blowing back from the crests, then towered, curled over and crashed down and forward in boiling grey-white foam, racing up the sandy slope, reaching for the tufted dunes and the palms, failing, sliding back as the next wave rode triumphantly over, reaching, reaching. The palms along the top of the beach thrashed, and here and there coconuts broke loose and rolled down into the sea, which carried them gradually down the beach, a little farther with each wave.

David ran steadily in his bathing trunks. It was no day for swimming. The old couple must have pulled the shark net in some time yesterday, when the sea began to get up, for it was lying in untidy coils near the beach house. David had not thought to swim, but he wanted exercise. The wind was warm and full of salt and he ran steadily north for a mile, then turned and ran back towards the south. From here he could see the black stone towers of Jumbhorn Wat above the trees round the royal beach house, though from closer the trees hid them.

Red crabs scuttled away before him in their hundreds, running sideways into their holes, claws raised defensively. He ran on.

She had stayed till four in the morning. She told him that Sidney Wilson had phoned her at teatime, inviting her to the Residency that evening for chess. When she had refused he asked where she was going. She had told him that was her business. 'I don't want to annoy him,' she said, propping herself up on one elbow in the bed. 'He can still make trouble for us. More important, he can still do good things for us ... but what else could I say?'

'Don't talk about it,' David said, and drew her down into his arms.

The Land-Rover also had been there till four, of course, parked under the portico. Wilson had quite likely driven out at midnight to find out whether Kumara had come to him. Well, if so, he'd found out.

As he approached the beach house he saw the grey Austin saloon that was the Wilsons' private car. He slowed to a walk. If he were to face Wilson, he had better not be out of breath.

Lady Anne got out of the car and came down towards him. She was dressed in street clothes, her heeled shoes sinking into the sand at every step. She said, 'You haven't been swimming in this storm, have you?'

'No,' he said, 'Just running.'

She said, 'I came out because I wanted to speak to you alone.' David glanced at the Gurkhas sitting on the steps of the beach house and the constable in the RMC Land-Rover twenty yards behind the Austin. Lady Anne said, 'They can't hear ... I want to tell you how happy I am for you.'

'For me?'

'And the princess. No, no one's told me anything ... Sidney came to the bedroom where I was asleep about one o'clock and said he was going immediately to Powlang to spend a couple of days shooting. Then he left. He looked very strange, white, trembling ... I've seen him once or twice like that before, when he was on the verge of doing something violent ... I wanted desperately to speak to you because, of course, I thought he'd gone to Powlang to be with Kumara, and he was angry because of something you'd said or done — you were at the Residency earlier, weren't you? — so I dressed and drove to Flagstaff House. I saw her car. Then I understood ... I ought to have guessed before — the way she looked at you when we all met at the club ten days ago ... but I was so wrapped up in my own troubles that I didn't see what should have been obvious — to a woman, anyway ... I am so happy for you.'

'Thank you,' David said. He supposed he ought to have denied the implication, for the sake of Kumara's reputation; but what was the use?

Lady Anne said, 'Of course it's taken a great weight off my mind even though it'll make Sidney impossible to live with until he gets over it – if he ever does. But all that matters is that she doesn't want him. She only wants you.' She put out her hand. 'And I hope she gets you. You deserve each other.'

'Thank you,' David said again.

'And if there's anything I can do, ever, for either of you, *anything*, please call on me.'

'Thank you,' David said for the third time. Lady Anne got back into her car and drove away. David began to change back into uniform, thinking. Lady Anne still loved her husband, even though he was infatuated with Kumara. She must have realized long since that Wilson had married her for the sake of her name and family connections. Women were very faithful creatures.

And what was *he* going to do, falling in love with the heir to the throne of Mingora, which, if all went according to the probabilities, in a few weeks would die in a welter of blood? Her blood, too.

The crowd at the University *padang* was thin but noisy. David thought there were about a hundred young men and women from the university come to cheer on their side in the blue shirts and white shorts, and across the field fifty fusiliers from A Company cheering the men wearing the vertically red and white striped shirts with the big black A on the left breast. A Land-Rover load of Military Police had come to watch and a dozen City Police to keep order.

Sally, standing beside him on the side line, said, 'It's really ridiculous that the university doesn't even have seats for spectators, let alone stands or a proper stadium.'

'I expect the Vice Chancellor thinks there are more urgent matters to spend his money on,' David said.

The fusiliers' team swept down the field in a burst of long diagonal passing. The inside left shot with both feet off the ground and the ball exploded into the upper right corner of the net before the university goalkeeper began his leaping attempt at a save. The soldiers in the crowd cheered. 1–0, David thought, in the first five minutes, and rather easily. A Company was stronger than he had expected; he hoped the match would not degenerate into a massacre.

Sally said, 'Tommy Yates told me the battalion is leaving before the 31st.'

'Oh?' David said. Tommy Yates was an engaging young subaltern of the Fusiliers, and a good golfer. Also a good talker, apparently. Well, the facts of the move had never been classified secret.

'Tommy said they're going by road, leaving on the 24th.'

'I believe it's about then,' David said. The A Company outside left centred a beauty, screaming just above head height across the goal mouth. The centre forward leaped in the air, jerked his head, and the ball shot into the net. 2–0. He clapped enthusiastically, and cried, 'Well played!' Across the field John Allen and Paul Whitmore, the company commander, and CSM Berg and the other fusiliers all clapped and cheered.

'You're being secretive,' Sally cried. 'You must know perfectly well when the Fusiliers are leaving. You gave the orders!'

'I do know,' David said cheerfully, 'but I have a Brigade Major and a D/Q to remind me what I have told people to do. Why do *you* want to know?'

'There's a golf tournament at the end of the month,' she said, pouting, 'and I wanted Tommy to partner me. Now he can't.'

'That's dreadful,' David said.

'So I'll have to get one of the 2nd/12th, and they don't have anyone as good as Tommy. I suppose *they'll* be here till the end of the month, won't they?'

'I think so,' David said, 'One company into June, even, to take part in the independence celebrations on the 1st . . . Oh, good shot!' The ball was in the University net again. 3–0.

Then, to David's relief, the University began to gain some cohesion, particularly in their attacking movements. They scored twice quickly and, just before half time, would have scored again, but their inside left was felled by a savage shoulder charge just as he was about to shoot into the open goalmouth, the Fusilier goalie having slipped and fallen. The crowd roared its disapproval in a storm of boos and hisses; but the referee did not blow his whistle – the tackle had been hard, but perfectly legal. Then, as play swept back and forth up the field, David heard a rhythmic chant rising in the crowd but could not for a time make out the words. He turned to Sally, 'What are they shouting?'

'Bully Whitmore – *out*! Bully Whitmore – *out*!' she said.

Then he heard it plain himself, as the chant was taken up by more and more students. Whitmore and Allen across the field heard it. David saw Whitmore turn to speak to Allen and Allen shake his head decisively.

Half time came and the shouting died down as the players sat on the sere grass drinking the fresh lime juice taken out to them. It was only a pause in the mounting tension. More students had been trickling down to the *padang* so that when play resumed there were about two hundred and fifty of them. Their team came out like lions, and scored a goal at once, equalling the scores at 3 all. Then a fusilier fouled a university player, who scored with the ensuing free kick, making it 4–3. The chant of the students rose again, triumphant now: 'Bully Whitmore – *out*!'

'How do they know he's here?' David said, more to himself than to Sally; but she answered shortly, 'His picture was in the papers at the time. And when this match was announced, they published that he was the commander of A Company.' But half the people yelling over there probably don't know what they're shouting, David thought to himself.

The game seemed to stagnate for a time, and the ball was kicked out of play a great deal. The soldier spectators began to shout derisively 'HLI!' The students could not be expected to know that the cry stemmed from a historic Army Cup final when the Highland Light Infantry, to guard a one-goal lead, had kicked the ball out of play at every opportunity throughout the second half. Since then, for half a century British soldiers had greeted delaying tactics on the field with shouts of 'HLI!' or 'Keep it on the island!' But the Mingoran students did not have to know the origin of the cry to sense the derision in the soldiers' shouts, and to hear the boos from across the field. They themselves began to jeer and boo every time a fusilier got the ball. David wondered whether he should tell Allen to quieten his men a bit. Better not interfere . . . though in Allen's shoes he'd have sent CSM Berg along the line with the word to pipe down.

The fusiliers scored again: 4–4. Soon afterwards, the university right half, momentarily up in the middle of the field, intercepted a fusilier pass and himself passed to his outside farther up. The referee's whistle shrilled and his arm flung out, pointing. 'Offside,' David muttered, 'by a mile.'

The university students began booing at the tops of their voices, and their players crowded round the referee, gesticulating, waving their arms, shouting. The referee, an artillery bombardier, folded his arms and stood motionless, a look of immense disdain on his square face. The fusilier players waited patiently in their places. Students began to stream on to the field, the city police striving to hold them back. David saw a student rush up to a fusilier player and swing a fist at his head. The soldier easily dodged the inexpert blow and pushed the youth in the chest; he fell over backwards. The police were shouting 'Back, back, back!' and swinging their truncheons menacingly. Two students knocked over a fusilier player and began kicking him. The soldiers' temper changed abruptly.

John Allen arrived, running, at David's side: 'Sir, these bloody people are out of hand!'

David said, 'Your man seems to be quite capable of looking after himself.' But, he thought, is he? Is Allen right? Wouldn't it be wiser to order the MPs into action?

The referee broke free from his assailants, and came trotting to David's side. He stood rigid to attention, and said, 'Sir, I'm going to suspend the game.'

David hesitated. John Allen broke in, 'But we've got to beat them! There are only four or five minutes left to play, and if the MPs cleared the ground, we could . . .'

The blurred mob, the untidy fighting and running to and fro seemed to freeze before David's eyes, as though held by a stop-motion camera. He said, 'The referee's right. Blow No Side, bombardier.' He sharpened his voice: 'John, get all your men off the field and back to barracks. Corporal!' he beckoned the corporal of MPs, who came running: 'See that the Fusiliers can get into their vehicles without hindrance. Just keep the crowd away from them – don't get involved out on the field.'

'Sir!' the corporal bellowed, and leaped into his Land-Rover. John Allen hurried away. A student with a camera had it poised and ready. David beckoned a city policeman and said, 'Sally, tell this man to arrest that student and hand him over to the Chief Minister's Intelligence people.'

'Why?' Sally said, 'he's not doing anything.'

'Oh yes, he is. He's waiting to collect evidence, which his friends are trying to manufacture, of military brutality. Of course, I can't order you to do it, but . . .'

Sally spoke sulkily to the policeman, who ran off. David said, 'And now, I promised you tea at the Gymkhana.' She was looking at him with a mixture of grudging respect and suppressed anger. 'You're not so simple as you try to pretend,' she said. 'I wonder . . .'

Sixteen

THE ROOM HAD seemed almost dark when the Prince Chamberlain ushered him in and the Queen no more than a faintly lighter shape towards the far end. Then, after the Chamberlain went out, carefully pulling the heavy curtains behind him, and the Queen began to speak, slowly his eyes became used to the gloom. He was to be alone with her. As far as he knew she had never been alone with any foreigner in her life.

'Come closer, brigadier,' she said, the voice weak and hoarse, 'The doctors say I must keep the fan on, though it makes much noise . . . and I cannot speak more loudly.'

David went forward carefully till he was barely five feet from where she sat, legs crossed, on cushions arranged on top of a low wide table. The light seeping through the drawn curtains was warm and red, and that alone, he realized, gave her face a look of life; all other evidence, the hollow cheeks, the deep lines of pain around her mouth, the sunken eyes, spoke of death. He was shocked at the change since he had seen her last.

'Sit down in the chair. You have faced death, brigadier, in the war?'

'Yes, ma'am,' David said humbly. 'And once or twice, more closely, in the Emergency.'

'Were you afraid?'

'Yes, ma'am, very.'

'But you did your duty. I am afraid too, sometimes, but not as much as I thought I would be when I was younger . . . I do not have very long to live, brigadier. A week, perhaps.'

David said, 'I hope you will be spared much longer than that, ma'am.'

'I do not. There is pain – all the time. There is no chance. Sir

Harry Johnstone arranged for two specialists to fly out from London to examine me last year ... They told me then what would happen, and it has. Last week they came again, in secret, in order not to disturb my people ... they were here the day of the plebiscite, and they have confirmed their verdict.'

She paused, breathing slow but shallow, like a weakened runner trying to regather his strength after a race. The fans made an undertone of metallic vibration but drops of sweat formed on David's face and forehead and round his collar. Outside, it was 97 degrees, with 95 per cent humidity.

The Queen said, 'My daughter has told me she loves you.'

David said, 'And I her, ma'am.'

'She wants to marry you.'

David said nothing.

'What would you answer, if she were to ask you?'

David sat silent, looking at the eyes, now seeming clear, sharp, widely distended. What would he say? He loved Kumara – the past weeks had proven that beyond any doubt. He loved her far more deeply than he had ever dreamed love could reach, even in the most passionate days of his infatuation with Lucy. But there had always been a limit to it, a barrier unstated but as definite as the end of a railway line ... on 1 June he must leave Mingora, and she could not leave, for she would soon be queen. A Queen of Mingora could never marry a foreigner, especially a Christian, and most of all not in the conditions of tension and danger which would follow the departure of the British, when every section of the populace would have to be wooed afresh, and fitted comfortably into a different set of circumstances.

The Queen said, 'You don't know?'

'I had thought ... I still think it is impossible. It is better for me not to think of it.'

The Queen said, 'Kumara has never been happy, until now. She has faced her lot with courage and dignity. The training of her daughter, Salimina, was taken out of her hands early, nor did Salimina truly love her mother, for it is in her nature to be jealous ... and perhaps, like all children, to go a different road from their parents. Now Kumara glows like a bride, and sings in her room – my women have told me. She is faithful as rock and will not change. She will always love you.'

There was nothing to stop him leaving the army and starting

again somewhere with her – Canada perhaps, even London; there must be something he could do in civilian life. He wouldn't earn much money, and she would not take much out of Mingora, feeling that it belonged here, as a part of the country's wealth, not something for her to have a good time with far from the land where it had grown. But what was he thinking of? She would not leave Mingora. She *should* not.

Queen Valaya said, 'It is the hardest thing I have done since I became queen, what I do now...because I love Kumara. Seeing her happy has brightened my days so that I feel glad, glad to be dying with that memory of her as my last...yet I must ask you to promise not to marry her. For our country.'

'I understand, ma'am,' David said abruptly, 'I...' He wanted to say *I promise*, but the words would not come out. No words came. The Queen put out her hand. David stood up, bent, kissed it quickly, and hurried out, his throat dry.

When he was ushered into the Resident's big study, Wilson motioned him to a chair, but David did not intend to sit. He remained standing, his swagger cane under his arm, his peaked red banded cap in his left hand.

Wilson said, 'I was just going to send for you when you called. To show you this.' He handed David a flimsy cable form, adding, 'That was deciphered half an hour ago.'

David read: 'COMMISSIONER GENERAL HAS CONSULTED WITH C IN C FARELF AND WITH THE LATTER'S CONCURRENCE REQUEST YOU INFORM OC BRITISH FORCES MINGORA THAT IN THE PRESENT DELICATE STATE OF ANGLO-THAI RELATIONS NO TROOPS ARE TO BE DEPLOYED NORTH OF TRANGLOEK WITHOUT YOUR PRIOR APPROVAL. OC IS ALSO BEING INFORMED DIRECT THROUGH MILITARY CHANNELS.

'Initial it, please,' Wilson handed him a pen. David put the message on the edge of the table, initialled at the foot, and stood up. He said, 'I want permission to move most of the troops to the Moirang-Thai frontier, and keep them there until the MPRP invasion forces move. If they haven't invaded by 15 June I'll bring our troops back here. They can leave Mingora immediately afterwards.'

'You have put this proposal to me before, and I have told you it is out of the question. Why do you bring it up again – especially in the light of this cable?'

David said, 'Because I think the present plan is immoral.' He had rehearsed this speech all the way back to his headquarters after leaving the palace; and, after Wilson had granted him an immediate interview, while being driven to the Residency. He continued, 'What we are proposing to do – and not do – is a national disgrace, and also a private disgrace on every responsible person who carries it out.'

'You have no choice,' the Resident said. 'You are a soldier.'

David said, 'I do have a choice, sir. The Nuremberg trials established that soldiers cannot plead that they are obeying orders when they do something immoral, even though their constitutional civil superiors told them to do it.' Wilson was watching him intently, tensed as always in David's presence, but with a hidden glint almost of happiness behind the pale, shining eyes. David said, 'In the last resort I must obey my conscience.'

The Resident said gently, 'Do you refuse to obey the orders, then?'

David said, 'Yes, sir. I do.'

It was out: now all Wilson had to do was pick up the telephone and speak to the C-in-C and he'd be on the next plane to Singapore. There would be a court martial at the end of it, probably; if not, an invitation to resign his commission and an ignominious end to his career; but anything was better than waiting here, loving Kumara more every minute, unable to see any future with her, and compelled to take part in the destruction of her country.

Wilson still had that faintly concealed look of pleasure, a suppressed gloat, behind the unmoving features. He said, 'You have all along expressed your opposition to HMG's policy. But what you *say* does not matter, only what you do. I have given you your directions. When you disobey them, I will have to notify your Commander-in-Chief. Until then, I shall assume that you will, in fact, loyally carry out the policy of your government. I don't want to see your career destroyed. Think it over.' He nodded in dismissal. David put on his hat, and saluted rigidly. As he turned to go. the Resident said, By the way, squash at five?'

'All right,' David said automatically. Then he was in the passage, his mind seething. He'd come here determined to get himself relieved of his command; Wilson had refused to accept his defiance. Why? He had told him to his face that he would not carry out the official policy but Wilson had in effect laughed at him and said, *You will, when it comes to it.* Why? The look of a stoat with a cornered rabbit came into his mind. Wilson wanted him to be here to the end, to see him swallow the bitter pill of failing the Queen and Kumara and the Minister and Sir Harry and all the others who had been harbouring some mad secret hope that he could save them and their society. Wilson wanted to see him suffer, because of Kumara. For many other reasons, too, but above all because of Kumara.

But – all power grows out of the muzzle of a gun, the Communist shits said. Well, he had the guns . . .

The outer door of the private second floor dining-room, leading to the wide verandah, was open, a faint breeze stirring the table linen. Overhead the fans whirred. The heavy seas of the previous week had abated, but the general build up of clouds continued to make the skies over Trangloek a chiaroscuro of blue, white and indigo. Light from the sea glittered and rippled on the high ceiling of the room.

Sir Harry Johnstone sat at the head of the table, the Chief Minister to his right, David to his left. They were savouring the dessert of iced mango fool, watched with trained indifference by the usual pair of club servants, now standing beside the outer door.

David said, 'Then that's settled: the special train to be ready day and night in the yards – not formed up to look like a train, but able to be made up and got going within half an hour.'

The Minister said, 'That will mean keeping an engine in steam twenty-four hours a day. I don't know much about steam engines, but I think it takes two or three hours to get the fire hot enough.'

'Have one ready all the time,' David said. 'It isn't going to be a long wait. The train is to be capable of carrying a full battalion, without vehicles, and also four field guns, with their quads. Check that Emergency Loading Ramps 3 and 4 are in good order, also 11 and 12, near Lepet, for unloading.'

'Are you proposing to move the other battalion by road, brigadier?'

David nodded. 'That's the Fusiliers. They're due to move off on 24 May – that's D minus 8 in *my* plan – four days from now.

Both battalions, and all the other troops, have started handing over immobile stores in their barracks.'

'I know,' the Minister said. 'We can't afford to lose the valuable material you're leaving behind . . . but we don't have men to guard against pilfering or full scale raiding by MPRP elements.'

Sir Harry, puffing on a cigar, grunted, 'I can lend you some of my mine guards, for a time at least. Go on, brigadier.'

'I'm putting the full emergency plan into effect as from 0800 hours 24 May – and that is to apply to all village Home Guards and auxiliaries.'

'It will be done,' the Minister said.

'. . . all bridge guards that we decided on, to be in place at the same time, harbour security to go on war footing – search junks and sampans coming down the west coast particularly – it will be the MPRP's best way to get arms and ammunition to the invaders as they move south.'

'We'll do our best,' the Minister said, 'but that west coast is very difficult to patrol except from the sea, and we have no navy.'

Sir Harry said, 'I have a big motor cruiser at Powlang, and some cargo junks at Deran. Make them your navy.'

'We can put constables in them, if your crews will remain as sailors.'

'They will,' Sir Harry growled. 'I'll see to that.'

For the moment, yes, David thought; but only if they outfaced the coming storm. Two weeks hence, if there had been heavy government defeats, those crews would not be found, nor the guards for the barracks, nor servants for this mighty Mingora Club, which had seemed as solid as the Bank of England . . . and that wasn't so solid these days, either, was it?

He said, 'There's one more thing, Sir Harry. You've given us money and men. Now I need one more thing. I need the *Mingora Times*, on 24 May, to publish the news, by wire from Singapore, that heavy rains broke there that day.'

Sir Harry took a large swig of brandy and soda, his head cocked on one side. 'Ahh! Ye're a clever boogger! A sight cleverer than Ah gave thee credit for!' He reverted to his normal English: 'But I don't know whether Mong Kla – that's the editor – will allow it. I don't like the idea myself. It's taken thirty-five years to build up its reputation as the most accurate newspaper between Tokyo and Suez. Mong Kla will resign if I tell him we're going to publish a deliberate lie.'

'Don't tell him,' David said. 'And it doesn't matter if he does resign – because if this doesn't work, you won't be owning the *Times* much longer.'

The Chief Minister said, 'Of course, the monsoons don't break on certain fixed dates here. But I know from experience that when heavy rains break in Singapore at the end of May, our heavy rains will begin four days later.'

David said, 'Sujak knows that too, and it's very important for him to get his Freedom Fighters into Mingora before movement off the roads becomes impossible. I think that when he hears of the Singapore rains, he'll move at once. That should be on the 26th, five clear days before the last of our troops are due to leave the country.'

Sir Harry said, 'Do you think the word about the monsoon will get to them, the invaders?'

David said, 'I'm sure of it. We've intercepted radio signals that can only be from a hidden transmitter somewhere in Trangloek – it keeps moving. There's nothing more important to them than the weather and the state of the roads – nothing! That news will be sent by radio at once. Then we have to keep all contradictory news out of the paper and the local radio for two days. By then they'll have marched, and be committed.'

'What about the Thai radio?' Sir Harry asked, 'They might be listening to that.'

'I doubt it. They don't speak Thai. In any case, the Thai radio is very unlikely to give information about rains in Singapore. Why should it?'

Sir Harry rose, walked heavily to the outer door, and stared out. He said, 'The success of this deception plan will depend a good deal on what sort of impression you made on Sujak bin Amin when you were his prisoner . . . whether he thinks you're capable of telling a lie, of acting differently from the way British officers are supposed to act.'

David said, 'I felt like an ordinary British officer – then.'

Sir Harry said, 'It might work. We've got no choice, as you say. All right – I'll see that it's done.' He sat down, glancing at his watch: 'Have to be off soon.'

David said, 'All communications out of Mingora must be

broken from the time the false report is published until say, mid-day on the 26th.'

'I'll see to it,' the Chief Minister said.

David said, 'One more thing. . . . If the Freedom Fighters invade, I am reasonably sure that we will be able to give them such a bloody nose that the revolution will flop completely, for the time being. But it is not certain. They may suspect the Singapore news. They may evade battle. I may be relieved or in some way prevented from getting the troops up there in time. Therefore it is imperative that we try to do as much damage as possible to them before they ever set out.'

Sir Harry grunted, his little eyes sharp in the rolls of fat. The Minister said, 'You are again thinking of a raid?'

David said, 'Not by land.'

No one spoke. After a long pause and three puffs at his cigar, Sir Harry said, 'H'm. How many aircraft?'

'Depends on the type and armament.'

'American Sabre Jets. The ones I could get are armed with six .50 calibre machine guns and two 20 mm cannon. '

'Three would do.'

'You're going to break me, lad . . . All right. Can do. When?'

'As soon as possible.'

The Chief Minister said, 'The only airfield in the country that they can use is Trangloek here, unfortunately. I wish there were a secret one somewhere, but there isn't.'

'It'll have to be Trangloek, then,' David said.

Sir Harry said, 'Send Crawford to me tomorrow. By then I'll know how and when they'll be coming, and arrange to brief the pilots.' He heaved up. 'Very useful meeting. Are you off too, brigadier?'

'Yes, I have a lot to do . . . now that I've made up my mind.'

'A difficult decision. When this is all over, I'll be glad to give you a job. You may need one.'

David said grimly, 'Thanks, Sir Harry. I'll remember.'

But, he thought, as the staff car headed back for Flagstaff House, he didn't want a civilian job; he wanted vindication as a soldier. Politicians seemed to think that Nuremberg was something they could bring up only when they chose, as when a soldier had obeyed orders which they disapproved of; but it worked the other way round, too: why should a soldier not use the precedent of

Nuremberg to disobey orders which *he* considered immoral and inhuman?

They dined alone at Flagstaff House, he at the head of the rosewood table, she at his side. They talked little during the meal, inhibited by the presence of Thomas the butler; but afterwards, when they had gone to the drawing-room and Thomas had been dismissed for the night, she said, 'Sidney spoke to me today ... warning me not to make a fool of myself over you. He said it had become a matter of state ... an affair of state, he said, but he has no sense of humour at the best of times. He said my mother's condition has altered my situation, and it was his duty to point out the danger to the queendom if the people came to despise me.'

'When was all this?' David asked.

'This afternoon.'

'And what did you tell him?'

'That I had to disagree with him. I said that it was my business, and my mother's, perhaps, but not the British Government's.'

'That explains why he was in such a state. We played squash.'

'I heard.'

'He broke another racquet. ... I suppose actually the private lives of royalty here are in his sphere, as long as Britain is committed to maintain the present set-up. And I can understand his jealousy. I'd be pretty murderous if our positions were reversed.'

She curled closer to him on the sofa and said, 'I thought at first that it – his being so jealous – would be bad for us, for me and Mingora, I mean. But now I think the opposite.'

'His being jealous of me isn't going to make him any keener to do what I think ought to be done.'

'No – but he hasn't had you relieved, has he? If he didn't care about you one way or the other, he would have, long ago.' Her voice was thoughtful, almost judicious. 'But he wants you to hang yourself, before his eyes. So you will be able to carry out your plan to save us ...'

'And then be hanged?' David said, smiling.

She jumped to her feet, leaned over him: 'Take me to bed, Dylan?'

'So soon after dinner?'

'I haven't seen you for two days. I love you, I love you ... I feel cold and hot, uncomfortable ... sitting, standing, lying. I'm empty and scratchy inside.' She planted her lips against his ear and whispered, 'And I'm a princess. I can't be kept waiting.'

He rose slowly, feeling immensely powerful as he stood over her, and lifted her in his arms and carried her up the stairs, while she explored his ear with her pointed tongue.

They made love for an hour, their bodies glistening and slippery against each other with sweat and the milk of love, her hair damp, her lips swollen and on his ears and neck and chest the deep marks of teeth, scratches on his back, blood in the hollow of his shoulder. Then they slept, locked together like animals by arms and legs. Then she again turned her lips to his, again they made love, and again slept.

The light went on and David stirred, feeling for her, but she was not there. He heard water running in the bathroom and saw that it was half past two in the morning. He got up and found her standing naked in the shower, the water streaming off her long shiny black hair and running in a stream between her breasts, making a river down her flat belly and dripping off the small dense forest of her loins. He held her from behind and stood under the shower with her, kissing her neck. The water was cold and slowly, as they stood, it washed away the lust that had held them for so many hours. But, David thought ruefully, it is only temporarily sated; he loved her more than ever, holding her so clean and cool, like this ... now she was drying herself on his towel, dashing his eau de cologne on her body, shrugging into a white shirt of his, which came down almost to her knees, sitting on the edge of the bed, patting it ...

'Come. Lie down. Here, wait till I prop the pillows.' She stooped and gently, almost humbly, kissed his hand: 'When are you going to marry me?'

David had been fearing this moment a long time. His worry had been drowned in the depths of their physical passion, but now it surfaced again. He said miserably, 'I don't see how we can.'

She was silent for a long time, her head resting on his shoulder; then she said, 'Has my mother been talking to you?'

David nodded; but added, 'It isn't only what she said. I had been thinking the same things myself. ... And I'm not a very exciting chap. My first wife ran away from me.'

And you think I will, too, after the novelty has worn off? I am not that sort of woman. I have lived all my life since I became a woman – twenty-five years – waiting for some man to both create the . . . love, passion . . . I can't name it, that you created in London, and fulfil it as you have done here. Ever since that night on Pulo Pattan, our first, I have been to the Old Pagoda every morning and prayed that we will become man and wife.'

'Kumara. . . dearest . . . how can it be? You will be queen very soon. The people don't want a British king or chamberlain or whatever I'd be.'

'Commander-in-Chief,' she said at once, as though she had worked all this out long since. 'That they would accept. That they would welcome.'

'I wonder. I don't know them well enough. Your mother obviously thinks they wouldn't.'

He felt a new dampness on his shoulder and realized she was crying, without sound. She said in an unsteady voice, 'I don't know, really. I am just so miserable at the thought of losing you, now that I've found you, that I don't think I can live without you. Or rule my country. I won't have the will.'

He put his arm round her as she sank lower against him, the tears damp on his naked belly, her lank hair wet on his chest. He stroked the hair, separating the strands with his fingers to help it to dry in the warm night air. He realized – he knew that she must realize it, too – that one event, at least, would enable them to marry: that was, the success of the MPRP revolution. Then, banished from her country, her royal future abolished, she would be free.

But he had just put the seal on plans, which, if successful, would ensure that none of that would happen. He held in a sigh, and kept his breathing even. Gradually her sobbing subsided, and she dozed in the crook of his arm while he lay awake, looking down at her, his mind full.

Seventeen

THE COMPANY COMMANDER bellowed the order, 'Royal salute – present arms!'

The ninety-six men of C Company 2nd Bn 12th Gurkha Rifles jerked their rifles up to the present and snapped the right heels behind the left. The white-clad band began playing *God Save the Queen*..........

Alastair Campbell-Wylie, standing with David, Sally, and the Commissioner of the RMC at the flank of the parade shouted 'No! Do that again. The two flags must go up together.'

The Commissioner nodded and spoke to the constable at the halyards of the flagpost carrying the Mingoran flag. The Gurkha pulled the Union Jack down, the soldiers returned to the order. Sally said, 'What am I supposed to be doing now?'

'Standing there, waiting. The Duke will be at the top of the ramp. He doesn't come down till both anthems have been played.'

'All right, sir?' the company commander called.

'Go ahead,' Campbell-Wylie said.

The company commander swung round, his sword vertical in his right hand: 'Royal salute . . . present arms!'

This time the two flags began to move at the same moment, and as the last notes of the anthem died both flags reached the peak, fluttering out in the hot sea wind.

The company commander bellowed, 'Guard of Honour . . . order . . .'

Campbell-Wylie shouted, 'No! Stay at the present until the Mingoran anthem has been played.'

'Sir.'

David said, 'Well, you have a week to get it sorted out. The main ceremony will be the next day, of course, on top of the old

Portuguese fort at Dhaphut Point. Are you going to be there, too, Sally?'

'No. My grandmother's going to try to go herself, but I expect it will have to be my mother.'

David turned back to Alastair Campbell-Wylie: 'How's the handing over going?'

'Pretty well, sir. I don't suppose there'll be a light bulb left by the time the Mingorans have any soldiers to put in the lines, or much window glass, or even beds, but that's their business. They need more police.'

'Which we don't have,' Sally said.

'And what they do have are all allotted to Internal Security . . . Do you think we're going to get away free and clear, sir?'

David said, 'I don't know, Alastair. But I want you to be ready for action right up to the last minute. You've been practising entrainment at the emergency loading ramps?'

'Yes, sir.'

'At night? Everything looks different at night.'

'Yes, sir.'

'I'd better be going,' David said, 'I have to see the Fusiliers.' He paused, his head cocked. The sound of jet engines grew in the south-west. It was too early for either of the BOAC flights, nor did this sound like a Comet. The sound increased to a bellow and three single-engined fighters swept low over the control tower.

David swore silently. These must be Sir Harry's Sabre Jets, come at last. They had been due to arrive at five p.m. yesterday, and attack the Freedom Fighters' camp half an hour later, in the first twilight.

'No markings,' Campbell-Wylie said, as the three planes circled and came in on a landing run, wheels and flaps down.

'I'll ask the control tower where they're from,' the Commissioner said, hurrying off. David wondered what answer he would get: he was not in the know about the aircraft, but someone in the control tower had to be, and had to have a satisfactory story to prevent the Sabre Jets from being impounded and their pilots arrested.

'They're American Sabre Jets,' Sally said, 'with long range tanks. I had a pilot friend at Stanford.'

The planes landed together, in arrowhead formation. The sound of the engines became deafeningly loud as they swung round on the tarmac behind the company of Gurkhas. David said abruptly to Campbell-Wylie, 'Wait here.' He walked quickly towards the planes. The engines were still bellowing, but a little less full-throatedly. The lead pilot's canopy slid back and he beckoned to David. David climbed up on to the wing and leaned his head into the cramped cockpit. The pilot took off his helmet and shouted, 'Can't stop the motor ... I have a message for Brigadier Jones or Sir Harry Johnstone.' The accent was Texan.

'I'm Jones.'

'Hey, that's a break ... Got arrested in Sumatra yesterday, though the bastards were paid off. We ran for it this morning and got the ships off the ground. Kept radio silence in case they or the British in Malaya sent fighters after us.'

'You know where your target is?'

'You bet! A guy briefed us in Manila yesterday morning. Maps and all. We got just enough fuel to do the job and get back here ... and that jail Sir Harry promised us had better be comfortable, with plenty of beer and dames ...' He rammed his helmet back on and raised a thumb. David climbed back down the wing and jumped to the ground. The jet roar rose, as the three fighters, like ungainly birds, waddled off towards the runway.

He hurried into the terminal building and towards one of the public telephones in the hall. Sally was coming out of the nearest booth. She said, 'I must run, David. 'Bye.' She walked away as David slipped into the booth and got through to his Brigade Major.

'Stork? Operation Wild Goose is under way. Tell Crawford and Sir Harry.'

'Right, sir.'

He hung up. It was seven o'clock. The Sabre Jets, now airborne, would hit the Freedom Fighters' camp in twenty minutes ... early enough, with luck, for all the enemy to be still in camp and not yet dispersed on exercises or fatigues. He climbed into his staff car and said, 'Fusiliers, please, Wood.'

The city seemed oddly quiet and people looked up at the car with the blue brigade pennant on the radiator cap, which in itself was unusual; normally no one turned his head at a passing car and if they did, once they had seen, they turned back at once to whatever they had been doing. Now they were holding their glance a moment longer than was comfortable – not quite a stare, but an interrogation, half stated. But he'd have to look into that later; now he was going to see off the 1st Battalion the Royal Oxford Fusiliers.

John Allen and his adjutant were waiting outside the orderly room when he stepped out of the staff car, and after salutes, led off quickly towards the parade ground. As they strode along David said, 'Any problems?'

'No, sir. We're ready to go.'

They reached the lines of vehicles and the men standing at ease in front of them. This might be the last time he saw the Fusiliers before his brigade re-formed – or ever. He began at the right of the line, Battalion Headquarters and HQ Company. His perception sharpened when he reached A Company, where he was surprised to find himself greeted by a tall lieutenant. 'Where's Whitmore?' he asked.

John Allen said, 'In his quarters, sir. You remember, he's not allowed to leave Mingora.'

'Of course, I forgot,' David said. He'd really have to get the Chief Minister to do something about the trial or Whitmore would rot here for ever.

He looked into each man's eyes, asked questions about homes, service and experience, and at the end, when he moved on to B Company, had not liked what he had seen.

When the whole inspection was finished he drew Allen aside, and said, 'A Company doesn't feel quite right to me, yet.'

Allen said bluntly, 'They're pretty fed up about the football riot still.'

David thought, Yes, perhaps; he had detected a certain surly belligerence towards him personally in some of the men; but there was something else.

'Is that all?' he said.

Allen said, the words coming out unwillingly, 'I'm afraid not. Paul's almost too much the opposite of Jimmy Spalding. He's such a tiger that the men are afraid of him. I spoke to Berg about it a couple of weeks ago.'

'The CSM?'

'Yes. He was my batman at the Rhine crossing . . . carried me forward when I couldn't walk. I can talk to him. He says that where Jimmy Spalding apparently didn't know enough of what was going on in the company, Paul knows almost too much. He breathes down the men's necks twenty-four hours a day. They feel that at night Paul's standing beside each bed, watching the man sleep, ready to pounce on him if he breathes out of rhythm.'

'Have you spoken to him?'

'Yes, sir, but it's not easy. I don't want to discourage a keen man . . . I think he'll have to learn for himself. The company won't win the football – they're good but too tense – they won't win the musketry – same thing – they won't win the drill competition – same thing . . . all of which he's sworn that they will.'

David nodded. As long as there was no great crisis, it would work itself out; if there were, some sudden call to battle, for instance, or one of those situations so common during the Emergency in Malaya, which demanded that all ranks knew and trusted each other, and could act together without supervision or formal orders, then A Company of the Fusiliers might run into trouble; and its commander into disaster.

'I notice that two of the ringleaders from December are back in the company,' he said.

'You recognized them?' Allen said, sounding surprised.

'I was looking at them for some time,' David said grimly, 'wondering whether they were going to shoot me.'

Allen said, 'Paul asked for them. They said they wanted to return to A, where all their mates were, and Paul said he wasn't afraid of them, he'd have them.'

David nodded. That was a good mark for Whitmore – and Allen. The Board of Inquiry found that there were genuine grievances in the company. All that these two men were ever accused of was pointing out the grievances. Men shouldn't be punished for that.

They were at the deserted Orderly Room now and he glanced at his watch. The Fusiliers were due to move in ten minutes. Wood was holding the door of the staff car open for him. He turned to Allen and said, 'You are to be ready for action to the last moment – which will be when your last vehicle enters Malaya. You've still got your Mingora maps?'

'Yes, sir. The RMC were complaining about them not being handed over.'

'Send them back from Taiping . . . Above all, make radio contact with my headquarters here every hour on the hour, on the new frequencies. If you don't get through, stop where you are until you do.'

'And send a DR back to find out what's happening,' Allen finished for him. 'It's in the orders.'

David said, 'Good luck, then,' and stepped into the staff car. To Wood, he said, 'Mingora Club, please.'

With the car parked outside the august portals of the Club he set off along the street that ran beside it up into the centre of the old city. He heard the measured tread of boots behind him and saw Tulbahadur following, as were his normal orders; but David wanted to feel the city as a man alone, unarmed. He was dressed as for a parade ground, wearing his slacks, bush shirt and Sam Browne, and carrying a swagger stick but no pistol. He sent Tulbahadur back to the car and went on slowly, alone.

Most of the shopkeepers in the tight packed stalls recognized his red-banded hat as a mark of senior rank, and rose from their squatting positions to touch their foreheads as he passed, to which he smiled and saluted. From time to time he stopped and asked how was business, was the man healthy, how was his family? When the shopkeepers didn't rise, they touched their foreheads from where they squatted, or waved a hand – nearly all. One or two men, not shopkeepers, turned their backs as he passed by, as though to indicate that he was not welcome; but as he came out into the open square round the old Pagoda he thought that on the whole there was nothing to worry about in the state of mind of the city at this moment – only, as he had noticed earlier, a sense of interrogation, which could be accounted for without postulating anything serious: an era was due to end a week from today – what would the future be like? Not in its general shape – for the people seemed confident that that would be much the same as now – but in its exact details. This was the question in people's faces.

The crowds were always thick round the Pagoda, for over the centuries it had been the gathering place for the citizens of Trangloek. There must have been five hundred here now, about half of them watching the expert manoeuvres of a group of old men practising kite-fighting tactics. The dragon and eagle-shaped kites, bright yellow and blue and green, swooped and soared against the banked cloud masses in the sky, the horns boomed inside the temple.

David glanced at his watch. A few minutes before ten. He smiled to himself and muttered – *fool*. She had told him she came here at ten every day to pray that they would become husband and wife. Here he was, and it was nearly ten o'clock. A pure coincidence? He smiled again. But he did not want her to see him. She'd come in from the north-east side there, from the direction of the palace. He started across the square, easing between the chattering women and the trudging men burdened with heavy sacks. Near the north point he stood back against the wall of a shop, under an *angsana* tree in flaming blossom, and lit a cigarette.

She came five minutes late, accompanied by a maidservant. The men who saw her bowed low and the women stooped to touch the hem of her long skirt. Her head was up, her face composed. She smiled slightly and murmured words to all who acknowledged her, but to David she seemed removed, as though her body was here to do whatever it had to do of royal duty or the physical functions – breathing, moving, seeing – but the rest of her, whatever was spiritual and of the mind, was away, untouchable because not present.

He watched hungrily. Six more days, six nights. He wanted to imprint her on his soul, as light on colour film; to impregnate his own skin and flesh with the feel of hers. She staggered and jerked upright, away from the wall. Something flashed, someone screamed. A man was close on her, arm thrusting, the maidservant clawing at him, screaming, Kumara falling. He broke into a frantic run, men and women stumbled and fell away from him. He reached her side in thirty paces. A policeman was running down the steps of the Pagoda, another man was running away, a long knife red in his hand. The crowd enveloped the man with the knife, then David saw no more for he was on his knees beside Kumara. The blood was staining her dress just under the Jumbhorn Ruby, to the right, trickling down her side on to the dusty paving stones of the square. She was white, teeth clenched. She murmured, 'I'm dying . . . darling . . . oh darling.'

The policeman was standing over them now, and David said, 'Get a car, the nearest. Hurry!'

The policeman ran off, shouting. David held her head and shoulders in his arms. She whispered, 'It doesn't hurt much . . . I love you.'

'Don't talk,' he muttered. God, would the car never come? Perhaps he should leave her and get his staff car, but that was half a mile away.

A car's wheels appeared and he saw that it was a big Chevrolet taxi. The taxi driver looked at Kumara and began to tremble. David ordered the policeman to take her hips while he took her shoulders. Together, holding her level, they put her on the wide back seat. David snapped to the policeman, 'Tell the Chief Minister what has happened – and that we're going to the hospital. Run!' He jumped into the back of the taxi and knelt on the floor beside Kumara. The taxi started off.

Fifteen minutes later she was in the operating room with the chief surgeon, a Scotsman, and his two top Mingoran assistants. David, waiting in the hospital administrator's room on the ground floor of the rambling three-storied building, was smoking his third half cigarette. The outer door burst open and the Resident strode in. He came up to David, his face white, his hands shaking. 'You were there?'

'Yes.'

'What happened?'

'A man came out of the crowd and stabbed her.'

'Why didn't you stop him?' Wilson's face was six inches from his own, his breathing heavy and irregular. David saw that the man was nearer the breaking point than he had known him, and that had been near enough, once or twice.

He said gently, 'I was not close. I was unarmed.'

The Resident said, 'Are they operating?'

David nodded.

The Resident's voice almost cracked. 'Is . . . did you see . . . is it . . . very bad?'

'I couldn't tell. It was in the chest or under the rib cage, on the right. I don't think it pierced the lung because there was no bubbling or bleeding from the mouth. But as to internal injuries – they're finding out now.'

He turned away and resumed his pacing. Wilson stood in the centre of the big room as though frozen, the sweat gleaming on his face. David thought, I should say something now – about how we both love her but neither of us can ever win her, so why don't we shake hands? But he couldn't; and, obviously, nor could Wilson. Their thoughts were tight closed on the same person, the wounded woman, but otherwise did not touch or communicate at any point.

Wood pushed the staff car fast down the main road towards the hospital. It was half past eight of a hot still night. For once the building-up monsoon clouds had been sucked back into the damp air, so that the sky was a dark blue canopy from horizon to zenith and down to the horizon again, blazing with stars. Lower down, palm trees cut black shapes into the blue, and pale trunks flashed by in regular procession along the sides of the road. In the morning, at half past eleven, the chief surgeon had come to them after an hour of operating, and said, 'It's a serious wound, but as far as we can see no vital part has been touched. Shock is setting in and she's weak . . . very. Now, will you please go home.'

The Resident burst out, 'But, McKenzie, I must know . . . is she going to live or die?'

The surgeon said, 'I can't tell you. By eight o'clock tonight, perhaps. Now, please leave the hospital and do not telephone. You may rest assured we'll call you as soon as we have any definite news, or if there's a change either way.'

By then the Chief Minister and the Prince Chamberlain were also there, and lesser officials squatting under the trees in the gardens outside.

David had driven back and buried himself in work, stopping only to have a cup of tea. It had crossed his mind to ask Wilson to play squash with him; today they would both play like maniacs. But he had not.

Five minutes ago McKenzie had called from the hospital: 'Brigadier? She's awake, and asking for you. I wish she'd go back to sleep but she won't till you get here.'

'How is she?'

McKenzie said gruffly, 'I think she's turned the corner. I just think, mind. And that's for your ears only. I'm not publishing that abroad. And by the way, you're the only one who's being allowed to visit her.'

'Thanks,' David said and hung up, yelling for Thomas to call Wood.

Now he was nearly there. McKenzie had not telephoned Wilson;

by now, he supposed, everyone knew about the Resident's infatuation, and presumably about Kumara's rejection of it. About her turning to him, too? What the hell did it matter now . . . or ever?

He ran up the steps, across the wide ground-floor verandah where in daytime many of the patients sat to enjoy the breeze. McKenzie was waiting in the passage, and led him to the right.

'Only a few minutes,' he said.

David nodded. The surgeon opened a door and he went in.

The bedside light burned and, squatting on the floor behind it, he recognized the young Mingoran maidservant who had been with Kumara in the Pagoda square. Kumara lay propped on a tilted bed, her head high, her feet low, heavy bandages visible above the single sheet that covered her lower body, a transparent muslin shawl over her bare shoulders, and two thick tubes coming out from under the bandages into receptacles set on a low table to her right side. Her eyes were open and she said at once, 'My dearest . . . I can't move . . . Kiss me.'

He stooped and placed his lips on hers. They were hot and dry, the eyes – so close now – burning, the cheeks touched with spots of red like a doll's. She whispered, 'I feel . . . miles away. Both of us together, miles from anyone else, high in the sky. Am I dying?'

He shook his head. 'McKenzie doesn't think so.'

'Have you been near death?'

Hadn't her mother asked him almost the same question? And why was it that now, lying there on the tilted bed, she resembled her mother more than she ever had? There was something about the way the skin was stretched taut over the bones, an appearance of being painted – though she was not – the strength of the eyes against the weakness of her body.

He answered her question: 'Yes . . . You must sleep now.'

'If I live, marry me, Dylan. Promise . . . promise!'

Again, her mother's words. Who was it here in the bed below him – Kumara, or the Queen's spirit enclosed in Kumara's body? But what was he to answer? For weeks now, whenever he tried to imagine what he would be doing, how he would be living a month, a year hence, no shape would appear, only a blank.

If his attempt to outwit and destroy the MPRP failed, then she would probably never become queen, and would have to flee Mingora for her life. They would be married, and he would love her and cherish her the rest of his years. If he succeeded, she would become queen, and then ... and then ... It was still a blank.

Looking into that blankness, he could not give his word to anything. As he had done to her mother, and for the same reason, he did not answer the plea.

She spoke with the pale brown lids drawn down over the burning eyes: 'You mean, they've told you I won't live?'

'No, my darling! You will, you will!'

Her breathing settled. The door opened and McKenzie muttered, 'That's enough, brigadier.'

David kissed her again, long and slowly on the lips. Her lips parted and her mouth lay open, helpless, begging to be filled. He went out.

Ten o'clock. David sat at the piano playing a prelude, as he had been since he came back from the hospital. As he finished each piece he found the music for the next, set it up, and began to play. In a momentary silence he heard the crunch of tyres on the gravel outside. He got up, took an automatic from the drawer where he kept it, turned out the lights and stood by the window. The attack on Kumara showed that the enemy were moving. The car was a big black Austin Princess saloon. Sir Harry Johnstone climbed out heavily and started up the steps. He had been driving himself. David reached the front door to open it before Sir Harry could ring the bell. He locked the door behind them, led into the drawing-room and turned on the lights.

Sir Harry said, 'Couldn't get them bailed out till half an hour ago, with all this excitement about Kumara, and then ...'

'Who bailed out?' David asked, puzzled.

'The Yank pilots, of course,' Sir Harry said. 'Ah, you've been thinking of nothing but Kumara, and I can't blame you. The pilots got back at eight this morning. They fired off all their ammunition at the camp, which was plain as a pikestaff, red flag on a tall pole, *bashas*, a few tents, latrines, everything ... except Freedom Fighters. They set fire to a lot of *bashas* but don't think they hit a soul.'

David's mind focussed sharply. The airport terminal building. The telephone booth. Sally coming out. She'd had time to telephone the man who ran the secret MPRP transmitter and give him the message; ten minutes later the camp could have been evacuated. 'Bad luck,' he said.

'They must have been tipped off,' Sir Harry said. 'Even if most of them had already gone out on manoeuvres, *someone* would have been in camp – but the Yanks say there was no one, nothing, not so much as a ruddy chicken.'

David said, 'Well, we'll have to do it the old-fashioned way, on foot . . . if they come.'

Sir Harry said, 'As to that, we've done our part. Seen the paper?'

'No.'

The old Yorkshireman held out a rolled paper: 'Page 5, bottom left. News that heavy rains hit Singapore this morning, 24 May.'

The telephone rang. David picked it up.

'Wilson here. I have to go to Singapore immediately. They're sending a jet to pick me up at 4 a.m. I'll be back some time late tomorrow night or early morning of the 26th. Nugent will be in charge. Please phone me at the Commissioner-General's if there is any change in Kumara's condition.'

'Yes, sir.'

He hung up. Sir Harry was looking interrogatively at him. David said, 'The Resident's making a flying visit to Singapore.'

'In the middle of the night? Must be something serious. Probably those Indonesian boogers. You've heard they're threatening to attack us in Sarawak?'

'Yes . . . Have the news blackout conditions been put into effect?'

'Yes. All cable and telephone lines out of the country out of action. No messages being accepted for radio transmission. Everything's going to stay that way till midday of the 26th, the Chief Minister assures me.'

The telephone rang: 'Brigadier? The Chief Minister here. There are a few things we ought to talk about, perhaps. Shall I come up or . . .'

'Is it about the Princess? Is she . . . ?' He controlled himself. The Minister had sounded a little strained, if you knew him well. And when he said 'a few things ought to be discussed' he was obviously playing it down in case someone was overhearing the conversation; in fact he would not call at midnight without serious cause.

David said, 'I'll come down.'

'If you would be so good. It will only be yourself present.'

David turned to Sir Harry. ' 'Fraid I've got to go out.'

'Can I give you a lift?'

David shook his head – 'I have to come back, anyway. But thanks.'

'More trouble?' Sir Harry said, the little eye cocked knowingly, 'But I'm not asking for details. I know you'll tell me if I need to know.'

'I will,' David said. He put out his hand suddenly – 'I don't know what we'd have done without you.'

Five minutes later he was again bowling down the road, the escort following, this time past the hospital, its lights gleaming, over the railway crossing, and down the spine of Trangloek's central ridge to the palace. A heavily muffled figure at the main gate stepped forward as he left his car, looked at him carefully, opened the door without a word, and followed him in. Inside, by the lights burning dim along the verandah, he saw that it was the Minister himself. The Minister led him in, talking in a low distraught voice: 'The princess has a good chance, Mr McKenzie told me . . . unless there should be some . . . tragic change. Here, brigadier.' He held aside the ornate curtains of a room on the right and David entered. He had been here before, only a few days ago. The Queen had been sitting on that table there. Now someone was standing behind it, his face hidden in shadow.

There was the same scent of sandalwood that the Queen liked, and a subtle perfume of hers, a woman's perfume, that she had used since the days of her beauty. Someone had recently been smoking cheroots in here, but that might have been the Queen herself, for he had seen her smoking once, in the first weeks of his stay, she and Kumara smoking together.

The man behind the table stepped out of the gloom and David saw that it was the Prince Chamberlain, the Queen's brother. The Chief Minister said sharply, 'Brigadier Jones, Queen Valaya VI died an hour ago.' His voice was quite different from what it had been while he talked as they came along the verandah – that, David guessed, had been for the benefit of anyone listening, or hearing, in the many rooms off the verandah. He added, 'It was expected, as you know.'

'Has a doctor seen her?'

'No. But there is no doubt. Princess Kumara will not be able to move for four days. Mr McKenzie said it might be much longer, but certainly not for four or five days which takes us to the 29th. We cannot have the country without a queen during these days.'

David said, 'It would be difficult.'

The Chamberlain said, 'Worse, brigadier. The people are very superstitious. The death of a queen always presages some great calamity.'

The Chief Minister said, 'We have decided to keep the Queen's death secret until Princess Kumara can show herself in public. Her Majesty had her own private quarters, kitchen, and dining-room through there —' he gestured towards the curtain behind him — 'together with bedroom, sitting room, and storerooms. There is a small deep freeze. We have emptied it and put Her Majesty's body in it. We can keep up the pretence that she is alive, though sick – as she has been for the past three months – for five days, perhaps six . . . which will be enough, if you carry out the actions we discussed at the Mingora Club, on the dates you proposed.'

David said, 'I will, unless I'm stopped. Or unless the Freedom Fighters fail to move.'

'Good. We do not propose to inform the Resident of this.'

'I understand.'

'The only people who will know the truth are our three selves, and an old maidservant of the Queen's, who found her dead.'

'The princess Kumara?'

'When she is fit enough . . . I must speak personally, brigadier. I believe the princess wishes to marry you.'

David nodded.

'I believe that you promised Queen Valaya not to do so.'

'She asked me to make that promise.'

The others looked at him keenly. The Chief Minister changed the subject: 'The man who tried to assassinate the princess has been questioned. He swears that the order to kill her was given to him personally by Sujak bin Amin.'

David said, 'I didn't think he'd do that.'

'Nor did we, once. But he's getting desperate now and thinks his revolution needs to terrify the people. Tomorrow I will inform the Binte Binte Mingora that Sujak ordered the assassination of her mother.'

'Sally? She's now the Perdana Binte Mingora, isn't she?'

'Yes, but we must not change our ways of thinking or speaking of any of the royal ladies until the news can be made public, or a slip of the tongue might give everything away.'

'Why do you say that you're going to inform Sally, in particular?'

'We are sure that there has been a link between this palace and the enemy. After long and very careful investigation, and elimination of many suspects, we are convinced that that link is the Princess Salimina.'

David said slowly, 'It all fits in. She knew Sujak before. Liked and admired him, I read in the reports. I saw her looking at him once or twice in a funny way, while we were his prisoners. I think now they may have been looks of love.'

'It is possible,' the Minister said. 'We are now certain that we can intercept any message she sends. We want to learn whether she is a true revolutionary or only a foolish young girl who wants progress and does not understand why we must move slowly . . . or what crimes the others will commit to gain their ends. That is why I shall tell her that Sujak ordered the murder of her mother. If that does not shock her out of infatuation with him and his party, nothing will . . . and we shall take other measures.'

David said, 'Did you have someone following her this morning, at the airport?'

'Yes.'

'She made a telephone call. Was it traced?'

'Yes. The security police arrested the man she called.'

'Why wasn't I told? Did they search the house?'

'Yes. You weren't told because there seemed to be nothing important about it – the security police found MPRP literature in the house – and dynamite, otherwise there would have been no cause to arrest the man. We don't know what the princess said to him. The operator said it was only a very short call.'

David said, 'But you didn't find a radio transmitter?'

'No.'

'What time was this?'

'Half past four this afternoon. The house was watched from eight o'clock in the morning on. At four the chief of security decided to move in.'

David said, 'That man has the MPRP's secret radio transmitter in Trangloek. Sally called him this morning because she'd seen the Sabre Jets land and guessed what they were going to do. He radioed an immediate warning to the Freedom Fighters' camp and they had time to disperse before the attack came in.'

'But we found no radio,' the Minister said tensely, 'And the man has been persuaded, strongly . . . He says nothing. Not a word. He never will.'

'He's got the damned thing hidden somewhere not far off,' David said, 'And we've got to find it. Do you realize that the *Mingora Times* comes out at five?'

The Minister said, 'What . . . ? Aaah! With the news of the rains in Singapore . . . and if the man was arrested at half past four he won't have seen it and therefore cannot have sent the information to Sujak at the Freedom Fighters' camp. This is disastrous, brigadier!'

David said, 'No good worrying now about what we should have done or shouldn't have done . . .' He stared silently at the two old Mingorans. He had to get a message to Sujak. Within twenty-four hours at the outside, though the sooner the better. Only radio would do it. Radio from an operator who would be believed. Who knew the wavelength used. And the location of the transmitter.

He said, 'Is Sally in the palace?'

'Yes.'

'Take me to her, but please don't come in with me.'

The Chamberlain nodded silently and led out, David following.

A servant girl was stretched out asleep on a mat outside the beaded curtains to the princess's quarters. She awoke silently at the Chamberlain's word and held aside the curtain. David went in. It was dark in the first room but a farther door was open and there a light shone. Sally's voice called in Mingora-Malay, 'Who's there?'

David said, 'May I come in?'

There was a long pause. Then, 'What do you want?'

'I want to talk to you.'

Another long wait, then, 'Come in.'

She was sitting up in bed, a book open on the sheet beside her. She was wearing a simple demure cotton nightdress, high at the throat. Her eyes were puffy and lined, the ashtray was full of cigarette stubs and she had a cigarette between her fingers.

David sat down on the bed beside her and, looking into her

eyes, knew that she knew that he knew. He said gently, 'I want you to do something for us, Sally.'

'What?'

'Send a radio message to Sujak. It's very important.'

'Why?' She spoke her monosyllabic words in a dry voice.

'Because if he doesn't get it, we will probably not be able to prevent his revolution succeeding – with all the murder of innocent people that would cause . . . people like your mother.'

'That was a madman,' she said, suddenly vehement. 'It was nothing to do with the MPRP!'

David said, 'The man swears that Sujak personally ordered him to kill your mother.'

'It isn't true,' she cried, 'they're making it up . . .'

'It's true,' he said, 'And you know it. That's why you've been crying.'

Tears began to run out of her reddened eyes, and her chest heaved, but she made no sound.

David said, 'I ask the Perdana Binte Mingora to help save a country of which, at any moment, she may become Queen.'

'*Perdana*? . . . my mother? . . . God, David, what are you saying?' She seized his arm. 'Is my grandmother . . . ?'

He nodded. 'Only five people know now . . . not including your mother.'

The girl got out of bed and walked away from him. At the end of the room she turned. 'He promised me he would never use violence against any of us. To give continuity, and to keep the old-fashioned people happier I was to be president for five years, while the People's Republic got on its feet, under him as chairman of the party. Mother was to be exiled, with a pension . . . What do you want me to do?'

'Take me to the transmitter and send a short message. Do you know how to work it?'

'Yes. I'll get dressed.'

The single bulb glowed dimly in the roof, directly over the transmitter on the table. Parts of other radio sets littered other tables and benches. They were in a cellar under the Physics Building of the University. The door, broken off its hinges, lay on the floor behind them.

253

Sally put on a pair of headphones, pushed a switch, waited a few seconds and then began to send the letters FFC in morse code, sending the group three times, then waiting a minute. At the third pause David, bending close to her, heard a faint buzz in the headphones, and read the letters FFC, then K. Sally sent the signal SAL. The distant station answered IMI, and Sally responded with LLR.

She muttered, 'That stands for "Long Live the Revolution". That's my private sign and countersign. Now they know it's me.' She began to tap the buzzer, sending slowly but accurately in Mingora-Malay the message David had written out for her in English.

At the end she began to send in English: 'You ...' and David moved involuntarily to stop her, but it was too late. Her message continued, '... promised not to hurt Kumara.'

Back came the answer: 'Join us soonest possible I will explain all.'

Sally sent: 'Will try. Ending.' She stood up. 'Do you want me to go to them?'

David said, 'You'd be dead as soon as they'd won. Or held as a hostage if they failed. No, you stay here, and say nothing. And thank you, Sally.'

The young princess said, 'I don't know whether I feel better, or worse ... I can't face the palace tonight, knowing my grandmother's in there, dead. I'm going to spend the night with a girl friend of mine. I'll tell the hospital where to find me if ... they have to.'

She went out, head bowed, past the police guard posted outside the wrecked door, to the waiting car.

Twenty minutes later David was back in Flagstaff House. The telephone rang as he entered the drawing-room. It was McKenzie. 'She's sleeping. Temperature 102. Better than I had feared. Goodnight.'

David went to the piano, lifted the cover and began to play Schumann's *Papillons*.

Eighteen

THIS WAS THE day. The 26 of May. Six a.m. If they had swallowed the bait, and moved yesterday evening, they'd reach Moirang about now. Six a.m., the light thin but growing fast. It looked like rain – heavy clouds, sultry air, oppressive heat. Even here on the upper verandah, where he was walking up and down in his pyjamas, smoking a cigarette, it was damp and uncomfortable. A bugle call sounded from the Gurkha lines, followed immediately by a trumpet blowing the same call from the Artillery lines. Blending with the trumpet he heard the trill of the telephone.

It was the Resident. 'I'm back,' he said briefly. 'Got in at half past four.' He hung up.

Odd, David thought as he replaced the receiver. No word about why the Commissioner General had called him down to Singapore in such a hurry, who else had been present, what it was all about . . .

That was beside the point, for him. The Fusiliers were in camp a mile inside Mingoran soil. At seven a.m., unless he gave them the order now, they would break camp and head south, passing out of his command as they crossed the frontier. There ought to have been some news from the north long before this . . . the Freedom Fighters should have been spotted by intelligence agents, they should have attacked a village Home Guard, they should have run into one of the many ambushes set by the RMC along the northern border . . . but they hadn't. Had Sally managed to warn Sujak, by some particular way of using the morse key, or her Mingora-Malay wording of his message, that it was false? Had Sujak somehow got correct information from another source? Or decided that he could afford to wait, in any case? Had . . . ?

Christ Almighty, all this, too, was beside the point for him, David Dylan Jones, at this moment. The point was – did he give the orders or not?

He walked quickly downstairs. Thomas was setting the table in the dining-room. Two gardeners were at work on the front flower beds. Tulbahadur was raising the Union Jack to the top of its staff outside the portico. He opened the cover of the piano and struck two resounding discords, slammed the cover shut and picked up the telephone.

'Get me the Brigade Major . . . Stork, Brigadier here . . . Send the Fusiliers the signal to open the sealed orders.'

'Any news, sir?'

'Not yet. But it's now or never.'

'Yes, sir.'

Now he was committed. He ran upstairs and began to wash and shave. There was much to be done. Warn Taiping that the Fusiliers would arrive late as he had ordered them to carry out an urgently needed training exercise. Keep Wilson ignorant, and as far as possible, busy, in the Residency. Five days to the end of his career . . . five days at the outside. The Chief might smell a rat at any moment, and send someone up to relieve him. But with luck he'd save Mingora if his plan was carried out with secrecy, precision, and above all, speed. And as Nelson said, something must be left to chance. It was impossible in war, ever, to make hard and fast plans for every contingency.

He must see Kumara, who didn't know yet that she was queen. What would her name be, as queen? He knew that the dead queen had not been named Valaya at birth, but had taken it on her accession, as popes take names that have already been used by previous popes. If he were to stay on here in Mingora after he was cashiered, he would need a job. In Kumara's government? Working for Sir Harry? But he might spend a few years in jail before that. And *could* he stay, not married to Kumara?

Quarter to seven, breakfast being served, yesterday's *Mingora Times* beside his plate . . . Thomas at his ear: 'Captain Whitmore outside, sir.'

'Whitmore? Ask him in.'

Whitmore came in, his cap under his arm, faded parachutist badge on his sleeve. David thought, meeting the man's intense gaze, that he was rather like a black-avised, wirier and younger version of Sidney Wilson.

'What is it?' he said. 'Want a cup of coffee?'

'No thanks, sir ... The Chief Minister's office rang me half an hour ago to tell me that the man who I beat up is withdrawing all charges. He has acknowledged that it was a put-up job, done for the MPRP.'

'Good!' David said. 'What made him confess, did they say?'

'He was so shocked at the attempt on the Perdana Binte Mingora's life that he decided he had to leave them. He turned himself in to the city police at midnight ... Can I rejoin the battalion now, sir?'

David said, 'Report to the Brigade Major right away. He'll see that you rejoin your battalion.'

Whitmore looked mystified and David said, 'I can't tell you any more now. And when you do hear more, keep your mouth shut.'

'Yes, sir. Thank you, sir.'

The captain wheeled round and marched out. David returned to his study of the paper. Thomas said, 'Lieutenant Crawford on the telephone, sah.'

The Intelligence Officer's public school accent was overlaid, in his excitement, by the inflections of his mother's Malay: 'Brigadier, sir! They're on their way! There was a clash with a village Home Guard four miles north of Moirang at four o'clock this morning.'

'How many of them?'

'Nothing accurate, sir. One report says five hundred, another says two hundred and fifty, with a lot of sub machine guns. I'm going to the office right away.'

David sat down once more and lifted his coffee cup.

'Duty officer on the telephone, sah.'

'Brigadier here.'

'Trouble in the city, sir.' David's heart bumped and steadied; this was *Der Tag* all right.

'What trouble?' he said.

'A policeman on duty outside the palace has been found dead, and others get shot at if they approach. Two other policemen – one city police and a Constable – have been seriously wounded. I've sent a warning order to the Gurkhas to alert their standby company.'

'Good man. I'll be right over.'

He hung up and turned towards the door. The phone rang again. He hesitated then turned again and picked it up: 'Wilson here. Have you had the news about the trouble in the city?'

'Yes, sir.'

'Meet me at the central police station right away.'

'Yes, sir.'

This time, when he heard the click of the Resident hanging up at the other end, he called the CO of the Gurkhas: 'Alastair – brigadier here. Meet me at the central police station, with your R and O groups – right away.'

'Right, sir. Shall I march the standby company down?'

'Start them at once, but hold them at the railway station.'

'They'll be there in an hour.'

To Thomas he said, 'I haven't eaten anything yet. Call the artillery major and ask him to have some breakfast sent down to me at the central police station.'

Ten minutes later, having picked up Crawford from his office, and told Porter to keep him up to date on all news from the north, the Land-Rover rattled over the railway line by Trangloek station, and headed on past the edge of the university. A bullet cracked overhead. He ducked instinctively, while Tulbahadur, perched up on the back seat with sub machine gun ready, peered at the blank walls and windows. Behind, the escort and a scout car followed on, all weapons trained. Another shot cracked over close, but there was no trace of the firer. A moment later they entered the narrow street leading to the central police station, a hundred yards short of the Old Pagoda on the broad back of Trangloek's central ridge.

David jumped down as the Land-Rover stopped. Campbell-Wylie was already there, talking to the city police chief with a large group of officers and signallers. The Resident arrived on foot, accompanied by two Residency messengers.

The Resident said, 'Everyone here? Where's the Commissioner of the Constabulary?'

'Touring the north, tuan,' the police chief said.

'Well, what's happening?'

The police chief straightened his tunic and rearranged the black cap on his head. 'Shooting at police, all over city, tuan.'

'And at us,' David said, 'from the university.'

'Some fires . . . people are not moving about . . . the streets are empty.'

'What about the palace?'

'I think it has been seized, tuan. I have sent a sergeant and six men to find out. Also the Radio Mingora building.' He cocked an ear to a loud-volumed radio inside the police station behind him, and said 'That is not one of the proper announcers. He is telling the people that freedom is at hand.'

A police sergeant came panting up from a side alley, followed by two policemen. He saluted and began to babble in Mingora-Malay to his chief. 'What does he say?' the Resident cut in impatiently.

'One moment, tuan . . .' The chief listened to another few minutes of rapid speech, with gesticulations. He turned to the waiting British: 'Tuan, the palace is in the hands of the MPRP.'

'How many of them?' David asked.

'We don't know, tuan.'

'How many loyal people inside?'

The chief said, 'Usually about a hundred people live in the palace, including Her Majesty, the Prince Chamberlain and the Chief Minister, and the two princesses. As far as we know they were all there when it was seized – except the Perdana Binte Mingora, of course.'

'Princess Salimina's not in there either. She's with a friend. Didn't your city police see any large body of men moving towards the palace?'

'No, tuan.'

David thought, then probably there is no large body of men. Suppose ten groups of three or four each wandered in from different directions – forty men at the outside. And they'd probably start chasing the loyal servants out soon, for fear they might turn on their captors.

Now, what to do? This was the diversion he and the Chief Minister had foreseen long since – designed to hold the security forces in Trangloek while the fate of the country was being decided at Moirang and Powlang. In his secret plan the Gurkhas were due to move north this evening; so if he used them here, it must be soon, and the job must be done quickly.

The police chief returned from a brief turn inside the building and said, 'The rebels are now broadcasting that the Queen has authorized them to form a new government ... that all land holdings over ten acres will be seized and distributed to the people, also free education through university level for all, and free medical care and old age pensions ... I have a clerk taking down all that they say.'

David thought, the Queen's dead, and in a deep freeze. He wondered whether the rebels had found her and if so what they would do about it. If they announced that she was dead, then the people would know that Kumara was now their queen, and as Kumara was not a prisoner she could deny all that was being put out on the radio ... once she could use a transmitter that could reach all the people of Mingora. He realized with surprise that he and Sally were the only ones not prisoners who knew that the old queen was dead. He'd have to decide whether to let the information out on the basis of what happened next.

He heard the Resident's exclamation – 'What's this?', and turned quickly. An ambulance had pulled up close by. A Mingoran whom David recognized as one of the senior doctors at the hospital tumbled out from beside the driver, ran round to the back and opened the doors. Kumara was there, lying on a stretcher, another doctor beside her. The Resident ran forward. 'Kumara! What are you doing here? McKenzie told me ...'

She raised a hand. She was pale, still bandaged. Her eyes on David, she spoke to him: 'I had to come. They have my mother in there. Sally's safe. She called ten minutes ago.'

The senior doctor cut in: 'Mr McKenzie says the princess must return to hospital in half an hour. He tried to stop her coming at all but she insisted.'

'Then let us not waste what time I have,' Kumara said. She turned to the Chief of police: 'Tell me what you know.'

The Chief spoke rapidly for five minutes, Kumara listening intently with eyes closed. David never took his eyes off her weary face, nor did the Resident. When the Chief ended she opened her eyes. 'Give me a cigar,' she said to the doctor, 'A Mingoran cheroot.'

'Madame ...'

The police chief stepped forward, fumbling. 'Thank you ... Light it for me.' She drew long on the thin cigar. A policeman hurried up behind the group and the Chief bent to listen to his urgent whispers. He turned to Kumara. 'The rebels in the palace have sent out all the women prisoners, and most of the men. They have kept the Chief Minister and a dozen others.'

Kumara said, 'What do you advise, Mr Wilson?'

Wilson said, 'I think there must be no undue haste. Let the troops surround the palace and allow no one in. The rebels will be starved out.'

'There's plenty of food in there,' the Chief said, 'Her Majesty had deep freezers installed several years ago so that the palace could have meat and fruit at any time.'

The Resident said, 'There is no cause for precipitate action. I know that the troops will soon leave, but we still have the Constabulary. It won't take many men to blockade the palace.'

'And the same with the Radio Mingora building?' Kumara asked.

The Resident hesitated: 'There perhaps an ultimatum might be given . . . that they must evacuate the building in, say, twenty-four hours. Meanwhile we can use military radio to ask Singapore to send us a transmitter which we can use to tell people the truth about the situation . . . and perhaps jam Radio Mingora as long as the rebels hold it.'

Kumara looked at David: 'Brigadier?'

'I think we must act quickly, and with the maximum available force. Everyone in the country is waiting to see what happens here. The ordinary man in the street can't afford to get caught on the wrong side.'

She looked at the police chief, who said, after a nervous side-long glance at the Resident, 'I think Brigadier Jones is right, *tuankana*.'

Kumara didn't hesitate: 'Very well. As my mother is a prisoner, on her behalf I declare martial law throughout Mingora, effective at once. I appoint you, Brigadier Jones, as martial law administrator . . . Try to save my mother's life, because she is my mother. For no other reason. Last time I saw her she was praying for a quick release from her suffering. Do not hesitate to use all force necessary, from the beginning. I much respect the Chief Minister, and of course I know personally all the servants and others now held prisoner, but if we hesitate in the hope of saving these few lives here, we shall sacrifice a hundred, a thousand, elsewhere.'

'One moment, *tuankana*,' the Resident said, 'You realize that

Brigadier Jones will be leaving Mingora in five days? And all other military officers?'

'We shall have to do the best we can, after that,' she said.

'Would it not be wiser to deal with this problem by diplomatic means now, since you'll have to after the 31st?'

'I do not think so.'

'As the British Government's representative, I have to tell you that I disagree with your policy.'

'I am sorry.'

'I am empowered to deny the ruler's requests in any case where in my judgment British interests will be imperilled.'

She lay still, looking at him, waiting.

After a time he said, 'In this case, I will acquiesce in your directive – for the time being. I reserve the right to countermand those orders and withdraw all British forces, including Brigadier Jones, from the administration of martial law.'

'Thank you,' she said formally. She lowered her voice and spoke so that David who was closest to her, could barely hear: 'Come and see me when you can.'

David felt a blush mantling his face and neck. She smiled and closed her eyes while the doctors officiously settled pillows under her head and gave the driver orders to return to the hospital.

As the ambulance disappeared up the street the Resident said, 'What are you going to do?'

David said, 'Clear the area. Order the Gurkhas to prepare an assault. Warn the rebels to come out, or else.'

'I'll be at the Residency until you're ready to act,' Wilson said. 'I have to tell London and Singapore of this . . . then BOAC will be asking whether it's safe to land their flights. There'll be a lot of questions.' He walked away, his two messengers at his heels. David found the burly form of Major Paul Stevens at his elbow, a white cloth over one arm and a loaded tray in his hands. 'Your breakfast, milord,' he said, grinning.

David said, 'What on earth . . . ? Is this for me?'

'Yes, sir. Thomas asked us to send a vehicle to take it down, but I thought I'd come myself and have a look-see.'

'Here, let's take this into the police station. Have you eaten?'

'I grabbed a bite.'

'Alastair, come along too.'

He sat down at a grubby pencil-scored table in a little office just inside the station. The chief said, 'Tuan, if you want a bigger room . . .'

'This'll do fine. Sit down with us.' He began to eat the scrambled eggs and grilled kidneys Thomas had prepared. Between mouthfuls he said, 'Alastair – prepare to seize the Palace and the Radio Mingora building . . . simultaneously . . . as soon as possible.'

'How many enemy are there supposed to be inside, sir?'

'No one knows. My guess is thirty or forty in the palace, ten to twenty in the other. The job must be done by noon, and your chaps back in barracks by two.'

'Yes, sir.'

'Paul, recce with Alastair. I think it would be a good idea to use artillery to blow in the main gate, perhaps follow with smoke into the interior then have the bunfaces go in from all directions, wearing gasmasks.'

The gunner's eyes were large. 'We're going to do quite a bit of damage, sir,' he said. 'And we can't guarantee not to blow up the Queen.'

David said, 'Forget the Queen.'

Now all looked quickly at him, and he said coldly, 'I mean it.'

The police chief said nervously, 'But, tuan, Her Royal Highness the Perdana Binte Mingora said . . .'

'I know what she said,' David said. 'I am the Martial Law administrator and I am giving an order. Is O'Grady here?'

'Yes, sir. Outside, with a couple of sappers.'

'He's to recce with you and Paul. If you want to use dynamite to blow a breach, go ahead. I'll leave the plan to you.' He turned to the Police Chief. 'Tuan, I want all the fire brigades of the city close here by the time the Gurkhas assault. You have some part-time police, don't you?'

'Yes, tuan, but they are only trained to handle traffic and crowds at big feast days.'

'That's all right. Call them all to duty, to be ready by early this afternoon.' He sat back and poured hot coffee out of the thermos. 'Any questions?'

Alastair Campbell-Wylie said, 'Sir, may I have that order in writing . . . about freedom to use artillery and explosives?'

David looked at him a moment. Alastair was a good soldier, a very good soldier, brave, very bright; yes, bright enough not to overlook the future prospects of Alastair Campbell-Wylie. A written order would cover him in the matter if anything happened to the Queen. David said, 'Peter, have a draft ready for my approval in ten minutes. Half a page should be ample.'

'Your command set radio's here, sir, at the back of the building,' Crawford said.

David got up: 'I'll try to keep out of your hair, Alastair, but there are political overtones here and I can't just go away as I would if it were a real battle. I'll be close, and interfering.'

'I understand. I'm glad of it,' the other said. 'This could get quite tricky.'

'All right. Get on with it.'

The soldiers trooped out. To the police chief David said, 'Wait here, tuan.' When they were alone he said, 'Don't worry about the Queen. '

The chief looked at him, uncomprehending. David repeated, 'Don't worry.'

The chief's face cleared. He did not understand the real truth, David hoped; but at least he understood that he would not be held responsible; perhaps he thought that Kumara's words had meant that really she wanted her mother killed. David said to him, 'Now, gather all your men, and start clearing the people out of their houses within a quarter of a mile of the palace in all directions. Don't leave police all over the city in ones and twos – they can't do anything and are just targets – in fact the snipers are sniping just to keep them scattered. Bring them in, and let the city stew until this is settled. It won't be long. Then we can deal with it. But hurry – I want everyone out in two hours – that's by ten.'

'Very good, tuan.'

Alone, David thought about the Chief Minister. If the rebels had left him in his own room, he could show Alastair where that was and the sappers and gunners could make sure not to direct fire or blast directly at it. If the rebels intended to use him as a hostage, that was a different matter. He might have time to go and see Kumara while the reconnaissances were being made and the area cleared. He shook his head – No, this could blow up at any moment, and his place was here. Suppose that the rebels inside the palace decided to make a sortie ... He looked out of the window and saw Gurkhas in battle order filing past. That danger was over.

He went to the next room and found the Chief listening to the radio. He said, 'What are they saying now?'

'The same, tuan. Freedom. Land. Money and education for all.'

'Nothing about what is to happen to the royal family and the aristocracy?'

'No, tuan.'

'H'm. That's a clever man in charge there. Keeps it vague ... No more messages as to what the Queen is supposed to have promised?'

'No, tuan.'

'No message from her in person?'

'No, tuan.'

'All right. I'm going to have a look round the palace and Radio Mingora building for myself. I'll have walkie-talkies with me.'

The circle of the binoculars wavered as David shifted his position. The heads of the two rebels on guard at the nearest corner of the palace roof jerked then steadied. Underneath them, hanging down the sloping roof was a large white sheet hand-lettered in red – *Workers and Peasants Arise!* – the motto of the MPRP. Those enemy sentries must be uneasily clinging on to the slope their side of the roof, for the Chief of police had confirmed that there were no flat places up there – though perhaps the rebels had knocked in a few planks or iron bars for their men to stand on.

He was hot, lying on his belly on one of the few flat roofs in this part of town, a ramshackle brick building overlooking the west end of the palace. At the back of the building, two twenty-five pounder gun-howitzers, hitched to their towing vehicles, waited in a side alley with their crews. The gate of the palace was straight ahead down the main street. Once the guns were towed out of the alley and positioned in the street they would be pointing at the west gate at about two hundred yards range. David shifted his gaze to the north-east, where he could see a knot of men gathered on a low roof that was clear to him but hidden from the palace by intervening buildings. The group were Alastair Campbell-Wylie and his command post. The walkie talkie lying under David's chin spoke tinnily: 'Alfa Charlie X-ray, for 9, over.'

David picked up the radio, 'Alfa Charlie X-ray, 9.'

'No problems.'

'OK Delta Foxtrot Delta, are you listening?'

'Listening.'

'Time now is ... ten thirteen.'

'Alfa Charlie X-ray, acknowledge.'

'Delta Foxtrot Delta, acknowledge.'

'Out.'

Two minutes to go. The Resident, lying beside him, said 'I will repeat for the last time – I advise you not to use artillery. It will look very bad in the world press.'

'I'm sorry,' David said formally.

Fuck the press, he said to himself. They had no responsibility. And he was beginning to read Wilson clearly. In the beginning, when he was breathing decisiveness and all for instant action, he had seemed a very model of what soldiers hoped for in administrators: a man willing to accept responsibility, who looked beyond the moment to the logical consequences of the action or inaction that he had ordered. But in fact Wilson was merely an acute reader of the political climate. When he acted firmly, as he had in the West Indies and still more in the Seychelles, it was not because he thought that was the right thing to do, but because he sensed that that was what his masters in Whitehall wanted, though political considerations prevented them coming out and saying so. Here, on the other hand, he had sensed that Whitehall wanted the velvet glove ... there might be some important treaty cooking with Thailand, or Burma ... the leaders of the MPRP, some of whom had certainly attended the London School of Economics, might have been promised trade deals or loans once they had got rid of the monarchy, which the government was finding awkward to support in the face of revolutionary or socialist parties all over Asia.

The blast of a gun below him made him start, though he had been looking at his watch, watching the second hand sweep round the face, while his mind wandered. Again, and this time bullets cracked down the street below. The west gate was a crumbling wreck, licked by flames. The enemy had a number of firearms in the palace he knew, for they had put a couple of shots close to him while he was reconnoitring, and Alastair's signal sergeant had been seriously wounded. Now, from the curtained outside windows, they were firing at the guns in the street below. But Paul Stevens had personally sited those guns, so that only a marksman standing in or above the west gate itself could hit them or the gunners crouched behind the shields. From right or left of the gate, other buildings blocked the direct line; and it was against the gate that the twenty-five-pounder shells were exploding with booming crashes. Each gun fired four rounds, carefully aimed at the corners of the gate posts and down the centre line where the double doors met; at the eighth shot the two gates collapsed, blown away. The guns kept firing but now, instead of the rumble and crack of high explosive where they burst, there was the weaker pop and hiss of smoke shell. From forward, where the Gurkhas had occupied the stalls and shops close to the palace, machine guns began to fire long bursts at the western façade. On the right tear gas grenades fired by the detachment of Constabulary with the Gurkha headquarters arched into the centre of the palace. Slowly the whole huge complex sank into a white fog, now the lower windows and verandahs drowning, now the long ornately carved roof lines vanishing into the swirling cloud. The guns were no longer firing. Ten twenty. The machine guns stopped. 'The Gurkhas' A Company's going in from the north now,' David said.

The Resident said, 'I'm going down.'

David said, 'Very well. I have to stay here. Walkie-talkie reception is not good down in the streets.'

He waited. Tulbahadur lay to his right at the edge of the roof, his gun thrust forward, the shapeless jungle hat pressed down on his round head. David listened to the walkie-talkie, his head bent. From the palace he heard a few short bursts of fire and one long human scream, faint and far. The Radio Mingora building, to the east of the palace, suddenly showed smoke at one window.

The voice on the radio was breathless, and speaking in Gurkhali, '2 *platoon, sahib. Pugyo! Tin dushman maryo, ath jana qaidi. Hamro dwui jana ghaile bhayo. Ago lagyo.*'

So the Radio Mingora building was taken, with three enemy killed and two Gurkhas wounded. The rebels had set fire to some part of it, but Alastair had been listening to that report and the leading fire brigade was under his command, its captain at his side.

He waited. Two minutes. The radio came up: 'Charlie, for 9.

Objective taken. Quite a number of rebel CT dead, but we haven't had time to count them yet.' The speaker coughed and retched. 'I've had one killed. Rifleman Karnabahadur Thapa – and several wounded.'

'What took you so long?' That was Alastair's voice.

'Couldn't speak because of the gas masks on. The gas is still bad . . . over.'

'Alfa Charlie X-ray 9,' David said, turning the switch to 'send': 'What about loyal civilians? And CT prisoners?'

'Can't say for sure yet. I know the Chief Minister was wounded slightly by the shell fire – he got a splinter in his leg.'

'Is your guard in position on the Queen's quarters?'

'Yes. But there's no one in there.'

'Doesn't matter. Just let no one in or out. *No one*. I'm coming down. Meet me at the west gate.'

David stood in an interior grass lawn of the palace, in the shade of one of the huge fig trees that were planted here by the great Queen Supaya IV three centuries ago in token of a victory over an invading Burmese army. Acrid smoke drifted across the grass from the western rooms, close to the gate which had been set on fire by the shelling. In corners of rooms and verandahs smoke and gas lurked, but the soldiers had taken off their masks and slung them again on their chests. Four Gurkhas with sub machine guns stood over twenty Mingorans squatting in a corner, the Chief of police standing among them. A dozen corpses were laid out in a row twenty feet behind the group under the tree.

The Resident said, 'You haven't found the Queen?'

The Gurkha company commander said, 'No, sir. We've searched every room. We found her old maid but she doesn't seem to be able to talk – paralyzed with fright by the shelling, the police think.'

'Extraordinary,' Wilson muttered. 'She must have gone out in the night . . . but I didn't think she had the strength. What about the Chamberlain?'

'He's in his room, sir. Says he doesn't know where the Queen is.'

David thought, the truth had better come out now. The rising had been put down here in the capital; Radio Mingora was in their hands again, and the Chief Minister was even now being carried over there on a stretcher to announce the suppression of the attempt. And he could tell the people that Kumara would recover.

The Chief of police came over from the group of prisoners.

'Anyone important there?' the Resident asked.

'Not alive, tuan. Two of the dead men were leaders – they both happened to be near the west gate and were killed by the first shell. But . . .'

'What have they done with the Queen? Have you explained to them that they are liable to trial for murder as well as high treason if she has been killed?'

'Yes, tuan. They swear she was dead when they got here. They were searching the palace for food, because they thought we would not attack, only try to starve them out, and in the Queen's kitchen they found the deep freeze. Her Majesty . . . her Late Majesty . . . was inside.'

The Resident stared, his skin turning grey.

David said, 'See that those prisoners are held incommunicado until the official announcement can be made. Commanding officers will see that no military or police personnel talk about this.'

Wilson snapped, 'Take me there.' The chief moved off, after a glance at David, who nodded consent. Alastair Campbell-Wylie was looking at him oddly, with admiration. He had guessed that David knew all along. David said, 'March your chaps back to barracks, except one company, but have that company ready to move at ten minutes notice. Open those sealed orders as soon as you get back to your lines. Get the police to take charge of these prisoners at once. Your men did a very good job, Alastair. Congratulate them, from me, especially Gurkha Captain Manjang.'

'Thank you, sir.'

'I'm going to the hospital to tell Princess Kumara, and arrange for the announcement of her accession. I'll be with Tac HQ. After that . . . well, you'll know when you've read the orders. I'd like you and as many of your officers as possible to be very visible this afternoon – playing golf, shopping, swimming. The idea is to *show* that we've won this round, not just announce that we have.'

Nineteen

IN ACCORDANCE WITH his own instructions David played golf that afternoon, with Stork Porter. He was tense, and played badly, but the game was never finished. Young Crawford intercepted them at the sixteenth tee and said to David, 'Sir, the leading group of the MPRP Freedom Fighters has taken Moirang. They are estimated to be three hundred strong. The local RMC – a hundred men – are holding a line south of the town, and will retreat slowly in front of the enemy, if they continue to advance.'

'I don't think they will, till they've consolidated Moirang. Probably after twenty-four hours. Any news from Powlang?'

'Nothing, sir. But everyone's tense. They're all waiting, ours and theirs, to see what happens next.'

'Good. No information about this is coming out through other channels?'

'Not as far as we know. The RMC have got all roads to the south and east blocked, but of course some one might slip through and spread the news . . . And, sir, the Ban Khao intelligence agents report that a second group of Freedom Fighters will move out of their jungle camp tomorrow.'

'Ah. I thought the numbers reported for the initial invasion were a bit low.'

'One more thing, sir. Princess Kumara telephoned just before I left, to ask you to attend an audience at six.'

'In the hospital?'

'No, sir. In the palace.'

'She's not fit to get up,' David exclaimed; then, 'We'll have to abandon this game, Stork.' He headed for the clubhouse, his mind racing. Why was Kumara holding an audience? He'd find that out soon enough. The plans for the night . . . He turned to

270

Porter. 'Listen. I want you to get hold of Lady Anne Wilson, alone ... and it's important that Wilson should not know that you have been passing a message to her. Ask her from me to ensure that Wilson sleeps all night tonight. She can get a suitable prescription from the hospital – saying it's for herself, of course. She is to stay up all night, answer phone calls, but tell the caller Wilson's left Trangloek, she doesn't know where – accept any messages in his name, but don't give them to him.'

'I understand, sir,' the BM said. 'Can I come with you tonight? I know I'm in the orders to stay here, but ...'

David said, 'I wish to God you could, Stork. I'll need you up there if anything develops – but I can't be in two places at once and there's important work to be done here.'

'I know. I was just hoping,' the lanky staff officer said.

'I'll call you when I get back from the palace. Probably Kumara's going to tell us when and how she will announce her mother's death and her own accession – but she may bring up something else.'

The smell of burning wood still hung about the palace, clinging to the heavy curtains that covered the inner door of the queen's audience chamber. There the woman David had known as the Perdana Binte Mingora, the Daughter-in-Line, his own Kumara, sat cross-legged on cushions on the low table. Lamps set low on the walls threw her shadow long across the room, and another on the table in front of and to one side of her painted a golden glow under her chin. White bandages showed above the top of her blue silk bodice. Below the waist she wore Thai silk pyjamas. At her breast, on the bandages, shone the Mingora Cobra, the queen's personal mark.

To the left the Chief Minister sat in a chair, his heavily bandaged leg and foot thrust out, resting on a stool in front of him. Sally sat in another chair to the right; the Chamberlain stood in the shadows behind Kumara, David sat directly in front of her.

Kumara said, 'Brigadier Jones told me earlier today of my mother's death. Thank you, all of you, for what you did ... I am now the Queen. My name is Supaya, the sixth of that line ... Come here, my child.' She beckoned slightly.

Sally stood up and went to the front of the low table. Kumara held out her hand and the Chamberlain leaned over and put a glowing red jewel into it. It was the Jumbhorn Ruby. She said, 'I should pin it on, as my mother pinned it on me, but I am not strong enough. Pin it on yourself . . . There . . . Now you are the Perdana Binte Mingora.'

Sally stood, head bowed, her thick-curled hair glowing in the yellow lights. David could not see her face, for she was standing in front of him. Kumara said, 'Don't you know what to do now? I have often told you.'

Sally mumbled, 'Yes,' and knelt down. Slowly she laid her forehead flat on the cushion between her mother's crossed feet. Kumara put her right hand on Sally's head, wincing, and Sally began to speak in Mingora-Malay. David recognized that she was swearing an oath of allegiance to her mother. Kumara was looking at him over her daughter's bowed body, her eyes deep, her face expressionless.

Sally stood up. Kumara said, 'Now, daughter, there are some matters that must be brought out, then put away and, I hope, never mentioned again . . . You took the photograph of Sir Harry and the other at the commercial banquet, with your miniature camera, and gave it to the revolutionaries that they might use it against us.'

Sally said unhappily, 'I did. It was because . . .'

'We know your reasons. You warned the men who were about to invade our country that they were to be attacked from the air, and enabled them to hide. You saved many of their lives – at the cost of the innocent whom those men are even now murdering.'

'I did.' The voice was low and miserable.

'You arranged for Sujak bin Amin to kidnap you. What was your purpose?'

'I told David – Brigadier Jones,' she muttered. 'I was to be the president for five years so that there would be less opposition from those who are loyal to us. He . . .' she stopped.

'He – what?'

'He was going to marry me when we were all equal.'

Kumara moved her head slightly and the Chamberlain came forward to hand Sally a large photograph. It showed a youngish Chinese woman with a baby on her hip, and obviously pregnant with another. Kumara said, 'That is Sujak's wife. She is a Chinese

Communist Terrorist who escaped to our country from Malaysia. My dear child, they tried to murder me . . .'

'He promised never to do it,' the younger woman cried. 'He swore . . .'

'And he would have killed you the moment you ceased to be of use to him and his party.'

Sally flung herself forward and Kumara reached out one arm and took her in it. For a while Sally lay half crouched across the low table, in her mother's arm, sobbing uncontrollably. Then Kumara said, 'Here, dry your tears. Brigadier Jones has told me how you sent the message that may save us. And if we are saved, you shall help me in leading our people to a new world.' She wiped Sally's face carefully with the silk handkerchief the Chamberlain gave her. 'Now sit down again. We will hold a council of state . . . I shall broadcast to the people at nine o'clock tonight the news that my mother is dead. I shall tell them about the invasion in Moirang, and that if I go north, you will stay here and issue any necessary edicts in my name. Now, brigadier, please tell us what has been done here and what you are going to do.'

David said, 'Early this morning the Fusiliers, who were near the Malayan border, turned round and headed north. They pass round the outskirts of Trangloek after dark – in an hour's time. They should reach Lepet near midnight. The Gurkha battalion and the guns and their tow vehicles will leave by special train at nine p.m. and will also reach Lepet near midnight. Their scout cars and Land-Rovers will go by road. All the Constables in Lepet will be allotted, in pairs, to our platoons as guides and interpreters. We have had no more news from Moirang, but I am sure that the leading rebel force, which is holding the government offices in the centre of the city, will not move until the second force reaches them. The Fusiliers will leave Lepet as soon as I have spoken to Allen, and should arrive just south of Moirang at about 0400 hours, while it's still dark. The Gurkhas will march at the same time, followed by their tactical vehicles, but it will take them an extra twenty-four hours to reach their objective. I am directing them farther north, to cut off the rebel forces' retreat. It is my intention that the Fusiliers bring them to battle in Moirang and the Gurkhas catch those who try to escape.'

*   *   *

273

'What about the security of Trangloek?' the Queen asked, 'Are you leaving any soldiers here?'

'No, ma'am. The more trained soldiers I can employ against the invaders, the more quickly and thoroughly we can do the job. Trangloek will be guarded by its own police and the specials I ordered to be embodied this morning. I have ordered the deputy-commissioner of the RMC to move his central reserve to Powlang, where it can act quickly to disarm and imprison any MPRP members who act in support of the invasion, as they will have been ordered to do in Sujak's plan.'

'That is clear enough. What if the Resident orders you not to move your troops?'

A heroic answer was on the tip of David's tongue, for his mind was made up; but he didn't think that bombast suited him, so he said, 'I shall have to wait to decide that in the circumstances of the moment, ma'am. I am meeting him at the central police station at half past seven.'

'Some soldiers will still be in the city then, won't they? I was told that he had insisted they stay.'

'They'll be there when he inspects,' David said. To himself he added, 'and five minutes after he's returned to the Residency they'll be marching to the rail yards to entrain on the special which is at this moment being marshalled for the journey north.'

'Do you have anything to ask Brigadier Jones?'

The Minister said, 'No, majesty ... except to wish him God's help to his task, and to pray for his success.'

David said, 'Thank you ... I'm sorry about your leg, but I had to.'

'Don't say another word. I understand very well. We had better prepare your speech, majesty, and then you really must lie down and rest.'

'Bring me a draft of the speech in quarter of an hour. You go and help them, Salimina. Wait, please, brigadier.'

In a moment they were alone. She rose with an easy flowing motion, stepped down, and held out her arms. David held her gingerly and muttered, 'Am I hurting you?'

'Yes ... but hold me ... I can't stay in that hospital bed any more. I was thinking of you. I could only stay if they had put you in the bed with me.'

She held up her mouth to be kissed. After a time she bent her neck away from him and said, 'Is it going to work out?'

'I think so. It's going all right so far.'

'What can I do to keep Sidney away from you?'

'Nothing. Lady Anne is.'

'Lady Anne? Is she . . . ? Dylan, is she your lover too?'

'Good God, Kumara!'

'I'll pull her hair out. I'll . . .' She laughed weakly, and then winced. 'That does really hurt . . . When are you leaving?'

'Nine o'clock. Earlier if I can get rid of Wilson by then.'

'I'm going to Moirang as soon as I can. I'd come with you if it wasn't for the broadcast.'

'No, you wouldn't! Please stay here, Kumara. There's nothing you can do up there, except have all of us worried for your safety.'

'I shall come as soon as I can.'

'I suppose I can't stop you.'

'No.'

'Promise you won't move at night, at least.'

'All right. Call me just before the broadcast. I love you.'

Wilfrid Porter was waiting for him at the Central Police station, a gangling figure dimly seen at the side of the main entrance, away from the light. David said, 'Any problems?'

'Nothing, sir. The matter you spoke to me about will be fixed at dinner.'

'Good.'

They started pacing up and down the narrow street. A pair of Gurkha sentries stood at the corner of the building, the street lamps gleaming on the polished steel of their weapons. A sergeant and four men appeared in patrol formation, three on one side, two on the other, hugging the irregular line of wall, store, and straggling tree. Two city policemen were clearly visible at the end of the street, in the Pagoda square.

The Resident appeared at their side, with a brief, 'I came by back streets. The Gurkhas seem to be patrolling everywhere. How many have you got on duty now?'

'One company.'

'Seems like more. Show me round please.'

'What do you want to see, sir?'

'Anything you think is important, especially in this part of the city. I haven't got a great deal of time, though – have to be back by half past eight for dinner and to hear the Queen's speech.'

'Right. We'll take the Land-Rover. Stork, stay here, please.' He climbed up into the back, leaving Tulbahadur to drive. The Resident got into the front passenger's seat. David said, 'Palace, *keta*.' The Land-Rover moved off, followed by the escort. At the Old Pagoda dim lights were burning, and torches flared on the tall stone posts at the corners of the platform. Several monks in orange robes sat, legs folded, near the entrance, but there was no sound of chanting or music from inside the building, only a single insistent bell. 'They know the old queen is dead,' David said. 'The bell is for her.'

Wilson said, 'When did she die?'

David said, 'I don't know.' It was a lie, and he hated lying; but at this moment he had no alternative. A few days ago he'd been trying to force Wilson to have him relieved of his command; now that must be avoided, at whatever cost – just for an hour or two more.

Sidney Wilson said, 'Kumara – the Queen – wouldn't allow an autopsy – which makes me suspect that she knows more than she is telling.'

Now, he'll say, 'Do you?', and I'll have to lie again, David thought. But Wilson went on, 'It seems to have worked out for the best, anyway. If the people had heard of Queen Valaya's death while they didn't know whether Kumara would live or die – it would have been bad. Sally could never have rallied them – even if she had wanted to.'

He was shrewd as well as intelligent, David thought, as long as passion or fury were not blinding him; for no one had told him about Sally's disloyalties.

They reached the edge of the university complex, and Wilson said, 'Any trouble here?'

'Not since the shots early this morning. The Chief Minister isn't surprised. He thinks, and my intelligence people agree with him, that the MPRP members in the university were ordered to lie low until the palace had been seized and Moirang taken.'

'The palace was seized.'

'I don't think they expected the violence of our reaction. By the time they were ready, we'd recaptured it.'

'And your Freedom Fighters have not marched south, after all.'

'No, sir. You seem to have been right.' Another lie, he thought unhappily.

He directed Tulbahadur to drive northward, through the poorer slum section of Trangloek. He realized suddenly that they were running alongside the railroad yards, and that ahead there the Gurkhas' special train was being marshalled. 'Left here, Tule!' he said abruptly. The Land-Rover plunged into narrow streets, David talking fast: 'This is the sort of section where you'd expect the most trouble ... but there wasn't any, the Police chief told me.' He had Tulbahadur stop the Land-Rover by a pair of auxiliary police and leaned out and spoke in Mingora-Malay: 'I am the brigadier. Is all well?'

The policemen peered at him, leaning on their long brass-bound staves. 'All is well, tuan. Is it really true that the Great Queen is dead?'

'I think so,' David answered, 'The Perdana Binte Mingora is to speak on the radio at nine o'clock. You must listen to her.'

'That we will ... but we thought she was in the hospital, wounded by a traitor – even killed.'

'She was wounded, but is getting well. Tell people who ask.'

'We will. Many ask us, tuan.'

'I understand.'

The Land Rover pressed slowly through the knot of men and women who had gathered while they talked, seeming to emanate actually from the walls of the buildings, rather than emerge through the doors.

They reached the sea front, where the surf on the long north-south beach that ran from Cape Rataphun to Malaya made a steady hiss and roar in their ears, and the wind blew spray across the sandy road and shook the palm huts lining it. Twenty minutes later, after passing behind the old Portuguese Fort and past the docks, they returned to the central Police station.

The Resident climbed down: 'Thank you. I'll walk back. It's only five minutes. When do you propose to ask for the repeal of martial law?'

'I haven't thought about it yet.'

'It wouldn't look good to grant independence to Mingora under martial law.'

'No, sir. The responsibility is not mine.'

'No. But you can volunteer your opinion to the Queen. Personally, I shall advise her to repeal it as soon as possible. One more thing. I would like to make another tour of the city tonight, at say, two o'clock. Please meet me here at that hour.'

'Right, sir.'

The Resident gave his customary curt nod and strode up the street towards the Old Pagoda. Stork Porter appeared from the shadows. David muttered, 'You heard? Do they sleep together?'

Porter replied, 'Same room, different beds.'

'Well, she'd better fix the alarm. He's the sort of person an alarm would awaken, whatever sleeping potion he'd been given. Get the message to her somehow.'

'Yes, sir.'

The red road glowed a paler red under the headlights as the scout car and two Land-Rovers hurried northward. At the sides of the road the heavy line of jungle showed that they had passed out of the cultivated land of Machin and were entering the province of Lepet. Eleven o'clock and all well. The Command set in the second Land-Rover was switched to 'receive' on the frequency controlled by Stork Porter back in Trangloek; but David's sealed orders had directed radio silence except in extreme emergency, and in fact no one had transmitted. The radio sat, hissing quietly to prove it was receiving the carrying wave from Trangloek.

Tulbahadur jammed on the brakes with a muttered Gurkhali curse and David looked up quickly, his carbine slipping down in his hand. A monitor lizard over five feet long waddled slowly across the road. As its long tail disappeared into the undergrowth on the left Tulbahadur put the Land Rover in gear again. David kept his carbine ready, the barrel pointed upward. There had probably been some attempt to set up ambushes on the road and railway during the evening, but the first victims to come along would have been the Fusiliers. Finding themselves faced by a whole battalion, the CTs would probably have had the sense to lie doggo, and wait for something more their own size to turn up ... like, for instance, the little convoy constituting a brigadier's command post.

A light gleamed ahead, on the right, and he stared at it,

puzzled. It was moving, but not as fast as his convoy, which was doing a steady 45 miles an hour. Then he saw a spot of red and recognized the tail lamp of a train on the railway, which here ran parallel to the road and was separated from it only by a thin strip of jungle. There was no passenger train at this hour, so he had caught up the special carrying the 2nd/12th Gurkha Rifles northward. Slowly he passed the darkened train, its presence now only obvious in the jungle by the glare thrown upward from the firebox on to the smoke and steam streaming back overhead. Then the headlight appeared, seen diffusely through the trees. It fell back.

Fifteen minutes later, with Lepet less than five miles ahead, as the lead scout car rounded a curve and dropped towards a short iron bridge over a creek, David saw a tree fall across the road just short of the bridge. His heart leaped to his throat, choking him. A savage blow on the left arm hurled him sideways. Tulbahadur had already swung the Land-Rover half way across the road, jamming on the brakes. The headlights shone on two crouching figures at the base of the felled tree. Sparks of light appeared from them, sub machine guns chattered, bullets clanged and cracked about him. The scout car was silent, wrecked against the felled tree. David fell out and crouched at the side of the road. His breath came back and he began to fire carefully at the dimly seen men, now running, by the tree. The Gurkhas of his escort ran by, firing. All other lights were out, leaving the headlights of his Land-Rover the only illumination of the scene. His arm hurt fiercely but he did not think a bone was broken. More firing began, from the left of the road now ... must be six or seven of them here – about the same as he had. He lay down, his carbine thrust forward, thinking. Tulbahadur was beside him, aiming carefully and firing single shots. Crawford appeared, crawling. David said, 'Peter, take our men round left. Force the CTs back towards the railway. Have at least two men covering the road north. The Gurkhas' train will be here in five minutes.'

'But, sir,' Crawford said, 'you can't stop it without standing in the headlights. They'll see you. Are you hit?'

David said, 'Yes. Not badly. We'll deal with it later ... Do what I say.'

'Yes, sir.'

The IO ran forward, crouching. David crawled back fifty feet from the stationary Land-Rover, its headlights bright on the iron bridge, the raw stump of the felled tree, and beyond, the dark green jungle. The night was full of sound – but seemingly aimless – the sudden clatter of the CTs' Chinese AK sub machine guns, single shots, human shouts. David crossed the road at a run as a couple of random bursts of automatic fire slapped the boughs over his head, showering him with twigs and leaves. He edged on through the jungle, his left arm hanging. After twenty paces he expected to find the rails, but there was no sign. He struggled on ... ten ... twenty more paces. Here they were, well away from the road. That was lucky in one way, for the CTs on the road would not see him; but if there were more CTs here, placed to ambush a train, then he would be out of supporting range, quite on his own. He walked down the tracks to the south. Mustn't go too far or the CTs would hear the train stop and have time to break off the battle and escape ... not too close or the train wouldn't stop at the right place. This would do.

As he stopped he saw the flash of the headlight to the south. He took off his red-banded hat and crouched beside the line. Now the engine had rounded a last bend and was coming straight at him, the rails shining silver ... maybe half a mile away. He glanced behind him. A girder bridge, like the road's, crossed the same creek; no sign of anyone there, but that proved nothing.

With the locomotive barely three hundred yards away he stood up, waving his hat. The small of his back felt cold and naked. The engine whistled furiously, and again. He heard the scream and grind of brakes. The engine passed him, the driver peering out ... thank God, there were two Gurkhas beside him, in the cab, who were gesticulating to the driver to stop. They had recognized David. The train squealed to a stop, the fourth carriage opposite David. A Gurkha captain leaned out of a window over him. David recognized him and called up, 'Quick, Manjang-sahib, all men out!'

The captain peered once, then his head snapped back. Volleys of Gurkhali abuse and orders echoed inside the carriage. Manjang tumbled down the steps, his carbine ready. From the road the boom of grenades interrupted the scattered small arms fire. David said, 'Sahib, CT ambush on the road bridge down there. About six or ten men. My escort to the left, CTs to the right.'

The captain nodded, and doubled up the track, the thirty

Gurkhas of his platoon clattering at his heels. A British officer appeared calling, 'Who's here? What the hell . . . ?' He peered; a flashlight shone in David's face.

'Turn that off,' he snapped.

'Sorry, sir, didn't know who . . .'

'Get another carriage-load up the railway, past the bridge there, and then over on to the road behind the CTs, who have sprung an ambush down there. Take command of the whole lot.'

'Yes, sir.' The young officer ran off. Another officer appeared. 'Brigadier, sir? Major Grant, A Company, here, I'm OC Train. The CO's following by road with all the tactical vehicles. He ought to be here any minute.'

David sat down carefully. 'Send for your RMO.' The noise was coming to a climax. He heard twenty automatics firing and at least thirty grenades bursting almost simultaneously. He felt keyed up and his arm throbbed in rhythmic thrusts of agony. He closed his eyes, waiting.

Someone was cutting the sleeve of his shirt. Someone had stuck a needle into his other arm, and he said sharply, 'No more morphine! I've got to keep awake.'

'It's only a small shot, sir.'

Time passed. He heard Grant talking Gurkhali and opened his eyes. Men were standing around, flashlights playing on faces and arms. 'Gurkha Captain Manjang here, sir. I'm back.'

'How did it go, sahib?'

'We found six enemy dead, sahib. The lieutenant doesn't think any of them got away. One rifleman of your escort killed and one wounded, three of my platoon wounded.'

'Thank you, sahib. How's my arm, doc?'

'Flesh wound through the upper arm, on the inside. The wound's clean, but I'll have to put it in a sling, and give you a tetanus shot.'

'A small one, please. I have a regular TT every year.'

'You ought to go back to hospital, sir . . . or at least rest in the train.'

'Sorry, doc, no can do. Take all the dead and wounded on to your train, Grant, and get going again. Meet you in Lepet.'

'Yes, sir.'

Ten minutes later, the sling in place, Tulbahadur was guiding him back through the jungle towards the road. The two Land-

Rovers were drawn up at the side. Someone was pouring water on to a seat, presumably to clean off blood. The Gurkhas had pushed the tree and the scout car out of the way. 'Get going!' he said to Crawford.

A short time later, on the outskirts of Lepet, Alastair Campbell-Wylie caught up with them from behind, with his battalion's scout cars and Land-Rovers. David told him to follow on, and together they rolled over the long bridge into the town. A Fusilier sentry, at the point where his battalion had bivouacked during the trouble at the beginning of the month, stepped out and directed them off the road. It was near one o'clock, almost an hour later than David had planned.

The Fusiliers' vehicles were parked in rows on the open space, a sentry at the front wheel of each, men sleeping on the ground all round, others inside the vehicles.

John Allen appeared from behind a hut and David stepped down. Allen peered at him. 'What happened, sir? I didn't know whether to go or wait . . .'

'You should have gone,' David said. 'We were ambushed on the road.'

Allen looked disgruntled in the dim light of the lanterns by the huts, and he sounded peevish, too; but that was because he had done wrong, and he knew it. His orders were to take his battalion to Moirang, arriving there at 0400 hours, and pen the CTs in. There was no mention of waiting for David.

David said, 'Any news from Moirang?'

'The CTs control the city altogether. They've seized the post office, bank, governor's house – everything.'

'Good. They'll still be there when you arrive.'

'And a man from Ban Khao came in to report that the second detachment of the Freedom Fighters left their jungle camp in Thailand at four o'clock yesterday afternoon, also headed for Moirang.'

'How many men?'

'A hundred and fifty, he said. Well armed, and they had carts loaded with some kind of rocket launchers.'

'H'm. I hope we'll be able to wipe them out before they join up with the others.'

To the right the headlight of a locomotive illuminated the station buildings and the palm thatch hovels beside the line a quarter of a mile away. The engine whistled long, and again.

David said, 'Any questions?'

Allen said, 'What about the artillery, sir? Am I to try to avoid damaging Moirang? You said in your orders that we were to avoid antagonizing the civil population, and I wondered . . .'

David said, 'I hope you won't have to use them until I get there with the 2nd/12th. And then we'll have to consider many factors – whether there are a lot of civilians or loyal citizens in the area, whether the use of artillery will tend to concentrate the CTs or scatter them, and others.'

Allen said, 'I understand . . . Sir, the RSM told me he'd heard a rumour that this whole operation is against orders.'

David looked at the locomotive, stopped now across the flat land beyond the serried vehicles. The Fusiliers were all awake and up now, ready to go. The Gurkhas and the guns had arrived.

He turned back to Allen and said, 'Is your second-in-command here?'

'Bannister? Yes, sir, but I was only asking because we're going to lose some men in this operation, and . . .'

'That is my responsibility,' David said, 'I signed those orders personally.'

'We noticed that it wasn't the Brigade Major's signature.'

David thought, you realized I was protecting Porter, and the reason you did not march at midnight, as ordered, was that you hoped I had been killed or incapacitated, so that you would then become Acting Brigade Commander, and be able to rescind the orders. He wondered whether Wilson had been speaking privately to Allen, and priming him what to do. But to ask would only waste time, and lead discussion into dangerous channels. He said, 'Call Major Bannister here.'

He took out his field note book, leaned over the Land-Rover and wrote. Bannister ran up, halted, and saluted smartly. David said, 'You have read my Operation Order Number 47?'

'Yes, sir.'

He gave him the torn out sheet from his notebook – 'Read that, aloud.'

The heavily moustached Bannister switched on a torch and read: *'To Major P. Bannister, Royal Oxford Fusiliers. If Lieutenant-Colonel Allen fails to obey Brigade Op. Order 47 in the letter and the spirit, arrest him, take command of your battalion, and carry out the purpose of the order. Signed, D. D. Jones, Brigadier.'*

'Is that clear?'

'Yes, sir.' Bannister looked thunderstruck.

Allen said stiffly, 'I don't think that was necessary, sir.'

'We'll see . . . Look, John, you will have some casualties, but there's no need to go at the CTs baldheaded. Conceal your strength, herd them in towards the centre, and we'll finish them off together, probably some time tomorrow.'

He climbed back into his Land-Rover and told Tulbahadur to drive him to the railway unloading ramp. As they jolted along he wondered whether Sidney Wilson was at this moment snoring in a drugged sleep, or radioing London and Singapore that he had a mutiny on his hands.

At the train, Alastair Campbell-Wylie came up as the Land-Rover stopped. 'My God, sir, you look bloody awful. Couldn't you . . . ?'

'No. I couldn't. Get a move on, Alastair! There's a second lot of CTs moving south and we've got to head them off at the pass!' He laughed with feeble near-hysteria; then pulled himself together as pain stabbed his arm. 'Send your doc here to fix up this Land-Rover so that I can get some sort of rest in it while we're moving.'

Twenty

DAVID TRUDGED ON west by south under the high sun. Twenty-seven miles done, fifteen more to cover before they would cut the main avenue of approach from Thailand to Moirang. The temperature was over 100 in the shade, but there had been no shade, except during the night hours, when they had been marching through and over the jungle covered hills of the Central Range. The cough of jungle animals and the startled shriek of night birds had been the only sound above the tramp tramp tramp of the Gurkhas' boots in the thick dust of the road. Now, since a little after eight in the morning, when the column emerged from the jungles on to the cultivated plains of the west, there had been the sun, and the dense air, stirring listlessly, and the reek of sweat, the dust rising to hang in a choking cloud, so that the Gurkhas marched with handkerchiefs tied round their mouths.

On leaving Lepet all his forces in the north had been free to send properly encoded radio messages on their VHF sets. There was some danger of the CTs picking up the signals and learning at least that there was military activity in the area, but at this stage the importance of communication between the various parts of his force overrode all other considerations. But the big set which communicated with his headquarters in Trangloek could be picked up as far as Taiping and beyond, and so he had ordered that it should maintain radio silence.

Near three in the morning the Fusiliers signalled that they had found their road ambushed at a point in the Central Range, but had had no difficulty clearing the ambush, finding two enemy dead afterwards and losing a man of their own. David had expected that; he had not expected the Gurkhas, marching parallel to the Fusiliers but ten miles farther north on a forest road, to meet any opposition; but there had been half a dozen CTs at a bridge over a narrow steep-banked torrent, in the early hours, near the rim of the jungle. The battalion quickly cleared the ambush – but the CTs had set fire to the wooden bridge the day before and nothing remained but charred timber and grey ash. All the vehicles had to stay on the east bank, with a working party of sappers and a platoon escort to get them over. Crawford and the brigade signal officer stayed with the vehicles; he himself had to get down and walk. Noon, and they had not come up yet . . .

His arm throbbed without cease now. He felt weak and tired and very thirsty. He wasn't as young as the Gurkhas around him, and even they looked drawn, the bunfaces dull with weariness under the masks of dust. But they went on, one foot after another, rolling slightly, the sturdy shoulders bowed under the weight of ammunition, weapons, water, and food. Campbell-Wylie, at his side, was as immaculate as ever, only looking concernedly at him from time to time – but he knew better than to speak. He had to go on . . . no news on the radio since the incident at the bridge, because he didn't have a radio – no one here did, until the Land-Rovers could catch up. What was happening . . . in Moirang? In Trangloek? In Singapore? He ought to let the men sing – each company had its piper with it – but the sound of bagpipes carried a long way. Farther than the cloud of dust would be visible at this time of day? No.

He mumbled to Campbell-Wylie, 'Have your pipers play.'

The colonel hesitated, then obviously worked out the same problem for himself, and spoke a word to his adjutant. A few moments later the piper of the leading company began to press and manipulate his pipe bag. After the usual preliminary wails and groans, he swung into *Scotland the Brave*.

Campbell-Wylie said, 'We'll alternate the pipes with *jaunris*.'

David trudged on. Kumara . . . naked beside the lagoon on the magic island of Pulo Pattan . . . Better not think of her, she was the Queen now. What an ironic tragedy it would be if after saving Mingora by a feat of arms, he were to destroy it by an act of love. His head was splitting. Where the hell were the Land-Rovers? Had Allen let the CTs slip through his fingers? Had . . . ?

The column stopped, the men dropping at the roadside, their feet up. A small tough Gurkha lieutenant came down the column,

joking in Gurkhali, 'Not far now,... You're not tired, just lazy
... tighten your arseholes, *nani-haru*, we're nearly there ...'

Up, on again ... two o'clock ... three o'clock, wavering voices
behind, the beat and throb of the madals:

Hamro Tenzing Sherpa – le
Himachal-a chuchura!

Four o'clock ...

Cock o' the North ... Cabar Feidh ... He'd been adjutant of
the 1st/13th and knew them all, in the long ago when they had
marched across the burning plains of India towards the North-
West Frontier ... *The barren rocks of Aden ... The 74th's Fare-
well to Gibraltar ...*

Five o'clock ...

Kati ramro jhyal a bhunyo
Bhane, makhura – le

The land swayed around him and he realized that a Gurkha
officer was marching on his left, supporting him, and Tulbahadur
on his right. 'Let go of me,' he said thickly, but they stayed at
their posts. Everyone was very tired now. Forty miles done,
the clouds piled high and the inky sky a bowl of hot lead all round.
He'd sleep for a week ... but the men were young, they'd bounce
back like rubber balls after an hour or two of rest.

The Black Bear ...

He turned to Campbell-Wylie. 'That's *The Black Bear* ... only
play that when you're marching into camp or lines.'

'I know, sir. Here's the road ... our objective. That village
over there is Bhraseng.'

There it was, stretching across, red-stone gravelled, rolled,
twenty feet wide, with a ditch on either side, running north and
south, straight to the south, to the north winding out of a patch
of woodland and jinking to cross an irrigation canal.

'This is the place,' he said, 'I'm going to reconnoitre and ...'

'Sir,' Campbell-Wylie said, 'I can do that. There's only my
battalion to dispose.'

'Quite right,' David muttered. 'Look, see those trees? Make
that the backstop. This area round the bridge is to be your killing
ground. The only way they can get away under cover is this
irrigation ditch, so make sure that anyone who jumps into that
doesn't get out alive. Send some RMC to see that no one moves
or signals from Bhraseng.'

'Right, sir.'

'No digging. The raw earth will show if they come before dark . . . or tomorrow morning. But I think they'll come by night. When the vehicles arrive, hide them all in trees, somewhere. Don't waste a moment.'

The colonel turned away, gesturing to his adjutant to follow. David stood in the middle of the cross roads, swaying. He heard the putt of motor engines and stiffened, his head clearing. They were coming, already, before the ambush was set up . . . in fact while the Gurkhas were sprawled in the ditch, asleep, waiting for the reconnaissance to be finished. But the sounds were coming from the east, down the forest road by which they had marched. A long string of scout cars and Land Rovers appeared, the latter festooned with Gurkhas of the escort clinging on to the back or sitting on the hoods, in addition to their normal loads. The Gurkhas' adjutant hurried up, barking orders for the concealment of the vehicles.

Tim Harington, the Brigade signal officer, jumped down and said, 'We got shot up, sir. There weren't many of them but it took a long time to drive them far enough off so that we could finish the job.'

'Did you repair the bridge?'

'No, sir. Cut a way down into the ravine and up the other side. Winched the vehicles up this bank. We've had two messages from the Fusiliers.' He handed over a couple of signal slips. David read them. The Fusiliers had reached report line A at 0511 hrs – that was the eastern edge of Moirang city. At 0843 they reported contact with enemy in the centre of Moirang, enemy strength estimated at 350, with rifles, sub machine guns, recoilless rifles, and knee mortars.

The Regimental Medical Officer of the Gurkhas, took him firmly but gently by his good arm and said, 'Now, sir, I'm setting up the RAP in the ditch back there and you must let me redo the dressings on that arm.'

David followed the doctor meekly. His head swam and ached, his whole body throbbed. The doctor said, business-like, 'Now, sir . . . H'm, a bit inflamed, I'm not surprised. Have to give you an antibiotic shot. Just hold still for a moment, while I get the swab . . . there . . . now we'll get on with this, and . . .'

The voice faded gently, slowly away, the twilight darkened, the hot air cooled.

'Brigadier, sir! ... Brigadier, they're coming!'

David awoke with a violent start. Where was he? Darkness embracing him, a voice whispering in his ear, his arm stiff and aching. In bed? But there was earth beneath him, and a smell of disinfectants.

He remembered; he was in the Gurkha RAP. 'What time is it?'

'Just after two o'clock, sir. The backstop company has radioed on the walkie-talkies that the CTs are passing them now.' It was Crawford.

'Take me to the Gurkhas' command post.'

'It's along here, sir. Up the ditch ... This way.'

David stumbled along the ditch in a foot of water. The night was thunderously hot and close, no stars visible. He was sweating, his clothes soggy. That bloody doctor must have put him to sleep. His eyes were getting a little accustomed to the darkness and he saw the grouped figures in the ditch and half way up one side before they saw him. A man crouching in the bottom, his ear to something, seemed to be whispering ... no, the whispering was coming out of the walkie-talkie in his hand. David stooped to listen, his head close to Campbell-Wylie's.

'... that seems to be the tail ... 150 altogether ... 100 of them with bikes ... three buffalo carts, couldn't see what was in them ... about a dozen RCLs being carried ... over.'

Campbell-Wylie muttered, 'OK. The head must be close to the killing ground now.'

They waited, tensed, still, silent. A frog croaked in the water down the ditch. Farther off, something fell with a splash. The Gurkhas breathed evenly, David tried to control his own breathing but heard it heavy and irregular against the bank of earth where his head was rested.

Twelve light machine guns opened fire simultaneously, and, all together, a dozen Very lights arched up into the night sky. The guns were firing to the right of the ditch where David and the personnel of the command post were sheltered – a never-ending deafening clatter. Mortars popped and bombs whistled through the air, followed by the crash-crash-crash of the bombs exploding.

Splinters whined across the flat paddy. David pulled himself up to the rim of the ditch, and surveyed a scene from a mediaeval painting. Lit by the hovering white ghosts of the Very lights, small figures of men crouched, sprawled in the road, ran across the paddy, to be suddenly cut down by the invisible scythes of the machine guns. Two carts blocked the road fifty yards away, their buffaloes dragging dead in the yokes. The metal of bicycles gleamed and flashed everywhere, everywhere there were humpd rows and piles of bodies, some moving, most still, the near ones seen to be black clad, red blood and white pulp garishly decorating the sombre clothing.

A mortar bomb whistled loud and burst twenty feet away. David ducked. That was incoming. The CTs had pulled themselves together very well. But this end of the Gurkha ambush had really caught the front half of the column; from what he could see – his head up again – that had just about been wiped out. Another CT mortar opened fire, then another. Four in all. They had not used their RCLs – no target for them to fire at, for the army's vehicles were invisible.

The machine guns stopped firing and only the mortars continued the battle, on each side. The heavy crumping continued steadily for fifteen minutes, then suddenly violent small arms fire broke out again, from up the road to the north. Campbell-Wylie let out a loud exclamation of relief: 'They've retired into the backstop company.'

David relaxed. The ambush was going perfectly. He said, 'I never heard your plan. What are you doing to prevent them escaping east or west?'

'I've got a platoon spread out thin to the west. We have a lot of machine guns with them, firing in enfilade. I couldn't put anyone to the east – there's no cover that way, and our LMGs would have been firing straight at them.'

David thought for a few minutes. Then he said, 'We've got to get down to Moirang as soon as possible. Leave a company here to hold the road block until further orders . . . they won't be attacked again. Tell them to mop up at first light. As soon as the rest of your battalion's ready, we'll march. Bring your casualties down in your tactical vehicles – if you've had any.'

He climbed up out of the ditch, helped by Crawford, and fumbled for a cigarette. Crawford lit it. Two thirty a.m., 28

May. He might drive south, fast, with his Tac HQ. It was a little over twenty miles to Moirang... but what was the point? He would have no troops with which he could influence affairs. Allen ought to be capable of dealing with the situation by himself until the Gurkhas arrived; and it would be risky. The double ambush at the forest road bridge showed that the CTs were well organized and tenacious. The Gurkhas would be dog tired by the time they reached Moirang – forty miles yesterday and another twenty now. But he'd probably have to put them into action at once. They'd have plenty of rest when it was all done.

A pale shape loomed in the darkness to the south. Crawford and Tulbahadur thrust forward their weapons. The shape said 'Dhaulagiri,' and Crawford answered 'Pokhra... That's the password and countersign for the night, sir.'

The shape materialized as a Gurkha signaller with a message: 'From the signal-officer-sahib. Just arrived.'

David dropped back into the ditch while Crawford shone a torch on the message. It read, 'G.45 OP IMMEDIATE – TO BRIGADIER JONES FROM H.B.M. RESIDENT IN MINGORA. RETURN ALL TROOPS TO TRANGLOEK FORTHWITH REPEAT FORTHWITH. ANY DELAY IN CARRYING OUT THIS ORDER WILL RESULT IN YOUR IMMEDIATE REMOVAL FROM COMMAND AND SUBSEQUENT COURT MARTIAL. ACKNOWLEDGE.'

'Did we acknowledge?' David asked quickly – but of course the signaller would not know; but the man was still here, holding out another slip. This was from Tim Harington the signal officer: THE BRIGADE MAJOR SENT US A PERSONAL MESSAGE BEFORE G.45. IT READS: FOLLOWING MESSAGE G.45 DICTATED PERSONALLY TO ME BY RESIDENT AT 0147 HRS. C-IN-C INFORMED AS STATED BUT NO MESSAGE FROM SINGAPORE YET. WILL INFM YOU WHEN IS. GOOD LUCK. PORTER. ENDS. WE HAVE NOT ACKNOWLEDGED EITHER G.45 OR BM'S SIGNAL BUT MAINTAINED RADIO SILENCE.'

David absently stuffed the slips into his pocket. Time was getting short, but part of the job was done. As long as he didn't acknowledge receipt of any of these messages they could order as much as they liked. But General Sir Rougemont Huntingdon was not the sort of man who'd take that for long; if he'd been informed, and didn't like what he heard, he'd be on the spot soon enough, even if he had to jump out of an aeroplane to get here. A hundred and fifty CTs written off here, say three hundred left in Moirang; he himself had twelve hundred men in hand. The job would have to be done before dark this day.

His watch showed eight when he first saw the spires of Moirang pagoda six miles to the south. The heat was building and he thought that by afternoon it would be worse than the day before. He sat back in the Land-Rover where it waited at the roadside, his mind working. All night the convoy of tactical vehicles had been stopping fifteen minutes, then moving forward until it caught up with the tail of the Gurkha column, then waiting again, so that the engines would not overheat by crawling along at the infantry's pace, and also to keep the dust and fumes behind the marching soldiers, though the soldiers raised plenty of dust themselves.

David lit another cigarette. John Allen had signalled during the night that he thought he had the CTs well boxed in; but he didn't know how long that situation would hold now that the enemy had had twenty-four hours to gauge the strength of the force opposing them. He advised that the Gurkhas should come down as fast as possible to act as a backstop to north and west of the enemy-held area, while his Fusiliers attacked and cleaned it up from south to north.

Six miles to Moirang – two hours marching. The 2nd/12th would get there at ten. Then it would take an hour to co-ordinate details of the attack. Allen should be able to go in at eleven, or soon after.

He threw down his cigarette and stubbed it out. The convoy moved forward.

The Fusilier attack began finally at 12.10 p.m. David watched from the verandah of a private house two hundred yards south of the city centre, where the CTs held the Governor's house and garden compound, the pagoda, the RMC station, the bank, the post office and a dozen other buildings grouped on the right bank of the Moirang River. The river, now shallow and wide between sloping muddy banks, would soon become a swirling brown torrent so thick with earth and uprooted trees and dead cattle that it would seem more like a stew than a river. The monsoon clouds were heavy and dark across the sky.

B Company of the Fusiliers was leading the attack, supported by C. The four twenty-five-pounders of 154 Light Battery were well forward, concealed and camouflaged in alleys and inside houses, ready to fire individually at targets which needed to be reduced – but they were not to fire except on David's personal order, for the CTs were holding some forty hostages, including the governor and other prominent loyal citizens; also, the wind was blowing in gusts and he feared that a fire, once started in those palm thatch and wooden houses, would cause tremendous damage and loss of life.

Rifle and machine gun fire crackled in the steamy noon. A moment later a light *thunk thunk thunk* told David that the enemy were using their knee mortars.

The minutes dragged slowly by. Bursts of fire from forward were interspersed with the crash and boom of mortar bombs, the occasional bump of a grenade and now and then the chattering clatter of enemy automatic fire sweeping the street. Stretcher bearers passed, carrying wounded Fusiliers. David counted seven – and that was only the wounded; there must have been some killed in that incident, whatever it was. Two Fusiliers half-ran, half-stumbled to his command post, dragging and carrying a black-clothed Mingoran with a long bloody gash across his face and one leg smashed. 'Prisoner, sir,' they gasped to Peter Crawford. 'Caught him trying to sneak out that way. Colonel said to bring him to you.'

Crawford began to speak to the prisoner, but he fell into a real or pretended faint. He's probably a messenger, David thought, sent out by Sujak to give orders to the second group – which he did not know had been annihilated. Then he wondered, would Sujak be here? He had been assuming that he was, and when he made his plans and gave his orders had had a clear picture of the man in his mind. His momentary doubt vanished. This was the decisive point, and Sujak would be here.

One o'clock . . . half past . . . He didn't want to bother Allen but he must go forward now and find out what was happening. He beckoned to Crawford to accompany him, when Tim Harington, at a signal set a few paces away along the verandah, called, 'Hold on a moment, sir. Message from FARELF coming in.'

David waited. He felt cool and at ease. This was it, the message from the Chief whom he had always respected and feared, the man to whom he owed his immediate duty. Harington handed him the message form, saying 'We got it direct from Singapore, sir. Rear HQ got it, too.'

David read: 'CINC 608. OP IMMEDIATE. PERSONAL TO BRIGADIER JONES FROM GENERAL HUNTINGDON AM ON MY WAY TO YOU BY FASTEST MEANS CAN NOT GIVE ETA OWING TO BAD WEATHER HERE MEANWHILE ALFA BREAK RADIO SILENCE BRAVO CEASE ALL MILITARY ACTION EXCEPT SUCH AS TO ENSURE SAFETY REPEAT SAFETY OF YOUR TROOPS CHARLIE ACKNOWLEDGE.'

He read it again, half aloud, though he had understood perfectly the first time; had, in fact, found it almost word for word the message he had been composing in his own mind, for the C-in-C to send, had he been down there as the Chief of Staff.

He gave the message back to the signal officer, saying, 'File it. Acknowledge. Peter, come with me.'

He started up the side of the street, Crawford and his escort following. Allen's headquarters was in another house a hundred yards closer to the CTs. On the way, David passed more wounded and saw several groups of British soldiers lying or sitting against the walls of houses, trying to find shade where there was none. Those that he saw looked exhausted. He saw by the yellow flashes on the sides of their jungle hats and on their shoulder straps, that they were B Company.

He reached the battalion's headquarters. The noise of battle was louder here, and the bullets smacked closer. Three figures in jungle green lay humped in the dusty street thirty yards farther up, and even from where he was David saw the red pool in which they lay. 'Ours,' Allen said briefly, 'killed by a mortar. The bodies are covered by CT snipers from the right. We're having a hard time. B lost about twenty casualties, only four killed, but they couldn't move, and I passed C through. Now they're pinned down all along. Snipers hidden not only up there but back here – we've definitely had one man killed by a bullet from in there somewhere' – he gestured at the warren of houses and stores and occasional taller buildings behind him.

'What do you want to do?' David asked.

Allen's freckled face was red and wet and streaked with mud where the sweat had made runnels in the dirt. There were rings of fatigue and strain under his eyes and his hand trembled slightly all the time. He said, 'God, I don't know, sir ... If we use the guns and blast them out, we'll kill the hostages ... but if we just go in straight, we'll lose a hell of a lot of men. Most of the CTs are pretty poor shots, but they've got guts. They're not going to pack in just because they see us coming.'

David thought, there's some gas available, not much, and the Fusiliers had their gas masks – but the lie of the buildings and the gusty winds would disperse the gas so that no one could be sure where it was having effect and where it wasn't. No good.

Crawford lit a cigarette for him. His left arm in the sling was as stiff as a board now, and useless to him. It was true that more soldiers would get killed if he didn't use the artillery, but that was what soldiers were paid for.

'How many CTs do you think you've put out of action so far?' he asked.

'It's hard to say ... I guess about a hundred. We've captured a third of the objective, and found forty dead and wounded. We've taken some prisoners, and it's reasonable to assume we've done some damage in the part which the CTs still hold.'

'About two hundred or two hundred and fifty still left?'

'That's my guess. With all their mortars and tommy guns ...'

'... but perhaps not much ammunition.'

David drew on the cigarette. Then there was the order from the C-in-C: cease all military action except such as to ensure safety repeat safety of your troops. He saw the general's bulging forehead and glittering eye and glowing rows of ribbons. A real soldier, shot to pieces in the Western Desert. A man to obey.

He said, 'Have your RMC with megaphones give them a surrender message right away. We'll spare the lives of all except those guilty of murder committed before yesterday. They'll be tried. Everyone to come out in ten minutes.'

'And if they don't?' Allen said, wearily belligerent.

'Have A Company assault, supported by B and C from their present positions. No artillery or heavy mortar support.'

Allen snapped – 'Right! I'll take them in myself!'

David had decided that, in all the circumstances, he must lead the attack himself, and therefore answered, 'That won't be necessary. I will.'

Allen growled, 'The men are jumpy ... the heat ... the snipers in the back ... and the rumour that this operation is illegal and unnecessary. They know that they were supposed to be out of Mingora forty-eight hours ago. And ...'

'And what?'

Allen said, 'One of your signallers talked about the message from the C-in-C. It was all round the battalion before I could do anything about it.'

David said then, 'I'm going to speak to A Company. You get the covering fire ready. Where are they?'

'Down the road, fourth street on the left.'

'Thanks.' David went out and back the way he had come. A hundred yards behind his headquarters, where Harington and the signallers were still in position, he found a hundred Fusiliers, sitting and sprawling against the houses, the black flashes of A Company on their crumpled hats. The company commander scrambled to his feet and saluted. David said, 'All your company here, Whitmore?'

'Yes, sir.'

'Good afternoon, sergeant major. Bit hotter here than on the Rhine, eh?'

The burly warrant officer wiped his sweaty face: 'Temperature's 'ot, sir, but the rest, cor, this is nothing. These kids don't know what a scrap is!'

David said, 'Well, we're going to show them. We're going to assault again, with your company, and I'm going in with you. I'd like to speak to the men. How are they?'

The captain said, 'Hot ... thirsty ... a bit fed up with waiting around.'

'The position the CTs have taken up means that we simply can't deploy more than one company at a time,' David said, 'Otherwise Colonel Allen might have been able to use the whole battalion right away, yesterday, and clean them up in a single big bite.'

Up the street he heard the garbled booming of the distant megaphones as the Constables shouted the surrender message to the CTs.

Whitmore said, 'We've had two men wounded by snipers, even back here, but never found anyone ... no one we could be sure was a CT – just an old woman of about ninety.'

'They can be the worst,' David said. Whitmore was a fire

eater, but even he seemed a little uncertain now. And this was A Company. Looking round at the men gathering under the beckoning of CSM Berg he recognized a face here, another there, from his meeting in the barrack room the day of his arrival six months ago. He could read nothing certain in their faces, except fatigue, heat, and, yes, a vague sense of hostility.

Whitmore said, 'You all know the brigadier. He wants to say a few words to you.'

'To us' would have been better, David thought, including himself and the other officers with the men, instead of by implication separating them.

He said, 'You may not have heard that at two o'clock this morning the Gurkhas wiped out the second group of these CTs, who were coming down, hoping to catch our forces in the rear. We killed a hundred or more of them and captured all their stores and heavy weapons. Our attacks on the CTs here have gone well, but slowly, because we don't want to suffer needless casualties. We've put about a hundred of them out of action one way or another. Now we have to finish the job before dark, which will come in about three hours from now.'

'Why?' a voice called from the crowded ranks in front of him.

He said, 'Because England promised to protect the people of Mingora. If we don't do our job now we'll have taken what the Mingorans have given us for a century and a half, and then backed off when it was our turn to live up to our part of the bargain. We didn't help them much against the Japs, but we can now. We should. And we will.'

The men packed in the narrow street stirred like leaves, but kept their faces towards him, still unreadable.

David continued, 'If we used the artillery point blank we could blast them out of most of the houses – not all – one at a time, but most of those buildings are wooden, palm-thatched, and we'd certainly set fire to the area and perhaps to the whole city. And there are about forty innocent people in there being held hostage. I have decided to attack once more without the guns. Colonel Allen has chosen you to do the job. I wanted to tell you why it has to be done this way, and that I'm going with you, with the leading section. I'll answer any questions you have now.'

There was a long silence. Then, just as Whitmore began to say, 'There are no questions, sir,' a fusilier near the middle of the crowd said, 'Couldn't we send them a surrender message, sir ... saying if they don't surrender we'll use the guns?'

'It's been done,' David said. 'But I doubt if they'll pack in. In my opinion they're more afraid of their leaders in there than they are of us ... so far. Anything else?'

An educated voice said, 'We have heard that this whole operation is unauthorized. Is that true?'

David said, 'I am the brigade commander. I have ordered it.'

'We could be charged with carrying out an illegal order.'

'You won't be. I think you know already that there is a disagreement between myself and the Resident as to what is necessary and what is not, but martial law has been declared and I am the martial law administrator ... which means in fact that I have dictatorial power, because martial law is no law – merely the right to do whatever the administrator considers militarily necessary.'

Another man cried out in a sing-song, 'We'll be the ones to get killed or wounded!'

'That's enough of that!' Whitmore said sharply.

David recognized his namesake, the fiery politician Fusilier Jones, and spoke a rapid sentence at him in Welsh. He added, 'For the benefit of the Sassenachs among you, that means, "Keep close to my red hat, and you'll stand a good chance."'

Kid Berg led a round of laughter, but David thought, this company's not right yet; perhaps he should ask Allen to give him another, or get a Gurkha company to assault – *they* wouldn't hesitate or ask questions. But fate had given him these men to achieve his object with, and he would be proved wrong in his whole case – that the ordinary people of Britain would not betray Mingora if they knew the facts – if he could not persuade them.

Another Fusilier said, grumbling, 'You wasn't so keen on us when the mob was beating us up after the football, sir.'

A hum of agreement passed round the crowd. How typical of British soldiers, David thought – they don't really mind the possible illegality, or the danger, but they're angry about the football game.

He said, 'Who got hurt?'

Silence.

He said, 'The students lost their tempers. You had a scrap afterwards. A good scrap. Forget it!'

A car passed in a swirl of dust, stopped with squealing brakes and backed up. Sidney Wilson jumped down from his big official Rolls. He strode into the group of soldiers, calling 'Make way, please. I am the Resident.'

David saluted as Wilson ran up the three wooden steps where he had been standing to address the soldiers, and faced him: 'You are under arrest!' he snapped.

'By what authority?' David asked.

'Mine.'

From the corner of his eye David saw the soldiers swaying forward, suddenly intent in a way they had not seemed to be before, their eyes moving back and forth like spectators at a tennis match.

'Has Her Majesty repealed martial law?'

'No. I have.'

'You do not have the authority to do so.'

Wilson swung on the soldiers, shouting 'What's he trying to make you do? Attack? Get killed? He's been forbidden to do so by me, our Queen's representative . . . and by his own Commander-in-Chief. Arrest him. You, you, you! Seize him!'

No one moved. David waited.

Wilson wheeled on Whitmore: 'Captain, arrest Brigadier Jones.'

The captain's face closed. He said, 'I have no authority to do that, sir.'

Wilson turned again to the men, calling, 'I'm telling you, obey him and you'll be liable for serious charges . . . mutiny, murder!' His face was dead white, soaking wet. David thought dispassionately, he's driven here, probably by Kusalung and Powlang, alone, through country where the CTs were all out and active, unaware of anything except his one obsession: get David Jones – kill, break, crush, smash . . . like a squash ball.

John Allen came into the alley, carbine slung, followed by two fusiliers. He came fast, hurrying through the dust. Then he saw Sidney Wilson. An expression of relief crossed his streaked face, to be replaced at once by a tensed look of strain as marked, or more so, than during the conference at his headquarters. He had realized what must come. He said nervously, 'Sir . . . brigadier . . . no CTs have surrendered.'

Wilson turned to him: 'Colonel Allen, I have relieved Brigadier Jones of his command. He has no official position. No one is to obey him. You are in command now.'

David said, 'Mr Wilson has no power to remove me from command.'

'Tell these men not to obey his orders, you damned nincompoop,' Wilson snarled at Allen, his voice grating like a knife across a plate.

Allen looked helplessly from Wlson to David, then at Whitmore and Berg. His eyes wandered round the circle of the Fusiliers. His mouth worked.

David felt a stiffening of resentment among the soldiers. John Allen was their CO, and a Victoria Cross. No bloody civilian in a feathered hat had the right to speak to him like that. He seized the moment, crying, 'We can't afford to waste any more time. Whitmore, Berg, bring the company forward.'

He stepped down into the street among the soldiers and Wilson leaped at him. A hard fist crunched against the bone of his cheek, and he struck back as best he could with his right arm. Then he was down, the Resident on top of him. Darts of agony shot up his wounded arm. He saw Whitmore leaning over Wilson and croaked, 'Leave us! Attack!' Then Wilson's hands were at his throat, banging his head up and down in the dust. The man's eyes were bulging, his mouth streaming meaningless obscenities, saliva and bubbles dripping from the corners of his lips. David struggled for his breath, jerked his knee up in the other's groin and punched up as hard as he could with his good arm. But the Resident was too strong, and he felt his senses going, and an excruciating pain in his left arm told him that the arm had probably been broken. He went limp.

Wilson eased his maniacal banging. From gathering darkness David called, 'Whitmore? Are you there?'

'Yes, sir.'

'Attack . . . now!'

He could see soldiers' boots all round him. Dimly he heard Kid Berg barking orders, but none of the boots moved. Then he heard a Midland voice say, 'The brigadier treated us right in December, didn't he? When we could all have been shot! Come on, you blokes.'

The boots began to move past the two men in the dust, leaving them a wide berth as though the boots belonged to women drawing back their skirts from defilement. David, his head slowly clearing, caught a look in one young fusilier's face that told him another reason why he had won, why they were obeying his order: the wound that handicapped him and made the Resident seem to be picking on a helpless man.

Slowly Wilson rose and leaned against a post, resting his head on his forearm. David followed A Company up the alley. When he caught up with them Berg looked at him and said, 'My God, sir, you oughter go to the RAP, sir. That arm's like a ruddy corkscrew.'

David said, 'Later . . .' He tramped on, reeling and dizzy. He heard Whitmore say,' If you'll wait here, sir, I'm going to check my support and start line.'

David sat down, leaned back against a wall and closed his eyes. Someone was giving him water . . . a Fusilier . . . a gunner bombardier was offering him a sip of rum. He took them both, coughed and looked about. Crawford had appeared, but where was Tulbahadur? With the Land Rover, back in cover somewhere. They were near the CT-held area now and no one moved in the open. He could see, across the street, down alleys, in open hut doors, the heads of soldiers with here and there the snout of a weapon or the gleam of a bayonet. The firing had almost ceased, though occasional drum taps showed where snipers on both sides were still at work.

A voice at his ear said, 'You think you've won, don't you?' It was the Resident, standing over him, his white suit soiled and torn, his pale face suddenly calm.

David said, 'I am trying to do my duty as I see it, sir.'

'Well, you don't understand . . . Every step we take to help this royal house is a step backward. Royalty has had its day. The Mingorans of tomorrow are the ones inside those buildings' – he nodded forward – 'and we ought to be helping them every way we can, because that's how things are going to go. How they have to go. Which side is England going to be found on? Holding up the old and dying, or reaching out our hand to the new and living?'

David said, 'And you've been interpreting, and stretching, your mission accordingly?'

The Resident said, 'Of course I have, because that was implicit in my orders. But for you we would have succeeded in giving independence to a regime that would have fallen to the new wave without a blow . . . peaceful exile of the royal family, break-up of the great estates, abolition of ancient privileges.'

David said, 'Peaceful exile of Kumara? They tried to murder her!'

Wilson ignored the remark. His voice rose: 'You've spoiled everything. In a year or two, or three – it doesn't matter when – all this will happen again, with more bloodshed, more bitterness . . . because that's the only way for these people to progress.'

'I disagree,' David said. 'And even if I did agree, our job is not to plan the future of Mingora but to ensure that the present government of it, which is allied to Great Britain by treaty, is not overthrown by force.'

The Resident said, 'Force! These people only use force when they have to. They'll listen to reason. Cease fire . . . and watch.'

He walked a few paces down the alley and out into the oven-hot street, the wind blowing in his hair and flapping his white trousers against his legs. David hobbled to the corner where the alley debouched into the main square opposite the governor's house. Wilson strode steadily forward, his arms spread. He was calling out in Mingora-Malay 'Hear me . . . I am the British Resident . . .'

Then Crawford murmured, 'He's saying, "This attack on you is a mistake . . . done without authorization. I have kept faith! Come out, with hands raised. There will be no reprisals, punishments, trials . . . the troops will retire . . ." My God, they're firing at him!'

Half a dozen shots rang out. David looked round the corner and saw Wilson, standing, his head up, hands outstretched beseechingly. A storm of machine gun and rifle fire from the Fusiliers crackled into the CT positions. Wilson started back, walking, not running, head erect. Bullets were flying round him, but he was not hit. He reached shelter and stood, looking straight ahead, seemingly unconscious of what was going on about him.

Whitmore returned and said, 'We're going to use mortar smoke, sir. It didn't work well for C Company, but it might for us. Two minutes to go.'

Bombs whistled over them from the city behind, and burst with hissing phtts in and among the buildings ahead. The white smoke thickened and David followed Whitmore into the square, his pistol drawn. Firing inceased as fusiliers came tumbling out of lanes and houses all round. David broke into a run, heading for the main door of the Governor's House. It burst open as he reached it and a crowd of men, women, and children ran out, coughing and retching in the smoke pall. Black clad CTs tumbled out with them, hands raised. From a house on the right an enemy automatic sent a stream of bullets into the right platoon and half a dozen men went down like skittles. The rest of the platoon turned and charged, all weapons blazing.

Three CTs ran out, tommy guns barking, to be cut down by the supporting machine guns of B Company. With a dozen fusiliers he burst into the Governor's House. The garden in the middle of the building was full of armed CTs. The fusiliers fired into them and three fell, the rest dropped their weapons and raised their hands.

Now the company had the bit between its teeth. He found himself alone with Crawford, soldiers with black hat flashes pouring past.

'We've got 'em, sir,' Crawford crowed exultantly. 'They're running into the Gurkhas . . . those who can move!'

Then the ground rose and Crawford's arm shot out to hold him, just in time. From far away he heard Crawford call, 'Stretcher bearers! Double!'

Twenty One

H<small>E THOUGHT FOR</small> a moment that he must be dead, for
Kumara's face hovered over him, and her hand was on his
forehead. But she looked worried and surely if she were appearing
to him in an after life she would be smiling, at the least. And he
heard the crack of small arms fire, slow now and staccato, but
there would be no battles in heaven – at least not with self-loading
rifles.

He said, 'Kumara . . . you're bandaged! . . . I remember. Isn't
the fighting over?'

'Not quite,' she said, 'We're in Moirang.'

'Oh, yes. Where have you come from?'

'Trangloek. I drove up as soon as I heard that Mr Wilson had
left. Don't speak.'

He was lying on a bed in a room with a shattered window.
Through the window he saw palm trees thrashing against an
indigo sky, heavily clouded, and light from a lowering sun. He
tried to look at his watch, but his left arm would not move. Ah,
Wilson had broken his wounded arm in a fight, but before that
he'd transferred the watch to his right wrist. He lifted it up.

'It's nearly four,' Kumara said, and now he saw Tulbahadur
behind her. John Allen came in, taking off his jungle hat and
dashing sweat from his face and forehead on to the floor.

'What's happening?' David asked.

'Thank God you've come round, sir. We cleaned up the
objective . . . took a lot of prisoners, including someone who claims
to be Sujak's right hand man. I believe the Chief Minister's
interrogating him now.'

'Is *he* here?'

'He came up with me,' Kumara said briefly.

'Any sign of Sujak himself?'

'No, sir.'

'Where can the man have got to?'

Allen continued, 'Apparently about fifty CTs had evacuated the objective before we went in. Sujak might be with them. They're holed up in the next section of houses, west along the river bank.'

'What casualties have we had?'

'My lot's had sixteen killed and forty-six wounded, till now. I don't think the Gurkhas have had more than four or five wounded.'

Kumara said, 'Please, colonel, the Brigadier is . . .'

David pushed her hand away from his forehead, so that he could see Allen more clearly, but still held on to the hand. He said, 'Why didn't the CTs run into the 2nd/12th?'

'I don't know. Probably a mixup of boundaries. But they're right up against them now. I've been talking to Alastair by walkie-talkie.'

David sat up and swung his legs off the bed on to the ground. His head felt a little swimmy and his slung arm, which he now saw was also in a splint, ached fiercely. He was dressed from the waist down, naked above.

Kumara said, 'Dylan, before you give any orders, you must know that General Huntingdon is arriving any minute by helicopter direct from Singapore, with Sir James Fortescue.'

'The Commissioner General?'

She nodded. David thought, if he ordered another attack right away, it might be finished before they arrived; if he waited, there was a chance that darkness would fall before the job was done and then inevitably, some of the CTs would slip away. He made up his mind – it must be done now. And quickly. This time the CTs were not holding any hostages, and field guns could fire on the isolated group of houses without such great danger of causing a universal conflagration.

He said, 'Crawford, give the CTs another chance to surrender Same terms as last time. Give them ten minutes. We'll attack in half an hour from now . . . that will be 1630. Run along! John bring me a walkie-talkie, and get Alastair on.'

'Right, sir.' The Fusilier colonel ran out. Kumara said, 'Can your radio here be linked with the Radio Mingora transmitter in

Trangloek, so that I can speak to the people from here?'

'I don't know. Someone, go to the signal officer and see if it can be worked out.'

Kumara said, 'You *must* rest. There's not much more to do and I'm sure Colonel Allen can do it.'

'This isn't an ordinary battle. I must give all the orders until the C-in-C gets here.'

She said, 'So that no one else can be blamed . . . I can't think why it took us so long, when you first came to Mingora, to realize what kind of a man you are, Dylan. And for me, there was no excuse.'

Allen came in. 'Alastair's on. Outside. Reception's not good enough inside the building.'

'Where are we, by the way?'

'In the Governor's House – you passed out in the passage just outside there, so we made this brigade HQ.'

Tulbahadur was at his side, helping him, and he walked slowly across the room and out into the sheltered glare on the long verandah. He picked up the walkie-talkie: 'Alastair? . . . I'm giving the remaining CTs ten minutes to come out. You attack from west to east at 1630. Start with artillery firing from north to south. The Fusiliers will hold their present positions. Any questions? Time now is 1608. Keep listening watch on this frequency. Out.'

Allen said, 'A chopper's landing in the square, sir . . . They're under fire from the CTs!'

David watched numbly. Getting the two top British officials in the Far East killed would crown his achievements. It would at least make his court martial more interesting. The green camouflage-painted RAF helicopter landed heavily, the door opened and a small red-capped, much beribboned figure stepped down and marched stiff-legged towards the Governor's House, neither hurrying nor dawdling. A tall man in a light grey suit and panama hat, carrying a brief case, followed. The chopper rose and drifted away across the jumbled houses, followed by a flurry of shots from the enemy-held enclave.

All the military on the verandah stiffened to the salute as the Commander-in-Chief limped up the wide wooden ornamental steps. At the top he saluted – 'Your Majesty . . . We have to speak to Mr Wilson and Brigadier Jones, in private.'

306

David said, 'I don't know where the Resident is. Last time I saw him he was out in the street.'

The Commissioner General looked round and said, 'There he is. He's coming now.' They waited as Wilson walked unhurriedly across the square amid desultory shooting, and up the steps. 'Good afternoon, Sir James,' he said. 'General.'

'Where can we go?' the general said.

David led back into the room where he had been lying. Sir James Fortescue sat on the edge of the creaky bed, the Commander-in-Chief on a bare chair, his wooden leg outstretched. The other two stood, facing each other.

The Commander-in-Chief said, 'This morning I ordered you to take no action except to ensure the safety of your men. You have disobeyed that order. Explain.'

David said, 'I considered that if the CTs were allowed to survive here, with the appearance of victory over us, there was a probability of communist risings all over the country, which would seriously menace the safety of my troops.'

As he spoke he was losing the nervousness which had gripped him as soon as the C-in-C reached the verandah. He was not afraid to lose his commission; meantime he had a case to present, and he would do so. Rougemont Huntingdon was a hard man, but never unfair. Yet the general was staring at him – glaring would be a better word – with an intensely hostile look, overflowing with barely suppressed rage. He said, 'You think there might be trouble in getting your troops back to Trangloek?'

'If we had not wiped out the CTs, sir – yes.'

'That risk wouldn't have arisen if you hadn't come charging up here in the first place, leaving Trangloek – airfield and all – guarded by a handful of ragamuffin auxiliary police. The Resident here radioed us about that before he left.' The blue eyes snapped electrically and the voice rose – 'And you did that with me – and the Cabinet – relying on you to provide the 'Guardian' force at an hour's notice! As we still are! The aircraft are standing by to fly up to Trangloek!'

David was taken aback by the C-in-C's fury, and he did not understand the reference to troops being ready at short notice, but he answered the first part of the general's complaint: 'I don't think anyone can say what would have happened if an MPRP force of 450 men, well armed, had been allowed to take over half the country without a fight from us, sir . . . There are approximately forty CTs left out of that 450 who invaded this country two days ago. They are being offered their lives now. Any who don't surrender will be attacked at 1630 hrs . . . that's in eight minutes from now. Do you direct me to cancel those orders?'

The general turned to the civilian. The Commissioner General said, 'This has become a purely military decision, Rougemont.'

The C-in-C looked hard at David: 'How many casualties have you had, and how many more do you expect to take in this attack?'

'We've had about sixteen killed and fifty wounded in the whole operation so far, sir. There are no loyal hostages in this last enclave, and we're going to use artillery. I don't expect more than half a dozen more casualties.'

The general's eyes bored into him for a long minute. Then he snapped, 'I shall order a Board of Inquiry into this whole episode later, and I am confident it will lead to a court martial. Meantime, with the situation here as it is – the situation you yourself have created – the best thing to do is finish the job. Carry out your plan.'

'Thank you, sir.'

'Where can we watch from? Those bloody fellows were shooting at us as we came in.' Sir James held up his brief case and David saw that there was a bullet hole through it. David led them out on to the verandah. Crawford was waiting by the door, and said hurriedly, 'They've had their ten minutes, sir. More. Five of them surrendered. Ten more tried to, but were shot down from behind by their own people. The bodies are on the river bank down there.'

'Only twenty-five left for us to deal with,' David said grimly, 'We should thank Sujak for doing our work for us. We'd better get behind something solid, sir. There are going to be a lot of stray bullets coming this way when the 2nd/12th start in.'

They waited behind a low stone balustrade. Motor engines throbbed from among the houses back from the river. The trees bent and groaned, the sky was nearly dark, lit by lightning flashes all along the southern horizon.

Without warning an artillery piece fired from fifty yards away. The shell burst against a strongly built wooden house which they could just see behind the left edge of the pagoda. The house shook and a timber flew into the air. Another shell followed the first, then all four guns of the troop were firing, though David could not see the other targets. Smoke began to rise from the building first hit, quickly followed by licking orange flames. The thunderous explosions of the guns, firing point blank over open sights, continued for four minutes. Suddenly they stopped. David muttered, 'The 2nd/12th are going in now.' He heard nothing over the scream of the wind and the cry of the trees. Wilson said, 'The city will burn!'

David said nothing; first things first. Now the saving of the city's buildings depended on how quickly the Gurkhas could clean up the CTs so that fire fighting could begin. Automatic fire rattled round the pagoda as the smoke thickened to a dense black pall which hovered low over the city, hunted to and fro like an uncertain hound, and finally streamed away towards the north-east, flames painting its underside orange and angry red.

Crawford, lying on the verandah behind them with a walkie-talkie, cried, 'Colonel Campbell-Wylie reports all houses taken. Resistance ended.'

David stood up. 'Give me that set . . . Alastair, get your whole battalion in to put out the fires. John, yours too. You have O'Grady with you? Tell him he's in command of all fire fighting. He can blow down houses, do whatever he thinks necessary, to stop the fire spreading.'

Kumara ran down the steps crying, 'Is it finished? Dylan, is it all over?'

'Yes, ma'am,' he said formally, but she flung her arms round his neck, laid her head on his shoulder, and began to weep. He patted her head, at first tentatively, while the general and Sir James, after a startled glance, looked away and began talking to each other in low voices.

After a time Kumara dried her eyes and said, 'Gentlemen, Brigadier Jones has saved Mingora.'

'At the risk of losing Sarawak,' the general said grimly. 'That cannot be overlooked, ma'am.'

'Sarawak?' David said. He felt faint and queasy. 'What about Sarawak?'

'Are you trying to pretend you didn't get the 'Guardian' warning order – to hold a Tac Brigade Headquarters, one battalion, and the whole of 154 Light Battery on Trangloek Airfield, at an hour's notice to fly to Sarawak?'

'We have had no such order, sir,' David said.

'Don't lie to me!' the general grated.

'I am not lying,' David said coldly. 'We have not received that order. When was it sent?'

The general looked at Sir James. The latter turned: 'Sidney, when did you pass our message to Brigadier Jones?'

'Immediately on my return to Trangloek from the conference.'

David said, 'You gave me no such message. There was an earlier order not to move troops north of Trangloek, but that arose from the political situation here and in Thailand – nothing to do with Sarawak.'

'One of you is lying,' General Huntingdon said bluntly.

David stared at Wilson, who met his gaze with cold precision. The man intended to ruin him.

Sir James Fortescue said, 'The matter was delicate, brigadier. We didn't want to make the Indonesians feel that they must confront us for face saving reasons. So, after the meeting in Singapore on the 25th the C-in-C here and I instructed Mr Wilson to pass the message to you verbally as soon as he had returned to Trangloek. It wasn't a complicated message and we didn't want to put anything in writing at that time.'

David said slowly, 'And I had all the troops ready to move, anyway – only the destination would have been different.'

'The Indonesian so-called volunteers are still on the move,' the general said, 'but they haven't crossed the frontier yet.'

The Commissioner General said, 'Wilson, you cabled me early in the morning of the 26th that you had personally given the message about 'Guardian' to Brigadier Jones. Later, General Huntingdon mentioned that he had not had an acknowledgement from the brigadier – but there was the rising in Trangloek to deal with and . . .'

'Then you vanished, with the troops,' the general growled at David.

David said, 'Mr Wilson gave me no message about 'Guardian,' then or at any other time.'

All the other men, and Kumara, looked towards the Resident. Wilson said coldly, 'It is his word against mine. As he has lied about his intentions in regard to moving his forces, and lied to me that he would obey my orders . . .'

David cut in: 'On the contrary, I warned you that I would disobey your orders, as being immoral. You said that was only talk, that you would know what to do when I actually did disobey. Well, I did disobey . . . but I did not lie.'

Kumara cried, 'You must believe Dylan! Mr Wilson became infatuated with me. Lately, I have made it clear that I love only Dylan. Mr Wilson has taken several steps to ensure that Dylan should defy your orders, and so have his career ruined . . . perhaps even be sent to jail. This is only the latest.'

Sir James said, 'I think General Huntingdon and I need to discuss this matter further, just with Mr Wilson and the brigadier. If you would be so good . . .'

'I'm going,' Kumara said. 'I have to make a broadcast.'

She went out. General Huntingdon said, 'We'll go inside. This is too public.' Inside the room once more, he glared at David: 'Now . . .'

David cut in, 'One moment, sir . . . Peter!' The IO hurried in. 'Peter, get accurate casualty figures and warn the D/Q how many are coming down, and when they'll arrive. Get them off at once in Fusilier vehicles. Check up on how the fire fighting's going and report to me. That's all.'

When the four of them were again alone, General Huntingdon said, 'I've changed my mind about the need for a Board of Inquiry. I will move direct to a General Court Martial. Let the Court Martial develop all the facts in this matter. Meantime, I propose to relieve you of your command and send you down to Singapore under arrest.'

David said nothing. Wilson was looking at him, but there was no hint of triumph in the stare.

The general, as though infuriated by David's silence, snarled, 'You've allowed yourself to be twisted round a woman's finger like a piece of wet string! For her you've sent British soldiers to their deaths! You bloody Welshmen always let your hearts rule your heads. I saw it coming months back, but I picked the wrong woman. And now that you've done what she wants, she'll say goodbye – with tears, I don't doubt, but goodbye just the same.'

David did not speak.

'Don't you have anything to say for yourself?'

'Yes, sir. But I'll keep it for the court martial. I think I should

311

have a look at the fire. Shall I tell Colonel Allen that he's in command?'

'No! Finish the job and then.... Go on, Get out of my sight. Come back in half an hour.'

'Perhaps you would be good enough to leave us, too, Sidney,' the Commissioner General said, speaking to Wilson.

David went out, his arm throbbing steadily.

It was very dark now, the smoke invisible, but leaping flames casting lurid irregular light on the pagoda and the tops of the houses. As he plunged into the narrow alleys off the pagoda square he entered an inferno, scores of Gurkhas running with buckets, the hoses of the Moirang fire brigade writhing like snakes along the walls, sharp explosions of bamboo, crash of beams, hiss and crackle of sparks towering up into the dark sky. He found Crawford with O'Grady, the engineer officer, and shouted in the latter's ear, 'How's it going?'

'Touch and go, sir. We're just going to blow down a couple of houses and then, if the Fusiliers can get the debris dragged away in time, we ought to have a fire-break.'

'OK.' David stood back, watching. The boom of the explosions sounded almost at once, and immediately a crowd of Fusiliers, naked to the waist, pounced on the debris and started dragging wood out and down to the river. Artillery quads backed up and Major Stevens, his barrel chest bare, yelled encouragement as the gunners tied chains round the bigger timbers and the quads towed them away. Everyone was coughing in the aimless flurries of smoke. David and Crawford walked round the fire and came to the other side, where the Gurkhas were working as hard as the Fusiliers. Among the wrecked buildings on that side they were finding corpses of Communist Terrorists, and a row of eight of them lay along the side of the alley, opposite the fire. Crawford said, 'We haven't found the body of Sujak bin Amin yet. But we've identified five other important leaders. And two more were in the party we ambushed at Bhraseng. The local RMC up there telegraphed in some time ago.'

'The governor all right?'

'No. The CTs murdered him – shot him in the back of the head.'

David looked at his watch. Time to go back to the Chief. He circled the conflagration, talked briefly with O'Grady, and reached the Governor's House at the appointed time. The flares along the stone balustrade had been lit, though their light was puny compared with the arched reflective curtains of the fire. Wilson was waiting on the verandah, looking out, silent. They went in together, not speaking.

General Huntingdon began without preamble: 'Sir James and I have been considering what will best serve the interests of Her Majesty's Government . . . of our country, if you like. He has been able to persuade me that your insubordination, or mutiny, could be punished by asking for you to resign your commission.'

Wilson spoke up sharply. 'Brigadier Jones has accused me of lying. There must be some public trial at which I am cleared.'

'Or found guilty,' David said. 'I agree. I demand a court martial.'

'Christ!' the general snarled. 'Here we are trying to save your reputations, and avoid a public scandal, and you demand that we wash the linen in public! And you, Jones, do you realize you can not only be cashiered, but face a life sentence for murder? Murder of the soldiers killed here carrying out an operation you'd been forbidden to undertake?'

'I understand,' David said.

Wilson said, 'The accusations made, the things that have been done, have been done too publicly to be disposed of in secret.'

His word against mine, David thought; and against my record of doing what I have thought necessary in this whole business. It didn't look good, but he saw no alternative.

There was a knock on the closed door. General Huntingdon cried, 'Good God Almighty, this bloody place is like Euston station!'

The door opened and the Chief Minister entered, swinging inexpertly on crutches. The general got up quickly and said, 'Sit here.'

The minister lowered himself gingerly, and laid the crutches down beside him. 'Her Majesty told me you were discussing the actions of Brigadier Jones,' he said. 'I felt it was my duty to lay before you certain facts which have just come to my knowledge.'

'To do with Brigadier Jones?' the general asked, 'We are quite pressed for time, and . . .'

'To do with Mr Wilson,' the Chief Minister said.

Sir James Fortescue leaned forward in his chair. The Chief

313

Minister said, 'You may have heard that Sujak bin Amin's deputy surrendered today. I have been talking to him.'

He fell silent. Everyone leaned towards him. He knows his theatricals, David thought.

'Well . . . ?'

'His name is Songgram, a Khmer-Mingoran, an Easterner.'

'Yes, yes.'

'Brigadier Jones here will recall that I told him that the Resident was making secret contacts with some group who could only be the MPRP. Songgram has told me that in the months of February, March, and April he held five secret conferences with Mr Wilson at various places in or near Trangloek.'

'It is true,' Wilson said, his voice still cold. 'I am authorized to make whatever contacts I wish, in the interests of Her Majesty's Government.'

The Chief Minister continued, 'At the last meeting after negotiations at the earlier ones, the Resident made certain promises on behalf of the British Government. First, that British troops would not be used against the MPRP under any circumstances, in any part of the country, after 15 May – providing of course that the troops or their families were not attacked.'

'You had no authority to make such a promise!' the Commissioner General exclaimed.

'Second,' the Chief Minister continued, 'that Britain would recognize the MPRP as the government of Mingora the moment it had effective control of any four provinces. Third, the Resident would use his best efforts to force the Queen and royal family into exile as soon as the MPRP rose in active rebellion, on the grounds that their continued presence in Mingora would endanger British subjects in the country. Lastly, that Britain, as soon as the MPRP was installed as the local government here, would make a new treaty of friendship with Mingora, to replace the outmoded and insulting Treaty of Trangloek.'

Sir James Fortescue was pacing the floor. He stopped, wheeling sharply, his normally placid face stern: 'Is this true, Sidney?'

Wilson hesitated, began to say something, then something else, finally, 'In part.' Watching him closely, David thought, now he's beginning to break up. Now he has to decide between expedience and truth, between honesty and his ambition, and he doesn't know which to choose.

314

'What do you mean, in part?'

Wilson said, 'There was the letter of my instructions – and the spirit ... It was clear that HMG intended to get out of Mingora and also wished to retain good trade and general relations with whatever group replaced the monarchy.'

'Why should it be supposed that the monarchy would or must be replaced?' Sir James said coldly. Wilson did not answer.

David said, 'The truth will come out at my court martial.'

Sir James waved his hand as though waving away a wasp. 'No, no, there can be no court martial! This is too ... disgraceful. Let us get back to our prime concern – what is best for our country, not for the individuals concerned.' He turned suddenly on Wilson: 'I think you forgot to give Brigadier Jones that message about 'Guardian' ...'

Wilson, his head hanging, the sweat bursting out on his face, did not answer.

'*Didn't you?*' Sir James grated, louder. 'Do you want a formal departmental inquiry into *all* your acts here?'

'Perhaps ... I may have forgotten ...'

'Good. You forgot to give Brigadier Jones the message, though you thought you had. Rougemont, if Brigadier Jones did not flatly disobey an order of yours, is it necessary to court martial him?'

The Commander-in-Chief stared a long while at David. Finally he said, 'I thought you couldn't have received that message. Disregarding the 'Guardian' warning wasn't like you ... No, Jimmy, I don't have to court martial him, and he can't demand a court martial, either.'

David said, 'Sir, Mr Wilson has accused me of lying, when it was he who lied. In making these contacts with the MPRP, and promising what he did, he put me and my men into ...'

Sir James said, 'That is a matter for us in the Commonwealth Relations Office to deal with, brigadier. You must trust us to do what's best for the country, even as we trust General Huntingdon. Wilson, if you'd come with me, we can talk about future arrangements here without disturbing these good soldiers ... We ought to leave in half an hour or less, Rougemont.'

'Right. I'll have the helicopter brought to the square here ... David, come outside.' They left the room.

'You've been walking a tightrope across a bottomless pit, David, and now you think you've made the far side . . . no demand for you to resign your commission, no board of inquiry, no court martial. That's what you're thinking, isn't it?'

David said wearily, 'I haven't had time to think anything yet, sir. I'm only glad it's all finished.'

The general said, a little more gently, 'And so are you, David – finished. You did what you thought had to be done, and you'll pay the price. I'm getting you out of Mingora – swopping you with Tom Hampton in Hong Kong. Why? Because there you'll be under the eyes of General Pearce. When you finish your time there, you'll be allowed to retire. Why? Because major-generals and lieutenant-generals have to work hand in glove with politicians, more and more as they go up . . . and no politician, from the Prime Minister downwards, is going to trust you again.'

David made a small angry gesture. Now that the Chief was putting it into such plain words, he recognized that he had known it all along, simply not admitted it to himself.

The general said, 'I know it's all wrong, but that's the fact. The only thing that'll save you now is a major war . . . You spoke to me once about Nuremberg and the precedent it set. You were right, but only for the politicians – because they can put us on trial. We can't do the same to them. Not without declaring a military state, martial law. That was the flaw in your argument. Anything I can do, personally, for you, I will. And let me tell you, now we're alone, I admire you, David. You've got moral guts. You'll always be able to live with yourself, which damned few of us can do . . . Now, I'm going to take you back to Singapore with us in the helicopter, and straight into hospital. I'll tell Allen he's in command till we can get Hampton in . . . Do you want to speak to the Queen?'

'I must, sir . . . If I applied to resign my commission, how long would it be before I could be released?'

The general looked at him keenly. 'Not long. In the circumstances, I could get you out in a week . . . in fact, as soon as they release you from hospital. But I warn you, our government is going to insist that the British military adviser to Mingora shall be of their choosing, with Mingora's approval, of course . . . but you won't get past the first hurdle.'

'I know, sir. If you'll excuse me . . .'

'Don't be long. Be back here in twenty minutes. I'm going to take a look round, talk to Allen and some of the men.'

David stood with Crawford at his side, waiting for his Land-Rover. All the orders had been given, everything decided and put in train, except the one thing that mattered. Several times in the past hour he had been on the point of collapse, but now he felt strong and almost fresh, though his arm hurt abominably. A huge drop of rain fell on his shoulder, splashing his cheek. Headlights bored through the murky gloom and stopped behind him. He got in, and Tulbahadur drove him across the debris-strewn square. The rain fell faster, making mud cakes on the dusty hood and filling the darkness with the penetrating smell of dampening earth.

Kumara's blue Land-Rover was parked outside the Rest House. David told Tulbahadur to wait and went slowly up the verandah steps. It was there, in that doorway, that she had first declared her love. He paused a moment, then passed on.

She was sitting at the big table in the main room, writing. She saw him and came at once to him, where he waited inside the door. 'My dear,' she whispered, 'when are you going to let them take you to hospital?'

'The Commander-in-Chief's taking me to Singapore. In a few minutes.'

'What are they going to do to you . . . about what you did here?'

'Nothing. Wilson broke. Admitted he'd lied.'

'So . . . you'll stay, and raise and train our new army?'

'They're posting me away. Another brigadier will replace me . . . and if you ask for me, they will refuse. Because the politicians aren't going to trust me any more. My career in the army's finished.' He wanted to say, 'but Sir Harry Johnstone has promised me a job here. I can get out, and come back and live here the rest of my life, with you.' There was something in her face, a distance almost like that of his first days here, that stopped him. The lamp on the table painted her face a dull glowing gold. The Mingora Cobra glittered on the bandages over her bosom, where so often he had seen the Jumbhorn Ruby, and now it seemed suddenly menacing, the hood expanded, the diamond eyes glittering. She laid her head on his good shoulder: 'Since I became a

317

woman I've tried to show a strong face to the world, because I was the Perdana Binte Mingora. Now I must do it for the rest of my life, because I am the Queen . . . but without you what is tender inside me will eat itself away, until soon there will be nothing left, only the hard outer shell.'

The rain drummed on the roof. Under it they heard music from the city, and the growl of truck and car engines. She said, 'My mother had her husband for many years, but I . . . ?'

The words came out at last. He said, 'I can come back, as a civilian. We cannot marry, I know, but . . .'

She did not speak for a long time, her head still resting lightly on his shoulder. Finally she said, 'Do you love me?'

'Yes. And you?'

'I never imagined I could love anyone so much. You know that I love you and always will. But we cannot marry. And for the other . . . Look at me.' She stood away from him. 'Do I look different?'

He shook his head.

'I am! Kumara is running out, like water out of a broken vase. The feelings and thoughts she used to have are vanishing, even as I try to keep hold of them. What is replacing them is Mingora . . . the state . . . my people . . . I am Queen Supaya VI. Kumara could have asked you to live here as her lover—'

'Kumara asked to bear my child,' he muttered. 'Kumara said she didn't care what happened to Mingora. At Pulo Pattan. By the edge of the lagoon. Kumara begged me to marry her – in Flagstaff House – in hospital.'

'Kumara did!' Kumara cried, 'But the Queen is another woman! Can't you see? That's why I asked you to look at me.' David tried to look at her, but saw only the baleful threat of the cobra's raised hood and bared fangs.

Kumara said, 'My God, Dylan, think how I feel! If they'd let you stay here as Military Adviser, there would have been a definite term on it. We would have three years, working together for the country, acknowledged lovers – and at the end, you'd go, and I would turn to my work, alone. Three years of happiness is more than I ever expected. But this . . . you always here, no term to it . . . that would only be possible in marriage and that cannot be . . . or if we were working together for Mingora. If you were Military Adviser, we'd have a thousand reasons for being together

... but with you working for Sir Harry, our meetings would be hurried assignations snatched from time I should be giving to my work ... Sujak's escaped, there are a thousand things to be done, now, tomorrow, every hour of every day ... No, no! I can not allow you to come back to Mingora under those conditions. Darling ... darling ... don't you understand?'

You've allowed yourself to be twisted round a woman's finger like a piece of wet string ... now that you've done what she wants, she'll say goodbye – with tears, I don't doubt, but goodbye just the same.

Sir Rougemont Huntingdon's words echoed in his ears. Had it really been like that? She was crying, true, but was it possible that the tears were not real? Was Kumara, lover, dead and only Supaya, monarch, living? Her face was a mask, the tears the only moving thing on it.

Looking steadily at her, consciously trying to see beneath the surface into her soul, he knew she was suffering as much as he, indeed more ... for the certainty came slowly to him, from the long silent locking of their eyes, that she loved him; and that if he made a move towards her she would break down, and accept him on any terms. But with that certainty came another; she was right in what she had said. He could not live here as a hanger-on of Sir Harry Johnstone, and spare-time lover of the Queen. Sooner or later that would destroy both of them, and perhaps Mingora as well. This was the revelation for which he had been searching, when so often he had tried to see the shape of his future with Kumara. The vision had always been blank, because in fact there could be no future. That blankness, and a premonition of what it portended, had held him from giving promises which at the time he had desperately wanted to give.

It was ended. He felt not so much sad as washed out, finished, wrung dry. He had loved, been loved, and done what ought to be done. Those were the only worthwhile realities of these six months. Somewhere close by a helicopter began to warm up its engine, its rotor thrashing the rain-filled night. He saluted, and said gently, 'Goodbye, Your Majesty ... my dearest,' and went out. Tulbahadur started up the Land-Rover.